TOMMY AND THE

ORDER
OF
COSMIC
CHAMPIONS

WRITTEN BY ANTHONY J. RAPINO

STORY BY ANTHONY D. GRATE

GREENLEAF
BOOK GROUP PRESS

Published by Greenleaf Book Group Press
Austin, TX
www.gbgpress.com

Distributed by Greenleaf Book Group

For ordering information or special discounts for bulk purchases, please contact Greenleaf Book Group at PO Box 91869, Austin, TX 78709, 512.891.6100.

Design and composition by Greenleaf Book Group
Cover design by Anthony Grate
Illustration on page 3 provided courtesy of João Florêncio.
Illustrations on pages 121,177, 226, 273, 310, 325 provided courtesy of Milos Markovich.

Publisher's Cataloging-in-Publication data is available.

Print ISBN: 978-1-62634-966-7

eBook ISBN: 978-1-62634-967-4

Part of the Tree Neutral® program, which offsets the number of trees consumed in the production and printing of this book by taking proactive steps, such as planting trees in direct proportion to the number of trees used: www.treeneutral.com

TreeNeutral

Printed in the United States of America on acid-free paper

22 22 23 24 25 26   10 9 8 7 6 5 4 3 2 1

First Edition

Part One

PROLOGUE

CHAPTER ONE
THE NIGHT BEFORE

The barrier wall was all that mattered, and Masculon was nearly finished. Though construction had taken months, the priests had faith. They knew what kind of power Masculon possessed, and with the protection of ironwood surrounding their small village, his secret may yet endure.

Masculon carried a great log on either shoulder, breathing the clean air of Evernitia, glad for twenty-six years of peace. What he didn't know was their hard-won tranquility was about to end.

An explosion rocked the outer wall, sending great pieces of lumber flying. Villagers and priests ran for cover, but Masculon remained.

Skullagar, the loathsome Skullarian king of the Bone Sands, rode his reptilian Draconican over the destroyed wall and held his staff of power high. "At last!"

The grizzled voice of the beastly villain caused Masculon's blood to run cold. From behind his horned skull mask, Skullagar smiled maliciously.

"You knew this day would come, boy! There is no hole you can crawl into that I cannot find."

From behind the corner of the blacksmith's quarters, Deleon, the priest who had saved Masculon as a baby, called out. "You must resist!"

He knew this, for if Masculon fell, so would his village, along with all those he cared for.

Skullagar dismounted his beast and strode forward. "Give me what is mine, and I'll consider not turning this place into a pile of ash."

Masculon touched the blue gem embedded in his golden headband. The twin to the stone on his ax, the conduit of his power. But he knew Skullagar's words were lies. He knew this as clearly as the violet sky of Teltam above. "Come and take it," he challenged the wretched villain.

Skullagar laughed in villainous tones. "I do admire your spirit, misguided as it may be." He spread his arms wide as a squadron of mechanized fighters appeared behind him. "Destroy them."

The air filled with noxious fumes from the robotic army. Villagers screamed as they ran to safety. Some of the men came forward, but Masculon sent them back. He knew what he had to do.

Retrieving his ax, he held it skyward and invoked its power: "Make the force of Myragran mine!" The gems erupted in an explosion of brilliant light as Masculon's mind and body surged with potential. He swung the ax into an enormous log, then threw it at a cluster of robots, sending them soaring through the air. They collapsed into a pile of sparking metal, crushed between rock and wood.

Skullagar gasped. "It's not possible."

Masculon replied, "Tommy! Do you hear me?"

The robots looked around, confused.

Masculon threw his ax down. "Earth to Tommy."

"What is this devilry?"

"Bedtime, kiddo."

Skullagar whined, "Come on, Ma!"

* * *

Planet Teltam melted away as the village in crisis became a pile of cardboard pieces and Tommy's *Order of Cosmic Champions* action figures toppled over.

"Ten more minutes?"

Tommy's mom checked her watch. She was wearing a robe, and her usually bouncy hair was as lifeless as Tommy's toys. It wouldn't be long before her face transformed into a blue mask of rejuvenating cream.

"Not a minute more. You should be fresh for your last day."

Fresh? Heck, he didn't even want to *go*. Some of his friends' parents were letting them take a senior skip day, but his dad claimed the tradition wasn't for elementary school kids. Tommy didn't know about that, but he sure would have liked to stay up a little later.

He knocked the cardboard town over. "Fine. I need EyeSpy and Vile-Ette to finish the story anyway." He smiled at his mom, hoping she got the hint.

Her response dashed all hope. "You're cleaning this up after school tomorrow."

"Sounds awesome." He got into bed and drew the covers up to his chin.

"Don't you get sarcastic with me, buddy." She sat next to him and kissed his head. "We have the whole summer ahead of us. What's one more day of school? Besides, the sooner you get to sleep . . ."

"The sooner I can start my day," he repeated in the standard monotone of well-worn advice.

"You betcha." She kissed him again for good measure. "Goodnight, kiddo. No sneaking out of bed to read comics."

"No sneaking out of bed for cake."

His mom's reaction made him smile. She obviously didn't know Tommy had discovered her little secret, but some nights (yes, when he was up with a flashlight and a comic), he heard her pad down the stairs into the kitchen. The next morning, there'd be crumbs and a slightly smaller cake. The deduction didn't require Sherlock Holmes.

"You know about that, huh?"

"Yup."

"Well," she stood and walked to the door, "I guess we all have our little secrets."

Tommy thought about her last words after she closed the door and went to bed. The excitement of what they implied kept him peering into the dark of his room. Even after sleep found him, Tommy thought about the words long into his dreams.

We all have our little secrets.

Part Two

THE
WONDER
YEARS

CHAPTER TWO
SCHOOL'S OUT

Time had stopped. That was the only reasonable explanation for Tommy Grant's continued imprisonment behind the wooden school desk, its surface etched with lamentations. He read them for the thousandth time. *Tony rulz. I'm sick with pac mania. Skool food suks. Tammy Toots.* He ran his fingers over the peace signs and hearts, wishing for an end to the drudgery. No other day had ever been as long.

Tommy dispensed with courtesy and peered over his shoulder to steal a glance at the time. The round clock mounted on the back wall was surely a cruel joke set upon the students, ensuring swift punishment for anyone brazen enough to check it during class. But this wasn't any regular day, and the teacher's scorn held no sway over Tommy. This, after all, was the last day of elementary school. What could old Mrs. Tither possibly do? As soon as the bell rang, he'd be gone from that place, and he'd never look back. Mrs. Tither could scream and threaten a trip to the principal's office all she wanted. None of it would matter.

Tommy's bravery paid off as he discovered only five minutes remained in his tenure at Golden Pines Elementary.

The teacher didn't even glance his way, which was weird for old Mrs. Tither—Withered Tither, as she was referred to in hushed tones on the playground—who was usually ever vigilant. So much as an implied note-pass was known to set her flying into an almost comical rage, her floral dress spinning around her wide frame like a helicopter propeller. Her face twisted into a flushed mask of indignity, deepening the creases and crevices of wrinkles as if to prove she was actually withering away before their eyes.

A worn copy of *To Kill a Mockingbird* whirred in the VCR, though no one paid the stuttering picture much mind. There had been rumors leading up to the last day that some teachers would show *The Karate Kid*. Other students claimed they'd get to see *Flight of the Navigator*. Tommy dug those kinds of movies—ones like *The Goonies*, *Explorers*, and *Stand by Me*. There was a new one he'd been dying to see called *The Monster Squad*, but he'd have to wait until movie night.

Now even Withered Tither was checking her wristwatch. Time had grown short indeed. A quick check over his shoulder confirmed, yes, less than a minute now! The other students around him became shifty in their seats. Lauren R. straightened her books into a neat pile. Tommy's best friend, Evan Winger, groaned audibly as he tapped the desk. The movie whirred on, ignorant of the students' disinterest.

"Settle." Mrs. Tither peered over her glasses, a stern disciplinarian to the end. "Settle now or I'll hold you after."

Could she actually do that?

Tommy looked at Evan, whose face lost all color. His mouth hung open. Other students gazed at each other questioningly, but no one had the guts to defy Mrs. Tither's order and risk having to remain in the chalk dust–covered room a moment longer than necessary. Enough of Atticus Finch. Enough of math and English. And as the prophetic rhyme said, "No more teacher's dirty looks." What else could they do with mere seconds left? They settled. They quieted. They tamped down all the joy and exuberance and excitement. Down, down, down to the bottom of their stomachs as the seconds ticked closer to 2:25.

Silence until the second hand found its home and the bell rang.

Tommy's stomach lurched, ready to spew anticipation like a shaken bottle of soda. But Mrs. Tither, that withered witch, had one last trick.

She held a finger up as she had so many times before: *Wait.*

Evan shot an expression of unbridled shock at Tommy. But the bell had rung! This was the last day of elementary school, and summer waited outside like an idling ice cream truck.

Where children once sat, only mannequins remained. No one dared move a muscle, or speak, or *question.*

Mrs. Tither continued to hold her finger in the air like a dictator brandishing some glorious blade of triumph. Her gaze held satisfaction, authority, and yes, a smidgen of malice. Tommy long suspected that Withered Tither hated children, and this last moment with her confirmed it.

Tommy's mother had once referred to his teacher as a schoolmarm, and that word returned to him as he sat stationary, praying for Mrs. Tither to lower her dreaded index finger, which had been imbued with such power that a single gesture could hold a classroom of children in their seats. What wizardry! What witchcraft! This raised finger alone could cease invading armies, but she instead used her power against innocent children wishing for parks and bike rides, ice cream and pools.

Her expression shifted and became villainous, a sneer quivering on red-painted lips, revealing teeth stained yellow from nicotine. Her eyes squinted as she gazed upon what Tommy assumed was her most satisfying plaything: a classroom filled with hopeful children. The enormity of that moment weighed upon young Tommy's mind, as if for the first time in his short life he understood the secret intentions of adults.

With her finger still stabbing the air, she said, "I expect you'd like to leave now."

Outside, the cheers and exclamations of luckier students rose into the clear air like balloons on the wind.

Mrs. Tither gestured to the row of windows and shook her head. "Go on then. Join your friends." A smile teased at her lips. "Have a wonderful summer, and promise me you will *savor* every moment." She lowered her finger as her expression shifted one last time to something Tommy could not identify. Something sad and lonely.

But he was only eleven years old, and even though he reconsidered his earlier judgment of Mrs. Tither, the thought was immediately drowned out by his uproarious classmates leaping from their seats as if they were on fire.

Sammy C. patted his shoulder and said, "See you at the new school." Lauren R. and Howard L. waved on their way through the door. There were other goodbyes and sayonaras, but they blended together in the miasma of excitement. Tommy grabbed his backpack and headed for the door where he expected Evan was waiting, but his best friend had left him behind.

His stomach twisted. *Why did Evan leave without me?* They had so much to talk about. What would they do on their first day of summer? Where would they explore? What games would they play? But he was gone, and without so much as a word.

The hallways were crowded with bustling children headed to buses or parents' cars. Some lucky few lived within walking distance and as fifth graders were allowed to go home on their own. A strange sensation descended on Tommy as he made his way to the front door. A bad kind of itch, somewhere between his heart and stomach. This would be the last time he walked these hallways. The last time he sat through a class with Mrs. Tither. No more lunches in a cafeteria that smelled of warming trays and disinfectant. No more gym class with Coach Marvin. No more field days, book fairs, or Hallway Halloween.

In the weeks leading up to this last day of elementary school, all of those notions had seemed like blessings. But now, as he left the building he'd occupied for five years, these ideas became awful. Would he even have classes with Evan anymore? A sadness for the end of school he never thought possible descended upon him, and it flopped around his guts like a dying fish.

Deep down, he feared these notions were an omen of things to come.

CHAPTER THREE

LAZY DAYS

"Tommy? Hey, Tommy-boy, where are you?"

Dave Grant entered the living room where his son lay on the floor watching that cartoon again. The one with all the weird costumes, sword fighting, and ray guns. He could never figure out why Tommy was so obsessed with the show in the first place. And the *toys*. So many action figures and playsets. Magazines, read-along records, stickers, and View-Master reels. He was convinced the only reason the show existed was to sell toys.

"Hey, Dad." Tommy's eyes were back on the set before he finished speaking.

Dave sat on the couch and took a sip of beer. Suzie was sure to nag him about getting started so early, but it was a summer Saturday and he didn't have work for two days. The sip turned into a gulp.

Tommy stretched, his skinny legs poking farther from his shorts than they had just the week before. In fact, most of his clothes were fitting too small lately. Maybe he'd finally stop wearing the ratty graphic tees he was so fond of once they bought some new clothes. "Hey, kid. Why don't you sit in a chair like a normal human?"

"Who says I have to be normal?"

A few more sips of beer helped him cope with the answer. "Why aren't you outside? You're gonna ruin your eyes watching so much boob tube."

Tommy spun around, his dark hair flopping in a shaggy mess. "Gee, Dad. Haven't heard that one before."

Everything about the boy was growing and changing. His hair and height, sure. But he also appeared more angular as he shed the baby fat. All knees and elbows. His nose was filling in too, more like his mother's side of the family with the Greek features and heavy eyebrows.

Dave shook his head and went for another sip before realizing he'd finished the can. "Tell your mother to bring you for a haircut already. That bowl cut of yours is turning into hippie hair."

"Hippie hair?"

"Long. Your hair is too long."

"Oh." Tommy stood and stretched. His Nintendo shirt lifted almost high enough to show belly. "I guess."

"Holy cow, kid. You've sprouted all right." He stood and ruffled Tommy's shaggy head, which was now only about a foot below his own. "You should think about joining the basketball team at your new school."

Tommy's face twisted and he looked down in that shy way of his. Dave hated when he did that. The expression reminded him of how he used to act as a kid, before he came out of his own sullen shell. No, that wasn't quite right. Before his father had *beaten* the shyness out of him. That was the truth, wasn't it?

"I thought you liked basketball."

"Yeah, at the park. We play horse or toss the ball around."

"Okay?"

"I don't want to play on a team. We just play for fun."

Dave shook his empty beer can instead of his head. "Call Evan, will ya? Get out for a while. I don't want to see you in the house when I get back from the kitchen."

He tried not to see the pained expression on his son's face. Had he been a little harsh? Maybe, but he hadn't hit the boy. And every day he was a better father than his own was a minor victory.

✳ ✳ ✳

When Dave returned to the living room with another beer and a bowl of potato chips, his son was no longer there. He thought he'd heard the door, but his mind had wandered to other things like how much weight he'd put on the last couple years and how badly his back hurt. He grabbed the remote and tried changing the channel away from the cartoon Tommy had been watching, realizing too late it was a VHS tape he'd gotten for Christmas. What a mistake that had been. Bad enough Tommy took every opportunity to watch the cartoon, going as far as highlighting every airing in the *TV Guide*. Then Suzanne had to buy episodes on tape so he could watch the damn show even when it wasn't on TV. The way Tommy was going through those tapes, he'd wear them out in a year.

Speaking of Suzanne . . . *Where* is *she?*

Dave had gotten up late that morning to find Suzanne already gone. Probably to the hairdresser or the mall again. She'd been going out on her own more often these past months.

He lifted himself from the scratchy old couch with some effort and stumbled past the coffee table. The small television sat atop a flimsy stand he'd found on the side of the road a couple years back. The rickety thing was in the rich neighborhood, which he sometimes liked to detour through on the way to the dealership. The trip wasn't faster, but he liked seeing the big houses with stone and brick faces, the paved driveways, the brand-new Caddies and Roadsters sitting shiny and proud.

He knelt in front of the wood-paneled set and stopped the VCR. The tape ceased its whirring with a few mechanical clicks. Standing pained his back, and he groaned, peppering in a few "ah hells" and "cripes" for good measure, knowing no one was there to hear or sympathize. Nope. No Suzie to fetch a beer and rub his back. Tommy, well, he'd sent him away after all, but he'd be of no use even if he was around. Always drawing or watching cartoons or playing with toys. He wished the kid would grow out of it already. Dave had had to give up on all the things he loved so he could have a family. Reluctance to do so only caused pain, and he had learned the hard way that having hope hurt. He'd save his son the torment if he could.

"Seriously, Dave?"

He dropped the remote and almost spilled his beer.

Suzanne stood in the doorway. A Macy's bag hung from her right hand, her brown pleather purse from her shoulder. Was her hair different? Shorter? Curlier? Certainly not colored; it was still the same old dirty blonde.

He straightened and put his beer on the coffee table. "Hey, hon. Your hair looks nice."

She rolled her eyes and closed the door behind her. "I didn't go to the salon."

"Yeah, well." He stood to greet her. "I just meant you look good today." After repeating the rote compliment, he realized she really *did* look good. Suzie had put on some healthy weight lately, and her curves filled out her jeans and blouse nicely. Her face had even taken on an elfish quality with the change.

"Uh huh." She peered around the room, then went to the kitchen and back. Her gaze rested on the staircase on the other side of the room. "Is Tommy here?" She said this with a little smile.

Dave glanced at the Macy's bag. "You didn't get him more of that Cosmos stuff, did you?"

Her grip tightened on the bag. "*Order of Cosmic Champions*. The least you can do is get the name right after all these years."

"Suzanne, he has enough—"

"It's just a little nothing. From the clearance rack."

"Doesn't matter, he has—"

"His birthday is coming up."

Dave threw his hands in the air. "Fine, so give the gift to him then."

Suzie shook her head, her hair bouncing. He'd be damned if she hadn't gotten it styled and lied so he'd feel stupid.

"It's just a little—"

"Every little thing counts, Suzie. He'll be glad for an extra present to open."

Her expression eased a little, and he could see his point had landed. But he could also see a hint of surprise there, which he didn't like one bit. As if being reasonable had become so rare that when he did divine a worthy counterpoint, Suzanne was shocked.

Her grip on the bag eased. "Yeah, okay. We'll wrap the toy for his birthday."

"Good."

"But don't think that means we're off the hook for a real gift."

Cripes, she couldn't even let him have one small win. Always expecting the worst. "I know. Didn't I just say—"

"Right, you're right. Sorry." She held her hands up, eyes closed as though she couldn't bear the sight of him. Her trips out alone. The increased frequency of TV dinners and ladies' nights. The book club, the drives to nowhere.

Yes, Dave thought. He was losing his wife, one fight at a time.

No. He corrected himself, because deep down he knew.

He was losing her one *beer* at a time.

CHAPTER FOUR

ALONE

Summer's lazy hum filled Tommy's senses. A mower growled in the distance, accented by a whining weed whacker. The air smelled like sweet grass, and the sky resembled the marbled eye of God. A satisfied warmth grew in his belly. Nothing ever felt so perfect as a summer day.

His dad acted like Tommy never went out, but that was because he wasn't paying attention. The truth was Tommy had been spending more and more time away from home. He didn't know if his parents thought he was in his room or if they didn't think of him at all. When they started in on each other, Tommy would slip out, hop astride his bike, and pedal fast away from his dead-end street.

Sometimes, when Tommy came back, his mom would be gone and his dad would be sitting in the living room with a half-eaten Hungry-Man dinner and a mostly empty six-pack of beer on the coffee table. Dad might look up with heavy-lidded eyes and say, "About time you came home" or "Hungry Man again, kid." What he never asked was, "Where have you been?" What he never said was, "I'm sorry."

Tommy shook off the oily thoughts, because oil stains if you don't clean it expeditiously. He refocused on the pleasant breeze at the top of his hill, where his house was located in a secluded cul-de-sac. The hill was high above everything except the trees and sky.

Tommy was king of the hill, astride his mighty green Mongoose. He'd saved up two years' of birthday money and allowances to upgrade to the green tires and chain, and boy oh boy were the adornments worth it. The Mongoose, his green machine, was the earthly version of Masculon's War Beast from *Order of Cosmic Champions*. Nearly every bare area of the bike's body was covered with *OoCC* decals.

Another cool breeze blew back his shaggy mass of hair. He surveyed his kingdom below. In reality, there wasn't much to see. Houses, trees, split rail fences. There was Mr. Redford pushing his rusty old mower around a rocky lawn. Mrs. Simpson yanked her primped poodle, Princess Penelope, away from the Montgomerys' mailbox. Squirrels capered and birds soared.

But Tommy saw past his mundane world. He saw beyond the accepted truths and spied an exciting planet before him. A place where the *Order of Cosmic Champions* lived and breathed. A place where he might stumble across buried treasure. Where secret spies wore human skin over their alien bodies. Mr. Redford was one. Most definitely. Look at his comical stride, as if he was hiding a third arm under that enormous gut of his. And Mrs. Simpson's poodle? A creature of the fourth dimension if he'd ever seen one. She doesn't even try to hide Princess Penelope's rear antennae or mass of venomous fur poofs.

Tommy let out a loud guffaw of laughter at the thought. *Wouldn't that be something?*

He kicked off and sailed down the steep incline from his hilltop, letting gravity do its work. His old Darryl Strawberry card clicked away

against the spokes, and the wind encased him in a forcefield of summertime perfection. A perfection that could only be penetrated by a strangely painful sensation that had only recently come over him.

Where had his best friend, Evan, gone? After his disappearance from the classroom on the last day, Evan remained MIA. Every time Tommy called, Evan's mom said he was busy. Maybe doing chores, maybe playing video games. The last time she even said Evan didn't want to come out to play. When Tommy asked why, Mrs. Winger clammed up as if she knew she had said something wrong. Her voice grew weird and soft. Tommy didn't know the word for it, but he knew what it felt like: lies and secrets. She hurried off the phone, and after that, his calls went to the answering machine.

Tommy gained speed so fast now, he couldn't pedal if he tried. The wind chipped away at the negativity, reminding him of where he was: the first month of summer break. The dead center of heaven.

Flying by at warp speeds, he raised a hand in salutation to Mrs. Simpson. She smiled and waved back, but in the split second before Tommy sailed past, he was sure her scalp had peeled back to reveal green reptilian skin beneath. As for Princess Penelope, she was too busy watering the grass to take much notice of King Tommy's descent to greet the peasants below.

Gravity grasped Tommy's Mongoose and flung him past the skating rink and right onto Branch Street. The main road would take him out of the woods and into Branchville, a small nothing of a town one could drive through and never know they had visited. But for Tommy, these little trips to town were the closest thing to a social life he had that summer, what with Evan's grand disappearing act. Besides, Branchville had everything he needed: a video store, a corner shop, a comic store, and a few arcade machines.

Momentum finally gave out, so Tommy pedaled to maintain his speed, making sure to check over his shoulder for cars. His mom used to

hate when he rode his bike into town. She'd freak on him, making him wear a helmet and never letting him go after dark. He'd thought she was nutso right up until an ill-fated rental of *The Toxic Avenger*.

He and Evan had been looking for a horror movie to watch after trick-or-treating the previous year. They didn't usually watch horror films, and most of the time their parents wouldn't let them rent any of the good stuff anyway, but that year Evan's dad had relented. Tommy figured part of the decision was because the box art made the movie look like a stupid comedy. But Evan's dad also commented that since the movie was "unrated," it was probably okay (he later realized his error).

In the opening scene of the movie, a young boy goes out at night to ride his bike. He's told to wear a helmet, and he does. But that doesn't save him. The kid is run down by some teen sociopaths who drive over his head and crush his skull!

Evan's dad had turned off the movie without a word, and Tommy was glad. Even so, after that fateful viewing he wouldn't ride his bike on the main road for weeks. Nightmares of the scene plagued him, causing Tommy to wake in the middle of the night, sweating profusely and grabbing at his own head to make sure it was still intact. Those were bad nights, but children's memories for such things are short, and it wasn't long before Tommy was back on the road without a helmet (which his mother didn't seem to notice anymore).

Not that any of it mattered. Branch Street might be a main road, but the two-mile bike ride rarely revealed more than a few cars and trucks, all driving the speed limit or below and giving wide berth to Tommy as they passed. Half the time, the drivers would even slow and wave, knowing either Tommy or one of his parents.

He stood from the bike seat and cranked down on the pedals. The video store awaited with its lonely pair of arcade games, and he had a few quarters burning a hole in his pocket.

* * *

Emerging from Branch Street, Tommy hopped his bike onto the narrow sidewalk of the intersecting road and came to a stop. He assessed Branchville's thoroughfare. Most called it Main Street for some reason, but its real name was Oak Drive. Maybe people got sick of all the tree imagery. He once listened in on a group of old-timers lamenting over the town's name. They sat around one of the rickety wood tables in front of the Luncheonette, sipping espressos and munching crumb cake. The gathering was always made up of the same three or four men, though Tommy only knew old Mr. Miller, the granddad of a kid from school.

He hadn't been particularly interested in their conversation. He'd only paused near their table long enough to open his 25-cent bag of O'Boisies and tip a few into his mouth. As he crunched away, bits of the old men's diatribe broke through.

"Seems a mistake to me."

"Sure, sure. Big mistake. Founders didn't know what—"

"Cut it out, now."

"You disagree? Calling the road *Oak* Drive and the town *Branchville*?"

"Yup, seems a mistake to me."

"Who cares, it's just—"

"The town should be *Oak*ville and the road *Branch* Drive."

"Yup, yup. He's got it now."

"Because branches lead to the tree, ya know?"

"Seems an awful mistake to me."

Mr. Miller was the only one who didn't care, but the other three pressed on, trying to convince him the founders had gotten everything backward and turned around.

Tommy was with old man Miller. Who cares? A name is a name is a name, and Branchville was as good as Oakville in his estimation. Besides, it wasn't like any *cool* names were on the table. If Fortress Darkheart, Evernitia, or something else from *Order of Cosmic Champions* were options, then he'd have an opinion. A strong opinion indeed.

Letting these memories take their rightful place in the far reaches of his mind, Tommy crossed the road on his bike, making sure to keep a careful eye out for sociopath teens hoping to crush some skulls with their car. He hopped the opposing curb and pedaled up Oak Drive. Old houses with expansive front lawns boxed in by elaborate wrought iron fences lined the road on both sides. His dad sometimes called this the "Richie Neighborhood," and Tommy could see why. The houses had a distinctly expensive appearance to them, though he wasn't entirely sure what gave that impression. He supposed all the brick and stone on the outside had something to do with it. And probably the way everything was perfectly manicured, from the lawns to the paint to the curtains he could see peeking through the windows.

As he worked his way to the business district, he noted how these houses always seemed abandoned. On a beautiful summer day like this, his neighbors would be out working in their yards, taking walks, grilling burgers, and playing catch. But this was a ghost town, no matter the season, no matter the weather. He wondered if real people even lived in those rock-faced behemoths, or if only the spirits of previous tenants haunted the property.

Tommy sped up. He didn't want to think about spooky stuff. Summer wasn't for scary things. The season was for bike rides and video games. It was for hikes and fishing. Exploring and friends.

Friends. Well, on that score at least, he wasn't doing so well. But he wouldn't let Evan's absence ruin his summer. There was still plenty to do and plenty to see. He'd just have to do and see everything alone.

Despite his optimism, the warm day became cold and the satisfied happiness in his belly dissipated. He crossed Elm Street and parked the green machine in a rusted bike rack on the shaded side of the Luncheonette.

He turned the corner to find the group of old men chatting in their exaggerated way. The pungent stink of cigar smoke enveloped the whole corner and rose above the group like steam from a witch's cauldron. Their laughs became cackles, and Tommy knew they were casting spells, perhaps to transform the town name to *Oakville*.

More spooky thoughts. What was with him today? He nodded at the group as he passed, but only Mr. Miller nodded back, an enormous smoldering cigar stuck into the corner of his mouth, his yellowed skin crinkled around the eyes.

The smell of hash browns, bacon, and coffee managed to escape the atmosphere of smoke and caused Tommy to waver on his feet with hunger. He found it fascinating how the Luncheonette always smelled of breakfast no matter the time, as if the decades of breakfasts served there had permeated the surrounding landscape with their odors. He wished he'd eaten something before leaving home. He had only had a bowl of Nintendo cereal (the Zelda side, of course), and now his stomach grumbled and complained.

He increased his pace to get away from the wonderful smells and dug in his pocket. He counted five coins and thought over his options. He'd planned on spending the entire haul on *Double Dragon*. He wasn't particularly good at the game, but with five quarters he might be able to finally beat Jick, the first-level boss. Now, though, he decided perhaps fifty cents should be relegated to a blue Little Hug Fruit Barrel and a bag of chips. Or he could go a couple of blocks down to the pizza place and get a slice and a Coke for the lunch deal.

The options were as endless as the summer days. The warm, contented feeling surged back. How could happiness stay away on a beautiful day such as this? Tommy continued along the sidewalk, kicking a stray rock until it skidded into the street. He stopped at the phone booth between the dentist's office and the Laundromat long enough to check the change return.

"Dang." Pure nothing. Maybe he'd collect a few cans to recycle, but that felt like work, and work was the last thing on his mind. Coming up were the trio of shops he longed for. He skipped over Quality 1 Video and Defender Comics to hit the corner shop for a snack. His stomach growled at the thought.

Tommy pushed the glass door—covered with posters and stickers of ice cream bars, snack foods, and cigarettes—and bumped into Evan Winger.

The impact caused Evan to stumble and drop his Fruit & Creme Twinkie. "Damn it!"

"Sorry. Hey—" Tommy tried to help, but Evan slapped his hand away. "Jeez. I said I was sorry."

Evan retrieved his snack cake and stepped outside, followed by Jonathan Miller.

"Hey," Tommy said, following them out. "Where have you been?"

Evan shrugged. "Around. You know."

"I've been calling."

Jonathan snorted.

"I was gonna play some *Double Dragon* if—"

"We already played," Evan cut in. "Out of money anyway."

Jonathan took a big bite of his own Twinkie, and strawberry jelly oozed from the bottom.

Tommy didn't like this feeling, as if he didn't belong. As if he wasn't welcome. It didn't make sense to feel like that around Evan. He was Tommy's best friend. They did everything together. They rode bikes every day, played Nintendo, and watched *Order of Cosmic Champions*. Or at least they used to. Until school ended and Evan got all weird and stopped coming out to play.

"Are you mad at me or something?" Tommy hadn't planned on asking such a direct question, but the way Evan was ignoring him was irritating. And Jonathan's stupid grin was even worse, as if he knew some big secret.

"Give me a break, huh?" Evan replied.

"Then what's going on?"

Evan kicked at nothing. "Listen, we don't have to hang out all the time, you know?"

Tommy's chest grew tight; his face became hot. He tried to play it off. "I know."

Evan nodded. "Look, I'm going to camp next week anyway. I won't be back till like the week before school starts."

Tommy felt his throat closing, and he pleaded with himself not to start crying like a diaper baby. He was eleven years old, almost twelve. He swallowed hard and chased away the threatening tears, but his stomach cramped even worse than when he'd only been hungry.

"My birthday is next week. Are you leaving before then?"

"I don't know, maybe I'll be there."

Jonathan tugged Evan's arm. "Come on."

"Yeah, we gotta go."

They walked off without waiting for a reply. Tommy said, "See ya," but his voice was far too low for them to hear. He didn't think it mattered, though. They were laughing as they walked and didn't look back once.

✳ ✳ ✳

Summer's warm embrace became suffocating. The season had Tommy in a stranglehold. Breaths came short and fast, and his vision darkened as he realized Evan might not be his best friend anymore. The worst part was that the transition had occurred with apathy and abandon, like a shrug of the shoulders. Did friendships really fall apart so easily?

Tommy stood outside of the corner shop with these thoughts buzzing his head like biting horseflies. His stomach ached, but with a pain deeper and sharper than hunger.

A lady his mom's age looked like she might ask if he was okay. The concern in her eyes and half-outstretched arm urged Tommy into action. He forced a little smile and shuffled over to Defender Comics to escape the inevitable questioning. If someone were to ask if he was okay, Tommy might burst into tears. He hated the clawing beast in his gut and wanted it gone, but the hungry thing was busy carving a hollow inside him. Once the grinding pain relented, Tommy would be left with something much worse: the agony of emptiness.

Inside the shop, the smell of new comics soothed Tommy's hurt. Not much. But it was something. A musky note of incense wove through the aroma of newsprint while reggae leaked like sublime molasses from the back room. His dad once said the place smelled like a head shop, whatever *that* was. He wore a strange smile when he said it, and Tommy's mom nudged him like he'd uttered a bad word. Mom tried to explain, but they got embarrassed and took him out for ice cream instead. Adults could be so weird.

Matty, the owner of the comic shop, had a neat system of comic-mailboxes for his regulars. Tommy had one such mailbox in which Matty placed relevant comics he thought Tommy might like, and he usually guessed correctly. Still, Tommy didn't have much money, and his parents were conservative with his allowance, going so far as to open a savings account where they deposited half of each week's bounty. He'd be happy for the safety net when he went to college, they said. But to Tommy, the money may as well have been Christmas socks.

"Hey, little buddy. How's it going?" Matty leaned over the glass counter at the back of the shop and grinned like an evil clown. Tommy thought the goatee made Matty look like he could work for the carnival. Or maybe the effect came from his tiny circular glasses and Rastafarian hat with nubs of short dreads peeking through.

"Hey." He tried to speak normally but ended up sounding like Eeyore from *Winnie the Pooh*.

Matty looked over the top of his glasses. "Why so glum, bud?"

Tommy forced a smile. He liked Matty okay, but he wasn't in the habit of dishing out personal details to random old people. Even ones he'd known all his life. Matty had to be like *thirty*. Maybe even older! He just wouldn't understand.

"Bored, I guess."

Matty pulled a shocked expression. "Bored? *Bored?*" He swept his gaze around the shop and held his arms out. "How could you be bored with all this *wonder* around you?"

"All I see are comic books and board games," Tommy said, playing the straight man.

"Dude."

A genuine smile teased at Tommy's lips, and some of the weight eased off his chest. "You've been watching too much *Ninja Turtles*."

"*Watching?*" Matty waved the idea away like a bothersome fly and dug under the counter. He returned with a bagged and boarded comic the size of a magazine: *Eastman and Laird's Teenage Mutant Ninja Turtles*. Only the turtles on the cover didn't look much like the cartoon.

"It's a magazine?"

"Naw, little bud. That's just how they printed it."

"It's in black and white."

Matty grimaced. "Oh no, not black and white! I'm melting, *melting!*"

Tommy laughed and said, "I didn't know they made a comic from the cartoon."

Matty placed the comic gingerly on the countertop and pushed it toward Tommy. "You got it backward. They based the cartoon on the *comic*." He tapped the counter. "This here is one of only 3,250 copies. I was there, man. I was at the convention when they first sold it."

"Whoa, so this is, like, worth money?"

"Big money, and it came out in '84! Imagine what it'll be worth when I'm old."

"You're already old, Matty."

"Hey! You just wait until you're my age. You won't think it's all that old then."

"Yeah, but that's like a hundred years away."

Matty's expression changed. He looked more like an actual adult. More like Tommy's dad. He returned the comic to its hiding spot under the counter, show and tell apparently over. "Listen, Tommy. You're a kid, and this probably won't make much sense to you now, but pay attention anyway. Pay attention like your life depends on these words— because it does."

A strange quiver ran through Tommy. This sounded dangerous. This sounded scary. He wasn't so sure he wanted to hear what Matty had to say.

"Right now, I bet your summer feels like it could go on forever. It's unending, like your childhood. Like your life. The truth is, time moves faster as you age, and before long the clock runs out."

"Matty—"

"No, listen. Even if you don't believe me, I want you to promise this one thing: Don't take even a moment for granted. Enjoy your child-hood while time is still on your side."

In a flash, old Mrs. Tither's final words came back to him. *Have a wonderful summer, and promise me you will* savor *every moment.* Her strange and lonely expression lingered in his mind, as if she were remem-bering something nearly lost. Something from long ago. Something she wanted back.

Tommy felt weird. He understood the message, but he also wanted the moment to end so he could go back to being a kid. "Okay, I will."

The comic shop owner watched Tommy's eyes for a few beats, then nodded. "Yeah. Yeah, I know you will. You're a good kid, Tommy." He straightened. "Why don't we see what's in this mailbox of yours?"

Matty meandered to the wall of mailboxes. A bunch of shelves were divided into narrow openings. Each section had a piece of paper with a name taped to the edge. Matty pulled out a small stack from a compartment labeled *Tommy G.* and returned with it to the counter.

"Let's see now." He flipped through a couple issues. "I have some different stuff in here I thought you might dig." Matty held each comic in turn. "*Adventurers, Book II.* Haven't had a chance to read it myself. First issue of *Alf.* Could be cool. A little more traditional, *Batman: A Death in the Family.*" He glanced sideways at Tommy to measure his reaction. "Any of these interesting you?"

"Well—"

"Fine, fine. I know what you're after." He slid a magazine from the bottom of the stack and presented it with a flourish. "The new *Order of Cosmic Champions Magazine* is in!"

"Awesome!" Tommy grabbed it out of Matty's hands.

"Yeah, thought you'd like that."

Like it? Tommy lived for it! The cartoon had been canceled, and except for the toy line and the promised comic series, this magazine was his only regular fix for new *OoCC* content. He ran his hand over the glossy cover, which depicted Masculon atop his fearless jungle cat, War Beast, ax outstretched and segmenting a violet sky. Skullagar, the main villain, had his staff raised in attack.

"Excellent," Tommy whispered. The artist depictions of *OoCC* on the magazine covers were like oil paintings, full of life and vibrancy. They appeared even more realistic than the animated version, a shocking revelation Tommy had when he purchased the first issue.

This issue—number seven—promised *two* full-sized posters inside. Past issues had come with only one poster, but even then, Tommy never took them out. His father had taught him the art of collecting, and rule number one was to never damage the collectible by opening the packaging, or in this case, removing a poster. Truth be told, the rule sucked. He wanted to plaster his room with the awesome artwork. Why did he have to preserve every little thing? It's not like he wanted to sell any of his stuff. Money didn't mean much to him unless it was for playing video games or buying—

"Uh oh."

Matty raised an eyebrow. "Uh oh?"

Tommy dug his five quarters out and plunked them onto the counter. "I only have a buck twenty-five."

"Uh oh indeed."

The cover of the magazine clearly read $1.95. Tommy was short.

Matty rubbed his fuzzy chin. "That's seventy cents you're missing. No small amount, little bud."

"I know," he said, defeated. The hurt of Evan's deceit slid back into his belly as he placed the magazine back onto the counter. "I can come back."

"Hold up." Matty rubbed his goatee again, pantomiming thought. "How about we make a deal?"

"What kind of deal?" Tommy was suspicious.

"Oh, nothing crazy. I'll let you have the magazine for a dollar twenty-five, and all you have to do is promise to *consider* selling me *Strange Tales #1*. Whataya say?" He stuck out his hand.

The comic Matty wanted wasn't something Tommy had been particularly interested in, but it *was* the first one his dad had ever bought, and he'd handed it down to Tommy as a birthday gift two years earlier. His dad was the one who had introduced comics to Tommy, brought him to the shop, and bought him his first issue ever. Collecting comics had been *their thing* for a while, until his dad got busy at the dealership. Around that same time Mom and Dad started having fights. Little disagreements at first, then big blowout screaming matches that made Tommy want to hide under his blankets.

Tommy had brought the comic into the shop one day to see if Matty could tell him what it was worth. His dad had said *Strange Tales* was valuable but hadn't said exactly *how* valuable. Matty had hounded Tommy to sell him the comic ever since, offering increasingly insane amounts of money. Hundreds and hundreds of dollars. He had of course almost immediately agreed, but then thoughts of his dad intruded. Dad had given him the comic. No, not merely *given*, but *handed down*. This implied Tommy was supposed to continue handing it down to his own children, then his children to theirs.

He loved the idea of passing the comic down through the generations, but he loved the idea of $800 even more.

"Gimme a break," Tommy said, looking at Matty's outstretched hand.

"No, give *me* a break. This is a lot of scratch we're talking about. And I've been on the level with you too." He brought out a price guide and flipped to the page listing the comic in question. "Look here."

Tommy scanned the page until he found the title, then ran his finger across to the prices. His eyes shot wide.

"Yeah, little bud. Prices went up again." He pointed at the mint price. "Look there, mint condition is thirteen hundred dollars." He grinned. "Don't get too excited, though. Yours is in good condition, but not mint. I have an eye for this, ya know. I'd call yours 'very fine,' and if you look here," he pointed at the price. *$1,050.* He closed the guide and shoved it under the counter.

"You'll give me a thousand bucks?"

"Well, no. But I'd be willing to do nine hundred. That's a hundred more than my last offer."

"And a hundred less than the comic is worth." Tommy grinned. He was good at math, and he was good at negotiating. He'd traded up for better comics with Evan a bunch of times and even sold some of his old toys to a kid at school for a pretty good price.

Matty raised his hands in surrender. "Just think it over. Like I said, the deal is I'll give you the magazine if you *consider* selling *Strange Tales*. I know your dad gave it to you."

He nodded. "Okay. Deal." He handed over the money and retrieved his magazine. "But I'm not promising anything."

Tommy turned and started to leave when Matty called out. "Little bud! You think you'll enter the contest? I bet you have some of your dad's talent."

"What—?" he began but stopped when he noticed the cover of his new magazine. It read *Create your own OoCC character and win!* He didn't even know what the prize was yet, but he knew the answer to Matty's question as surely as he knew his own name.

He responded without looking away from the magazine. "Totally!"

✳ ✳ ✳

When Tommy got home, it was almost dusk, and the air had become cool and dewy. He knew eventually the real heat of the summer would take hold, so he breathed deep, enjoying the weather while it remained pleasant. He parked his bike outside the garage and stampeded up the porch steps with his magazine in hand. Before he even opened the door, his parents' voices penetrated the walls. They were yelling at each other again. Tommy hesitated, his hand on the knob, wondering if there was anywhere else to go. Some wonderful place of escape, where friends called you back and parents didn't scream.

His stomach protested. Hunger had finally and completely gripped him, and he meant to satiate the craving with something other than a Hungry-Man dinner, fighting parents or not. As soon as he opened the door, Mom and Dad's voices cut out as if he'd turned off the television. They were both in the living room, standing dead center. Dad's face was red; Mom's eyes were glassy.

"Tommy, honey. We were—"

"Just talking," Dad cut in.

Sure. Like Tommy didn't know what he had heard. "Is there dinner?"

"We ordered some pizza," his father said. He glanced at Mom, and his features tightened. "Hey, looks like you got a new magazine there, huh? What do you think about taking it to your room for a bit, until the pizza gets here?"

His mom nodded, the edges of her mouth turned down, her eyes on the floor.

"Yeah, okay." Tommy beelined around the edge of the room and up the stairs. He paused at the head of the staircase and noticed his parents' bedroom door was closed, which was weird. They pretty much always left it open except when they were sleeping. Why would they close the door when they weren't even in the room?

Tommy stepped closer to their end of the hallway, curiosity tickling him behind the eyes. Then he hesitated. His birthday was in a week. Maybe they'd bought presents but hadn't had time to wrap them. Images of the newest *Order of Cosmic Champions* figurines danced through his mind. He'd been asking for a new EyeSpy figure ever since he lost his last one. The pyramid-headed bad guy was one of his favorites. Or maybe he'd finally get that rad Vile-Ette baddie. He'd held off asking because he was afraid his dad might say something about a female action figure. Dad already had the tendency to call the toys *dolls* despite Tommy's repeated corrections.

Since he loved a good surprise, Tommy retreated to his room rather than intrude on his parents'. There was the new magazine to enjoy, and pretty soon a hot pizza. He nearly drooled at the thought. *Pizza*. And maybe he could convince his parents to watch *The Goonies* again while they ate. He'd love to stop thinking about—

Evan.

Why had his supposed friend snubbed him like that? Evan was obviously hanging out with Jonathan, so why not invite Tommy along? Why not answer his calls?

Skullagar spoke inside his head: *Because he doesn't like you anymore.*

No, that couldn't be true. They were best friends. That meant something. It was a forever bond.

He said you didn't have to spend all your time together. Take the hint.

"Shut up!" Tommy screamed, shocking himself. He didn't think much about hearing the voices of characters in his head. The action figures often spoke when he played. He'd set up sprawling battle scenes and act them out, speaking for each character as their voices came to his head. It was just his imagination, and imagination was good. At least, that's what all his teachers would say. Plus Mom always complimented his drawings and stories. His father would even call him "a chip off the ol' block" when he caught Tommy sketching. There was nothing strange about imagination. Nothing weird.

So why did he feel uneasy about replying to the voice of Skullagar?

Because it's one thing to speak for your toys. It's another to have a conversation with them. He shook the thought off and closed his bedroom door.

His room was a bastion of wonder. Everything he loved was represented. Nintendo posters hung all around the room: *Zelda*, *Super Mario Bros.*, and *Metroid*. These of course weren't of the collectible variety, so they were okay to display. There was a Garfield alarm clock, magazines, books, and comics. His *OoCC* bedsheets and action figures. He even had his very own TV, though it only picked up antennae channels.

When his parents first gifted the spare television to him, he couldn't believe his luck. He constantly wished for another way to watch Saturday morning cartoons and a reprieve from the boring soaps and sporting events his parents watched. But the best thing about having a television in his room was he could tune in to the late-night movies he wasn't supposed to see. After his *Toxic Avenger* experience, he'd been a little gun shy about exploring more adult cinema, but he quickly found that the censored fare broadcasted on network television barely lived up to the hype. Still, he loved a good monster movie, and the local horror host, Count Frankenwolf, was too corny to actually be scary.

Besides, the network stations were his only option. A second VCR was out of the question, and the Nintendo was in the living room so everyone could enjoy the console. His dad was known to kick some major butt in *Duck Hunt*. Even Tommy, a veteran light gun slinger, couldn't keep up with his old man. When that dumb dog rose out of the grass to laugh at him after a miss, his dad would mimic the taunt, making the loss a hundred times worse.

Tommy flopped onto his bed and admired the cover of the magazine again. *Create your own OoCC character and win!*

"Awesome," he whispered to himself. This was a chance to flex his drawing muscles. But even better, to win something. But *what?*

He started flipping and found the ad for the contest on the fourth page. The instructions were explained in comic strip style, with Masculon exclaiming that every entry wins a free gift! But even better, the first-prize winner would get his character made into a real toy, receive a college scholarship, *plus* be "president for a day" at Telco Toys!

Tommy read through the rest of the comic strip feeling more and more confident about his chances. Didn't he draw every day? Didn't he already have a dozen or more *Order of Cosmic Champions* characters in his binder? It was like someone had peeked in on his life and designed a contest specifically for him. Not only was he an artist who was obsessed with the show, but he also had plenty of time to work on an entry, given that Evan was leaving for camp and didn't seem interested in hanging out anymore.

The thought made his heart ache a little. Any other day, Evan would have been the first person he called about the contest. They would have brainstormed and critiqued each other's entries, and if either of them won, they would share in the glory.

Downstairs, the doorbell chimed and, like Pavlov's dog, Tommy began to salivate. When he opened his bedroom door, he found his parents' door was open again too. Maybe they had sneaked up to wrap his presents while he was in his room. Curiosity clawed at him, so he bypassed the stairs and peered into their room. The bedroom smelled of Mom's perfume and carpet cleaner. Everything in his parents' room was usually perfect and neat. That's why the open suitcase with clothes hanging out looked so out of place. There were more piles of clothes next to the suitcase and Dad's little bathroom caddy that he took with him on vacations.

Were they taking a surprise summer vacation? Why hadn't they told him, and where was Mom's bag? The childlike faith that had soothed the day's hurt also concealed what was right in front of him. He saw, he even understood, but the thoughts flitted away like fireflies. Until—

"Tommy! Hey, Tommy-boy, dinner's here!"

His father's voice sounded *wrong*. Some hidden thing had tightened his vocal cords and caused him to stumble through the words.

"Come on down, son. Your mother and I—"

The whispered voice of his mom cut his dad off in a panic.

"Just come on down. The pizza is here."

Tommy glanced again at the suitcase on the bed. The lone suitcase that his father had half packed. He gazed at this innocent thing and Tommy knew.

Nothing was ever going to be the same again.

CHAPTER FIVE

HAPPY BIRTHDAY

Suzanne Grant stared at the backyard, decorated with all the *Order of Cosmic Champions* stuff she could find in the party supply store. Gold and red streamers were draped from tree to tree. The folding picnic tables were covered with paper in the same color scheme. Masculon and Skullagar toppers were placed equidistant from one another, surrounded by *OoCC* napkins, cups, and plates.

The decorations had cost far more than Suzanne wanted to spend, but Tommy had been insistent. She even bought the special *OoCC* Carvel ice cream cake, which alone cost as much as the main present (wrapped in *Order of Cosmic Champions* paper, of course).

Normally, Suzanne would have told Tommy to limit his requests, but with everything going on the past week, guilt outweighed frugality. They couldn't keep up this kind of spending, and she refused to spoil the boy long term. But it *was* his birthday, and the split was still new and painful for everyone.

The night of the uneaten pizza (as she'd come to think of the awful experience) reasserted itself in excruciating detail. They'd sat Tommy down at the table and served two slices each. Her little boy looked so worried, his eyes darting between the two of them, lingering longer on his father, as if he knew. Maybe that's why she'd blurted out the confession as Tommy took his first and only bite of pizza.

Why had she done that? Why couldn't she have waited?

The look of horror on Dave's face. The way Tommy stopped chewing as if he'd taken a bite of roadkill. The tears spilled immediately, like they'd merely been waiting in the wings. He had pushed his food away and stood so fast the chair toppled behind him. What he did next, Suzanne didn't think she could ever forget.

Tommy fixed his watering eyes on Dave and pointed at him, accusingly, like he'd discovered an alien spy had been wearing his father's skin. He shook and quaked while pointing the accusatory finger, his mouth working with no sound until finally he screeched a single word: "*You!*"

Dave's face was a horror-show mask of terror and confusion. Why hadn't she waited like they'd planned? Why hadn't she let her sweet boy have dinner before crushing his world?

Had Tommy actually howled like a dying animal or was memory assaulting her with terrible lies? She wasn't sure, but Tommy *had* taken the news of his father moving out hard. They'd called the decision "a break," but Tommy was a smart boy and had immediately asked if they were getting divorced.

Suzanne's stomach twisted at the word. *Divorce*. So final. The truth was, she didn't know. Neither Suzanne nor Dave had done anything to hurt the other. There had been no cheating, no lies or manipulations. Only a slow drifting apart, like a spreading pool of molasses.

"Mom?"

Suzanne held her hand to her chest. "How long were you standing there?"

"Are you okay?"

"Sure, just thinking." She motioned to the backyard. "What do you think? Not bad for a one-person decorating crew, huh?"

Tommy smiled as his eyes danced across the landscape, taking everything in. "It looks great, Mom." He surprised her with a big hug, his arms wrapping all the way around her, his forehead resting against her shoulder. When had he gotten so *tall*? The growth spurt was like his body sprinting to his twelfth birthday, keeping pace with the ever-increasing speed of time.

He released her from the hug, and she felt momentarily like she was peering into a mirror. He resembled his father too, of course, but the heavy eyebrows, slim nose, and golden-brown mass of hair—those were hers.

"Did Evan's parents call you?"

"No, I haven't heard from them. Why?"

He shrugged. "He never told me if he was coming."

This caught Suzie off guard. Tommy and Evan were best friends. They were basically attached at the hip. Why *wouldn't* Evan be there?

A horrible thought occurred to her: *I have no idea what is going on in my own son's life.* The notion spread like frostbite across her body. Had something happened between her son and his best friend, and had she missed it? Of course, she didn't know the answer because Suzie hadn't the faintest idea what Tommy had been doing this summer. She and Dave were still in the thick of marital tension when school had let out, and Tommy had slipped through the cracks.

No, not cracks. *Chasms.*

She had to close the distance between them before her son drifted beyond her reach. "Is something going on with you two? A fight?"

"No," he answered quickly. "Not a fight anyway."

"What—?"

"Will Dad be here?" Tommy cut in.

She let her previous question dissolve on her tongue. He obviously didn't want to talk. She squeezed his shoulder. "Of course, honey. He wouldn't miss your birthday; you know that."

He looked at her, eyebrows low, mouth in a knot. The expression asked: *Do I, though?*

✳ ✳ ✳

Over the next couple hours, the backyard party filled with neighbors, family, and friends. Suzie brought out the portable boom box and played a variety of Tommy's cassette tapes, though she kept it low enough to be mostly background noise. Partly to be courteous and partly because she didn't particularly like most of the music. He didn't listen to any of that awful heavy metal at least. She'd heard stories about bands hiding messages in their songs about Satan and instructions detailing how to raise the dead. She wasn't sure she believed the gossip, but then again, you never know.

Suzanne's mother and sister were sitting at the farthest table, each with a plate of french fries. Her mother also had a hot dog that she shouldn't have been eating with her high blood pressure. They were coddling Tommy, probably asking him a million questions about his summer and what he was hoping to get for his birthday.

Some of his schoolmates were playing badminton. Others were busy scarfing food. A couple parents stayed, but most brought their kids and begged off for various reasons. The funniest having been Tina's mother, Denise, who confessed she had a bad case of diarrhea from the spicy Tex-Mex they had for dinner. Suzanne laughed awkwardly, embarrassed by the admission and trying hard not to think about Denise on the toilet.

She checked the time. Already four o'clock, and she'd told everyone the party would go to about 5:30. They still hadn't done the cake or the presents, but Suzanne had been holding out hope that Evan would show up.

As if summoned by her constant worry, Evan pushed the fence gate open and stepped through with another boy she didn't know. Tommy's reaction confused her. His face at first registered happy, then immediately disappointed. Still, he waved to Evan and walked over. They spoke, and the other boy—a stocky kid who looked older—gazed around the backyard with a sneer she didn't care for.

No matter. Evan had arrived, and the time was slipping out from under them. Suzanne went into the kitchen to get the ice cream cake and found Dave standing at the counter, his hands planted flat on the surface, staring at nothing.

"Are you drunk?" She said it without thinking. Suzie immediately regretted the reflex.

Dave didn't respond right away, nor did he appear angry. His expression was one of deep thought and melancholia. The look of a man who'd been told he was dying of cancer. After another beat, he replied, "No."

She chided herself for the attack. It was the sort of knee-jerk accusation Dave said he was sick of. The sort of mean-spirited salutation he'd grown tired of enduring. And Suzanne understood. She even agreed that she treated him unfairly at times. But she also couldn't stop herself. After years of respectfully requesting changes in his habits, and years of being ignored, she had finally and irrevocably grown at first distant, then aggressive.

She shook her head. Marriage was harder than her parents had ever let on. "Sorry, you just look out of sorts."

He spat a joyless laugh. "I'm *visiting* my house for our son's birthday after sleeping in a motel for a week. Yeah. I'm out of sorts."

"Don't speak to me that way—"

"But you can accuse me of coming to Tommy's birthday drunk? You can kick me out of my house? You can . . ." he trailed off, the anger fizzling before he could get going. "Forget it."

Her throat tightened, and she feared another bout of crying would follow if she didn't busy herself. So she brushed past her husband and retrieved the Flip Grip cake from the freezer. The mohawked hero with his robotic arm appeared a little worse for wear in cake form, but the decorators had done their best.

"Can you get the candles? They're in the junk drawer."

Before Dave could answer, the sliding door shot open and Tommy strode in. He closed the door much too hard, causing plates and cups to rattle in the china cabinet. His face was red and his mouth a sealed line.

He made to rush past them, but Dave put his arm around Tommy and held him fast. "Whoa there, kiddo. What's going on?" He held his son at arm's length and took a good, long look at him. Then he gazed out at the party. "What happened?"

Tommy shook his head. He appeared angrier than Suzanne had ever seen him, and on the verge of tears. "I don't want to talk about it."

"About what?" she said, coming closer.

He shot her a look. "*Nothing.*"

Dave released Tommy's shoulders. "Alrighty, no problem. Forgotten. But don't get too far. We're serving cake in a few minutes."

Suzanne understood what Dave was attempting, but from the expression on her son's face, the feigned merriment was a lost cause.

Tommy backed away, shaking his head. "I don't care. I don't want cake, I don't want any presents, and I don't want to be at this stupid party!"

Suzanne's stomach sank. She knew he didn't mean it, but the words hurt all the same. What hurt even worse was seeing her baby broken and disappointed on his birthday.

"Tommy! Your mother put a lot of—"

"It's okay, Dave."

"I'm sorry. I didn't mean the party's stupid." He fixed her with a pleading expression that broke her heart. "Please don't make me go back out there. *Please.*"

Dave glanced at her, concerned. And she understood why. Tommy never acted like this. Even as a baby he hadn't thrown tantrums. During teething he barely made a sound. Through the terrible twos, Tommy was thoughtful and kind. This just wasn't like him.

She tried to keep the concern from her voice. "Are you hurt? Is there anything we need to know?"

"*No.*" He stared through the glass door as if afraid someone might come in. "*Please.*"

"Fine, go to your room. But we are talking about this later."

He started to go, and she called to him, "And we are serving your guests this cake!"

"We'll save you some," Dave added.

She shot him a face but was glad he'd said it. She didn't know what had happened out there, but she knew Tommy wouldn't have abandoned his own party without a good reason. In the meantime, she meant to find out what was going on, with or without Tommy's cooperation.

CHAPTER SIX

REWIND

I t was June 26th, 1988, and Tommy was officially twelve years old. Friends from school were running around and playing party games in the *OoCC*-themed backyard. Some of the younger siblings were spellbound by a small balloon pit his mom had set up in the sandbox. He mostly considered himself far too old for the sandbox, but it did make a perfect place for desert battles in The Undying Expanse of planet Teltam.

Some of the other kids were setting up a badminton game that he was thinking of joining when Grandma Winnie called him over. Aunt Katherine was at the table too. She was a little younger than his mom and always struck him as kind of weird. Well, not weird exactly. Surely out of place with her tattoos and piercings. She had a streak of pink in her frizzed blonde hair that he couldn't believe Grandma hadn't yelled at her about.

"Come give your grandma a hug, birthday boy." The monolith of a woman spread her arms, but she didn't stand from the flimsy folding chair. He'd already hugged her when she arrived but knew better than to refuse a grandma her due. She clasped him hard around the back and shook him from side to side, making him laugh. She smelled of rose water and beauty parlor hair.

After Grandma released him, Aunt Kathy said, "Don't worry, you're all paid up with me."

Grandma said, "Are you excited for the new school this fall?"

"For sure!" In truth, he hadn't given school a single thought. What kid in his right mind thought about school in *June*?

"You're growing up so fast."

Aunt Kathy said, "No kidding. Look at him, Ma. Musta grown a few inches."

Tommy smiled but didn't know what to say. Sure, he was growing, he guessed. But wasn't that what kids did?

Aunt Kathy reached into her leather purse (covered with all kinds of strange heavy metal pins) and said, "Come here, kiddo."

Grandma tutted and made a show of looking the other way. "I don't see anything. I don't *know* anything. I'm just an old lady."

"Come on, Ma. Cut it out." Aunt Kathy retrieved a small rectangular gift from her purse and handed it to Tommy. She whispered conspiratorially, "I snagged this from work for you. Doesn't officially come out until next month, but we had boxes of them in back for release day."

Grandma shook her head and continued to stare in the opposite direction. In a singsong voice, she said, "I'm not listening."

"You *stole* it?"

At this, Grandma Winnie snapped her neck around and fixed her youngest with a stern face.

"I paid for it. I was just able to get one early because I work there."

Chin high, eyes half closed, Grandma looked away again.

"Thanks, Aunt Kathy."

"Save the present for later. Open it when you're alone. You know how your mother gets."

"Sure thing." Tommy hugged his aunt. Just then, he saw Evan walk through the backyard gate.

Tommy's heart leapt. Evan came! He honestly didn't think his friend would show. Not after the last time they spoke. Not after a full week of being blown off. But there he was, and . . . and there was Jonathan Miller, walking in behind him. Tommy's shoulders slumped. "Oh," he muttered to himself.

Aunt Kathy seemed like she wanted to ask what was wrong, so he said, "Thanks again for the present." He put it in his pocket. "I'm going to go say hi to Evan."

"Okay, kiddo. Happy birthday."

Grandma finally turned back to her daughter and Tommy, smiling in her knowing way. Tommy wondered how his mom had become more uptight than her own mother, but figured it was one of those secrets of the adult world he'd never understand.

Both Evan and Jonathan remained near the gate with weird expressions on their faces. Jonathan nudged Evan and nodded at the tables. They both grinned, but the smiles felt mean somehow.

"Hey, Evan. Hey, Jonathan. I didn't think you were gonna come."

"Yeah, well, we were bored."

"Oh, okay . . . ?"

"Yeah," Jonathan added. "Better than sitting around doing nothing."

"Um, there's hot dogs, hamburgers, fries, and cookies. And we're gonna have cake." Tommy's spirit lightened. "My mom got me the Flip Grip ice cream cake! You know? The one from Carvel with the gumball eyes. You can have one of the eyes if you want."

Jonathan looked bothered, so Tommy added, "Sorry, there's only two, and I wanted one because it's my birthday, and Evan is my best friend, so he gets the other one, but maybe—"

"I don't want the stupid gumball," Jonathan said.

"I didn't mean to—"

Evan cut him off, "Dude, no one wants the gumballs."

Tommy felt as if someone had punched him in the gut. Why was Evan acting like this? Why had he brought Jonathan here? He wasn't even invited, and Tommy was being nice anyway.

Evan kept gazing around the party, shaking his head. His face looked sour like he'd stepped in poop or drunk old milk. "This is so stupid."

Tommy honestly had no idea what he was talking about. "What's stupid?"

"This whole dumb party."

Jonathan said, "Yeah, *Order of Cosmic Champions*? *Really*? They don't even make the cartoon anymore."

Evan was nodding his head as if he agreed, which didn't make any sense.

Tommy said, "But you love *Order of Cosmic Champions*. Between us we have all the action figures, and we've seen all the episodes! Last Halloween we both went as Masculon, and—"

"Shut up!" Evan appeared somehow both embarrassed *and* angry.

"Aw, you both went as Masculon? So cute. Little girlfriends playing dress-up together."

Evan shoved Jonathan.

"All right, all right." He held his hands out in surrender and refocused his jabs at Tommy. "I bet you watch *The Goddess of Good*, now that *Order of Cosmic Champions* only airs as reruns."

Evan laughed sharp and hurtful. "Yeah, totally. He totally does!"

"But you watched it with me."

"Yeah, right. Shut up, wuss. Big wussy liar."

"Come on, let's get out of here," Jonathan said. "I told you this would suck."

Before he left, Evan landed one last gut punch. "Stop calling me already. You're bothering my mom." He hesitated at the gate, staring at his own feet. "I'm not your best friend anymore, so screw off."

Tommy's feet were encased in cement as he watched them stomp out of his backyard and disappear beyond the fence. His whole body tingled, and his eyes stung. The world turned gray around the edges. He wanted to crawl out of the bright summer sun and hide in a dark cavern.

"Tommy, honey?"

His grandmother's voice brought him back before he could escape into his mind. When he turned, a few of his guests were watching with sad expressions on their faces. His grandma and aunt both looked the same way. Like he was a sick, lost puppy.

They heard. They heard everything, Skullagar's voice taunted in his head. *Now they think you're a loser. A big baby loser on his birthday.*

"Are you okay, sweetie?" Aunt Kathy asked.

The earth shifted below Tommy's feet. He grew dizzy and nauseated, like that time they drove to New Hampshire on the twisty mountain roads. He wanted to lash out and yell at them to leave him alone. He wanted to scream for the other kids to go away.

Skullagar said, *Yes! Stomp the vermin!*

"No!"

His grandma and aunt met eyes.

"I mean, I—" Tommy's mouth was dry and acrid. "I don't feel so good." He walked away fast, skirting past his grandmother and aunt, bypassing his school friends who were trying to ask if he was okay.

He spotted his parents through the sliding door, talking in the kitchen, and he knew they'd ask what had happened. He'd have to tell them something, because there was no way he was staying at his party. Not now. Not after everyone had watched his best friend make fun of him. His face burned hot, and his palms grew sweaty.

He wanted to go to his room and be alone.

Please, God. Please let them understand.

CHAPTER SEVEN
FAST FORWARD

After fighting past his parents, Tommy got into bed and curled up under the covers. He was afraid that the tears would finally come then, but they didn't. Instead, the ravenous ghoul reappeared to carve his insides with bleak, excruciating sadness. He'd been ambushed at his own birthday party by his best friend. In his short life, Tommy never imagined anything so cruel could happen to him.

"Former best friend," Skullagar corrected with malice from the side of the bed.

Had Tommy not been so absorbed in his own pain, he might have worried about the disembodied voice of Skullagar finding shape and form in the real world. He was only an apparition, yet somehow more real than the cartoon. Calculating green eyes stared from behind his bleached skull mask. The fur covering his body was matted and ugly in comparison to the action figures. Tommy even thought he could smell a musky animal odor in his room.

The beast inside kept carving and scooping. He was creating a comfortable hole inside Tommy. A pleasantly hollow place. Tommy cramped with the needling pain of a lost friend and ruined party. Of being made fun of in front of his grandma and aunt. And what made everything worse was he didn't know why Evan had turned on him. He acted like . . . well, like what his dad called an "A-hole." Tommy was old enough to know what the "A" stood for (schoolmates said it often enough), but he also knew how disappointed his parents were when he cursed. And if he started *thinking* the words, they'd start slipping out.

He threw the covers off and sat. Skullagar was gone, but in the spot where he had been lay the *OoCC* magazine. Tommy had already read most of the articles and peeked between the folds to see the posters, but he hadn't started work on the contest entry yet. He'd been waiting for his birthday. Waiting to talk to Evan and see if he'd want to do the contest together.

At this thought, the goblin inside his belly disappeared, cavorting off to trouble some other unlucky child. In its place, the vile creature left only a dark cavern. Tommy sensed the missing pieces of himself that had been devoured. The emptiness inside was like the time he'd gotten lost at the mall, the faces of strangers all around him. The word *lost, lost, lost* repeating in his head.

Tommy dug out the present his aunt had given him, hoping this would clear his mind of malice. He knew the gift was a cassette tape because Aunt Kathy worked at a music store, and the shape of the gift was unmistakable. He would have preferred a CD, but his dad insisted they were a fad and refused to invest in a completely new music library. Tommy rolled his eyes at the idea and tore the wrapping paper away, revealing a bloody skull staring back.

"Holy cow!" He ripped away more paper and saw the name of the band, Slayer, was scrawled inside one of those devil star things they sometimes showed on the news while the concerned anchor talked breathlessly about corrupted youth. Even the title was blasphemous: *South of Heaven*. Tommy wasn't a dope; he knew exactly what that meant. No wonder his aunt said to open the present alone. There was no way he could let his mom see, and in truth, even he was a little scared to hear what was on the tape. Still, it seemed a fitting gift, given his mindset as of late, and especially after the scene outside.

Evan wasn't his friend anymore. There'd be no more sleepovers. No more awesome action figure battles. No more Nintendo contests. No more trips to King's Island. No more screaming their heads off on the tree-lined rails of The Beast, fearing their arms would be lopped off in the tunnel of the roller coaster.

In other words, no more *summer*. Because what kind of summer could he have all by himself? Riding his bike alone, playing video games alone. He'd already had a taste of a solitary vacation, and he didn't like it one bit.

Flipping to the contest page, Tommy thought he'd try to enter anyway. That was something he could do alone. He didn't need Evan to enter. And if he won, he didn't have to share the spoils either.

Skullagar began whispering again. Explaining ideas for a new character. One that could house the spirit of Skullagar should he ever fall in battle.

"A *villain*," Tommy mused. He liked the idea of drawing something a little bad. A little evil. He always sketched the heroes of *Order of Cosmic Champions*, but he wasn't feeling very heroic anymore. No, he was feeling vengeful. Angry. *Mean*. Maybe he'd even play the new Slayer tape while he drew. He didn't like acknowledging the sensation. Certainly Pastor Roberts wouldn't approve. But in those defiled moments, Tommy wasn't so sure he cared.

The dark thoughts didn't make him feel completely better, but they did fill the hole in his gut. Anger blunted the sharp edge of pain. He might even want some cake after all. Besides, it was his party. His cake. *His* presents.

Tommy stood and placed the magazine on his desk. Maybe the summer wouldn't be so bad. There was still no school, and the endless summer days held a magic Tommy would regret squandering. He left his room and ventured back to the birthday party, a new, dark hope swelling inside like a gorging tick.

CHAPTER EIGHT

THE SUMMERTIME BLUES

Suzanne peeked into the living room where Dave was playing Nintendo with Tommy. *Contra*, she thought, but it could have been anything. Suzie never was one for the electronic games.

She ducked back into the kitchen and slapped the poultry, watching its naked flesh jiggle. "Ugh. I really hate you, chicken." But rotisserie chicken was Dave's favorite, so rotisserie chicken it would be.

She wondered for the hundredth time if letting Dave move back in had been the right call. After Tommy's mini-meltdown at his birthday a few weeks back, Dave and Suzanne had a serious talk about the separation, which by all accounts had been a runaway train headed for Divorce Land. *The happiest place on earth!* Then Tommy dove headfirst in front of the train, and would you look at that—the brakes were still functioning after all.

They agreed to give it one last try. There was still a chance. A small, glimmering hope they could rekindle the dying flame. Summer would be the trial period, until Tommy was settled in the new school. At least that way they wouldn't completely ruin his vacation.

"Chicken, Suzie. There's a chicken to cook."

"You talking to yourself again, Ma?" Tommy had sneaked up on her while she wrestled with her choice.

"Never. Me and Mr. Slippery Bottom here were discussing where he'd prefer I jammed the skewers."

Tommy pulled a shocked face and started laughing. "Jeez. Go easy on the poor guy."

She laughed along with him, not sure where the passive-aggressive remark had come from. Maybe the pressure of holding in all the complaints she wanted to fling at Dave had caused cracks in her shiny mom-veneer.

"Say, are you and your father getting along okay?"

Tommy rolled his eyes and went to the fridge. "Sure. Are there any Wild Cherry Pepsis left?"

Suzanne grabbed some spices from the cupboard and indiscriminately sprinkled a variety of things onto the chicken. Lemon pepper, salt, garlic powder, paprika—

"Is that cayenne?"

Suzanne stopped short. "Crap, crap, crap." She ran for a paper towel, balled it up, and blotted at the slippery skin. "I thought it was paprika." As she blotted, pieces of paper tore away and stuck fast to the chicken skin. "Oh, *crap*."

Tommy popped the top of his soda, releasing a satisfying hiss.

She grabbed the can before he could have any and drank a gulp.

"Aw, Mom! Your gross chicken hands!"

She nearly snorted a stream of soda from her nose. "Calm down. I don't want you drinking so much of this sugar water anyway." She took another gulp.

"Oh, sure." He held his hands out. "Presenting the reigning queen of hypocrisy."

"Hey! Don't get sarcastic with *me*!" The smile crept back on her face despite her seriousness. "Where did you hear that word? Hypocrisy?"

Tommy took the soda back and made a sickened face at the greasy fingerprints. He brought it to the sink and carefully rinsed off the sides. "What, you think I'm a dope?"

"*Tommy.*"

"Okay, okay." He took a long drink and smacked his lips. "I've been reading a lot, I guess." His expression drooped then, as if he'd thought of something sad.

Ever since his birthday party, Tommy had spent most of his time locked away in his room either reading or drawing. He still emerged for cartoons, video games, and the occasional bike ride, but not nearly as often as he used to. And he was sullen. His feet dragged, literally. He slouched more too. Dave attributed it to the sudden growth spurt, but Suzanne wasn't so sure.

Tommy started back to the living room when Suzanne surprised herself with a question. One she didn't think she'd ask again, not after the way he'd reacted before. "You feel like talking about what happened on your birthday?"

His entire body tensed. He was facing away from her, but she could tell he was not happy. "*Mom.*"

Don't push it, don't push it, don't push it . . . "You'd feel better if you—"

"Nothing happened, okay?"

From the other room, Dave called in, saving her from making things any worse. "Come on! The game ain't gonna play itself!"

Tommy left without saying anything, and she was okay with that. They were having such a nice moment and she had to go and ruin it.

Her mom and sister had filled her in on what little they'd witnessed.

Kathy said they couldn't hear the boys but did know they were being mean and stomped off, leaving Tommy shellshocked. Now she was the one left stricken. Her family was fractured, and the cracks were healing crooked. She didn't know what the last couple weeks of summer would hold, but it looked to be more of the summertime blues.

CHAPTER NINE
CONTEST ENTRY

Tommy retreated to his room not long after the weird conversation with his mom. Everything had been fine until she'd asked about his party. For like the six billionth time. Why couldn't she take the hint and leave him alone already? His dad was even worse because he went too far in the other direction. He didn't ask *any* questions, reducing their every interaction to an uncomfortable mono-syllabic conversation about nothing. Whenever he wasn't working, his dad tried to hang out with him, which was nice, he guessed. But the hang sessions also felt forced. He sensed his father watching for Mom to poke her head in so he could score points. Every beer he *didn't* drink, every hour he spent with Tommy, it was like he was keeping score and waiting for Mom to pat him on the head and say, "Good, David. Now isn't that a good David? *Yes*, good *boy*."

Tommy knew his father's interest in hanging out wasn't about him, and that was the painful part. His parents were fighting this secret war with each other. Mom trying to prove Dad was just faking, and Dad trying to prove he was on the level. Tommy was caught in the middle.

He plunked down at his worn wooden desk and opened the drawer. He took out two drawings and laid them next to each other. He had sketched nearly a dozen different designs for the contest, but finally narrowed his choice to two. On the left was Robo-Champ, a half human, half cyborg hero of Evernitia. He could be outmatched only by Masculon. His main weapon was a quantum ray, and his secondary weapon was a rocket arm. Tommy considered the sketch and read over all his character notes again. Robo-Champ was a solid creation.

To the right was his second choice, Mechani-Ghoul. Similar in theme, but Mechani-Ghoul was a villain and *way* cooler. He'd sketched this one with Slayer blaring through the headphones of his Walkman, fueling the devious design. The creature's cavernous body would act as a storage container for Skullagar's soul if he were ever killed in battle. This monstrous mixture of science and magic was completely robotic, with titanium armor, a giant bladed arm, and a built-in laser defense system. Even better, while Skullagar was still alive, he could control Mechani-Ghoul's every action through mere thought.

A smile overtook Tommy's face. The more he thought about the options, the more he realized . . .

"Sorry, Robo-Champ, but this once, the bad guy is going to win."

Skullagar laughed menacingly inside Tommy's head. "A second in command I can trust! Excellent, *excellent*. You did admirable work, Tommy. Good, good work indeed."

"Thanks, Skully."

"What did I say about calling me that! You take it back!"

Tommy laughed to himself, then concentrated on putting his submission together. He carefully tore out the entry form along its perforated edge, reminding himself to buy a spare copy of the magazine if Matty had any left at the comic shop.

At the mailbox, Tommy closed his eyes. "God, I know we're not sup-posed to pray for stuff. Pastor told us not to, and I know you're not Santa or anything. But I thought just this once, maybe you could bless my entry." He opened his eyes. "Um, amen?" He kissed the envelope and stuffed it into the mailbox.

This contest was as big as a rocket ship, and Tommy had strapped himself into the cockpit, into which he'd also packed every last remnant of hope. When the shuttle blasted off with Tommy riding shotgun as the winner, everything could go back to normal. His parents would love each other. They'd be a happy, normal family. Evan would want to be his friend. The crappy summer would be erased and replaced by an amazing first year of junior high.

Tommy knew, with this win, everything would be okay again.

It had to be.

Part Three

GROWING PAINS

CHAPTER TEN

SCHOOL'S IN

How could the summer be over already? Tommy glanced around his room at the pile of new school clothes (lots of striped shirts and earth-tone trousers), his new backpack, spiral notebooks, a pencil case, and all the other trappings of a new school year. The only good thing to come from the shopping trips was his blue and white Reebok high-tops.

He'd originally wanted an *Order of Cosmic Champions* Trapper Keeper, but after Evan and Jonathan made fun of *OoCC* at his party, he didn't know how well the binder would go over in junior high. They probably all had race car and jet plane folders. *Too cool for school.*

The last day of summer vacation was already half gone. Before long, he'd be waking up to catch the school bus. His parents used to drive him every morning to Golden Pines, but the new junior high was too far away, and the bus pickup was right at the end of their street. A fluttering of nerves danced in his stomach at the thought of the new morning routine. Some of the local kids would be on the bus, but he didn't hang out with any of them. Who would he sit with? Would people think he was weird if he sat alone? These were all new worries to Tommy. Before this, everything had always been *right*. Everything had been perfect.

Until elementary school ended, and his parents split. Until his best friend abandoned him. Then every little thing bothered Tommy. His body felt wrong, like it didn't belong to him. Creepy crawly thoughts invaded his peace of mind on a whim, ruining otherwise pleasant moments.

He saw the Nintendo posters on the back wall, the loose game manuals piled on the floor. On the small desk across from his bed, he had set up a few *OoCC* figures in a mock battle. On one side stood Masculon and Groppo. The tiny blue wizard creature was usually a bumbling mess and always managed to screw things up. Masculon, the bulging, ax-toting hero, was none too pleased with the sidekick selection.

In his booming voice, laden with reverb, he said, "I'd prefer Flip Grip or Defendra. Will you obey, Tommy of Earth?"

"Sorry, Masculon. Not today." No, he didn't feel much like helping the fantasy fighter. In fact, he thought he'd like to see Masculon lose for once.

On the opposing team stood Skullagar and EyeSpy (one of his birthday gifts). A much more formidable pairing. Plus Munch Mouth hid waiting behind a pile of comics, ready to ambush the heroic duo. He chomped impatiently with his mechanized mouth, drooling over the prospect of sticking it to those damn do-gooders.

The battle would be difficult, even with the chips stacked in Skullagar's favor. Fate, that invisible hand controlling their actions, thoughts, and words, favored Masculon. Tommy repositioned the villain's arms to be outstretched overhead in a pose of anguish.

"Cruel fates!" the menace screeched.

Tommy laughed at the theatrics playing out in his mind. *Poor Skullagar. He never stands a chance.*

The skeletal face of his action figure snapped toward Tommy, its eyes blazing. "Like you, Tommy. You don't stand a chance either."

The boy screamed and swept his arm across the desk, knocking the figures onto the floor. He fell back, his breath coming fast. What the *heck*? Did Skullagar actually move?

Tommy approached slowly. The figures lay still on the carpeted floor. No signs of life. He stepped closer and drew his foot back to kick the toy.

The door shot open and Tommy yelped.

His mother gasped. "What's wrong?"

"Cripes, Mom! Wouldya knock?"

She held her hands in surrender. "Sorry, sorry. I called but you weren't answering." She jerked a thumb over her shoulder. "Dinner's ready."

His breathing stabilized even as his heart continued to thud. "I'll be down in a minute."

She fixed him with a patented warning expression as only a mother can. Her face said all it needed to, but she added, "Two minutes and your little butt is at the dinner table."

"Aw, Ma," he groaned. "I wish you'd stop talking about my butt."

"Ha-ha-*ha*." She tapped her watch. "Two minutes."

She left without closing the door, and Tommy figured that was A-OK. In case Skullagar started to move again, he had a clear line of retreat. He understood imagination, but this—this was different. The toy's head had *moved* . . . hadn't it?

Yes, he was sure of it. A fast twist of the neck until those brilliant green eyes fixed on Tommy. He shivered at the thought. Or was the hallucination only his mind playing tricks?

He approached the pile of figures and kicked them. They scattered but didn't move any more than his own foot had made them.

"Tommy!" his father yelled from downstairs. "Dinner! *Now!*"

Ugh, like a dog. Tommy, here. Tommy, sit. Tommy, eat.

"I'm *coming*!" he screamed with a little too much anger. His father didn't reply, but Tommy suspected he would get a talking-to later.

"Whatever," he muttered, hating this feeling of apathy and frustration. Everything sucked, and the only thing he ever looked forward to was finding out if he had won the *OoCC* contest. Weeks had passed since he entered. An announcement had to be coming soon. Then things could be okay again. He'd be president for a day at Telco Toys, his toy would get made, and he'd have a big scholarship for art school.

For the hundredth time that summer, Tommy convinced himself that everything would get better. The hole in his stomach was packed so tight with this hope, he couldn't feel the warnings he'd buried deep underneath.

* * *

Standing at the top of his hill, Tommy perceived the summer slip between his fingers. He'd woken that morning before the sun, and even now with its bright heat just over the horizon, the far-off chill of approaching autumn teased on the wind. Real autumn wasn't until the end of September, but for him and every kid returning to school, summer was officially over.

Starting the long walk to the bus stop, he knew there'd be those crossover weeks when schoolwork hadn't yet reached a crescendo and the days were still warm and pleasant. But he also saw the world with the clear, cruelly honest eyes of a child. He knew what the end of summer was like because he'd seen it before. All children knew the omens, and they read them like fortune tellers at street fairs.

Stores shifted their summertime merchandise—ice pops, coolers, and beach gear—to folders, pencils, and backpacks. The ice cream truck stopped coming around as much. Back-to-school commercials overtook the airwaves. Trips to Toys "R" Us morphed into shopping for school clothes at Kids "R" Us. What a nightmare.

Ahead, the older kids from the neighborhood walked to the bus stop. They talked loudly and laughed, as if the first day of school wasn't an abysmal and treacherous thing stalking their every footfall across the warming pavement. Tommy thought to call out for them to wait, then changed his mind. An unfamiliar fluttering batted inside his chest and stomach. Something like fear, but not exactly.

Mrs. Simpson was scooting Princess Penelope away from a neighbor's lawn. She waved to Tommy and called out, "Have a great first day back!"

"Thank you, I will!" Though he wasn't so sure.

The cool morning breeze blew his hair back from his eyes. He tried to enjoy the moment but found his mind remained occupied by annoying thoughts of the kind that had kept him awake most of the night. Would he see Evan today? Would they ignore each other or make up?

Skullagar cackled inside his mind, which was answer enough. No, he was still mad at Evan. His friend had ruined his birthday party and never even apologized. Earlier in the summer, he wanted nothing more than to have his friendship with Evan go back to normal. Now, as he approached the small group of kids waiting for the bus, he decided Evan would have to work to regain his trust and friendship.

A group of three kids stood at the corner, across from the roller-skating rink. Two of them were brothers, but their parents dressed them like twins. Today they wore acid wash jeans and Nike sneakers. At least they had the sense to wear different color shirts. The third was a girl he'd never seen before, maybe from a family that had moved in over the summer. She had platinum blonde hair held back with a neon pink headband, blue-green eyes, and the most timid smile he'd ever seen.

She looked up as he approached, her mouth twisted in a bow. "Hey."

"Hey." Tommy joined the circle. "Hey, guys," he said to the brothers, trying to remember their names. Kyle and Jeff? No, Frank and John?

The one he then thought might be Randy said, "Damn, Tommy. Been eating your Wheaties, huh?"

His brother—Sam?—laughed way too hard, but Tommy ignored them.

He nodded awkwardly at the girl. "Did you just move here?"

"A couple weeks ago."

"Nice," Tommy laughed. "Just in time for school."

She giggled dutifully and nodded the affirmative.

Tommy bit the inside of his cheeks. "What grade are you in?"

"Sixth. You?"

"Same."

The brothers elbowed each other and bowed their heads together, laughing. "Watch out for sparks! Boy, are they flying!"

"Yeah, like, totally smoldering conversation, you two."

The girl blushed and hit the younger brother. Humphrey? Andy?

She turned back to Tommy, still flushed, but obviously not too bothered. "I'm Miranda."

"Tommy."

"No. That's not right." She held her hands up, framing his face. "You look more like a . . ." She frowned appraisingly. "Tony. Yeah, definitely *Tony*."

"Sorry to disappoint."

Her smile grew less timid. "I'm not."

The older brother laughed. "Sparks, I tell ya. Sparks!"

✳ ✳ ✳

The group chatted a few more minutes about their summers. Tommy left out the more disappointing aspects of vacation, which didn't leave a whole lot for him to say. He discovered Miranda was from New Jersey, and he thought that was pretty cool because of how close it was to New York.

Before long, the bright yellow bus clattered down the road, creaking and hissing to a stop. The bus was already half filled with morose and sleepy kids. Tommy wouldn't have to seek out someone to sit with at least, as long as Miranda didn't mind.

The brothers (Ambrose and Titus, it turned out) got on the bus first, then Miranda, and Tommy brought up the rear. Ambrose and Titus slapped five with a few kids on the way down the aisle and plopped into a seat together. Miranda stepped slower through the aisle, looking back and forth for a place to sit.

Tommy willed her to take one of the empty seats near the rear so he could ask to sit with her. She was new after all, so she wouldn't know anyone else.

"Miranda! Over here!" A mousy girl with braces waved her over.

Miranda waved back. "Hey, Tonya!" She hurried over and sat down.

Tommy blew out a breath he didn't know he had been holding and took one of the empty seats near the back. He scooted all the way in, then leaned his head against the window.

The bus hiccupped back to life, causing Tommy to bump his head on the window. "Ouch," he said to himself. Yeah, this was going about as well as he'd imagined. He rubbed his head. What the heck was wrong with him anyway? He was always grumpy and sad lately. Little things bugged him, and he dwelled on innocuous stuff. Was this what growing up was like? If so, he didn't want any part of it.

Ambrose flopped into the seat next to Tommy and threw an arm around him. "Hey, buddy." His breath smelled of breakfast.

Tommy peeled the boy's arm away and hoped he'd take the hint. "Hey."

Ambrose straightened and folded his arms. He scrutinized the interior of the bus with the shrewd glare of a security guard and spoke through the side of his mouth conspiratorially. "Listen, Tommy. I like you. You seem like a good kid, is what I'm saying."

"Okay. Thanks." Tommy shifted and tried to squeeze closer to the window.

"I'm an eighth grader, so I've been around. I've been where you are." He turned to inspect Tommy with that analyzing gaze. "Do you *know* where you are?"

"On a bus."

"Oh, har de har har." He blew out an exasperated burst of air. "No, Tommy." He jabbed him on the shoulder five times, once with each word: "You. Are. A. Sixth. Grader."

"Don't poke me."

Ambrose laughed, but Tommy understood his reaction was because of the deadpan delivery. "Okay, okay. But listen. Some eighth graders roast the incoming babies."

He didn't like the sound of that. "Roast?"

"Yeah, you know. Like hazing."

"Oh."

"Yeah. *Oh.* So keep your eyes peeled. They have a few go-to moves. There's the hot neck." He paused and smirked, drawing out the suspense. "That's when they sneak up behind you with a wet hand." He leaned close again. "They slap the back of your neck as hard as they can. And if their hand is wet with only water, you're *lucky*." He rubbed his own neck as if remembering his sixth-grade year. "Hurts like hell."

Tommy started to sweat. "They really *hit* kids?"

"You bet they do, and that's just one of the pranks. There are also swirlees, rug burns, the jelly roll, pantsing, and commander butt crack."

"You can't be serious."

"We'll see if you feel that way after school."

Tommy only knew what some of those pranks were, but commander butt crack? The jelly roll? He couldn't even begin to fathom what those would entail. What he did know, beyond a shadow of a doubt, was he didn't want to experience *any* of them. "So what do I do?"

Ambrose sobered. "There's *nothing* you can do." He grabbed Tommy's arm with both hands and twisted the skin as hard as he could. Tommy's entire arm blazed as Ambrose cackled and twisted his hands, pulling Tommy's skin in opposite directions.

"Get the hell off me!" Tommy yelled. He rammed Ambrose with his shoulder, and the eighth grader released his grip, nearly toppling into the aisle. He continued to laugh as he stood.

From the front, the bus driver yelled, "Get in your seat!"

Ambrose ignored him and leaned in. "I meant what I said. I like you. You seem all right." He shrugged. "But I'm a sucker for tradition. What can I say?"

Miranda turned around at some point, her eyebrows low with what looked like concern.

"No," Skullagar said inside Tommy's head. "That's not concern, boy. That's *pity*. And you best get used to it now if you don't start standing up for yourself."

He was right. Ambrose may have hazed him, but he had also warned him. Junior high was going to be war, and he had better arm himself.

CHAPTER ELEVEN

SCHOOL DAZE

When the bus pulled into the parking lot, Tommy lifted his backpack from the floor and stood.

The bus driver activated his intercom and said, "Sit down and be patient. Security radios when it's time to exit the vehicle."

Ambrose seized the opportunity to land another blow. "Yeah, kid. Sit down!"

Tommy sat and gazed out the window, praying the day wouldn't get any worse. Starting a new school was supposed to be exciting, not terrifying. Near the end of elementary school, everyone talked about how cool it'd be to run into each other in the hallways, but no one seemed to notice they'd all be in different classes and nothing would be the same.

A radio squawked at the front of the bus, and the security guard gave the go-ahead to exit. Tommy waited until everyone cleared the aisle before getting up. He especially wanted to give Miranda a head start so he wouldn't have to talk to her. At least not so soon after all his little embarrassments.

Compared to the elementary school, the junior high building loomed like an enormous prison, all brick and concrete. The school was constructed in the shape of a horseshoe, the intervening courtyard lined with benches and tables, presumably for outdoor lunch and breaks.

The staggered bus exits helped with crowd control, but there were still far more students than at the elementary school. Seeing all these people but not a single friend, a numbing cold spread inside Tommy's belly, reminding him of the hollow place. That dark, empty pit where he had shoved the past summer's activities in the hope he'd become whole again. He'd fed character sketches, cartoons, video games, and trips to the comic store into that gnawing pit. He'd plated and presented each distraction just so, serving up the contest entry on a silver platter as the final, most filling course. The banquet worked for a while, but over time the starving void became harder to satiate. Like a black hole, its craving was too vast to contemplate.

"Wake up, Tommy. You in there?"

Sammy C. walked beside him as they exited the bus and approached the school entrance. He was wearing an Alf shirt and blue shorts that made him look even younger than he was.

"Sorry, I was thinking."

He nodded seriously as though to suggest he knew all about this, and perhaps he did. "What homeroom are you in?"

Tommy pulled a yellow schedule card from his pocket. "Um. Mr. Roth, room 409."

Sammy perked up. "Me too!" He held his hand aloft.

Tommy slapped him five. A smile crept across his face and some of that chill inside his belly warmed. "You want to sit together?"

"Yeah." Sammy looked around at some of the other students walking through the front doors. "I don't recognize anyone else yet. I was getting kinda worried."

"Me too." Tommy regretted being so honest, but he figured Sammy wouldn't blab. He was always nice in elementary school. They'd even hung out a couple times, but for whatever reason hadn't become close friends.

"I heard you and Evan had a fight this summer?"

Crap. Word must have spread. "We didn't have a *real* fight."

They pushed through the big doors and into the air-conditioned lobby of the school. It somehow smelled both clean and old at the same time, as if they were storing millions of moldering books in the basement and no matter how many times they mopped, the stink still won out.

The kids in the lobby were divided into two distinct groups: the seventh and eighth graders who knew their way around and the sixth graders who were completely lost. Luckily there were monitors and teachers wading through the sea of students to help direct traffic.

Sammy said, "What do you mean not a real fight?"

"You know. It wasn't a fist fight."

Sammy seemed confused. "Really? Because he's telling everyone he kicked your ass."

This caused Tommy to stop walking. Someone bumped into him from behind and said, "Watch it!"

He ignored this. "*What?*"

Sammy grabbed Tommy's arm and pulled him to the side of the lobby and out of the main traffic. One of the teachers noticed and started over.

"But we didn't even fight. And there were other kids there! They saw!"

Sammy shrugged. "Oh, okay. I don't know why he's lying if—"

"First day at Ende Junior High? Let me see your schedule cards." The teacher had braided black hair and glasses almost bigger than her face. Her attire reminded Tommy of the women in that movie his mom liked to watch, *9 to 5*.

Sammy said, "We're both in 409."

She smiled brightly. "Mr. Roth. He's a goodun. You'll get along just fine." Pointing down a side hallway, she said, "Head thataway. Make the first right into the stairwell and go on up to the fourth floor. You'll see the markers from there, but if you get lost, just ask one of the teachers."

"Thanks—"

"Mrs. Jaffee." She shook Tommy's hand, then Sammy's.

They rejoined the throng, swimming through the treacherous waters of Ende Junior High and hoping to arrive in homeroom without receiving a hot neck or jelly roll. Children shoved and bumped through the crowded hallways. Every little nudge caused Tommy to spin around and cover his neck. An attack could come from anywhere.

Sammy eyed him with curiosity. "Why so flinchy?"

"Huh?" Tommy turned in a complete circle as they made their way to the stairwell. There were a group of older kids behind them. One locked eyes with Tommy and smirked menacingly.

"You seem nervous or something."

"I'll tell you later."

"Tell me what?"

The older students pushed ahead, gaining on Tommy and Sammy as they rounded the second-floor landing. The menacing kid smiled wider. His teeth were stained, and his hair stood out in all directions like he hadn't showered in a week. If Tommy had learned anything from those after-school specials, it was to avoid kids that looked like this one. He was trouble. He was a smoker and probably a drug addict, and worst of all, he was a *bully*.

Tommy increased his pace, pushing against the backs of those in front of him as they reached the third floor. "Hurry up."

A girl with a purple *My Little Pony* backpack turned long enough to sneer. "Stop pushing."

Sammy said, "Sorry." He nudged Tommy. "Cut it out."

The crowd on the stairs thinned as they rounded the third-floor landing. Behind him, the small group led by the unwashed bully came closer.

Skullagar laughed in his head. "Hot neck imminent! Ha ha ha!"

He took the stairs two at a time, leaving Sammy behind.

"Wait up! Jeez."

The bully stepped to the left of the staircase during a lull in traffic and ran the remaining stairs, closing the gap as they neared the fourth-floor landing. The greasy kid locked eyes with Tommy and said, "Hey." Tommy braced himself for the inevitable, but the kid simply ran past and shot through the doors leading to the fourth floor.

Tommy slowed and exhaled all his panic. Had the after-school specials led him astray? Because the obvious bully had greeted him kindly, and he hadn't doled out any wedgies or swirlees after all.

As they exited onto the fourth floor, Sammy said, "So what did you want to tell me, because you're acting really weird."

"You know Ambrose? He lives in my neighborhood. I don't know his last name, but he has a brother that always tags along with him?"

"I dunno, maybe. Why?"

"He told me the eighth graders like to haze new kids."

Sammy pointed to the left. "Go that way." He checked behind him as they turned the corner. "What do they do?"

"Your standard bully stuff, I guess. Pantsing. Swirlees. Slapping your neck with a wet hand—they call that a hot neck. Things like that."

"Oh, jeez." Now Sammy was the one checking over his shoulder every couple seconds, his eyes wide and unbelieving.

"Yeah. Look what Ambrose gave me after he told me about the hazing, like some kind of mean information tax." He held his arm out to display the red, irritated skin.

"Oh, *jeez*."

"Yeah. Keep your eyes peeled. You watch my back, and I'll watch yours."

"Deal."

They slapped five and continued on to homeroom, taking seats next to each other near the back, just in case.

Skullagar chimed in one last time. "Villains don't follow rules, Tommy. Caution is your only defense."

Yes, he thought. He should be cautious.

* * *

The school day played out in a series of boring activities and endless introductions. Tommy's initial fear and anxiety calmed, soothed by the mundaneness of it all. With every trip through the hallway that didn't result in a rug burn, with every bathroom break that didn't end with a swirlee, Tommy began to realize Ambrose had been messing with him. The eighth graders weren't hazing sixth graders.

One of the things Tommy had been most worried about was running into Evan. Miraculously, after an entire day of traversing the new building, Evan hadn't appeared. Tommy couldn't believe it. He was about to escape the first day of junior high with limited damage. He even thought he'd be able to talk to Miranda again. The embarrassment of the morning had all but vanished, and he was confident she hadn't judged him too harshly. Besides, she was new in the area and could probably use more friends.

Tommy leaned against the wall outside of his last class and dug out a handful of important documents. He had a new locker number and combination, his schedule card, a lunch pass, and a list of rules he was required to sign with his parents. The document boasted declarations so obvious they came dangerously close to insulting. Statements like, "I promise to do my very best at Ende Junior High" and "I will come prepared with an 8.5 x 11-inch loose-leaf notebook and pencil."

"What a joke." He pocketed everything but his locker information. He only had about ten minutes to get to his bus, but he wanted to check the locker before he left. It was one of the few things he was actually kind of excited about. He'd never had his own locker before. Sure, the locker was only supposed to be used for books and jackets, but Mr. Roth said they were allowed to decorate the interior as long as the adornments weren't lewd. Mr. Roth then had to define "lewd" for the class, which resulted in the inevitable giggles and jokes. Tommy had thought up a pretty good one himself but knew better than to say anything out loud. He wasn't looking to score detention on the first day.

By the time he arrived on the third floor where his locker had been assigned, there was only a smattering of students left. A few were inspecting their own lockers. Some were speaking with teachers. Another group entered a nearby bathroom.

Tommy counted down the metal-lined hallway until he arrived at locker 313. He ran his hand over the outside of the cold metal and pretended it was a giant safe filled with untold riches. He was infamous safe cracker Reginald Blunderbuss III. He pressed his ear against the safe and listened carefully as he turned the knob.

Click, click, click, clank.

"Ah ha!" Reginald exclaimed. "The first number is thirteen. Unlucky . . . for *some*." He let out a triumphant laugh and threw his hands into the air.

"Tommy?"

Later, he'd tell himself he didn't yelp like a scared coyote. And later, he'd almost believe the lie.

Miranda laughed lightly, and Tommy would have been embarrassed if her smile were not so kind and the laugh not so full of delight.

"Oh," he said lamely. "Hey."

Her smile continued to shine brightly. "What were you doing?"

He attempted to adopt an expression of extreme cool. He put one hand halfway into his pocket and loped a couple steps away from the locker. He threw a thumb over his shoulder. "Just making sure my combination works."

She pursed her lips and nodded. "Sure, of course. I always throw my hands into the air like a lunatic when I get the combo right too."

The facade of cool melted away like ice cream in the sun. "You saw that, huh?"

"Oh yeah. I saw." She laughed again, and it still held no malice. "You coming? Buses leave in like five minutes."

"Yeah, just want to check out the locker."

Something in her reaction suggested disappointment. Was she asking him to walk with her? He began to sputter a recantation, but before he could get anything decipherable out of his mouth, Miranda walked away. "Okay, see you on the bus then. But hurry!"

"I will!" He almost said *save me a seat* but remembered Tonya and figured Miranda would sit with her again. That was okay, though. He still had the walk home with her after the bus dropped them off. Well, her and the Bozo Twins.

Turning back to the locker, he abandoned his safe-cracking act in the interest of time. The interior of the locker was bare and empty. It was a little disappointing until he considered the many possibilities the blank space offered. Some of his sketches would look mighty good on the inside of the door. With decoration ideas fluttering through his head, Tommy slammed the locker shut and recoiled when a broad face appeared from behind the door. The kid's hair was so blond and his skin so pale, he almost looked albino.

"Hey," the kid said.

Tommy didn't recognize him, and yet there was something familiar in his pallid smile and dull eyes. He leaned too close to Tommy, the stink of cheap cologne lingering like a department store mannequin's fart.

Tommy backed away, holding the straps of his backpack. "Hey . . ."

At some point between his arrival at the locker and that moment, the hallway had cleared of students and teachers. The only sounds were that of his own breathing and the buzz of the fluorescent lights.

The boy's smile turned into an evil clown grin. "*Sixth grader.*"

"Huh?" He backed away another step.

"Sixth grader. Sixth grader. *Sixth grader!*" He clapped his hands together. "We got ourselves fresh meat!"

It's real, he thought frantically. *The hazing is real!* He turned to flee and ran face-first into a group of three shaggy eighth graders who grasped his arms and legs, then hefted him into the air in a single, well-rehearsed movement. These were the kids who had ducked into the bathroom earlier, he realized. All with varying degrees of long hair and jean jackets, like some juvenile biker gang. This wasn't happening. This *couldn't* be happening!

The eighth graders jostled Tommy, chanting, "Fresh meat! Fresh meat! Fresh meat!"

"Let me down!"

The kid who had scared Tommy at the locker said, "Be proud, little buddy. You're taking part in a tradition that has existed from time immemorial."

What the hell was going on? What kind of kid talked like that? Maybe not a biker gang after all. More like a satanic cult! The group continued to chant and carry him down the hallway, and before long, their destination became clear: the bathroom.

"Come on, you guys, stop it!"

They bulldozed through the bathroom door and spilled Tommy onto the wet and sticky tile, knocking the breath from him. Two of the boys dropped to their knees and held his arms and legs as he wriggled wildly in a crazed attempt to get free.

"Holy crap, Ray. This kid is going nuts!"

Tommy bucked and ripped his arm away from the long-haired kid on his right.

"Hold him!" Ray, the pale one, dropped and grabbed Tommy's feet. When he tried to lift him, Tommy kicked out and knocked him back. He fell into a seated position, his blond hair flying around his face like a hurricane of straw.

The kid on his left arm laughed stupidly. "Kid kicked you on your ass, Ray."

"Shut up and hold him! Steve, help me with the legs."

The fourth guy had been watching quietly from the sinks, leaning there with a cigarette hanging from his mouth. He had a scraggly goatee that looked like he'd pasted hair onto his face. Steve plucked the cigarette out and pushed it behind his ear.

He sighed and rolled his eyes. "Yeah, sure."

Tommy was getting tired, so he used Steve's obvious lack of enthusiasm. "Hey! Hey, Steve? Just tell them to cut it out. This is *stupid*."

Real convincing.

Ray grabbed his feet and held them tighter this time. "Get moving, man!"

Steve's slack expression changed from disinterested to suddenly now engaged. Tommy couldn't tell if this was an improvement or not.

"Stupid?" Steve knelt at Tommy's feet along with Ray. "*Stupid?*" He grabbed Tommy's ankles and smiled. "Naw. This is *tradition*."

So *not* an improvement then.

"Lift!"

"No!" Tommy squirmed, but his energy had been spent.

The eighth graders lifted him by his legs and held him upside down while wrestling him into a stall.

"Stop! This isn't funny!"

"It is from our end, little buddy."

The water inside the toilet was clear, but the sour smell of urine permeated the bowl and turned his stomach.

"On three! One—"

"Stop it! *Please!*"

"Two."

Rather than say anything else, Tommy closed his eyes, held his breath, and prepared for the inevitable.

"Three! Dunk him!"

In an instant, Tommy's head was plunged into the cold toilet water. Someone above him flushed while his head was held in place, completing the famous swirlee and placing the proverbial cherry on top of Tommy's first day at Ende Junior High School.

* * *

Once the ceremonial dunking had been completed, the four bullies ran off, leaving Tommy soaked in toilet water and near tears. He expected Skullagar to chime in, but no taunts came. There remained only the silence of the bathroom, the grinding of Tommy's teeth, and the creeping realization that growing up wasn't going to be easy.

There had been no indication that the eighth graders would continue to bully him. They'd played off the whole traumatizing experience as if it were a one-time offering to the dark lord of tradition. But Tommy was also learning to be dubious of hope. As the story "The Monkey's Paw" warned, be careful what you wish for. He had hoped his parents would work things out, but they'd reunited like an improperly set fracture, crooked, jagged, and grating against each other. He'd hoped his friendship with Evan would be rekindled and was rewarded with a summer of silence.

His last remaining hope, the one everything hinged upon, was that he would win the *OoCC* character contest. That gleaming beacon upon the hill guided him in his darkest moments. And so it did again as he sat broken, soaked, and close to resignation. If he won the contest, if Mechani-Ghoul took the day, Tommy would be reborn. The hopeful and worry-free child would return.

Over the loudspeakers mounted in the hallway, a woman spoke, "Buses are leaving in one minute. Last call for buses."

Tommy's heart spasmed into a jackrabbit race. "Wait!" he yelled to no one. He scrambled for the door, only to realize he'd lost his backpack.

His mom was going to be so mad at him. He'd begged for the green JanSport bag with the suede bottom. This shocked his mom at first, as she assumed he'd want some kind of cartoon-themed bag. He tried to explain the thematic connection between his bike (the green machine), the War Beast from *OoCC*, and a green backpack, but she lost interest the second she saw the price tag. Tommy soldiered on, arguing everything from popularity to durability, but in the end, it was the lifetime warranty that sold her. She'd said, "This will be the last backpack I ever buy for you. Understood?"

And now it was gone! There's no cashing in on a lifetime warranty without the backpack itself. He completed one last sweep of the bathroom with no luck, then raced into the hallway, figuring the bullies had stolen the bag. To his amazement, he found it outside his locker, forgotten during the ambush.

Grabbing the bag, he raced to the stairs. He took them two steps at a time, holding on to the railing and leaping the last four. The secretary made another announcement. He couldn't make out what she said, but it had to be something about the buses. Inside his head he screamed, *GO, GO, GO!* Tommy rammed through the first-floor doors and skipped to a stop a few feet from a stocky teacher with a pencil-thin mustache. He'd had social studies with him earlier in the day.

"Whoa there, young fella." He put his hands out in a *stop* motion. "What happened here? Did you fall in?"

"Huh?" he said dumbly.

"You're all wet, son. You look like you dunked your head in the—" He caught himself and nodded slowly. "A victim of first-day pranking, I take it?"

Tommy searched his mind for the man's name. Yet another one lost in the scrambled egg casserole in his head. He studied the man's kind face and understanding eyes and the name returned: Mr. Johnson.

"Who did this, son?"

"Um. No one?"

"I see. You ain't no rat then, huh?"

"What?" He'd never heard a teacher slip into slang like that before. The easy transition caught him off guard. It was almost as if Mr. Johnson were impersonating something he saw in a movie.

Mr. Johnson shook his head. "If you want to report the incident, you can. Your call." He paused as if something had only just occurred to him. "Is someone picking you up?"

Tommy looked past the teacher and down the deserted hallway, trying to decide how to answer. If he'd missed the bus, he didn't want to be held late and made to call his parents. At the same time, he didn't want to be stranded.

"I recognize you from class. What's your name, son?"

"I'm in your third period. Tommy."

Mr. Johnson put an arm around Tommy's shoulder and guided him down the hall. The exit to the buses was in that direction, but so was the front office, a place he didn't feel like visiting on his first day. "Tommy. Right, right. I struggle to memorize so many names every year. But my old brain still has a few rounds left."

Tommy enjoyed Mr. Johnson's class. He had a way of speaking that made even the boring stuff fun to listen to.

"So, Tommy. Did you miss your bus? Because if you did, you know we can just call your parents lickety-split and get you a ride home. No muss, no fuss. How's that sound?"

In truth, the suggestion sounded *horrible*. Tommy blurted, "They're picking me up."

Mr. Johnson stopped walking and inspected Tommy's face. "Okay, then. So you *didn't* miss your bus?"

"Nope."

"I see." He urged them into a speedy walk and escorted Tommy to the exit.

There were some cars outside, parents waiting for sons or daughters. But beyond those cars, not a single bus remained. What was his endgame here? What was his plan? He hadn't the faintest idea, but he did know he had just lied to a teacher and didn't relish the idea of coming clean. Besides, he remained steadfast in his decision to not call his parents.

"Thanks, Mr. Johnson. I think I see their car."

Mr. Johnson nodded in a way that made Tommy suspect his teacher knew exactly what was going on. "Well, I'll be right here if you can't find them." He waved his hand in a shooing motion. "Go on, then."

Tommy paused at the door, his hand on the cold metal handle. "See you tomorrow, Mr. Johnson."

Yeah, more like see you in two minutes when I realize I have no way to get home, he thought.

"Have a good day, Tommy."

CHAPTER TWELVE

A RIDE HOME

O utside, the sun glinted off metal and glass, dazzling his eyes, imbuing them with visions of Evernitia. If only he could escape to that mystical land where magic and science mingled with astonishing results.

Tommy checked over his shoulder and spied Mr. Johnson watching through the glass doors. He was pretty sure he knew how to get home from the school, but he also knew the walk would take forever. Maybe more than an hour. His parents would be freaking out by then, probably calling the school and the police. This thought killed his forward momentum.

Would they actually call the police? The answer came to mind almost as swiftly as the question: *yes*. As paranoid as his mother had been about Tommy getting hit by a car while riding his bike, she was infinitely more fearful of him getting abducted. Last year she started watching a new show called *Unsolved Mysteries*, and of all the episodes, the ones about unexplained disappearances affected her most deeply.

Nope, that decided it. He had to call them for a ride. Tommy turned around and began playing through the excuses he could use with Mr. Johnson. Maybe his parents were supposed to have picked him up but forgot? Would Mr. Johnson check on something like that? He *supposed* there was always the straight truth. That would be Pastor Roberts's suggestion, of course. *I have no greater joy than my children walking the path of truth.*

Tommy glanced back, expecting to see his teacher wearing an expression of concern. Instead of Mr. Johnson, Evan Winger and Jonathan Miller stepped through the doors.

Evan recoiled as if he'd gotten an eyeful of his naked mom. Jonathan appeared not to recognize Tommy at all. They continued walking, ignoring him with the concentration of expert golfers, and went to a muscle car waiting at the curb—red, sleek, and with one of those raised bumps on the hood.

Mr. Johnson leaned out the front doors and held his hands, silently asking Tommy, *What's going on?*

Evan called out before Tommy could begin the march to his doom. "Hey."

"Yeah?"

His face still looked like he'd sucked a lemon. "You need a ride?"

Tommy squinted in the sun, attempting to appraise Evan's sudden change in attitude. Maybe he finally wanted to make up. Or more likely, he felt bad for Tommy, standing there like a goon.

"Well, yeah."

He waved him over. "Come on then."

Saved! He waved goodbye to Mr. Johnson with an elevated sense of triumph. He didn't have to confess his white lie, and his parents wouldn't have to know he missed the bus on the first day of school. If things worked out *really well*, no one except the bullies even had to know he'd gotten a swirlee, assuming they didn't go around telling everyone.

He ran to the car and hopped in the back. Jonathan got in front then twisted in the seat to look at Tommy. "Hair's wet, dude."

"Freak water fountain accident."

The guy in the driver's seat erupted with laughter. "Ha! Funny little guy." He turned and lowered his sunglasses, and Tommy understood immediately this was Jonathan's older brother. They both had the same bleary eyes and squared-off jaws. The same scary look of superiority. "Oh, not so little, I guess."

"Growth spurt. I'm still getting used to looking down on people."

The brother chuckled again, though Tommy wasn't quite sure what was so funny. They pulled out, leaving the school behind, and Tommy sighed with relief that he'd gotten through the day.

"You know Jonathan." Evan didn't meet Tommy's eyes as he said this. "That's his brother, Travis. He's a senior in high school."

As if to prove his maturity, Travis lit a cigarette. "Where we headed, big-little dude?"

Jonathan whispered something to his brother, then said, "We're gonna make a pit stop first."

"Where?" Evan asked.

"Just a cool spot I found. Claw Rock. You know it?"

Tommy shook his head. "Nope."

Evan squinted at Jonathan. "Near the bog, you mean? In the woods?"

"Well, not all the way in. I stashed something just off the trailhead."

Evan seemed surprised. "Okay, but I have to be home soon."

"No sweat." Jonathan patted his brother's shoulder. "Travis drives fast."

✳ ✳ ✳

After a fifteen-minute drive in the wrong direction, Travis pulled onto a gravel path surrounded by trees. The sports car didn't handle the potholes well, and all four occupants bounced and jostled for the better part of two minutes, until they reached the opening to a trail that, Tommy assumed, led to "the bog."

He checked his *Order of Cosmic Champions* watch and groaned. "Hey, you guys? It's getting kinda late."

Jonathan rolled his eyes as the car came to a stop. "Quit bellyaching, dork." He laughed at his own insult and exited, followed by his brother and Evan. Tommy studied the surrounding forest. The long summer days were still holding out, and the sky was bright and clear. His mind wandered to thoughts of his parents, and a particularly awful one clawed its way to the surface: What if they decided to wait at the bus stop since it was his first day? What would they do when he didn't get off the bus?

Police.

No, that was ridiculous. Maybe Miranda would see them and put two and two together. No doubt she realized he had missed the bus. But then his parents would drive to the school, and—

Mr. Johnson would say Tommy got into a car. They'd think he was taken by a stranger!

He grabbed his backpack and leapt from the vehicle. "Hey, guys? I have to get home, like *now*."

The three boys were clustered together at the metal gate of the trailhead. Jonathan had a grim smile on his face. "Not yet."

"No, seriously. My parents are gonna freak if I'm not home on time. I missed the bus and—"

"Shut up!" Jonathan lunged at Tommy and punched him in the stomach.

Tommy dropped, his head buzzing with confusion, his gut burning. He tried to stand, but Jonathan kicked him back down. He fell backward onto his backpack and lay prone. "Why—" He gasped. "Why did you do that?"

"Because I hate you. Because you're a little cartoon-loving baby."
The bigger boy paused as he thought something over, his expression
crinkling like a raisin before smoothing out again. "Because I *want* to."

Evan hadn't moved or said a word. His face was pallid, eyes glazed
over. Tommy thought about what he had said in the car. Evan had asked
where they were going and was confused as to Jonathan's decision to drive
out to Claw Rock. *He didn't know.* This realization brought little comfort.

Finally, Evan said, "We made our point. Come on."

Jonathan turned on Evan with a wild look in his eyes. "You didn't do
anything yet. Hit him!"

Tommy scooted away and got to his feet. He wanted to run, to
get out of there before all three boys attacked him at once, but his legs
wouldn't let him. No, not his legs. His *heart*. His *mind*.

"What did I ever do to you?" He pointed at Jonathan. "I don't even
freakin' *know* you! And Evan?" He threw his hands in the air and looked
at the sky as if searching for divine guidance. "We were best friends! You
don't wanna be friends anymore, fine. But why *this*?"

"Shut up already!" Evan screamed, his eyes moving from stupe-
fied to angry.

Travis lit a cigarette and leaned against the metal gate. He appeared
to have little interest in joining in, but sure didn't mind watching.

Evan pulled at his own hair and paced in the dirt, kicking stones.
"Why couldn't you just stay the hell away from me?"

Tommy laughed sardonically. "You asked *me* if I needed a ride. I
haven't spoken to you since you made fun of me at my birthday party.
If anyone should be pissed, it's me!"

"I told him to let you in the car." Jonathan spit on the ground. "For
the fun of it."

"No," Tommy said, realizing something. "You're jealous." He
pointed with a shaking finger. "Jealous that I used to be his best friend.
And that you'll *never* be."

Jonathan growled and rushed Tommy, grabbing him around the neck. "I'm not jealous!"

This was a real fight, he realized as the boy throttled him. *A real fight, and I'm getting my ass kicked.* Tommy panicked, swung wildly, and clipped the boy's chin.

The hit did nothing but enrage Jonathan, who continued to growl like a rabid dog. He threw Tommy to the ground and kicked him. Pain shot through his body even as his mind darkened, stealing him away from what was happening.

"All right, get in there," Jonathan urged Evan.

Evan said, "Let's just go. He's hurt enough."

"Not until you kick him."

"I don't—"

"Do it." Jonathan motioned toward his brother, who nodded tiredly and pushed away from the gate.

"Listen to him." He flicked his cigarette at Evan's face, and Tommy began to understand something he hadn't before: Evan was as trapped as Tommy was.

His old friend approached. He looked younger somehow, his eyes glassy, his mouth puckered as if holding in cries. He stood there beside Tommy, fists clasped, face growing redder by the second.

"You don't—" But Tommy never completed his thought.

Evan kicked him in the stomach. He waited a moment, then kicked Tommy's thighs. Then his stomach again. With each hit, Tommy curled tighter, trying to block as much of the impact as possible. He kept expecting a kick to the face or head, but it never came. It didn't have to.

They'd done their job.

The tears Tommy had held back for the better part of the summer— the sobs for a lost friend, a crumbling family, and an ever-changing world—erupted from him like a long dormant volcano. He cried hard. He cried uncontrollably. Releasing the tears after so long would have been a relief had the three boys not been standing over him, laughing and calling him awful names.

Eventually, the bullies ran out of creative ways to verbally eviscerate Tommy. Lost in a miasma of ignorance and hate, they piled into the car and left him lying in the dirt, alone and utterly broken.

Even as he lay on the ground in excruciating pain, he knew he had to get up. Had to get home. The walk ahead of him would take hours, and his parents had probably called the police by now. Before, the prospect of involving the police had only been a child's fear.

Now, he knew it was a real possibility.

CHAPTER THIRTEEN
REVELATIONS

At least I didn't lose my backpack.

This thought recurred every few minutes as Tommy backtracked to the main road. He'd be thinking about getting beat up, his parents freaking out, the devastating betrayal of his former friend, and then—

At least I didn't lose my backpack.

His ribs ached with every step. Scratches on his palms stung. His pride hurt even deeper. And then—

At least I didn't lose my backpack.

This new mantra was all he had. The repeated reminder that not everything had gone wrong that terrible day. His expensive backpack had been saved from a near loss that would certainly have compounded his mother's anger and disappointment. No doubt she'd berate him for having not called them when he missed the bus. Didn't he know better than to accept rides from strangers?

His future self argued back inside the imagined scenario, "But they aren't strangers, Ma!"

Only, that wasn't true, was it? Evan had become a stranger as surely as Skullagar would always be a threat to Evernitia.

But, hey. *At least I didn't lose my backpack.*

As the long walk home continued, Tommy started wishing he *had* lost the backpack. The heavy load of new textbooks caused the straps to cut into his shoulders. Sweat soaked his shirt and dripped down his face. The sun dazzled his eyes, causing strange mirages to float past. Mechani-Ghoul chugged by, brandishing a razor-sharp machete arm. His eyes were dead sockets, but once Skullagar's soul inhabited the mechanical host, they would glow yellow and deadly.

Miranda was next in the parade going through his mind. Her smile had been the only good thing about the day. He could have spent the afternoon walking her home if only he'd left his locker check for tomorrow. If only he'd listened to her warnings that the buses were leaving soon. Maybe they'd even be riding bikes together at that very moment. They could have explored the wooded area near the end of the road, or maybe gone to the Skate-A-Way roller rink together. Instead, he was walking down the side of the road, his feet sweaty, his ribs sore, and his mind haunted.

At least I didn't lose my backpack.

At least I got to meet Miranda this morning.

At least Sammy is in homeroom with me.

These *at leasts* were a miserable consolation prize for surviving the worst day of his life. Had he survived though? No, not yet. The sun was still in the sky, and he was still miles from home. Opportunities for disappointment still remained.

✳ ✳ ✳

The walk home took close to two hours, and the sun was low in the sky by the time he ambled onto Wild Vine. His parents must be worried sick. That sickness transferred to Tommy with every thought.

His feet ached, he was thirsty, and the dull thud of bruises had settled deep into his bones, but he began to run, nonetheless. The sooner
he could get home, the sooner he could explain himself. The better off
everyone would be.

His backpack bounced with each stride, kicking him in the back,
bestowing upon him yet another pain. His breath came short and
fast, and he sweat from every pore. None of this mattered as much
as getting home. He admonished himself for being so hard on his
mother and father the past weeks. They were doing their best, and
he knew they were trying to work things out for his sake more than
their own. His heart flooded with love. After a full day of proof that
the world was hard and cruel, at least he knew his parents loved him
and would be there for him. Even if they *had* called the police, they'd
have done it out of fear for their little boy. They would have done it
out of love.

Tommy sprinted up the hill. He blew out a breath of relief when he
saw there were no flashing police lights outside his house. There were
no search parties, no frantic neighbors going door to door. Everything
looked normal and quiet. Finally, some good news.

Still, he knew his parents had to be worried. Maybe they'd called the
school, and Mr. Johnson told them Tommy had not gotten in a *stranger's* car, but that it had been with Evan. Sure, Tommy was still super late,
but if they'd been told he was with Evan, perhaps the alarm bells had
yet to go off.

He walked through the front yard and to the door, noting how dark
and quiet everything appeared. One last jolt of fear suggested his parents hadn't called the cops but had gone out looking for him instead.
As ridiculous as all of Tommy's imagined fears had been, that scenario
was the most outlandish. They'd never leave the house without knowing
where he was. He reached for the doorknob and pushed the door—

But it didn't open.

He tried it again, hoping with the wild imagination of a child that the door was just stuck, but it held fast.

Heart beginning to race again, he dug the emergency key out of his backpack and unlocked the door. He ran into the dark foyer, then the living room, flipping on light switches as he went.

"Ma? Dad?"

The coffee table was covered with empty beer cans and a half-eaten TV dinner. The sight gave Tommy uneasy flashbacks of earlier that same year before his dad had been exiled to the local motel. "Dad?"

Still no answer. He went to the kitchen and turned the light on.

There was a note taped to the dingy yellow refrigerator with Tommy's name scrawled on top. His heart raced but not for the same reason as before. Slowly, as though he didn't want to see what the note said, he plucked the piece of paper off the fridge door.

> Tommy,
>
> I hope your first day of school went well. Sorry I'm not there to congratulate you, but I had to step out. There are TV dinners in the freezer.
>
> I love you,
> —Mom

At the bottom of the note, in his father's handwriting, there was an addendum:

> Went out for something. Be back soon. There's mail for you on the counter. First day of junior high in the books!
>
> Proud of you, Tommy-boy.
> —Dad

Tommy stared at the note for a long time. The aches felt far away, as did his thirst and hunger. He stared and stared, not seeing the note anymore, and instead imagined his parents. Imagined his father coming home from work with a sixer and his mother admonishing him for his lack of willpower, which in turn led to him drinking faster and more deeply, which led to his mother nagging more relentlessly, which led to raised voices, screams, thrown cans, then—

His parents had left the house without the faintest notion that their son had been hours late. Without knowing he'd been bullied at school, beaten up by his former friend, abandoned in the middle of nowhere, and left to walk home.

And here he had been agonizing over being late and making them worry. Terrified his frantic parents would call the police or go searching for him. That they'd be scared out of their minds and tear Mr. Johnson a new one for letting him get in a strange car.

He had tortured himself over nothing.

His parents didn't even know he had been gone.

* * *

Tommy didn't fully absorb the note for many minutes. He especially didn't think much about the one bit his father wrote: *There's mail for you on the counter.* Why would he? He couldn't move past the feeling that his parents had abandoned him as thoroughly as Evan had. The sudden reappearance of beer cans, the reliance on TV dinners, the great disappearing acts. The road was all too familiar, and Tommy knew where it led. Divorce with a capital "D."

Eventually, he put one of the frozen dinners in the microwave and flipped through the stack of envelopes. Publisher's Clearing House was very excited to tell them they could be the next winners of a million dollars. Columbia House was equally ecstatic to declare their twelve-tapes-for-a-penny deal. There were rumors that if you wrote *cancel* on the first bill you could keep all the tapes without paying more than the first cent. Howard L. claimed he did just that with no repercussions. Lauren R., always the know-it-all, explained they could get away with the scam because they were minors. Tommy didn't have the nerve to tape a penny to the mailer and find out for himself, but he suspected they were telling the truth.

He considered the mailer a second longer, but the envelope had his dad's name on it, so he kept digging. At the bottom of the stack he finally hit pay dirt: an envelope from Telco Toys. A chill of excitement ran along his spine.

Finally, after weeks of waiting, the contest results for the character creation contest were in. The frozen dinner forgotten, he ran upstairs with his mail and slammed the bedroom door behind him. The house was empty, but he needed the extra security of his sanctuary for this pivotal moment.

The terrible, horrible, awful day suddenly made sense. To prove his worth, he had to endure the worst day of his life. Trial by fire. This win was so big, he had to pay up front, plus karmic interest. Yes, the whole horrible day made sense now. This winning entry balanced out every dreadful event. Heck, Tommy would have actively *invited* Evan's treachery had he known what awaited at day's end.

He sat at his desk and took a breath. This important moment deserved reverence. In a burst of inspiration, he dug under the desk for action figures and set them up around the envelope as if in prayer. He took his time adjusting their arms and feet, then placed a few weapons on the desk as if to say, for this venerable occasion, good and evil would stand side by side without raising arms.

After a moment's thought, Tommy went to his closet and retrieved his favorite *Order of Cosmic Champions* shirt and the fan club pin he had mailed away for. These new adornments in place, he addressed the audience.

"Gods and villains of planet Teltam, we come together today to celebrate the birth of a new member: *Mechani-Ghoul.*" A smile overtook his face as warmth bloomed within. "My creation will be among your ranks soon." He nodded solemnly. "I *know* it."

With those words spoken, he tore the envelope open and dug out a single sheet of paper.

His eyes rolled over the text too quickly to read, scanning for words like *winner* and *congratulations*. They would not reveal themselves, so Tommy slowed and read more carefully. He was so convinced of his winning entry, long seconds passed before he understood.

Dear Contestant,

Thank you for entering the official OoCC character creation contest! We were overwhelmed with thousands of amazing entries, and while we would have loved to choose every single one, we had to limit our decision to three winners.

We'd like to thank you again for your interest in OoCC with this free prize for entering! Watch for the official announcement of the winners in the next issue of OoCC magazine!

Yours,

—Deacon Rupert
President of Telco Toys

Tommy turned the paper over, then checked inside the envelope where he found a holographic Masculon sticker. His free prize for entering. He contemplated the letter and sticker. Everything had gone numb. His mind, his body, his hope. How could it be? And yet, this was right.

This made sense. Hadn't the world warned him these past months? Yes, with every moment of his summer, every second of his first day of school, the world had screamed, *Give up! Stop trying. Stop hoping. Stop caring. Just give up.*

Voices of Teltam invaded, speaking over one another until Tommy's head was filled with a clamor of confusion. These voices crept through his veins like tendrils of dread until they reached the chasm inside. The hollow place. There, they cavorted, giddy with ill intent.

Cartoon vocalizations, an unending spree of catch phrases and mono-logues, wrapped around one another, filling the chasm with a murky nebula. Then, quietly at first, barely recognizable beneath the throng, an unfamiliar voice spoke. The slithering syllables gathered strength. The words grew in power, their cadence rising above the other noise.

This unknown voice rose in the gloom of Tommy's cavern.

He knew as surely as he'd lost the contest, this was the voice of his losing creation.

Mechani-Ghoul repeated only a single word.

Father.

CHAPTER FOURTEEN

THE TIME WARP

Time passed like a fever dream, each day worse than the next. When he came to school on the second day, limping from deep purple bruises that had cropped up on his thighs and torso, people began to whisper. Before long, Jonathan filled in the blanks of their gruesome backwoods encounter. Evan corroborated the story, and Tommy didn't bother denying it.

He'd been wrong about the eighth graders who bullied him, too. They had no desire to keep their grand prank to themselves, especially in the wake of Jonathan's story. The news of Tommy's humiliation spread like disease. His name was canonized alongside other unlucky sixth graders like Wilbur Jenkins, who had been given the commander butt crack a record twelve times in a single day. Or Amanda Perkins, who'd had water poured on her while she was on the toilet.

No one except Sammy would sit with him at lunch. If gossip of his misfortunes was a spreading disease, then Tommy most assuredly was patient zero. He began finding anonymous notes in his locker with varying degrees of insults. Random eighth graders would trip him in the hallway. Kids would make fart sounds as he passed.

However, the most cataclysmic of catastrophes was that Miranda stopped talking to him. Or maybe he stopped talking to her. Tommy had trouble discerning which, because after the relentless bullying, the weight of embarrassment bent his tall frame until he stooped with shame. Maybe Miranda tried to speak to him. Maybe she tried to reach out. If she did, Tommy didn't notice. He was too busy exploring the pavement and investigating his shoes. Too worried about avoiding potential torment.

Weeks went on like this, until the air began to chill and the leaves grew bashful. The colors of autumn turned, and with them whispers of Halloween, candy, and the holiday season. Even in October, children looked forward to the days when they'd be granted reprieve from chalky hallways and schoolwork. Magic flooded the air like jet streams of fairy dust. Adults barely noticed, but kids—they knew.

Just as summer brought with it the firefly light of endless daydreams, autumn conjured bonfires of ghostly capers. Fallen leaves and orange pumpkins littered porches. Lone howls echoed through dense nighttime fog. The balance of power between living and dead shifted, and all who cared to listen could hear the coming change.

✳ ✳ ✳

Tommy was listening.

He lay in bed with his window cracked open. The waning October nights had grown chilly, but he loved the smell of autumn in his room. On the night air, there lingered a faint whiff of sweet smoke. Far off, a bonfire burned alongside piles of smoldering leaves. Half in the waking world, Tommy felt the campfire scent wind around him like snakes, whispering dreams in his ear.

A desolate expanse spread in his mind. A land of vines and decay, stones and moss. A place concocted of desire and dread.

Night air continued to pump into his bedroom, and Tommy pulled the covers close under his chin. He saw himself traversing this new land, his backpack heavy with gear. Dream logic dictated his bag held food, clothes, and money. Of course. Tommy needed these things. His journey through the wasteland, to a shining city on the coast, would be long and hard.

Someone walked beside him, but he couldn't turn to look. He couldn't focus his eyes. As hard as he tried, Tommy could not see who traveled by his side.

Without warning, massive bonfires sprang up all around him as if lit by magic. Witches congregated around the pyres, waving craggy sticks in the air as green steam arose with a noxious odor. Other sprites and hobgoblins cavorted about the travelers' feet, picking at their laces and spilling strange blue liquid about their footfalls. None of this fazed Tommy, who knew this road was the right road. Who knew this traveling partner was the correct companion.

Who knew he had a job to do.

CHAPTER FIFTEEN

THE COMIC SHOP

The bell rang and everyone in class launched out of the seats as if their butts were filled with rocket fuel. Tommy did not. He watched the other kids shove books into their packs and flee the classroom, but Tommy waited. He always waited. There was no one he wanted to catch up with or talk to, and no reason to rush into the hallway when it was packed with students. The more students there were, the better the chance one of them would decide to do something mean to him.

Mrs. Jaffee said, "Tommy? Can I speak with you before you leave?" She adjusted her enormous glasses and fixed him with a face that suggested this wasn't really a question.

"Yes, ma'am?" He approached the desk, his eyes on his feet, his arms wrapped around his torso.

"Tommy. Could you look at me, please?"

The act of lifting his gaze was akin to hauling a two-ton boulder above his head. But he did, and he hated what he glimpsed in the teacher's eyes. Tommy may have been young, but he recognized pity when he saw it.

"Is everything okay at home?"

This caught him by surprise, and he sensed his features contract at the mere suggestion of problems at home. In a small, defensive voice, he said, "Yes."

Mrs. Jaffee watched Tommy through those enormous glasses. Her dark hair was braided so tightly that her face appeared to be retreating toward her scalp. "I've tried calling and keep getting the answering machine. I've left messages."

Time stretched across the desk between them as neither spoke, and Tommy finally realized what she meant.

"I didn't erase the messages!"

"You can tell me if—"

"I didn't! I don't know why they haven't called you, I swear!"

She held her hands up to stop him. Maybe she detected the tears in his quaking voice. "I believe you. What about here at school. Are the other boys—"

"No."

"Tommy, if you're being bullied—"

"I'm not."

Mrs. Jaffee nodded and shuffled some papers around. The nod slowly morphed into a shake. Her mouth became tight. "You know, when I was in school, the girls—"

She broke off and glanced at the door. Tommy got the impression she was checking to make sure no one else was there. Mrs. Jaffee lowered her voice and leaned forward. "The girls called me *Cow*leen." Realizing she'd forgotten to mention it, she added, "My first name is Colleen."

"*Oh.*" The name wasn't nice, but it also wasn't a head dunked into a toilet and a kick to the ribs. Still, he liked Mrs. Jaffee, and she was trying. The attempt was more than he could say for his parents, who hadn't even noticed anything was wrong. "I'm sorry, Mrs. Jaffee. That's awful."

Her expression was soft, urging Tommy to confess. And he wanted to. He wanted to tell her everything. Because here was an adult who cared enough to ask. He almost spilled the beans, too. *Almost.* Then he imagined the bullies redoubling their efforts because he ratted.

"I can't help you if you don't tell me what's going on, Tommy."

He shoved his hands into his pockets. "Everything's fine."

She sighed and pushed over the most recent math quiz. "I haven't handed these back yet. Look at your score."

He did. "Yeah?"

She took her glasses off and rubbed her eyes. "That's three Fs in a row, Tommy. Look, I understand if this is because of something going on at home or here at school, but you have to tell me so I can help. Either way, I need to speak with your parents. Immediately."

"Okay." He took the quiz and placed it into his backpack.

"This is serious, Tommy. Tell your parents to check their messages and get back to me."

He liked Mrs. Jaffee, but at that moment, he wished she'd just stop bugging him.

✳ ✳ ✳

When Tommy got home from school, his parents were on opposite ends of the house and not speaking to each other. He told his mom about Mrs. Jaffee's request. She responded by asking Tommy to tell "his father" that he'd better clean the kitchen before dinner. In a weird way, Tommy wanted to be punished. Wanted his parents to yell at him for the bad grades. At least that would mean they knew he existed.

Instead of attempting to break through his parents' stupor, he pulled on his hooded sweater and rode his bike into town. Dinner wouldn't be ready for hours by the looks of the disastrous kitchen. Plates were piled high in the sink, empty beer cans littered the counter tops, and the garbage can overflowed as if playing a losing game of chicken with his father. The smell of rotting food wafted as far as the living room.

This same situation had played out a dozen times in the past weeks. His mom would complain that Dave had to clean up before she would cook. His dad would say "okay," only to disappear into the shed or garage to work on "important household projects." They'd fight. Mom wouldn't cook dinner. They'd both retreat to opposite sides of the house, or on really bad days, opposite sides of the town. Tommy figured it'd only be a matter of time before they retreated to opposite sides of a courtroom.

He didn't bother telling his parents before he left. They never asked anymore anyway.

At the top of his hill, Tommy gazed down at the cresting auburn treetops, then pushed off. He didn't relish the ride like he used to. The pride and joy of soaring down his hill had all but vanished. Only a shadow remained of the young Tommy who had cherished each golden moment and felt as light as the drifting leaves. On the way down, he spotted a few ash piles and remembered the previous night's dream. For a moment, the journey persisted like a haunting memory, the mysterious figure soaring alongside him like an old friend. As he coasted down the hill, leaves shooting out behind him like twin jet streams, the chill air cascading over his face, Tommy could almost believe he was recalling a past life.

Before long, he arrived in town. Shop owners had plastered their windows with die-cut Halloween decorations. Black cats popping out of pumpkins, ghosts, witches flying across big yellow moons. There were dried corn stalks tied to the streetlights, straw-filled scarecrows sitting atop hay bales, toppling gourdes of a dozen varieties, fake spider web pulled across hedges, and an army of hanging ghosts dancing in the wind. The decorations worked at Tommy's discontent, chipping away at the bad feelings, and even filling his hollow place with something more substantial than the high fructose junk food he'd been feeding it of late.

He parked his bike in the same old spot and plodded past the table of blathering old men complaining about rap music and baggy pants. Walking into Defender Comics, he barely registered the wonderful smell of new books and packaged toys. A numbness had overtaken him, and many of the things he had once loved now raised no joy. Small twinges of happiness would come calling, such as when he saw the town's Halloween decorations, but rarely did they penetrate the dull haze.

"Hey, Matty. What's up?"

"Just checking out the new issue of *Aliens*." He glanced over the top of the glossy comic and his eyebrows fell. "Everything okay, kid? You're looking morose."

"Huh?"

He dropped the comic onto the counter and rolled his eyes. "You're obviously not reading enough. Gloomy. Sullen. You look *sad*."

"I'm fine." Tommy picked through a rack of Archie comics and avoided eye contact.

"Yeah, right. And I'm a ladies' man. Seriously, what's eating ya?"

"Seriously." Tommy repeated in an obnoxious tone. "*Nothing*." *The New Archies, Archie Digest, Betty and Veronica.*

Matty adjusted his ridiculous glasses and stroked his goatee.

Tommy tried not to notice the penetrating stare. He moved around to the left of the store where Matty kept the long boxes of back-catalog comics. There were mostly old Marvel and DC. Stuff Tommy had little interest in. But he'd rather look through old comics than be at home.

"I have a few things in your mailbox if you wanna have a look?" Matty continued to watch Tommy with inquisitive eyes.

"Anything good?" Tommy abandoned the long boxes and returned to the counter.

"It's *all* good. Just a matter of what you have the money for." He pulled a small stack from the mailbox and laid the comics on the counter. "*Uncanny X-men, Strikeforce . . .*" He trailed off. "Yeah, I know. No interest?"

"Not really."

"I have something you'll like." Incense smoke rose around Matty as though he were performing some mystic ritual. He flashed a grin as he presented the newest issue of *Order of Cosmic Champions Magazine*. On the cover, bold lettering declared: **The Winner Revealed!**

A strange mixture of excitement and resentment flowed through him. The painful, empty place inside ached as though he hadn't eaten in days, hungering for something other than food.

His expression must have revealed great discomfort, because Matty said, "Whoa, you okay?"

He straightened his posture and forced a smile. Something tickled inside his head. Something about the dream he'd had and the mysterious figure. "Do you still want to buy that comic from me? The one my dad gave me?" He didn't know why he asked, but there it was.

Matty didn't appear happy about the offer, which confused Tommy. He hesitated far too long before saying, "Maybe. Only if you want to part with it, though." With Tommy's consent, Matty rang up the magazine. But when Tommy placed the cash in his hand, he hesitated again. He pushed a loose dread under his colorful hat. "I've known you a long time, kid. Probably before you even remember."

That came out of nowhere. "Um, okay?"

"Your dad used to come in here, you know. Back when I opened the place. He was probably one of my first customers. Older than me and a hell of a lot more knowledgeable about the vintage stuff. Used to chat with him for hours."

Tommy's feelings of confusion turned to curiosity. The musky odor of incense became oppressive. "I didn't know that."

"This was right before you were born. He used to be an artist. The old man and I even had plans to start our own comic. Did you know *that*?"

Tommy didn't. As far as he knew, his dad had always worked at the dealership, starting out in sales, then moving to management. Heck, he thought his dad always wanted to own his own dealership. Wasn't that what he was working toward all these years? "An artist? Really?"

"He used to work freelance, little jobs here and there. Guess it paid the bills for a while."

Tommy leaned against the counter, everything else forgotten in light of his father's hidden history. If his dad had any reaction to Tommy's drawings, they were usually that of indifference, and sometimes even irritation. "What happened?"

Matty shrugged. "Life." He retrieved a new stick of incense and brought it to his nose. "It's hard to make a living as an artist. Anyway, once you were born and he got the new job, Dave didn't have time to hang out as much. Our comic idea got shelved too. But every once in a while, he'd roll a stroller into the shop, filled to the brim with chubby baby."

"Aw, come on."

Matty laughed, cheeks jolly and bouncing. His eyes nearly closed with glee. "You were a huge baby." He laughed some more, remembering something, and nearly toppled over in delight. "He told me your mom said it was like giving birth to a Thanksgiving turkey!" Matty erupted with another burst of laughter.

"Oh, gross!" Despite his utter disgust at the thought, Tommy couldn't help but laugh as well. His tall frame bent and his eyes teared. The more he laughed, the harder the guffaws came.

For the first time in a long time, Tommy felt good.

✳ ✳ ✳

The sky darkened early as autumn devoured the summer sun. Tommy pulled up the hood of his sweatshirt and pedaled faster, eager to get home where he could curl up in his bed and read the new magazine. He hoped his mom had made something for dinner. Maybe mac and cheese, fried chicken, and greens like the old days. The *better* days. His mouth watered at the thought of biscuits piled high with chicken and gravy. Of course, he knew better than to hold out hope. He'd learned that lesson the hard way.

As Tommy rode home, he got the idea that Matty had tricked him. Not in a devious way, but in a concerned, parental way. Like how a guidance counselor might trick a student into choosing a class they hadn't planned on taking. When Tommy had first arrived at the store, he was feeling broken down and terrible. The world weighed about a million tons, and it had fallen firmly on Tommy's shoulders. He had precious little to be happy about.

When Tommy refused to talk about his troubles, what did Matty do? He circumvented the issues and got right to the job of cheering him up. No matter if he didn't want to reveal his true problems, no matter if he had no desire to talk it out, Matty had penetrated every layer of protective armor and ignited in Tommy a spark of happiness.

Had Matty told him all that about his father because he'd brought up *Strange Tales #1*? After all these months of hounding him to sell the comic, all of a sudden he gets sentimental? A little strange, but Tommy figured the shift made sense. He knew Matty and his dad were acquainted, but from the sound of Matty's story, they used to be pretty close. Maybe even *friends*. Why hadn't his dad ever mentioned the connection? Why hadn't he ever told Tommy about being an artist?

What had started as happiness began to transform. His dad knew Tommy loved to draw. Had watched him sketch on countless occasions. Why hadn't he offered to teach him? Why hadn't he revealed his old occupation? His plans to create his own comic? None of it made sense to Tommy, but he was sure his dad would find some stupid adult way of justifying everything.

With that thought, Tommy made a decision: He wouldn't ask his father to elaborate. He wouldn't even mention Matty's story. His mother's words from so long ago came back to him in a horrible recollection: *We all have our little secrets.* Now he knew how true those words were, and it gutted him.

Well, he thought. *They can keep their secrets, and I'll keep mine.*

For somewhere deep within his mind, far from the reaches of conscious thought, a dangerous plan took form.

CHAPTER SIXTEEN

AND THE WINNER IS . . .

There was no fried chicken. There *was* macaroni and cheese, albeit of the boxed variety. At least it was the dinosaur–shaped pasta, which made dinner a little better. Still, he'd have preferred his mom's ooey-gooey baked mac and cheese with the little pieces of feta and crunchy bread crumb topping. Sitting at the kitchen table, Tommy ate a big forkful of the pasta while thinking about his mom's cooking. He concentrated and thought he could almost taste the sharp bite of feta cheese.

His mom was leaning against the counter next to the stove, a tired expression aging her face beyond its years. Her blonde hair looked shorter and bouncier, and he wondered if she'd gotten it styled again. She was always going out for makeovers, lunch with friends, or spa days.

Suzie chewed her lip while watching him eat, though he had the distinct impression she was actually seeing *through* him.

"Mom?"

Her eyes refocused. "Need something, honey?" She glanced into the living room, where his father watched the evening news. Her features constricted.

Something about that look on her face needled Tommy. He hated the way the family was spread across separate rooms all the time. The way they spoke to one another with glares and thinly veiled aggression. He didn't mean to say anything, but the urge rose in him like hot lava until he spewed, "Are you splitting up again?"

She staggered as if hit by a cannon ball. "What?" She put a hand over her mouth and glanced at Dave. His dad had heard, and he was standing in front of the coffee table staring into the kitchen. Everyone remained frozen. His parents watched each other, perhaps waiting for the other to say something encouraging. Or something honest.

Neither spoke.

With every unspoken second, his mom's eyes became glassier until tears spilled over her high cheeks. She shook her head and wiped away the tears with what Tommy read as anger. "I'm going to bed." She left, nearly running, brushing past Dad and up the staircase. That Mom hadn't verbally answered his question hadn't mattered. She'd answered, nonetheless.

Dad stared a moment longer before sitting again and staring at the television.

Tommy pushed the bowl away and grabbed his magazine. As he walked through the living room, his father said, "Stopped at the comic shop?" He sat straighter. "Anything good?"

Here was his opening. If he wanted to know more about what Matty had told him, he could ask. Dad adjusted his glasses and scratched at the five o' clock shadow. Instead, Tommy said, "Just some *Cosmic Champions* stuff. Nothing you'd like."

"Right. Well—" He shrugged as if to say *to each his own.* Before Tommy could get to the stairs, his father added, "Don't say that kind of stuff to your mother." He removed his glasses. "We're trying."

"Sure seems like it."

As he climbed the stairs to his room, he wondered if Dad detected the sarcasm in his voice.

✳ ✳ ✳

And the winner is . . .

Aaron Beltzer of Brooklyn, New York, with his entry Fierce Phantos!

On top of winning the grand prize package, Aaron had been gifted a full page in the *OoCC* magazine for his announcement. They'd created a rad background of flying meteors and deep space imagery. Over top, they placed a picture of the winner, an illustration of his design, and a detailed write-up.

The picture of Aaron appeared to have been taken by a school photographer. He wore a forced smile that spoke of mandatory attendance and had chosen the popular *lasers* backdrop. When it had been time to choose, Tommy broke with convention and went with *green fog*. His mom said the color brought out his eyes, but he'd chosen the background because it reminded him of War Beast.

The reveal was too much for Tommy to take, and a deep-seated anger clawed back into the hollow place. The worst part was the abysmal winning design. Aaron had named his character Fierce Phantos. *Of course a hero won.* He wore some kind of spacesuit with a giant helmet covering his head. A nest of hoses and wires connected the helmet to the suit, but for some reason the character's face was fuzzy with static and distortion. Probably because Aaron wasn't a good artist. "So dumb."

Tommy skimmed the article, and after a couple paragraphs he found an explanation for the fuzzy appearance. "A holographic helmet?"

The article went on to explain that Fierce Phantos could project the holographic image of his choosing onto the helmet. The images often would have a ghostlike appearance, hence the name Phantos. Further, he had a hologram gun with which he could project phantoms of himself and other illusions.

He hated to admit it, but the character was actually kind of cool. Being able to project any image he wanted on the helmet was storytelling gold. On the one hand, he was glad he'd been beaten by a worthy opponent. On the other hand, this contest had been his last lingering hope, and the loss tore his heart out. He'd done some healing since he first received the rejection letter, but he'd also been dogpiled with unending bullying and problems at home. Enough so a scab had time to form, only to now get torn off again.

Magazine in hand, Tommy retreated to his bed and got under the covers. He continued to read about the winner. Aaron Beltzer of Brooklyn, New York. He studied the drawing of Fierce Phantos, tracing the lines of muscle with his finger, pretending to color in the red and blue of his suit. He continued until he knew every stylistic flair and tiny detail of the sketch. He did this until his eyes grew heavy with the exhaustion of adult problems. Then he slept and slept well.

For behind his sealed eyelids, there awaited a mysterious figure with a cryptic message.

CHAPTER SEVENTEEN

FIERCE PHANTOS

When Tommy opened his eyes, he inhabited the same desolate expanse he had explored many nights before. Unlike his previous dreams, however, everything appeared clear. The murky fog that previously obscured his surroundings had vanished.

He stood atop his hill, but everything was changed.

Time—always starving, always feeding—had stripped the houses bare, leaving only sticks of rotted wood and piles of debris. Small fires burned in mounds, not unlike piles of leaves from the waking world. A murder of crows perched on neon-flashing tree branches, their caws the sound of video games. A huge pile of pumpkins lay at the base of this tree, torn bus tickets scattered around it like fallen leaves. The silhouettes of five children lingered at the edge of visibility, surrounded by fog and mist.

Dread goblins of October dreams whispered secrets. They opened the eyes inside his mind even as his physical eyes remained shut. Dream logic directed his gaze to the horizon, where he again beheld the shining city. Only now he knew the skyline to be that of Manhattan.

The smoldering piles of debris stung his nose and made his eyes water. He tugged at his backpack straps and remembered he was going somewhere. Every time he had this dream, he was about to embark on a journey. The words *embark* and *escape* became entwined, and Tommy suspected for him, they were one and the same. But escape to where?

A distorted voice spoke like grumbling thunder, "The shining city."

Tommy recoiled. A mysterious figure stood next to him. The figure *always* stood beside him, in every dream, but he had never been able to make out its features.

Until now.

Fierce Phantos laughed, his voice layered with static as if coming through a walkie-talkie.

"Phantos!" A jolt of anger and fear shot through Tommy's heart as he grasped a heretofore invisible hilt and unsheathed his sword. Light glinted off unbreakable metal, mined from dreams, forged in the fires of youth. "I should have known it was you!"

Fierce Phantos raised his hands. The face projected within his helmet was a ghostly image, more android than human. "Easy, boy. Easy."

"Give me one good reason I shouldn't cut you down where you stand, Phantos!" He jabbed the razor's edge of the blade deadly close to the hero's chest, tightening his hand on the ornate dragon scale grip. The cross-guard resonated with magic from embedded griffin feathers. The pommel, a rare gemstone of pure hope, pulsed vibrant orange. He knew this sword. He'd wielded it in dreams before, but the name of his blade eluded him.

The image on Fierce Phantos's helmet flickered, taking on feminine qualities. The previously bald head sprouted platinum blonde hair in long waves. A neon pink hair band appeared nested in the locks; the face shrank in size until it was that of a young girl with blue-green eyes. *Miranda*.

"Please don't hurt me, Tommy!" she squeaked.

Tommy staggered backward and dropped his sword with a metallic clatter. "I didn't mean to—"

Before he could finish apologizing, Fierce Phantos began laughing uncontrollably, still in Miranda's voice. Her face shifted back to the original projection. He drew a laser pistol and said, "Leave your sword where it lies, villain."

Tommy's heart beat fast and sweat pricked his skin. "I'm not a villain."

"Then why do you attack a hero?"

Somewhere deep in his mind, Skullagar murmured incomprehensibly. Words of war and death. Words of hate. They overtook him momentarily, nearly bringing him to his knees. The words spread like an infection. The heat of life drained and Tommy's extremities stiffened.

His sword's pommel pulsed orange and true. Tommy reached out.

"Careful, boy," Phantos warned.

Tommy managed, "You startled me. That's all." The cold ate deeper, feeding on the warmth of his core.

Phantos thought this over, his hologram face glitching approximations of human expressions. He put the gun back in its holster and boomed, "Apology accepted!"

"I didn't apolo—"

"The shining city is Manhattan," he cut in, apropos of nothing.

Tommy breathed ice water as Skullagar's lamentations penetrated deeper. Each word was like an icicle stabbing his heart. He concentrated on the warmth of his blade, the pulsing gemstone, the pure light it exuded. He extended his nearly frozen arm. The sword thawed Tommy as he reached for the hilt, then grasped it and sheathed the blade. The second the sword was with him, Skullagar's voice extinguished, and as if he'd drunk a healing tonic, Tommy felt himself again.

"Manhattan. Right, I know."

"You also know Brooklyn is one of the boroughs of New York."

"So?"

Fierce Phantos stared at the shining city on the horizon and showed no intent of elaborating.

This was flat out the weirdest dream Tommy had ever had, and he'd had some doozies. He spoke if only to fill the void of silence. "I went to New York once for a Broadway show. I've never been to Brooklyn, though."

Phantos snatched a magazine out of thin air like a magician doing a card trick. He opened to a page and handed it to Tommy. "Maybe you should go."

It was a copy of the *OoCC* magazine, and the page Phantos had turned to was the announcement for the contest winner.

And the winner is Aaron Beltzer of Brooklyn, New York.

Tommy stared at this for a long time. Tendrils of conscious thought wormed through dreamland, connecting independent ideas. Notions Tommy hadn't realized he harbored. A ticklish sensation erupted in his belly.

Finally understanding some previously hidden epiphany, he repeated Phantos's words. "Yeah. Maybe I *should* go."

✳ ✳ ✳

When Tommy woke up, Fierce Phantos was sitting on his bed. The face projected inside the helmet flickered and ran through with scan lines. The hypnopompic hallucination didn't sink in right away. Crossing between sleep and wakefulness often drew relics of dreams into the waking world. That Phantos had traversed the eldritch veil made perfect sense to the drowsy child.

Then his alarm went off and shocked Tommy fully awake. He twisted on the bed, groaning as he reached for Garfield's bulbous, disembodied head.

He poked the nose to snooze the alarm when Fierce Phantos said, "Best to rise early. We have errands."

Tommy threw himself against the headboard, drew the covers to his neck, and screamed like a horror movie actress.

Fierce Phantos stood fast.

Tommy pointed and stammered, "What—? I mean, what's—Uh. But . . ."

"Oh my. I've broken the poor lad." His face transformed into a cartoon nurse. He leaned close, speaking extra slow and extra loud. "Are *you. Having. A stroke?*"

"What is this? What's going on?"

"*Do you smell burning toast?*" The cartoon nurse inside his helmet removed a slice of blackened bread from a smoking toaster.

Tommy continued to push backward against the headboard of his bed until he slipped off the side onto the floor, tangled in a nest of blankets and sheets. He pointed at the imaginary hero standing large as life in the middle of his bedroom and screamed, "You're not real!"

His bedroom door slammed open. "Tommy!" His mother's eyes were wide with shock. She dropped to the floor and moved the blankets around, searching for something. Probably blood, Tommy realized.

She unburied him frantically. "What happened? Why did you scream?" Not finding any sign of injury, his mother stood and held a shaking hand to her face. "You scared the heck out of me."

He stood and put the blankets on the bed. Phantos wasn't there anymore. He'd vanished the second his mom barged into the room. And yet there was a lingering sense of dread in the pit of his stomach. Something sharp and venomous stabbing his guts.

"Bad dream, I guess."

Mom's laugh held no humor. "Bad dream? Sounded like a world-class nightmare, kiddo. One for the record books. You sure you're okay?"

Tommy patted himself. "Nothing broken. Maybe just my brain."

She laughed this off, but Tommy had been serious. It was one thing to pretend the Order of Cosmic Champions were talking to him when he played with his action figures. To hear their voices in his head like far-off commentators. It was something else entirely to see and have a conversation with one standing in his room.

"Since you're awake, why don't you help me with breakfast." Her bemused expression faded. "There's something I want to talk to you about before you leave for school."

Her voice gave everything away. This would be about Dad. This would be about what Tommy had said the night before. "In a couple minutes."

Before leaving, she looked around his room as if seeing it for the first time. "Clean this up later. Your room is starting to look like the inside of a crazy person's head."

"You don't know the half of it," he muttered to himself.

With his mom gone, Tommy tiptoed around the room searching for any trace of Fierce Phantos. A footprint on the carpet, a stray space suit fiber, anything. The memory resurfaced of Skullagar's action figure turning to look at him. Those green eyes, the bestial head peaking from beneath a skull mask. Had the toy truly moved on its own? Tommy didn't think so. It'd been a trick of the eyes. And this? Probably a hallucinatory event brought on by a tired mind still trapped in dreamland.

"I was still dreaming. Still asleep."

The justification made sense, and yet the words held no comfort. Deep down, Tommy was certain it had all been real.

✳ ✳ ✳

The pancakes were as fluffy as cartoon clouds, and the maple syrup with tiny puddles of melting butter was ambrosia. Tommy enjoyed breakfast cereal, but for his money, nothing beat homemade pancakes with a side of bacon.

He crunched on a strip of oily, salty, melt-in-your-mouth deliciousness. Mom hadn't made a breakfast like this in weeks. She sat opposite Tommy at the kitchen table with her own small plate but hadn't taken a bite for so long that the syrup had soaked into the pancakes, making them look soggy and unappealing. Rather than eat, she watched Tommy, her initial smile fading over time. Maybe she didn't want to make the same mistake she had last time, blurting out awful news right before Tommy chowed down. The memory caused him to put his fork down and swallow the lump of pancakes as if it were a jagged rock.

"You wanted to tell me something?" He'd noticed the distinct absence of Dad that morning, and while he did sometimes go into the dealership early, this felt like something else.

His mom pushed her plate of food aside. Her eyes were appraising. "You're done?"

"Yeah. It was good, thanks."

"You're welcome, sweetie." She picked at some crumbs on the table. "I'll be cooking more again soon."

The thought of regular meals sounded great, though he wondered what the trade-off would be.

His mom got control of her hands and placed them on her lap. She locked eyes with Tommy. "Your father and I love you very much. You know that, right?"

The speech sounded ripped directly from an after-school special or one of those lousy made-for-TV movies his mom loved. He tried to keep from grimacing and nodded, all the bad feelings flooding back.

As his mom spoke, his mind drifted to the shining city. While she talked about his dad staying at a motel again, Tommy thought about his dream. When she spoke of a more permanent solution, the magazine announcement reasserted itself. And when she mentioned divorce, his body flooded with a keen desire to embark on a journey. No, that wasn't right.

He felt the keen desire to *escape*.

CHAPTER EIGHTEEN

GATEWAY TO HALLOWEEN WEEKEND

On the way to the bus stop that Friday, all the gears inside Tommy's head were spinning at full speed. He knew what had to be done, and he knew that weekend, Halloween weekend, was the perfect time to do it.

Miranda came around the corner ahead, and as usual, Tommy slowed his pace. A deep-seated embarrassment lingered inside him, disallowing any kind of discourse. As if proof his life was about to change, Miranda glanced over her shoulder and locked eyes with him.

She stopped walking and waved. "Catch up!" Her hair was tied back with a green scrunchie. She wore pink earmuffs that matched her jacket and fiddled with her knitted scarf as Tommy urged himself to jog over.

"Hey," he said lamely.

"Hey," she repeated.

They walked in awkward silence. Miranda's perfume smelled like cotton candy, lending her the aura of a confectionery.

"So." Tommy looked around as if only just noticing something. "No Ambrose and Titus today?"

"Went away for the weekend, I think. Got off school early to start the trip."

"Lucky." Even as he said this, he thought he might soon find the same kind of luck.

"Yeah." Miranda watched her feet as they continued. She twisted her mouth and stopped walking. "Do you hate me or something?" Her eyes glistened wet from the cold air. The tip of her nose and cheeks were flushed red from the chill. She refused to drop her gaze, a fierce look in her eyes.

He didn't have the wherewithal to answer with any kind of grace or even a modicum of understanding. He sputtered, "*What?*"

This caused Miranda's face to bunch with fury. "It's a simple question. You've been avoiding me like I have cooties! Why do you hate me?"

He couldn't believe this. *Hate* her? She was the most interesting person he knew. "I don't hate you," he said, hearing the defensiveness in his voice. "I'm just . . ." The words stuck in his throat. He started walking again.

Miranda caught up and kept pace. "You're what?" She pushed his shoulder.

Through clenched teeth, he said, "Embarrassed." The word burned his tongue. When Miranda didn't respond, he sneaked a glance and recoiled at the strange smile on her face. What a mistake! Now she'd make fun of him too.

Only, when she finally spoke, her words weren't barbed like the other kids'. "You shouldn't be embarrassed. The bullies should be embarrassed. They're the ones acting like . . . well, like—" She glanced around slyly and then whispered, "*Asses.*"

Tommy had never heard a curse uttered so adorably. His embarrassment melted like so much butter on pancakes.

"Don't ever tell anyone I said that."

"I won't." He smiled dumbly.

She shoved his shoulder again. "I *am* mad at you, though." She played with her scarf and looked down her nose at Tommy. "For thinking I was so shallow that I wouldn't want to talk to you after you got bullied."

Shame surfaced like a hungry shark. Miranda was right. She had only ever been welcoming and kind to Tommy. This newcomer to town treated him better than any of his longtime friends did, barring Sammy. Certainly there were plenty of other kids who were cordial, or at the very least, paid him no attention at all. The real bullies, the ones who had hounded his every footfall through the halls of Ende Junior High, were few and far between. It only *felt* like everyone bullied him because his subconscious had become an interloper in his own body. The reality was Tommy could name his tormentors and count them off on one hand. And he did. Almost every night as he lay awake in bed, praying for life to go back to normal.

Evan Winger. Jonathan Miller. Ray, the eighth-grade bully. Steve, the other eighth-grade bully. After each name, he'd clench his jaw and pray for them, because Pastor Roberts had warned against vengeance, and Tommy was scared, no, *terrified* for his mortal soul. Because deep down he hated them. So he prayed not only for their sake, but also for his own. And to keep that other voice out of his head. The one of Skullagar, who whispered dark thoughts and villainous ideas.

Tommy knew only one phrase to soothe situations like these, and he used it freely. "I'm sorry."

As they found the end of the road, Miranda asked, "*Why* are you sorry?"

Tommy frowned at the question. No one had ever asked him to explain before. They'd just accept the apology, and everyone would move on with their lives.

Why *was* he sorry? For making her feel bad? Well, sure, but was that the answer? Fierce Phantos spoke to him in the same disembodied way Skullagar used to. The angel to Skullagar's demon. Only this time, the words made sense and fit neatly within his moral code.

He repeated them. "I'm sorry I judged you unfairly."

The smile returned to Miranda's face. She tugged at her scarf and nodded once, firmly. "Apology accepted."

✳ ✳ ✳

When the bus arrived, they climbed the stairs and went to their usual seats. Miranda sat with Tonya, and Tommy sat alone near the back. The cold plastic seat ate right through his pants and he shivered, thinking that if he could get through this last day, tomorrow everything would begin to change. He opened his backpack and removed the *OoCC* magazine and his father's comic, *Strange Tales #1*. Funny how he still thought of the comic as his dad's, even after it had been handed down to him. Maybe the comic would always belong to his father. Even after his dad died and Tommy handed it down to his own son, the comic would still truly belong to Dave Grant.

And what if he sold *Strange Tales* to Matty? What then?

Miranda appeared next to his seat. "Move over."

Heart pounding, he slid closer to the window and Miranda sat next to him. "I told Tonya I wanted to sit with you today." She looked at the magazine and comic in his lap. "What's that?"

He presented the comic. "My dad gave this to me. It's worth a ton of money."

Miranda's eyes were wide with wonder. "How much?"

"Matty at the comic shop said he'd give me a thousand big ones!"

She waved this away. "Liar."

"For real." He carefully placed the comic in his backpack.

Miranda's eyes lingered on the bag as if she had X-ray vision. "That's so cool. What about that?" She pointed to the *OoCC* magazine.

Tommy opened to the winner announcement and handed the magazine to Miranda, who read the article carefully. When she finished, she said, "Aaron Beltzer? Did you vote for him?"

"No. I entered the contest with my own character. I lost."

"I'm sorry. What was your character's name?"

"Mechani-Ghoul."

"Was he a bad guy?"

Tommy shifted in his seat. "Yeah, I guess."

"Oh. Well, bad guys are fun to draw. Can I see him?"

Tommy retrieved the magazine. "I don't have the sketch with me." A little tickle in his chest urged him to spill the beans. To tell her the big Halloween weekend plan. He was excited, nearly bursting. He shouldn't say anything. Still—

"If things work out, maybe I can give you one."

She shifted in the seat and twisted her legs into a pretzel so she could face Tommy. "If what works out? One what?"

He ignored the first part of the question. "A Mechani-Ghoul action figure."

She lowered her eyebrows and pushed her lips out in thought. "But you didn't win."

"No, I didn't," he agreed.

"Then how?"

Tommy almost revealed his secret. Almost went through with a complete explanation just to savor his grand plan, like the villains in all his favorite cartoons. A full rundown of every little detail. But he knew it'd be a mistake, and with great effort, Tommy clammed up.

"I dunno. I guess I meant a sketch. I'd draw one for you."

"Oh! Okay!"

The immediate joy and excitement on Miranda's face reawakened something that had been buried since the beginning of the previous summer. Some childlike happiness that had been snuffed out. His hollow place became a little less hollow in that moment. Tommy cultivated this small patch of fertile soil Miranda had so graciously gifted. He planted a seed there and generously watered it. For the rest of the day, Tommy cared for this small plot, making sure to allow in a shaft of nourishing sunlight. As the soil warmed, so did his heart.

This new friendship did a lot to soothe the hurt, but it changed nothing about his plans. Come tomorrow morning, Tommy would be gone.

CHAPTER NINETEEN
THE NIGHT BEFORE

After school, Tommy went directly to Defender Comics and surprised the hell out of Matty when he put *Strange Tales #1* on the counter.

Matty lowered his glasses and stared at the comic for a full minute. Finally he regarded Tommy. "Why is this here?"

"You said a thousand dollars."

"I did say that." He picked up the bagged and boarded comic. "May I?"

"Sure."

Matty dug out latex gloves and swung a bright light over the counter. He removed the comic from the bag and looked it over. "It's in really good condition. *Really* good. But not mint."

He swung the light away. "Does your dad know you're selling it?"

A little white lie here and there couldn't send him to hell, could it? He'd just have to pray extra hard for a while. "Yeah, he wasn't too happy."

"Oh?" He pushed his dreads back.

"I told him it'd go toward my college account."

"Is that right?"

"Yeah. He said as long as I saved the money, it'd be okay."

Matty examined the comic, shaking his head with increasing determination until finally pushing it back to Tommy. "I can't."

"Are you kidding? You've been bugging me for months!"

He lit some more incense, as if the place wasn't already filled with the stuff. "Look, kid. I told you. Me and your dad go way back. I don't believe for a second he'd let you sell it."

"I told you, he—"

Matty threw a hand up like a crossing guard. "Kid. He knows as well as I do this comic will do nothing but increase in value. If he really thought this was for your college fund, he'd tell you to hold on to it for as long as possible. Any interest the money gains in a savings account will be pennies compared to the gained value of the comic."

"Yeah, but—"

"*Tommy.*" He took his glasses off. "I ask about the comic because it was a big deal for Dave to pass it on to you. I like to remind you the comic has value. Both monetary *and* personal. I never thought you'd actually sell it!" He waved his hand in the air and smiled. "It was like, our thing. You know? I'd tell you how much I'd pay; you'd say, 'Not happening, comic dude.'" He rubbed his head. "But Tommy, I can't steal from you. And this *would* be stealing."

His plan was falling apart around him, and he hadn't even gotten started yet. If he was going to get to Brooklyn, he needed money. This comic was the closest thing to money he had, except his college fund.

Matty watched Tommy with far too much scrutiny. "If you're not selling the comic for your college fund, then why *are* you selling it?"

"Who said the money wasn't for my college—"

"Come on, kid. We've already established your dad knows better. You're too young to be on drugs." Matty squinted. "You're not on drugs, are you?"

"No!"

"No." He laughed. "'Course not. So what's up?"

He couldn't tell Matty the truth. There was no way he'd let Tommy run away to Brooklyn without alerting his parents. There was only one other answer he could come up with. The more he thought about the explanation, the more he realized it was true. Tommy didn't *need* to sell the comic to get the money. His college fund was in a savings account, and he could access it. His parents trusted him with the deposits, and every now and then—with their permission—he'd taken out a few dollars for comics or video rentals.

So then why sell the comic that his father had handed down to him? "Because my parents are getting a divorce."

Matty's face went slack. "Oh—"

"I guess I'm mad. I wanted to get back at my dad. Wanted to do something to hurt him the way they're hurting me." Even as he said these things, he knew they were true. Every word, every syllable. All true.

Matty, his father's friend, *Tommy's* friend, quietly nodded. He scratched his goatee, his chubby cheeks flushed. "I get that, ki—" He shook his head. "I get that, man. Divorce is heavy stuff. Hard to get through. Harder to get *over*."

"You're telling *me*."

"I'll tell you something else too. Selling this comic or doing *anything* to get back at your parents. You'll regret it."

Tommy backed away unintentionally, not wanting to hear this advice.

"Listen, I'm serious. You *will* regret it, no matter how good the action may feel right now. In the long run, vengeance is poison."

"Poison." His features constricted. There was something else weighing on him. Another mistake? Perhaps. But he couldn't hold in the words or worry, and Matty was an adult who might have answers. "I've been seeing things too."

"Seeing things?" He took his Rastafarian hat off as if he'd entered a church. "What kind of things?"

Tommy's hands stung from rubbing them together. "Characters from *Order of Cosmic Champions*. Skullagar. That kid's winning entry, Fierce Phantos." With exertion of will, he fixed his arms at his sides and balled his hands into fists. "They talk to me."

Matty's demeanor changed slightly, though Tommy had trouble pinpointing how. "What do they say?"

Here, Tommy knew he couldn't be completely truthful. "Advice, mostly. Like how to deal with my parents splitting up, or the bullying at school."

Matty's expression softened. No, he looked *relieved*. "Gotcha." He rubbed his goatee in thought, taking on the mannerisms of a wizened philosopher. "If you went to a head shrinker, I'm sure they'd feed you some garbage about the voices being manifestations of your conscience. Like the little angel and devil whispering on your shoulders."

"Okay?"

A possessed expression came over Matty's round face. He closed his eyes, and in a deep monotone unlike his normal voice, said, "Countless worlds upon worlds. Worlds without end. In these galaxies, every possible reality exists." He waved his hands around like a magician. "And what is reality in any new world is mere fantasy in all others." Pause for dramatic effect. "Here, all is real, and all is illusion. What is, what was, and what will be start here with the words: In the beginning, there was . . . *Howard the Duck!*"

Tommy groaned and rolled his eyes. "You dork. I'm being serious."

"So am I." He stepped out from behind the counter and waved Tommy along. "Totally underrated film, by the way."

"It's trash."

"I'm gonna pretend you didn't say that." He pulled a couple long boxes from behind the counter. The ones with more valuable stuff. "I'm no therapist. I'm just a lowly comic book fan." He flipped through the comics for a minute, then said, "Here we go. In 1953, DC Comics introduced the idea of an alternate earth in *Wonder Woman number 59*. They expanded on the idea in 1961 with *The Flash number 123*, and Marvel took a swing at the alternate universes in 1977's *What If?*" He held up a copy of *The Daredevils number 7*. "But in this comic, we discover what we thought of as the real world was actually Earth-616."

Everything Matty explained sounded cool, but Tommy didn't grasp the point. "So there were six hundred and sixteen different earths?"

Matty put the comic away and threw his arms out, his eyes wide with excitement. "Infinite worlds, Tommy! A multiverse!"

"What does this have to do with me?"

Matty scoffed and sat on a stool. "A shrink will give you a whole load about your conscience and the trauma of your parents splitting up causing you to see things. But as I said, I'm not a shrink. So here's my explanation, and I think it'll be more appealing. If there are infinite worlds, then there are infinite possibilities. Other earths that are almost exactly the same as ours except for a tiny difference. Like maybe Masculon is called, I dunno, He-Man or something. And then there are other earths that are completely different, where maybe humans are all giant ducks. You follow?"

Tommy nodded, his mouth hanging open in wonder.

"Well, who's to say there isn't an earth where the Order of Cosmic Champions are real? And maybe, in that universe, they invented some wild contraption that lets them visit the other worlds in the multiverse, like spirits in a vast haunted house?"

The idea burst inside of Tommy like colorful fireworks, lighting his mind with a wondrous notion. "You're saying the things I'm seeing are *real?*"

He chuckled and waved the idea away. "Well, not really. But isn't it a far-out idea? Something a little nicer to believe in. That the heroes of Evernitia have traveled through the multiverse to help you cope?"

"That's pretty awesome." He thought briefly about Skullagar's poor advice and wondered if Fierce Phantos was also leading him astray. Maybe this whole plan was an excuse to get back at his parents. One of those things he'd regret, like Matty had warned.

In his head, Phantos said, "You're not running away to hurt your parents. You're not running away at all. You're going on a hero's journey to reignite hope. To reclaim your lost world."

Tommy didn't know if what Phantos said was true, but it *felt* true. Enough so that Tommy understood what he had to do. He'd listen to Matty and save the comic, but he would not abandon his quest.

Tommy would find Aaron Beltzer in Brooklyn, and he would convince the *president for a day* to use his ultimate authority over Telco Toys to have Mechani-Ghoul turned into an action figure. He hadn't won the contest, but Tommy would not accept defeat.

If that meant emptying his savings account, so be it.

✳ ✳ ✳

After the comic shop, Tommy went home and found his mom gone and his father packing a bag in the bedroom.

"Tommy?" His dad stepped to the doorway and held on to the jamb as if clinging to flotsam from a sinking ship. "Come here for a second."

Tommy met his father in the carpeted bedroom. The room smelled like his mom's perfume and his dad's aftershave. There were also other homey scents, things he usually took for granted but found himself fixating on that night. The tiny decorative bowl filled with a lavender-heavy potpourri. The carpet powder his mom used when she vacuumed. Newsprint from the pile of old papers and magazines his dad had piled

142

in a box. These scents swirled around like a nostalgia tornado, infecting Tommy with memories he'd carry far into the future, long after that specific combination of smells no longer existed, save for in his mind.

"Hey, Dad." Tommy's throat grew thick with an unexpected sob he managed to hold back at the last moment. The idea that his father may never set foot in this room again reminded Tommy of earlier that year, when he left elementary school for the last time. Change, he had come to realize, was painful.

It overtook him all at once. The sense that everything about his perfect little childhood was about to be broken into fragments and scattered across the town. The idea that this coming Christmas would be a pale facsimile of the holidays of his first eleven years. None of this was okay and only added to the desire—no, the *need*—to escape. If he could convince Aaron Beltzer to have Mechani-Ghoul made into a toy, he'd no doubt become rich and famous, and then he could make everything okay again.

"I guess you already spoke with your mom." The five-o-clock shadow was back in force. His glasses were fogged over with dirt, and his eyes had dark bags under them.

"Yeah. You're going to the motel again."

He looked away for a second, as if the words coming from Tommy's mouth were bullets. "That's right."

Tommy had to swallow hard to get the lump out of his throat. "And you're maybe not coming back this time."

His father placed a neatly folded pile of shirts into the suitcase. "Maybe not." His mouth twitched and he added quickly, "To live. But we're still gonna see each other. All the time. And I'll still come here." He went back to packing. "But unless there's some kind of miracle, no, I won't be living here anymore."

Tommy kicked the side of the bed. "*Why?*"

"Didn't your mother—?"

"Yeah. But why couldn't you fix it? Why couldn't you *do* something?"

The way his father looked in that moment, Tommy never wanted to see him that way again. Crumpled and balled up like a used piece of paper. Discarded. "We tried, Tommy-boy. We really tried."

He wanted to hug his dad. Wanted to say he loved him and that everything would be okay. Or maybe he wanted his dad to say those things. But neither of them did, because they were both broken, fragmented into an amalgamation of sharp edges no one could touch without being cut to ribbons. They remained that way for a while, perhaps afraid to leave each other's side. In the end, they never said goodbye. Never hugged or expressed their love.

Tommy simply walked out of the room, and Dave let him.

✳ ✳ ✳

Back in his own room, Tommy closed the door and began packing his JanSport bag. He shoved items into it, his mind far away, not seeing anything. A lost boy.

"Good evening, Tommy!" Fierce Phantos boomed, knocking Tommy onto the bed in fright as he yelped and kicked away.

Phantos was not at all like a cartoon. The fuzzy projection on his gleaming helmet, the metallic vents and rubbery hoses, the vibrant red and blue—were *real*. Instead of a smooth spacesuit, there were loose threads and textured rubbers. Scuff marks and dirt.

His holographic face became a bashful puppy. "I'm sorry. Did I— how do you humans say—scare your pants off?" His helmet projected the image of a pair of jeans flying through the air.

Tommy's shock and fear bubbled into a near hysteria as he watched the animation play out inside Phantos's helmet. He slapped his forehead, expecting the intruding hallucination to disappear. When it didn't, Tommy said, "You're kind of a cornball, huh?"

The image disappeared and became a humanoid face again. "Why do you think I am a ball of corn?"

"Forget it." Tommy stood cautiously, keeping his distance. Whether hallucination or visiting being from another universe, Phantos seemed harmless enough. Tommy packed some clothes in his Midland Falls duffel while keeping a close eye on the strange visitor.

Phantos pressed a few buttons on his armor and a tiny glowing screen appeared. On this, he began to write stuff using his finger, the cursive words transforming into perfect digital type as he went on. The digital pad was see-through, and from where Tommy stood, the words were backward. There was also a little clock, or something like it, on the screen.

"What are you writing—?"

"Call me F.P.," he suggested. "Notes for the quest ahead." He pressed a button and the digital screen fizzled out. "I am glad you have taken my advice. According to my intel, this quest is imperative to your future." He nodded firmly.

"Your advice?"

"To travel to Brooklyn. To find Aaron Beltzer."

Tommy shook his head. "That was my idea."

F.P. shrugged. "If you say so."

Could this Fierce Phantos be from a real alternate universe? Could he have implanted the idea to run away in Tommy's dreams? Or was Tommy just going crazy? Matty did say there was also a headshrinker interpretation, which had to be more realistic. But what had realism gotten him? A spoiled summer, parents in the midst of divorce, and a gang of bullies who haunted his every step.

In his closet, Tommy retrieved some of his old Boy Scout gear. He had a mapping compass, canteen, and a map of Ohio. He shoved the latter into his bag and hung the compass from a keychain ring on the zipper.

"Good thinking. We don't want to get lost in the overgrown wilds of"—F.P. tapped at his holographic keyboard—"Cincinnati."

"You know, for a universe-hopping superhero, you have a terrible sense of direction."

"Thank you!" His grin stretched to the outer limits of his helmet.

Tommy thought, *If this guy is a reflection of my inner self, I'm doomed.* He inspected the man . . . if he could call him a man. Slowly, tentatively, Tommy reached out and poked him in the stomach. He made contact with a stone-like surface and jammed his finger. "Crap!" He stepped back and shook his hand. "You're—"

"Real?"

"How is this—?"

"It is complicated. A conversation best left for another time."

"Can other people see you too?"

"Only you, Tommy."

That was the kicker. The giveaway. And though the figure standing before him seemed real enough, Tommy was mostly sure this was all in his head.

Mostly.

CHAPTER TWENTY

HERE I GO AGAIN

Tommy sat astride his Mongoose at the top of the hill. He left behind a note for his parents. If by some miracle they noticed he was gone, the letter would keep them from getting worried. As angry as he was, he still loved them and didn't want to freak them out. This trip wasn't about vengeance. It was about healing.

Gazing down the steep slope, he had a sense that this descent would be unlike any previous ride. This time, he was free. He could go anywhere.

And that's just what he planned to do.

Tommy pulled on a wool hat and buttoned the emblazoned jean jacket over his green "I saved the Triforce" shirt. The lined jacket was his armor, rife with pins and iron-on patches: Nintendo Power, *Ghostbusters*, *OoCC* fan club, a DeLorean, and so much more. Checking the straps of his backpack and the duffel he wore across his chest, the world shifted to make room for this new player.

He kicked off and soared through the October air. Yard signs had popped up over the past weeks, declaring support for Bush and Quayle or Dukakis and Bentsen. Most of the leaves went from vibrantly colorful to dead brown, but Tommy felt alive. He pedaled hard down the slope, pushing his speed more than ever before. His insides boiled with potential. His mind burned with anticipation.

"That's right, Tommy." Fierce Phantos kept pace next to him, riding a winged spirit creature, ghostly streaks of vapor trailing behind like a comet's tail. "Now take us into hyperdrive."

Nodding the affirmative, he stood on the green machine and pumped the pedals. Adrenaline and fear became an intoxicating cocktail surging through his veins until he was sure he'd explode.

The spirit creature spread enormous scaled wings of silver and rode a gust of wind into the overcast sky. Fierce Phantos yipped with glee and called out, "Savor this moment, Tommy!" Then he was gone like a streak of silver paint on canvas, receding into vast oblivion. As they had before in Matty's shop, Mrs. Tither's words echoed deep in his mind: . . . *promise me you will* savor *every moment.*

Tommy stopped only once, at the corner of Wild Vine and Branch, to check for traffic. The wind carried a sweet voice calling his name, and he smiled at the thought of Defendra of the OoCC awaiting him around the next turn. He left his street behind, savoring the crisp morning air and the pleasant burn of leg muscles as he raced to town. The morning was still new, but he had tracks to make and much to do before day's end.

* * *

Saturday morning in Branchville wasn't as deserted as Tommy had hoped. By 8:30, there were dozens of shoppers at the local farmers' market in Courthouse Square, past the cluster of businesses Tommy usually patronized. Not being middle aged and boring, Tommy had forgotten all about the weekly gathering of local farmers and businesses, each with their own little tent and table. The usually quiet streets were lined with cars and people walking around with bags of produce. The stores all opened early on Saturdays to take advantage of the influx of morning shoppers too.

Phantos hadn't returned, but Tommy figured the invisible entity wouldn't be any help here anyway. He walked his bike down a narrow alley between Defender Comics and the Luncheonette, intending to stash it there.

Behind the buildings there were a couple of enormous dumpsters. The one behind the Luncheonette smelled like a bowling shoe filled with barf, but the one behind Matty's place wasn't bad. There was still a sour smell, but it was only filled with cardboard boxes. His first idea was to hide the bike in the dumpster. The only problem was he didn't know when the garbage got picked up.

"Bad idea."

"*Phantos*," Tommy growled. The space-suited hero was a constant reminder of his loss. Why he had to go and imagine Aaron's winning entry as his sidekick, he couldn't fathom.

"I hope you weren't planning on hiding your bike in the dumpster." Phantos tipped his helmeted head over the open lid. "It smells like a family of raccoons might have died in there."

Not a bad riff, but Tommy thought he could do better. "It smells like a Limburger-lined jock strap."

"Ha!" F.P. slapped his leg. "No, wait, wait. It smells like a skunk with diarrhea!"

"Oh, *gross!*" Maybe F.P. wasn't so bad after all. "I bet you can't even smell anything through that helmet."

"I have vent holes."

"Yeah, but do you have a real face?"

Phantos answered this by changing his hologram into the words *Real Face*.

"So funny I forgot to laugh." Tommy looked around the back lot for another option. On the left there was a small strip of scrub brush and trees that separated the lot from some houses. There wasn't much cover, but maybe—

Tommy leaned over the edge of the dumpster and grabbed a couple boxes. He walked his bike and the boxes to the wooded area and placed his bike in the brush. He then laid the flattened cardboard over the top. The boxes didn't look out of place among the empty chip bags, cans, and other litter scattered in the grass.

He stepped back and appraised his work.

Phantos did the same, rubbing the bottom of his helmet the way Matty sometimes rubbed his goatee. "Not bad."

"It's the best we're going to do, I think."

"The best *you're* going to do anyway. I could have done much better." A first-place trophy appeared in F.P.'s helmet.

Tommy shook his head and repositioned his duffel bag and backpack. After a second, he said, "The dumpster smells like a rotten fish fart."

Phantos nodded solemnly. "Good one."

* * *

With his bike stashed, the next stop was Midland Falls Bank. When Tommy turned ten, his parents took him to the local branch of Midland Falls Bank to open a savings account. They gave him all kinds of free junk, like the Midland Falls duffel bag that depicted a gleeful man going over a waterfall in a barrel. Below, instead of water, there were piles of gold coins. Tommy also got a plastic cup in the shape of a barrel and an "I'm saving for my future" T-shirt with the Midland Falls logo on the pocket. It was like winning a slightly boring sweepstakes, where all the prizes were *almost* cool.

The account was what the bank called joint savings. Because of his age, his parents had to sign most of the paperwork, but when it was all over, the banker gave Tommy his own ATM card (even though Branchville had no ATM machines yet), a small pile of deposit and withdrawal slips, and a tiny booklet where he was supposed to keep track of his savings. His dad had showed him how to do this and even bought him a little solar calculator to use so he didn't get anything wrong.

His account had started out with a whopping $500, thanks to his parents. They said the money was his birthday present that year, but it sure didn't feel like a gift at the time. What good was $500 he couldn't touch? And they had been very clear about that, because technically Tommy *could* withdraw money on his own, but they warned him that the account had to have at least $500 in it at all times so they wouldn't get charged a fee. At least for a little while, he could only put money *in*.

And put money in he did. Half of his allowance every week, half of all the birthday and Christmas money he received, and an occasional injection of cash from his parents. His dad especially enjoyed throwing an extra $25 at the account when he made a big sale. After a little over two years, Tommy's account had grown to $1,362, not counting any accrued interest; those calculations were too hard for him. He stared at the figure in his little booklet, then took out his calculator. He subtracted $500 (the amount that had to remain so they weren't charged fees) and got $862. It wasn't the $1,000 he had been hoping for, but he thought it should be plenty to get to Brooklyn and back. Not that he had any real idea of cost.

The larger problem, he suspected, was withdrawing the money without raising suspicion. The bankers at Midland Falls knew him pretty well. For the first year or so, his parents had brought him to do his banking. Not long after his eleventh birthday, they started letting him ride his bike to town alone, and he'd make deposits all by himself. The first time he took money out, the teller asked if he had permission from his parents. Soon after, they didn't bother asking at all.

But that was only for small amounts. A dollar here, two dollars there. The most he ever withdrew was five bucks, and that had caused Mrs. Rutherford to raise an eyebrow. He figured there was no way he could take out all $862 at once. No way, no how.

* * *

Tommy yanked his wool hat low and kept his eyes on the ground, hoping to avoid the notice of farmers' market patrons.

The early morning October sensation worked its magic on Tommy, eliciting tiny shivers of excitement for Halloween and the coming holidays. The town had amplified the All Hallows aesthetic with a plethora of jack-o'-lanterns around the previously hung decorations. The farmers' market itself was like a glowing beacon of holiday cheer, all orange pumpkins and red apples. A local bakery sold apple cider donuts and pumpkin pies at their stall while their neighbor piled high an array of gourds, daring the stacked vegetables to fall.

Tommy was drawn to the festival atmosphere, mindlessly veering toward the spectacle of apple bobbing and cake walks. An acoustic band stood under a hay-lined gazebo, plucking away at some old tune about the harvest. A banner strung across the road, from streetlight to streetlight, announced the month-long Harvest Fest, held every Saturday during the farmers' market. No wonder there were so many people here. A cluster of little kids waited in line to get their faces painted by a lady dressed as a cat. She turned the children into a horde of cavorting goblins with pumpkin or witch faces. They screamed bloody murder and chased each other around the gazebo until their parents plied them with candy apples or cotton candy.

For the briefest moment, Tommy thought about abandoning his plan. His child's heart beat fast and strong, anticipating the taste of caramel and the weight of a Halloween treat bag heavy with candy. Maybe he'd just go buy a pumpkin and a pack of donuts, crunchy with a layer of cinnamon sugar, moist with appley goodness. His mouth watered. Yes. Donuts, pumpkins, and candy. And maybe just a glimpse of the apple bobbing station. Somewhere behind him Phantos spoke, but Tommy didn't listen. The season had gripped him, until—

A woman standing in line at the bakery booth caught his eye. She was digging in her purse, her black hair hanging down, hiding her face, but Tommy was pretty sure . . . She looked up, and her hair fell back to reveal Mrs. Winger, Evan's mom. Who knew Tommy. Who knew Tommy's *mother.*

"*Tommy,*" Phantos urged.

"Yeah," he said, pulling himself away from the glamour. Remembering his purpose. Realizing no number of donuts or pumpkins would ever change what was happening at home. The only thing that could *maybe* change the course of his ill-fated future was finding Aaron Beltzer. Somewhere deep, deep down, he knew it was only a child's hope. Maybe even a *childish* hope. But a hope just the same.

He turned away from the farmers' market and back onto the sidewalk, picking up speed and hoping Mrs. Winger wouldn't spot him. He kept moving until he reached the bank and nearly walked smack dab into his father.

Tommy's breath caught in his throat. The wool hat felt suddenly stifling.

His dad was standing on the sidewalk, his head down, counting through a few bills. He hadn't seen his son. Not yet. Tommy backed away a step, then another. His father dug the wallet from his pocket, and while he was still distracted, Tommy turned and ran for the corner.

Fierce Phantos ran beside him, his face a giant blinking green *GO! GO! GO!*

He didn't look back until he escaped around the side of the brick building. He slammed against the wall, arms outstretched, and gasped with equal parts terror and exhaustion.

"Tommy, look." Phantos peeked around the corner.

His dad walked to the farmers' market. He hadn't spotted Tommy.

"What the heck is he doing here?"

"Perhaps he desires his face to be painted."

"Oh, shut up."

His dad wandered over to a stand with pumpkins, then purchased the biggest one. At first, Tommy couldn't understand what he was seeing, and then the obvious occurred to him. Dave was buying his son a pumpkin for Halloween.

The notion caught Tommy off guard, but before he could let the sentimentality of the gesture further degrade his resolve, he jogged back to the bank. He kept a watchful eye on his father, but the man was far too involved in his present purpose. He smiled widely as he lugged the giant pumpkin around, saying hi to people he passed. When Tommy last saw him, he had been heading for the bakery stand, probably to buy Tommy the donuts he so loved.

More than anything, seeing his father alone at the Harvest Fest broke Tommy's heart. It felt like a last-ditch effort to save his family. Too little, too late. He shook the sadness from his limbs and focused. If he didn't play things just right, the bank teller might not give him his money.

Or worse, she could call his mom and ruin the whole plan.

CHAPTER TWENTY-ONE

MIRANDA

Saturday mornings were Miranda's favorite. There was something about the air. The diffused sunlight, the smells, and sounds. There was so much to take in during her morning bike rides, from the chirping birds to the cavorting squirrels. From the sweet smell of leaf decay to the sharp odor of fireplaces. Everything was a delight.

However, something more called her from the warm embrace of her bedroom that morning. As she untangled her legs from the crumpled mass of Strawberry Shortcake sheets, Tommy's promise of an original sketch lingered on her mind. After weeks of being ignored, she'd finally coaxed him out of his shell, and what she'd feared had proven true. He had been bullied into submission. The happy, carefree boy she had met on the first day of school had fled and left in his place a sheepish shadow.

She still thought boys were dumb, gross, and annoying, but Tommy had been nice when they first met. She felt comfortable around him.

As Miranda rode her bike, she thought that morning she'd turn left instead of right. Tommy's house was the last one, all the way at the top of the hill. She knew this because one day she'd waited at the corner to see which driveway he walked to. Early in the school year, after a few days of silence passed between them, she had planned to confront him at his house. But she'd lost her nerve.

This was different. Tommy had promised her a sketch, and even though it was still early, it wouldn't hurt to knock on his door and inquire. Maybe he'd invite her in so she could see his room. She was infinitely curious about boys' bedrooms, having no brother of her own. In her mind, they were messy nests of action figures, dirty socks, and video games. She wondered if Tommy's room would be a pigsty. Would he have his drawings taped to the walls? Would he have real books or just comics strewn about the floor?

Her head was so filled with images of Tommy's room that she nearly didn't notice him fly past the side street on his bike, headed down the hill. She started to call his name and her voice caught in her throat. Tommy was gone already, the momentum of coasting from the top of the steep hill having built to supersonic speeds.

"Dang it," she muttered. Miranda stood to pedal, trying to catch up with Tommy. She figured he was probably riding to the roller rink. Sometimes the kids in the neighborhood would mess around in the parking lot, erecting ramps out of plywood on the small curb to jump their bikes over, hitting the brakes to come to a skidding stop. They acted as though they'd performed some death-defying stunt, but one time after the boys left, Miranda tried a jump herself. The experience was underwhelming, and she wondered why the boys were always whooping and hollering like conquering heroes.

By the time she turned onto Wild Vine Road, Tommy was already nearing the bottom of the hill. She called out, "Tommy! Wait up!" but her words were caught in the autumn wind and blown away like a whiff of smoke. He was going so fast, even with those two bags he had strapped to his back. She didn't think she'd ever seen anyone ride the hill like that. Miranda put a little more muscle into her own pedaling until the incline took over.

Ahead, Tommy slowed and veered to the left where the rink was, but to her surprise he glided right past the parking lot and came to a stop at the main road instead.

"Tommy!" Miranda tried to pick up speed, but she was already coasting faster than she could pedal. "Wait up!"

Tommy's head tilted to the side as though he'd heard something, but then he pedaled onto Branch Street.

"Dang it." She kept gliding down the hill until she reached the corner. Tommy was already out of sight on the winding, tree-lined road, probably headed to town. She bit her lower lip and gripped the handles of her bike. Should she follow? Her mom and dad were both still in bed. They always slept late on Saturday mornings. If she rode into town after Tommy, her parents wouldn't know. They'd most likely sleep through her absence, and even if they didn't, they'd assume she was still riding around the neighborhood.

It's not that Miranda wasn't allowed to go into town alone, but usually she had to tell her parents first. Plus, they liked her to be with a friend. Her earmuffs became too hot on her ears, and her neck grew itchy underneath the scarf. Wind whistled through the colored leaves in the treetops above. A crow cawed somewhere in the wooded roadside, and Miranda jumped at the sound. Feeling silly, she laughed at herself, not understanding why she was uncomfortable and annoyed. As if she was chiding her cowardly decisions.

And that was exactly the problem. So often she was made to feel incapable and weak. Sure, she was just a kid, and she figured most kids had rules to follow. But why were boys her age allowed to escape on adventures while she had to ask permission? Even then, five times out of ten her parents denied the request just on a whim.

Miranda stopped chewing at her lip and gritted her teeth. She narrowed her eyes and kicked off onto Branch Street. As the wind cooled her face and the itchy, annoyed feeling dissipated, Miranda understood her decision was no longer about the sketch. It was no longer about Tommy. It wasn't even about her parents.

She had made the decision to go into town alone, without permission, to prove she *could*.

* * *

Arriving in town, Miranda swelled with an overwhelming sense of pride. The day unfolded before her like a great map of the world, illuminating the destinations she could discover and explore. Her life suddenly became very big.

With this new sense of autonomy still revealing itself, Miranda biked onto Main Street and to the bustling street fair ahead. She couldn't quite read the banner in the distance, but remembered her mother talking about the Harvest Fest. Things clicked into place, and she realized this is why Tommy had come to town. She rode to the edge of the market and parked her bike in a metal rack.

Canopies lined both sides of Main Street, running the entire length of a block. There were orange detour signs for cars wishing to pass, and a couple local police officers directing pedestrians and traffic. Each canopy was a different business, and each boasted some Halloween extravagance: pumpkins, apples, corn stalks, confections, face painting, and dunk tanks.

The caramel apples and donuts caused Miranda a sudden pang of regret that she hadn't told her parents where she was going. If she had, they probably would have given her a dollar or two for some treats. As it was, she only had fifty cents. Just as her disappointment reached a crescendo, a woman dressed as a scarecrow offered Miranda a Halloween treat bag from a basket. The woman's yellow-painted face smiled down, tufts of fake hay poking from her collar.

"For free?" Miranda asked.

"If you know the magic words."

This stumped Miranda for only a second. She was, after all, a twelve-year-old girl well versed in Halloween traditions. "Trick-or-treat!"

The scarecrow smiled wider and handed her a stapled paper bag emblazoned with a black cat in front of a giant yellow moon.

"Thank you!"

"You're very welcome," the scarecrow said and then skipped off to approach other children with the same offer.

Miranda wondered if Tommy had gotten a bag. In fact, where was Tommy? The fair wasn't so big as to hide him in the crowd.

As she searched, a man carrying a giant pumpkin and a pack of donuts smiled at her and said, "Hello there" as he left the market. She nodded a greeting and wondered if he was someone from the neighborhood.

After walking around for twenty minutes (and collecting a few more treat bags), Miranda abandoned the search. Maybe Tommy hadn't come to town for the fair after all. Maybe he'd just gone out for a ride and circled back home on a different road. While this scenario was likely, something nagged at her. Something about the way he'd been acting on Friday, and—

"Why did he have those bags with him?"

Tommy had been wearing a backpack, which wasn't unusual. But he also had a big duffel hanging across his back. A strange notion surfaced like a sea monster.

Tommy is running away from home.

A shiver coursed through her spine. Miranda didn't know where the strange notion had come from, but the more it nagged at her, the more real it became. Maybe she'd check Tommy's place, just to be safe. And if he wasn't back, she'd tell her parents. Miranda wasn't sure if her concern was valid, but the worry clung to her like wet clothes, cold and slimy.

She had to find out if Tommy was okay.

CHAPTER TWENTY-TWO

ON THE RUN

To Tommy's great surprise, he'd been able to withdraw a whopping $50 without Mrs. Rutherford raising any questions. Her eyebrows *did* nearly jump off her face when she saw the withdrawal slip, and she watched Tommy pretty hard for a few seconds, but in the end the reserved woman counted out ten five-dollar bills and placed them in a small paper envelope. She held the money back long enough to say, "Be careful with this. It's a lot of money."

It *was* a lot of money. The most Tommy had ever carried with him outside his house. He'd only once had more in his hands after a particularly lucrative holiday season when a seldom-seen aunt compensated for years of missed Christmases with a crisp hundred-dollar bill. Of course, his parents swooped in and made sure the money went straight into his savings account. *Joke's on them*, he thought, feeling the thick envelope of bills in his sweatshirt pocket.

"Heed the elder shaman's warning, young Tommy. She didn't become the guardian of a dragon hoard without a vast knowledge of the world." The idea of a slumbering serpent atop cascading piles of gold in a vault below Midland Falls Bank caused Tommy to reevaluate his opinion of financial institutions.

Tommy and Phantos continued to walk through a residential area on the way to the bus station. Halloween decorations and pumpkins littered nearly every porch and lawn. Tommy and Evan had come out this way the previous year for trick-or-treating, and the haul was beyond imagining. There was plenty of the common fare, but what excited Tommy the most was the sheer variety of rare candies, seldom seen in his treat bag. Fun Dip, Mr. Bones, Pixy Stix, candy cigarettes, wax bottles. On a few occasions, people actually gave out crisp dollar bills.

"The money," Phantos said, pulling him back to the daytime sidewalk, not yet filled with marauding ghouls fixated on a sugar high. "Put some in your shoe, some in your backpack, and keep only what you need access to in your pocket."

"Why?"

"Have you ever had this much money on your person?" Fierce Phantos didn't play any tricks with his helmet projection. Not this time.

"No." Tommy put three fives in his Velcro wallet.

"And have you ever traveled alone?"

Tommy bent over and pushed $15 into his sock. "Well, *no*. You know that."

"It's a dangerous world. A dangerous, unforgiving world. Don't think for a second a grown man won't steal from a child. Or worse."

The blood drained from Tommy's face as he stashed the last $20 in his backpack. "Worse?"

Phantos remained uncharacteristically serious. "Much worse. We are on a hero's journey. A *quest*. These sorts of expeditions are known to be somewhat . . ." Phantos trailed off.

"*What?*" Tommy's breath came fast.

Phantos muttered, barely audible, "Perilous."

"I can't hear you."

He threw his hands in the air. "Perilous!" he boomed like a thunder-clap. "Dangerous, dicey, precarious. *Treacherous.*"

The lack of goofy helmet projections worried Tommy. Traveling away from home, he knew he might run into some problems. And sure, maybe the trip was dangerous. Scary even. But *treacherous*?

As before, when enveloped in carnival happiness at the farmers' market, Tommy's dedication wavered. Not much, but enough so that he didn't feel as confident about getting to Brooklyn and back without incident.

The terminal loomed in the distance, an unassuming building with a large parking lot occupied by buses. As they drew closer, Tommy noted the vacant, lonely mood of the place. On a solitary outdoor bench sat a man whose face was nearly as crumpled as his old brown suit. An unlit cigarette stub hung from his puckered lips. Where his face wasn't wrinkled, it was covered with stubble. A worn briefcase sat at his feet, and his eyes were closed against the light of day. For the briefest moment, Tommy wondered what it was like to be that man. Wondered if perhaps, one day, he would be like this lonely traveler.

A few other people milled around, waiting for a bus. Across the street, there was a rundown Mobil station with a small convenience mart. Beside one of the regular pumps sat a large pickup truck, the wood-slatted bed filled with pumpkins in large cardboard boxes.

Some people fixed Tommy with a curious glance, but no one's eyes lingered for long. The crumpled man on the bench never even opened his. The smell of gasoline, oil, and smoke permeated the entire area, and Tommy perceived he had crossed over an invisible line between Branchville and the greater world. Everything felt different. *Real.*

He pushed through the glass doors at the front of the building and entered a waiting area lined with benches and reeking of bathroom smells run rampant. People waited on the benches. A family of four here, a lone traveler there. The line at the front window was only three deep, four once Tommy queued up. On the wall behind the teller, a giant board listed destinations, times, and costs.

Columbus, Athens, Dayton, Cincinnati, Cleveland, Pittsburgh, Philadelphia, and there—

"Manhattan is twelve bucks. Twenty for round trip."

Phantos knelt so his massive height was closer to Tommy's. "Is that a great sum?"

He whispered, "When you only have fifty bucks, yeah, kinda."

The woman in front of him turned around. "Excuse me?"

"Just talking to myself."

The woman's features tightened, and she nodded curtly before step-ping forward as far as she could.

"See what you made me do," Tommy hissed, eliciting another wor-ried glance from the woman.

So far, Tommy hadn't exactly kept a low profile, but for a twelve-year-old boy out on his own for the first time, he thought he was doing pretty good.

Phantos pointed at a sign on the window ahead. It read, *No unac-companied minors.* "I think that means you."

Tommy swung his backpack around and dug a piece of paper from the back pocket. He may have been young, but he wasn't stupid. He'd read plenty of young adult novels and watched lots of movies. He knew to expect this.

When the woman ahead of him had finished her transaction, he stepped to the window. "Round trip to Manhattan, please."

The man behind the window peered over his glasses and twitched his nose. His ears poked out from beneath a Red Fox Bus Lines visor. He'd have fit right in with some whiskers and a tail. "Are your parents here, son?"

Tommy shook his head and pushed the piece of paper across the counter. "I'm visiting my grandmother."

The man nodded and opened the note, his eyes darting across the lines Tommy had typed in computer class. A letter that ended with a forged signature. One he had traced from an old permission slip his mom signed. The lettering was a little shaky in places, but he thought he'd done a passable job after a few practice runs.

F.P. leaned over to see what was written and nodded approvingly. A big thumbs-up appeared inside the helmet. "Admirable work, young Tommy."

The clerk, on the other hand, didn't appear impressed. For one thing, he was taking a long time to read the short note. He rubbed at the signature with his thumb, then looked around the terminal as if searching for someone. His nose twitched. He said, "I see. Your mother has taken ill?"

"Yes, sir."

"And your grandmother will be looking after you. In Manhattan?"

"Yes, sir."

His nose twitched again. "I see." He scratched his cheek. "Do you have identification? Required to travel, I'm afraid."

Tommy dug his wallet out and tore the Velcro open with a satisfying rip. He handed over his school library card.

The man inspected this and said, "Master Thomas Grant?"

"That's me." Tommy smiled wide even as his heart sped to a gallop.

"Your mother's name is Suzanne. Your father's name, please?"

Tommy didn't like the question. Why ask for his father's name? But he had no choice but to answer. "David."

Twitch-twitchy-twitch went the man's nose. "Everything seems to be in order." He extended an index finger. "Give me one second." The clerk retreated to a back room, closing the door behind him, though the door didn't latch completely and swung open a crack.

Phantos's projected face morphed into a magnifying glass. He side-stepped the window for a better look into the office. "The mouse-man is investigating a white book of names."

Tommy took a look for himself and his stomach fell into his shoes. "That's a White Pages. He's looking up my last name." His mind spun round and round and landed on the obvious answer. "That's why he wanted Dad's name. He's gonna call my parents."

"Does this mean we don't get to ride atop the giant Red Fox?"

"There's something seriously wrong with you."

F.P.'s ghostly visage returned with a shocked expression. He pointed toward the room. "The mouse-man is dialing!"

That did it. Before his quest even began, the plan collapsed around him. It wasn't like he could ride his bike to Brooklyn (though he did consider the idea for the briefest moment of ecstatic wonder). "Let's get out of here."

The family waiting on one of the benches watched him flee; the parents bent their heads together. As Tommy burst through the doors and back into the chill of October, he wondered what kinds of bad things they were saying about him. Maybe telling their children not to be like the hoodlum running away as if he'd stolen a wallet. The idea hurt Tommy, like a painful stab to the heart. He had his darker moments, and sure, he liked cartoon villains sometimes. But deep down, he thought of himself as a good kid. He was young enough to still want approval from adults, even if they were random strangers sitting on a bench at the bus terminal.

Outside, a bus prepared for departure, and a short line of patrons climbed aboard. Tommy started toward the line, thinking maybe he'd be able to sneak on somehow, but Phantos stopped him.

"They'll want a ticket. They'll ask where your parents are."

"Crap." The hero was right, like usual. As much as the revelation hurt, he had to accept defeat and go home. If the clerk had already spoken to his mom or dad, he'd deny the accusation. And if he'd left a message, Tommy could erase it before they listened.

"*Tommy!* He's coming! And he still has your library card!"

"Crap, crap, *crapola!*" He scurried around the side of the building and out of view of the windows. "Should I go back for my card? Tell him it was a prank or something?"

Phantos wasn't listening. His face had turned into the giant magnifying glass again. He crept around the corner of the building and across to the small Mobil gas station.

Tommy hissed, "Yo, where are you going?"

When F.P. didn't answer, he followed behind, crouched over in a way that made him feel more silly than sly. He caught up with Phantos at the side of the convenience mart. Phantos stared at the pickup with the open bed filled with pumpkins.

An old man in overalls stood over another man sitting in a rickety wooden chair outside the building. They were jawing away, talking about the weather and the coming holiday. All Tommy could think about was getting home, but the conversation took an interesting turn.

The gas station attendant said, "Why aren'tcha at the market, then, Phil? Got enough gourds to start yer own parade."

Phil the farmer rocked back on his heels and played his overall straps like a fiddle. "Naw, the market's for suckers." He tapped his gray dome. "You gotta think, now. Plenty farmers with pumpkins around here, driving down the prices. But where ain't there farmers, Jack?"

The other man thought this over a minute. "The city?"

Phil touched his nose. "The city. That's where I'm headed. I can sell these here pumpkins wholesale and *still* get three, maybe four times the price."

Phantos spun around and grabbed Tommy's shoulders. "Get in the truck."

"What?"

He slapped his helmet and it bonged like a crystal ball. "You heard the farmer. He is going to the city." Phantos pointed at the gourd-filled open bed. "Get in the truck!"

The idea of hiding in the back of a random stranger's truck was insane. Buying a bus ticket was one thing. The trip would have been relatively safe. But *this*?

"Look behind you, Tommy."

He did, and what he saw chilled his bones more than the thought of hitching a ride with the unsuspecting farmer. The mousy clerk was standing in front of the bus terminal with a security guard.

"No way."

"Get in the truck."

"But—"

"Do you want to be arrested?"

"They can't arrest me for—?"

"Are you *sure*?"

"I don't think, I mean, I can still just go home."

Phantos stood, stretching skyward like a conquering god. "*Can* you?"

All things considered, his question wasn't the most convincing argument. Even so, Tommy knew the answer as surely as the clerk still had his library card. He stared into the static-laden face of Aaron Beltzer's creation. A gigantic heroic hallucination somehow manifest in the real world, its features rendered in glass, rubber, and metal. Tommy gazed deep into those ghostlike eyes, and he said, "No. I can't. Not until this is done."

His imaginary guardian nodded. "Then go, young Tommy. And go *now*!"

The boy wasted not a second more before running full tilt for the back of the pickup truck. He watched the men talking at the front of the building, but they were too preoccupied with their gossip and banter.

Tommy reached the back of the bed and very carefully, very quietly, dropped the gate.

"Watch out!" Phantos cried.

The sudden warning made Tommy's stomach plummet.

An off-balance pumpkin rolled across the truck bed for escape. His heart lurched as the gourd dropped over the edge, headed toward ruin. Tommy caught it at the last second and held it to his chest, breathing hard. Had they seen? Had they heard? He peeked through the slats.

No, still chatting the day away.

He placed the pumpkin back on the bed, then crawled in and hid behind the big boxes as best he could, piling mounds of hay and lifting a soiled blanket over him and his bags.

Once in position, he waited quietly until minutes later a door opened, then closed.

The truck started roughly, coughing fumes into the clear air.

As motion alerted him to their departure, Tommy had just enough time to think, far too late, *what* city was Phil driving to?

Tommy, of course, hadn't the faintest idea.

Part Four

UNSOLVED
MYSTERIES

CHAPTER TWENTY-THREE
MORNING BLUES

Suzanne lay in bed listening to the early morning sounds of a quiet house. She was sprawled across the bed because Dave wasn't there. Not anymore. Not ever again. The thought seared her as much as soothed, and she curled up under her plush blanket, trying to blot out the myriad worries plaguing her every waking moment. Worries about what she would do for money, who would get the house, and how they were going to handle custody of Tommy.

Suzie groaned and hugged herself tightly. None of these changes were okay, but all of them were necessary. Her mother had warned her against divorce, reminding her of the pledge she had made to God, if not to Dave. Her sister wasn't as worried about appearances and her shaky relationship with the almighty. Kathy's only real advice was, "Do what makes you happy, sis."

Do what makes me happy.

It wasn't as simple as that because the decision to dismantle her marriage made her miserable. At least, it did in the short term. In the long term, Suzie knew her choice was the right one. She loved Dave, but she couldn't stand being around him. He blamed her for the way his life had turned out, screaming his frustrations in drunken rages only to apologize the morning after as if none of his actions were real. Suzie knew better. Everything he said was the truth, and even as Dave begged her to stay with him, she suspected he wanted the divorce as much as she did.

Quiet footfalls creaked down the stairs in the hallway. Suzie checked the bedside clock and groaned. Why was Tommy awake before eight? She started to get out of bed. One foot even made it to the floor. But something stopped her. Perhaps it was the boundless exhaustion inside her muscles and mind. Or maybe depression had settled so deep in her bones that it weighed her down like lead. She collapsed back onto the bed and pulled the blanket over her head like a child hiding from the boogieman.

Suzie had yet to discuss the divorce with Tommy in detail. She needed time. Did Tommy need time too, or did he need his mother? In those veiled moments of darkness and uncertainty, Suzanne didn't care. She had to recharge her mommy battery. There wouldn't be any big pancake breakfasts or movie nights. Not for a little while at least. Not until she found herself again.

So she let Tommy sneak down the stairs. And when she heard the front door open after twenty minutes, she let that happen too. An hour later, when Suzie finally rolled out of bed, Tommy's bike was gone, but this didn't worry her. He'd become rather independent over the course of the summer, going off on his own and exploring the town. He had even learned how to fix his own dinners, albeit the easy, frozen kind.

Suzie's mind drifted to the mundane worries of a soon-to-be-divorced single mother. She retrieved the Saturday newspaper from the front stoop and turned directly to the want ads.

Her coffee was bitter, her breakfast cold, and her mind lost.

✳ ✳ ✳

When the front door opened, Suzanne assumed her son had finally come home from his autumn excursion. She had her blouse half on and one of her nicer skirts laid out on the bed as she fumbled to get ready.

She called, "I'll be right down, Tommy! I want to talk to you before you go disappearing again."

Suzie pulled on the sleek black skirt and tucked in her blouse. She checked the vanity mirror and groaned at the frizzy nest atop her head, then grabbed the brush. As she tamed her hair, Dave's image appeared in the mirror. He wore a sheepish smile, and apologetic eyes peered from behind his large glasses. The same expression he'd use the morning after a particularly bad fight. His shaggy brown hair was combed more neatly than usual, and despite it being a Saturday morning, he was wearing a shirt and tie with a pair of his nice brown trousers.

She spun around and pointed the brush at him, ready with a mouthful of fighting words. Then she saw the giant pumpkin cradled in his arms and all the fight drained out of her. "What are you doing here, Dave?"

His mouth twitched and the soft expression nearly turned hard. She knew she shouldn't have challenged him right out of the gate; they'd been married long enough for her to divine his reply. Something about this still being his house and how he's the one who pays the mortgage. He'd lunge with *we're not divorced yet*. Suzie would parry with a stinging *the operative word being "yet,"* followed by Dave's riposte of *what about Tommy?*

Instead of this rehearsed exchange, Dave recovered from Suzie's *en garde* and replied with a measured response. "I'm just dropping off some things for Tommy." He left the room without another word.

Suzie stood stunned, her hairbrush still pointing at the spot where Dave had stood. It wasn't like him to pass up the opportunity for a fight. She hurried down the stairs and caught Dave as he was about to leave. "Hold on."

He stopped, his hand on the doorknob.

"You went to the Harvest Fest this morning?"

He turned, a sad smile on his clean-shaved face. "Wasn't the same without you and Tommy."

She looked down, angry at what she felt. "No, I guess it wouldn't be."

"Well, anyway . . ." He turned to go, and Suzie stopped him again. "Dave."

He hesitated, head lowered.

"Did you see Tommy in town?"

"No. He isn't here?"

She flattened her hair nervously. "He left early. Thought maybe he went to Harvest Fest too."

Dave watched her for a moment, perhaps looking for the lie in her words. Or maybe he was just concerned. "Probably at the comic shop or something."

"Yeah." She waved away her worry. "Or the roller rink."

Dave shifted nervously on his feet. Something played behind his eyes. "I saw the want ads on the kitchen table. Is that where you're headed? Applying for jobs?"

His words weren't accusatory. Merely inquisitive. So she answered as even-tempered as she could. "I figured better to get a head start. I'll need the money."

"You know I'm going to—"

"Yes. I know. But I can't rely on you forever, Dave. I need to do this."

He nodded, smoothed his hair behind his ears. "We haven't been there for Tommy."

A flare of anger shot through her belly. She wanted to spit fire, but most of this anger was because she knew he was right. She wanted to place all the blame on Dave, what with his late nights at the dealership and his drinking, but she'd played plenty of her own disappearing acts. "That's why we're going through with this. When we're together, things are worse for everyone."

He flinched at her words, the hurt plain on his face. But she also detected resignation there. The understanding and yes, even agreement. "We have to do better for him." With his back to Suzie, he said, "I hope we can now."

To the closed door, she replied, "Me too."

✳ ✳ ✳

After Dave left, Suzie finished getting ready. There were a few promising listings in the newspaper, and while she wasn't completely qualified for the best options, she was determined to apply. Dave liked to complain about his lost art career, but he rarely expressed concern over Suzie's unused college degree. Why would he? She was a woman. Wasn't her place in the home, raising their child and keeping hot meals on the table?

These rinky-dink jobs weren't exactly her dream occupation, but they were a start. A foot into the working world. And maybe once Tommy reached high school, she could start looking for something permanent. Something that would feed her soul more than a receptionist or assistant manager job.

But first, she needed to apply, so Suzie grabbed her purse and stepped through the door just as the phone began to ring. She checked her watch, half in the house, half out. A restless little itch inside her belly demanded she not waste another moment. She hated the feeling, as if every lost second resulted in another applicant getting the job before her.

Suzie huffed and said, "The machine'll get it," before locking the door and leaving.

Inside the house, the red light on her answering machine started to blink a silent alert that no one would see for hours.

CHAPTER TWENTY-FOUR

THE CITY

The truck jerked to a sudden halt and woke Tommy from an uneasy slumber. Phantom images, leftovers from the dream-world, danced around piles of pumpkins. Nothing stuck firm except the fleeting notion he had donned Phantos's suit and fought divorce lawyers and schoolyard bullies in an epic battle spanning the whole of Branchville.

A door slammed, dragging Tommy's consciousness to full alert. Phil the farmer was talking to himself. Cursing, really. Something about toll prices and lost profits. Tommy peeked through the wood slats on the side of the truck and saw they were stopped at a gas station.

Phantos crept up beside him. "Where is the farmer?"

This was a good question. There were lots of people out there, but no one in faded overalls. No one with a shiny bald head or the gait of a drunken scarecrow. Had he slipped through the crowd and into the mini-mart already? Tommy threw off the soiled blanket and got onto his knees for a better view.

"Hey! Whattayou think you're doin'?"

The words were a cold blade thrust through his chest. He fell back and hid behind the large cardboard box.

"I see you! Get outta there, kid!" His voice was a gravel pit. "Whattayou doing, huh? Stealing from me?" Stone grating against stone. "I can *see* you!"

The pickup gate dropped, and the bed shifted with the weight of a new body. Tommy froze. He'd run away from home, taken money out of his college fund, and stolen a ride in the back of someone's truck. The realization unfurled that he may have, in a single day of poor decisions, become one of the *bad kids*.

Phil grasped the child's shoulders and brought him to a standing position. His rheumy blue eyes stared fiercely into Tommy's. Anger and confusion resided there. "Well? Whattayou doin'? You stealing from me, boy?" His eyes flickered to Tommy's bags, and Phil's expression grew grim. "You *are*." His breath smelled like stale coffee and pipe tobacco.

The situation had changed so suddenly, Tommy barely had time to register the trajectory. Even as Phil dragged him by the collar, pulling him out of the truck and plunking him onto the pavement like a bundle of sticks, Tommy was only just hearing the accusation ringing in his ears.

"I'm not stealing—"

"You stay there!" Phil warned, his bony finger stabbing the air. He climbed back onto the pickup bed.

"But, Phil—" He caught himself. "Sir, I didn't steal anything, I—"

"Evidence!" The man reappeared holding Tommy's backpack and duffel bag. Lowering himself to the ground took an effort, as if the anger that fueled the old man was waning.

He unzipped the duffel and thrust his hands into the recess. "What's this?" Phil rummaged through the assorted clothing and gear, then checked the backpack to find more of the same.

"I wasn't stealing, sir. I swear."

Phil looked the boy up and down, assessing. "Wait here." His voice had softened in a way Tommy did not like one bit. A familiar expression crossed his face before he wandered off, searching the lot with a sense of urgency.

"Like the clerk at the bus terminal," Phantos said. "He's looking for the police."

Tommy groaned. "Not again." Phil crossed the lot and entered the store. "Are you sure?"

Phantos tapped his helmet. "Think. Even if he isn't going for the police, if we stay here, our quest is over. Is that what you want?"

His conviction had wavered a number of times already, and again Tommy wondered if he perhaps *did* want this to end. He had to make the choice. Wait for the old farmer to return and ask for a ride home. Or run. Inside his chest his two choices assembled like warring factions at opposite ends of the battlefield. His stomach churned as they charged one another, weapons out, screaming cries of war. The decision of whether to move forward or go back lay in the outcome.

Before the battle could end, another began with a flash of light high overhead. At first Tommy thought it was lightning, but there was not a cloud in the sky. Then came another flash, even brighter than before, followed by a sonic boom that knocked Tommy back.

Phantos said, "Oh, no."

"What is it?" The light fell through the sky, a green tail blazing like an alien comet. Tommy looked around to say something, but no one else reacted to the explosion or the falling star.

Fierce Phantos placed a heavy, gloved hand on Tommy's shoulder. "I hope you're ready." He peered into the sky at the falling comet. "Because the fight has come to us."

✳ ✳ ✳

"What fight? Who said anything about a fight?"

Phantos surveyed their surroundings. Tommy followed his line of sight and took in the bustling city streets of Manhattan for the first time since being dragged off the truck. He wasn't used to sidewalks filled with pedestrians, or congested streets lined with cars. The buildings around him nearly blotted out the sky, but not so much as to obscure the green streak of blinding light headed right for them.

"There!" Phantos pointed across a side street to a cluster of buildings. No, not the buildings, but the narrow alleyway between them. "We need cover. Go!" Phantos took off running.

Tommy checked the mini-mart. Phil was nowhere in sight. He knew he could stay behind, stick with the old farmer, and go home. Logically, that was the best option. But he was so close to Brooklyn already, why go back? Besides . . .

The green comet continued its fiery descent, urging Tommy to make a hasty decision, not unlike being pressured onto the pickup truck back home. His mouth dry and head still foggy from sleep, he grabbed his bags and followed Phantos, who'd already crossed the street and stood at the mouth of the alleyway. The smell of exhaust and the strange, unnatural heat of surrounding cars enveloped him as he serpentined around the vehicles stuck at a red light. His duffel bounced off the bumper of a truck, and the driver honked repeatedly.

As he passed the double yellow, a red sports car squealed around a corner.

Phantos yelled, "Stop!" and held his hand out like a crossing guard.

Tommy jumped back as the insane driver flashed by, inches from his feet. Sweat pocked his forehead. Had he almost died like the poor kid in *The Toxic Avenger*?

"Look!" Phantos yelled.

The green comet had grown threefold as it continued to descend at increasing speeds. Still, no one reacted to the coming calamity.

Tommy shook the shock from his legs and crossed to Phantos. The alley stank of old rot. The kind of smell that accumulated after decades of neglect and layered filth. Through gasps of breath, he said, "It smells like baby diarrhea."

F.P. boomed with laughter, apparently not out of breath at all. He retorted, "More like a mountain of moose manure."

"Good one."

The comedic duo's stand-up routine was short lived. Ahead, the alley dead-ended with a chain link fence. On either side were the brick walls of neighboring buildings that rose four or five stories into the air. There were doors and windows, and a couple fire escapes.

"We can jump the fence," Tommy suggested.

Fierce Phantos pointed into the narrow slit of sky above the alley. The green streak was as long as a racetrack and ended with a giant, red-tipped ball of superheated matter. The air around them grew hot, and a sound like that of a jet engine shook the ground beneath their feet. "We were never running away, Tommy. We were merely looking for a quiet place to do battle."

Battle? That was even worse than the word *fight*. Neither was an experience all that familiar to Tommy. Sure, there were those little wrestling matches he'd had with Evan, in the heat of an intense game of manhunt. And that one time Kevin L. called him a crybaby in the schoolyard, which resulted in the two boys circling each other with raised fists until the recess monitor broke it up without a single punch ever being thrown. And there was of course the wonderful memory of getting his ass kicked by his former best friend. The memory of lying prone on the ground like a helpless baby didn't exactly inspire confidence.

Tommy tugged on F.P.'s arm. "Battle *what?*"

The green streak of cosmic fire sliced the sky in two. The red beating heart of its superheated center grew to the size of a boulder and homed in on their location. The air sizzled and cracked. Sweat prickled Tommy's face. None of this could be real, and yet he experienced every sensation. His eyes watered against the sun-bright spearhead. A thunderclap split his head as the falling object broke the sound barrier, rippling clouds and exploding the sky in a vast ring of vapor.

He fell back, shielding his face with a burning hand, screaming nonsensically, the panic biting deep. He hollered and yelped for Fierce Phantos, but the hero stood his ground, feet planted, arms raised in attack.

The last moments of the meteorite's descent were a blur of seconds, where at once the alien rock was miles away and then—

Boom! Contact.

Pavement exploded, and the force threw Tommy into the air like a leaf caught in the wind. He spun, airborne, catching glimpses of brick, shattering windows, green rock, fence, shards of flying debris, broken pipe, and when his body struck the fence at the end of the alleyway with a sharp jolt of stabbing pain, oblivion.

Floating in the obscure ether of unconsciousness, voices came and went like buzzing gnats.

> —devious scoundrel! How did you—?
> —to stop you, Helmet Head!
> —can try, but Good will always—
> —plan will fail—
> —time to fight, Metal Mouth!

Even in Tommy's half-conscious state, the words sounded rehearsed and stilted, not unlike the cartoon he so loved. His eyes fluttered open as pain shot through his body, bringing him fully awake through sheer discomfort. He stood and threw the backpack and duffel from his

shoulders. He was about to complain of the pain when his eyes refocused where the mouth of the alleyway used to be. In its place was an
enormous raised crater of pavement and concrete. In front of this monstrous mountain stood Fierce Phantos, circling a green bulging creature
with a metal face and one stone hand. He was partially wrapped in
tattered and stained bandages. Tommy immediately recognized the
menace as Munch Mouth, a villain of *OoCC*.

Overwhelming his previous fear, a sudden sinking sensation overtook him as he realized his hallucinations were getting worse. It was bad
enough he traveled with an imaginary friend, but now characters from
the *Order of Cosmic Champions* were falling from the sky like meteor-
ites? Tommy was young enough to still believe in magic but old enough
to understand these visions were not normal. Something had to give
soon, and he hoped it wasn't his mind.

The hero and villain continued circling each other, only there would
be no schoolyard monitor to stop this fight.

"Tommy!" Phantos called to him. "Are you okay?"

His body ached, but he was still standing. "I'm fine," he said, wondering if he was lying to himself.

Munch Mouth said, "Stop stalling and fight."

"Shut your bear trap."

Tommy shook his head. "Your insults are so lame."

Munch Mouth didn't seem to think so, as his metal-hinged jaw
dropped open in shock. "You'll pay for that, Phantos!" The hulking
green beast launched at F.P. with his stone fist.

F.P. dodged to the right, but Munch Mouth anticipated this and
spun to grab F.P. in a sleeper hold.

"You see how powerless your savior is, boy?"

"Don't—" F.P. wavered on his feet. "Don't listen to him."

Munch Mouth tightened his stone grip and redoubled the hold.
"Skullagar sends his regards, Tommy-boy."

A small flame flickered inside his chest. The nickname set his teeth on edge. The mention of Skullagar rendered him speechless. Had the voice in his head been more than his subconscious? Had the action figure actually moved that day in his bedroom?

"You're one of us. Search your black heart for the horrible things you desire to befall those who offend you." Munch Mouth laughed grimly. "Remember your anger. Remember your *rage*."

Tommy shook his head in defiance. Despite his recent choices, he knew he wasn't a bad kid. He wasn't a villain.

"*No!*" Tommy screamed, feeling the flame inside grow. Not rage, as Munch Mouth portended, but something stronger.

"*Yes*. Leave this sniveling android. Skullagar extends his most sincere invitation to you, Tommy."

Something ignited in his chest, and it blazed like the heat of a newly forged blade. He knew the answer as surely as he knew his own name. "Never!" Tommy ran toward the battling Goliaths, realizing too late that he hadn't the faintest idea of what to do.

He had no weapons save his two small fists. The power inside faltered; the flame flickered. Tommy panicked and swung wildly at Munch Mouth's wrapped stomach. His fist contacted what felt like a brick wall. The jolt nearly collapsed his wrist. Pain shot through his arm and into his teeth.

Tommy's eyes popped wide with pain as the green beast laughed, his metal mouth opening and closing mechanically, his beady red eyes blazing with maniacal glee. "Without Skullagar, you are nothing."

Tommy backpedaled, nearly tripping over his own feet, pain and defeat washing over him. He clumsily grabbed a hunk of broken concrete and threw it at Munch Mouth, who chomped down on the flying debris, crumbling it to dust. "You must join us."

The fire inside Tommy's chest snuffed out beneath the suffocating verbal attacks. The bullies were winning again.

Fierce Phantos took advantage of Munch Mouth's distracted attention and twisted out of the sleeper hold. He pummeled the green Goliath in the gut with three fast blows.

Munch Mouth recovered quickly. He lunged, stone fist raised to crush F.P.'s helmet.

Phantos fell back, drew his gun, and shot a red laser blast with the speed of a seasoned gunfighter. The beam struck Munch Mouth in the chest and knocked him against the raised mountain of concrete.

City sounds were far away, as if filtering through thick mesh. Nothing in the alley had changed, yet it all appeared vibrant and oversaturated. Munch Mouth wasn't a flat green cartoon; he was covered in pockmarked lizard skin like an alligator. Phantos's suit was littered with white dust from the unscheduled road construction.

Every detail popped and crackled, even as Munch Mouth lifted himself from the ground and brushed pavement from his bleeding arms. "Still standing."

Despite the overwhelming sense of failure, Tommy still shook his head at the lame banter. These mighty warriors were as real as the brick walls of the alleyway, and yet they spoke as if scripted by hackneyed writers. In many ways, it made Tommy feel like he was back at home, watching an episode of *OoCC*.

"Not for long." Phantos flipped a switch on his gun and fired repeatedly at the ground. None of the shots hit Munch Mouth. Where the blasts hit, tiny bursts of flickering neon light danced. Tendrils of shimmering light erupted from the orbs, nubs at first, then tentacles, then arms. The holographic light continued to spasm and grow until an entire squadron stood in the alley, and they were all exact clones of Phantos.

The villain's red eyes darted from hero to hero. "I know your tricks. There's only one of you."

"But can you find me?"

The squadron shuffled as though playing a game of Three-card Monte. They drew their ray guns and blasted Munch Mouth, though only one beam struck true.

"Ah!" Munch Mouth fell back, a small burn mark appearing where the blast hit. By the time he recovered and lunged for the Phantos that had shot him, the group had shuffled again, and the metal-mouthed deviant fell through a hologram and collapsed to the ground.

Every one of the specters shot the sprawled figure, his skin searing and bubbling.

He stood and attacked, only to soar through another hologram.

"Wrong again."

Munch Mouth spun and pulled throwing knives seemingly from thin air. He threw them at one, two, three figures, and they sailed through every single one. He threw the fourth wild. It clattered against the brick wall Tommy had backed against.

"Time to end this." The Phantos army began to shake and vibrate like a tuning fork.

Munch Mouth held his hands up to shield his face. "What's this?"

"*This*," they said in unison, "is your defeat!" The air vibrated with a high-pitched humming. All the Phantos clones pulled back their fists, and as they swung, the army phased together into the one true Phantos, delivering a devastating blow. Munch Mouth's metal face dented, and the force threw him over the raised concrete crater like a rag doll.

He landed hard. The lower jaw fell open, hanging by only one bent hinge. Munch Mouth tried to speak, but the words came out garbled and unintelligible.

Phantos replied anyway. "Go back to your master and tell him to stay in his hole. Tommy is protected."

The villain stared with red eyes and malice for only a moment before retreating behind the raised concrete of the alley.

With a grim expression on his ghostlike face, F.P. said, "As much as I'd love to believe Munch Mouth will deliver my message, I fear this is not over. And by the end, I will need your help."

∗ ∗ ∗

The world grew pale and dusty, like one of those horror movies his dad liked to rent. *The Last Man on Earth* or *A Boy and His Dog*. Clouds of filth obscured his vision. Gone were the vibrant colors of cartoons and toys. The spectacular, rumble-packed daydream of childhood was fractured, like the concrete crater Fierce Phantos shuffled Tommy past. The sharp edges of cement caught his jean jacket and bags but didn't stop F.P. from dragging him into the throng of the city.

People walked by, lost in their own worlds and paying no attention to the young boy who stood as if on a boat sailing over rough ocean. These random passersby also didn't acknowledge the newly formed hole in the cement behind them. This didn't surprise Tommy. No one could see Fierce Phantos, after all. Why should they be able to see the crater? Or the living meteorite that had fallen from the sky? Or the insane fight that took place in a hidden alleyway?

Because all of it exists in an alternate layer of reality.

Isn't that what Matty had alluded to? Couldn't the notion be true? Certainly it was a better alternative than Tommy going loony tunes before he even hit puberty.

"Keep moving, Tommy. We must abscond from this place."

He craned his neck as Phantos continued to tug him along the sidewalk and caught a glimpse of Phil the farmer scanning the area around the gas station. The expression he wore was a peculiar combination of worry and relief. Tommy didn't fully understand how both disparate emotions could sit so plainly on one's face. How a man could feel two opposing things simultaneously. Once he did a little bit more living, the notion would no longer seem quite so strange.

Another tug on his arm and Tommy traveled farther away from the salvation the old farmer represented. A quick way home. His *only* way home. And yet with every retreating step, another feeling began to simmer, then boil. His racing heart was the bellows that fanned a growing fire underneath his cauldron stomach.

Excitement.

The dimness of the day fractured, and the light of hope shined through. No, Tommy would not be going home. For the third and final time, he committed himself to the decision he'd already made.

Tommy ceased checking behind him.

He yanked his arm from Phantos and attained a steady stride next to the phantom hero. He didn't know where he was going, but he was done being unsure of himself and his choices.

Phantos eyed the boy with a knowing grin. "What changed?"

"I'm tired of questioning myself." The words were good. They were a return to the way his mind had worked before the cruel summer. Before his befouled birthday. This commitment felt like a homecoming.

"Good." Fierce Phantos nodded assuredly. "Because I'm going to need you at your peak if we are to defeat Skullagar's minions *and* find this Aaron Beltzer."

An idea surfaced like a whale coming up for air. Tommy dodged a few oblivious pedestrians walking along the busy sidewalk. He sidestepped a trash can and sped up, watching Phantos, trying to decipher the hero's expression. He'd have fared better attempting to discern the mental state of a puddle. Still, he needed to know. "Do you know who Aaron Beltzer is?"

"Why, of course! He is the boy we are looking for."

"Right." Tommy straightened his backpack and duffel. "But do you know *who* he is?"

"My dear boy." Phantos chuckled arrogantly. "He is the winner of the *Order of Cosmic Champions* contest."

"Right, but—"

"And," he interrupted, "you are going to convince him to use his president-for-a-day power to get your illustration turned into an action figure."

That was all true, of course. It had basically been Fierce Phantos's plan from the beginning, egging Tommy on in his dream only to come bursting into three-dimensional reality and further push him along this destined path. But that wasn't Tommy's point.

Continuing to walk along the sidewalk, the taller buildings thinned out and a nagging thought nibbled at Tommy's concentration. Something was wrong. He felt a strange sense of both familiarity and hesitation. The familiarity, he thought, made sense. Hadn't he been to Manhattan once before? He took in the buildings, the people, the streets, then fought his way back to the question he'd wanted to ask F.P.

"I know you know the plan, and that Aaron was the winner of the contest, but do you know *your* connection to him?"

Phantos's stride slowed. He placed a hand on his helmet and held it there a moment before whispering, "I was the winning design. Aaron. He drew me."

There was more Tommy wanted to ask. So much more. But as they stopped at the curb to wait for the light, he had a dark epiphany. He stared at the blue street signs mounted atop lights running across the road. These signs specified that Tommy and Phantos stood at the corner of Penn Avenue and Stanwix Street.

"Oh, *no*." A shot of electricity ran through his nerves as dread overtook him. "We're not in Manhattan."

The light changed and people pushed past Tommy, bustling through the crosswalk. He stood in place, staring at the break between the tall buildings. His eyes ran across Penn Avenue, lined with autumn-colored trees that led to Point State Park ahead, where his elementary school had once come on a class trip.

Through a dry mouth and cracked lips, he said, "We're only in Pittsburgh."

CHAPTER TWENTY-FIVE

FOLLOWING CLUES

The whole ride home, Miranda puzzled over Tommy's strange disappearance. Each blind curve heralded a new hope that Tommy would appear ahead of her once the road straightened. The anticipation of spotting her new friend caused Miranda to pedal harder until she was panting and sweaty under her puffy pink jacket. Of course, no matter how fast she rode or how far she went, Miranda never did catch up with the phantom rider. Rounding the corner on her road, she slowed once again to check the roller rink's parking lot. There were a couple older kids there she didn't recognize waiting for Skate-A-Way to open at eleven, but no Tommy.

This didn't worry Miranda. She had spent quite a bit of time at the Harvest Fest, exploring, collecting candy, and becoming enchanted by the autumnal atmosphere of the small town. Tommy had probably gotten home a while ago. This idea perked her up as she again remembered the sketch. Would he give her a drawing he had lying around, or would he create something new for her? Perhaps something from *The Goddess of Good*. Miranda liked the idea of a drawing that depicted a strong woman warrior defending the good of all Evernitia. Frankly, *The Goddess of Good* was fast becoming her favorite show, even more than *My Little Pony* and *Strawberry Shortcake*. She had wanted to talk to Tommy about it, knowing how much he liked *Order of Cosmic Champions*, but she figured he'd be a dumb boy and act like he didn't watch *The Goddess of Good* since it was a "girls' show."

What did that matter anyway? She'd watched plenty of *OoCC* and even *G.I. Joe* and that new one, the *Teenage Mutant Ninja Turtles*. Then again, she never did tell any of her friends out of fear of being called a tomboy. A pang of guilt reverberated in her stomach, the realization causing her to sweat even more than the bike ride home.

One of her teachers (who had been discussing politics) used a word that came back now with sickening clarity. Most of the lesson had gone over her head, but the word *hypocrite* stuck. Miranda understood the definition on an academic level, but it wasn't until her self-deception that she truly comprehended the meaning. She hated the oily feeling of this epiphany.

Miranda continued pedaling past her road and up the hill toward Tommy's house. Mr. Redford was raking leaves. The old guy was always in his yard working. Even now, with barely a dozen leaves scattered across his immense manicured lawn, he toiled away as if the president were coming to inspect his property. She waved back and called out, "I think you missed one!" then laughed delightedly at her quip.

Mr. Redford however didn't get the joke and scanned his yard with mild alarm for the errant leaf.

Poor old guy. She hoped he had other hobbies to keep him busy.

She stood on the bike and pedaled harder as the incline increased. With each pump, a decision—one she was initially unaware she'd made—became more solid. She'd tell her friends about the shows she liked to watch. She'd stop hiding her true interests. She'd cease being a hypocrite. Her deception would have probably sounded innocuous to most, but Miranda wanted to be true to herself, whether or not anyone else actually cared.

Reaching the top of the hill, she hopped off the bike and leaned on the handlebars to catch her breath. Young though she was, a fast ride back from town followed by a nonstop rally to the top of Tommy's hill was enough to cause spots of light to appear in her vision. She kept trying to catch her breath as she pushed her bike into the driveway. There weren't any cars there, so probably only Tommy was home. She set her bike on its kickstand, went to the door, and knocked. Her heart raced, and she acknowledged it had nothing to do with the bike ride. When no one answered, she knocked again then rang the doorbell. Maybe Tommy was in the bathroom or didn't hear the knock from upstairs.

With every passing second her heart slowed. She went to the front window and peered through, then around the other side of the house to try and see into the kitchen.

The house seemed empty.

Tommy's duffel bag and backpack became more ominous. Was her brief fear that he had run away actually correct? She'd tried to ignore the impulse to jump to conclusions, but too many colliding circumstances painted a dire picture in her head. Tommy being bullied at school, the rumors he had been beat up by his ex–best friend, his sheepish demeanor, the way he seemed to be hiding something from her when they spoke on the bus. Then he disappears into town with two overstuffed bags?

The fear was too real to ignore.

Miranda ran back to her bike and headed for home. She had to tell her parents. They'd know what to do.

* * *

Miranda arrived home with a million alarms blaring inside her head. Some of them were for Tommy's safety, but there were a few reserved for her own defense. How much should she tell her parents? Would they ground her? Would they yell at her?

She raced into the living room where her parents were watching the morning news with a late breakfast of pancakes on the coffee table. Seeing them in quiet Saturday morning cocoons, Miranda shook off her fear of reprisal. She'd made a pact with herself not to be a hypocrite, and though this wasn't exactly the same thing, she knew the full truth unencumbered by self-preservation was the only road forward.

Her parents turned away from the television only long enough to say good morning. They didn't notice the terror in her eyes, the sweat on her face, or the need in her expression.

Dad calmly sipped his black coffee, which matched both his eyes and hair. He was always composed, as if sitting through church. Until he wasn't. Miranda feared those moments of rage the most, when her father's six-plus feet of thickly layered muscle no longer promised protection. Still watching the screen, he said, "Long ride this morning, Panda." His comment was merely an offhand observation, and yet sounded accusatory in his mouth.

When Miranda's mother's eyes fell upon her daughter, she stopped chewing. Her fair complexion revealed a red flush of worry. "What's wrong?" asked Emma.

Cole put his coffee down so hard he spilled a few drops. "Did something happen? What is it?" He stood but didn't move from the couch.

Miranda had to extinguish some of the concern before her parents spontaneously combusted. "I'm fine; nothing happened."

Some of the visible tension eased from her father's shoulders.

"But I think Tommy may have run away."

Emma lowered her eyebrows and tilted her head. Neither parent said anything, and in the silence, Miranda realized they had no idea who she was talking about.

"*Tommy*," Miranda repeated as if this would clear things up.

Her father glanced at his wife for help.

"Tommy Grant. From the top of the hill."

Cole's face crinkled. "*Dave's* kid. Right, right."

"Dave?"

"You know. He works at the Toyota dealership outside of town."

"Oh, *him*."

Miranda followed this conversation with growing unease. Neither parent picked up on the important part. "Tommy's *gone*."

"Gone where, dear?" her mother asked.

"Well," she shifted, waving her hands in the air for some kind of divine assistance. "I don't know *where*. I saw him ride his bike into town this morning with two bags, and he just disappeared!"

Cole sat down and went back to enjoying his coffee, splitting his attention between the television and his daughter. "I'm sure he didn't disappear, Panda. Don't be hysterical."

"I didn't mean literally—"

"Why do you think he ran away, honey?" her mom interrupted.

"It's like I said, he had two bags with him. One was his backpack, and the other a huge duffel bag. It was super early, and he rode off toward town. When I got there—"

"*What?*" her father said, a scary edge to his voice.

Miranda forged ahead. "I went into town after him."

The resulting silence was worse than screaming. Both of her parents glared with terrifying disappointment. Her mother shook her head. Her father balled his fists.

Miranda broke the silence. "I'm sorry."

"Not yet you aren't," Cole said, his face growing red. "You know the rules, and you know the consequences for breaking them. Isn't that right?"

Righteous rage lingered just under the surface of her father's otherwise manicured persona, and it stayed her tongue.

"Well?" he pressed.

She looked to her mother, who turned away to let *the man of the house* take care of disciplinary matters. Mostly, Emma ignored these uneasy moments, then pretended they didn't happen at all. Maybe she was afraid of Cole's anger, an unruly beast held down by meager restraints. Or maybe she thought the strong fist of rule was the right way to handle their daughter. Either way, Miranda's mother never interfered.

"Yes," Miranda answered. "I know the rules, and I know the consequences for breaking them."

He stepped closer to his daughter. He leaned forward, his face red, his jaw clenched. "Then why *did* you?"

She flinched away at each word. "Tommy's in trouble."

"You *know* that?"

"I told you, he went into town and now I can't find him. He had bags with him like he was—"

"Do. You. *Know*? Or is it possible he went to town to meet his parents. Or to visit a friend for a sleepover. Or a hundred other possibilities?"

"He seemed—"

"I don't care what he seemed. You don't know. That's the point. You do not know, and you broke the rules of this house for some car salesman's kid. Is Tommy more important to you than your own family?" He swung around and pointed at Mom, who was holding her head in her hands. "Just look at what you've done to your mother!"

"Can you at least call Tommy's dad?"

Her father's mouth dropped open, as if he couldn't believe the audacity of Miranda's request. "You could have been kidnapped. You could have been taken by some pervert in town!"

"Tommy could have too!" she yelled, unable to control herself. She'd dealt with her parents all her life, and she understood her father's motivation for keeping strict rules. But *this*? It was like he'd lost his mind or something. Ever since they'd moved to Branchville, he'd gotten worse and worse. She was surprised he let her even ride her bike around the neighborhood.

"Tommy is not my kid. He's not my responsib—"

"*Cole*." Emma stood from the couch, her tone reproachful. "He's just a boy. No matter what you might think of his father, couldn't you call?"

"Seriously?"

"You'd want them to call us if Miranda was in trouble."

His expression constricted. He glanced at Miranda, perhaps imagining if she had gone missing. He sat and rubbed his temples.

"Dad?"

"You're grounded for the rest of the weekend." He shook his head and continued to rub his temples. "I'll call David Grant. I'll tell him what you've told me." He pointed at his daughter. "But our involvement ends there."

A wave of relief washed over Miranda. He'd call. She understood her father needed to reserve some measure of rule in the house, thus her punishment, but at least he had come to his senses.

Mom smiled and blew a kiss at her thankful daughter. She'd come through, and the power had shifted ever so slightly that day. Miranda could only hope things would continue to change, because as it was, their house sat on a crumbling foundation destined for ruin.

CHAPTER TWENTY-SIX

LOST

The highlights of Point State Park for Tommy were the forking rivers and the enormous fountain located where the three rivers met. Or more accurately, where the Ohio River became the Allegheny and the Monongahela, lending the Point State Park Fountain a much cooler name in Tommy's humble opinion: The Soaring Fountain at Three-River Meet Point. Behind the fountain, at the center of the park proper, there was a marker for the former site of Fort Duquesne. And even farther back toward the city, the site of Fort Pitt.

Staring at the meeting rivers, the chill air blowing his hair back, Tommy tried remembering what else old Mrs. Tither had told the class on their trip. There was some history about the Native Americans who'd lived there, and then some more recent information about the stadiums across the Allegheny. Beyond all of that, Tommy had been mesmerized by the fountain, shooting a jet stream of water that seemed to touch the heavens. Mrs. Tither had told them the water reached 150 feet, but Tommy knew she was lying. 150 *miles*, maybe. He had a notion that with the right flotation device and a proper breathing apparatus, he could hop into the fountain and ride that geyser of water straight to the moon.

The other kids had laughed at him when he explained his hypothesis. Everyone except Evan, who in elementary school had still been his best friend and accommodating of Tommy's wild imagination that bucked off other unsuspecting riders. But Evan knew the untamed reaches of Tommy's mind, and he'd been a reckless purveyor of their limits right alongside him. If they had an air mattress and snorkels within reach, both boys would have leapt headfirst into the fountain then and there.

Still squinting into the distance, though his gaze was trained inward, Tommy muttered, "I was so *stupid*." He shook himself back to the present, where Evan had metamorphosed into a mutant butthole of epic proportions.

"Why were you stupid, Tommy?"

He flinched, having forgotten Phantos for a moment. "Nothing. Just thinking about the silly ideas I used to have."

"Ideas are never silly. Ideas are seeds that grow into great trees, branching ever outward. They can be good; they can be bad. But never silly."

Tommy thought about his fountain moonshot and said, "I disagree." He turned away from the river and climbed the small set of stairs, removed his bags with a sigh of relief, then sat on a bench. He rubbed his sneakers over the dirty cobblestone, feeling the rough vibrations run up his ankles. His stomach grumbled and he checked his watch. Almost two o'clock, and he hadn't eaten since breakfast.

Phantos sat next to the boy. "Do you suppose we'll be bothered?"

He unzipped his backpack and dug around for lunch, happy he'd stocked up on food from home and the corner store. "I dunno. I'm tall for my age, but I guess I still look pretty young. They wouldn't even sell me a bus ticket."

"Which begs the question . . ."

Tommy took out a peanut butter and jelly sandwich wrapped in wax paper that he'd made at home, a pouch of Shark Bites fruit snacks, and a blue Little Hug Fruit Barrel. "Which begs the question, how do we get to Brooklyn?"

Of course, the thought had occurred to him once he realized they hadn't actually arrived in Manhattan. And how stupid he was for thinking they'd somehow traveled across two and a half states while he napped. Heck, he was lucky "the city" Phil the farmer had been talking about wasn't Columbus, Ohio.

He tore open the fruit snacks and wished his biggest worry was whether or not he'd find an elusive great white shark gummy in the pouch. They weren't always there, after all. And sometimes you only got one or two. He'd spent many a disappointed lunchtime staring forlornly into the empty paper pouch with only the distant fruit smell to remind him there was always next time.

Tommy reached into the bag and plucked out a great white gummy on the first try. He stared at the chalky treat in awe. "It's a sign."

Phantos glanced at the unsuspecting snack. "A sign?"

"A *good* sign."

"Ah, I see." The holographic face inside his helmet became a magnifying glass. "A *harbinger*!" Phantos grabbed the shark gummy and held it close to his helmet. He pointed with his other hand. "Tell us what you know, tiny prophet! It's no use resisting. I will have your knowledge even if I have to squish you into jam!"

"Give me that." Tommy snagged the gummy and popped it into his mouth.

Fierce Phantos gasped. "*Diabolical.*"

"It's not alive, weirdo. I just meant it was, you know, a good omen. That things are gonna work out."

F.P. nodded slowly. "I understand." The pale android face reappeared. "Does this mean you have a plan?"

The smell of the river washed over him on a breeze, and he pulled his hat down against the cold. "No, but we better figure something out before it gets late."

"We can try another bus line."

He bit into the sandwich and thought this over. Just because the clerk at his small-town terminal had been cautious didn't necessarily mean every attendant would be as rigorous in their duties. And if not a bus terminal, maybe a train. And if that failed? Would he have the courage to hitchhike?

The eerie theme song from *Unsolved Mysteries* played in his head. What if he got into a stranger's car and disappeared forever? Would Robert Stack be talking about "The Peculiar Case of Tommy Grant" next year? This idea caused a cold shiver of terror to run through his body. Not because he was scared of being kidnapped, but because he hadn't even considered for a second how badly running away would affect his mother. All of the terror she'd experienced watching those abduction episodes, all the worry and fear she'd exhibited, and Tommy was about to inflict the real thing upon her.

The sandwich turned sour in his mouth and he suddenly felt nauseous. A scratchy video played in his head of his mother running around the house, screaming his name in an exaggerated horror movie exhibition.

The note, he reminded himself. Yes, he'd left a note behind telling his parents he was spending the weekend with Sammy. He'd banked on their being too distracted with their own lives to bother calling Sammy's parents to check in.

Then Tommy remembered something else. *The bus terminal clerk.*

The clerk had called his house. Had he spoken to anyone? Had he left a message? Did they already know he tried to get on a bus? "This is a disaster." The sounds of water crashing down in the fountain and people talking as they walked past weaved a fabric of unease. "My parents are gonna kill me."

"They were always going to find out, one way or another."

Tommy shook his head. "My note was supposed to throw them off the trail until I got home."

"Did you really believe that?"

He absently fished around the Shark Bites pouch. "Mom and Dad haven't paid any attention to me for months. If the clerk didn't leave a message, I bet they still don't know I'm gone."

Phantos lifted his arm and looked at his wrist as if checking a watch. The holographic keyboard appeared, and he tapped out a few words with ringing bleeps and bloops, then consulted the various displays that appeared in thin air around his arm. Green and blue light danced in a series of charts and numbers. Words in another language, or perhaps symbols. He nodded as he went through the readouts.

"What?" Tommy shifted to see clearer.

Phantos tapped a few more keys, and the holograms collapsed into nothingness. "You are correct. They do not know . . . *yet*. According to my calculations, there is a 97% chance that both of your parents will know you are missing no later than nine o'clock this evening."

"How could you—?"

"My calculations are rarely wrong."

Tommy wrapped the rest of his sandwich and put everything in his bag save for the drink. "They're gonna freak."

"You should give them a little credit, Tommy. They love you."

He stood fast, wanting to run from the conversation as much as he wanted to argue. A young couple gave Tommy the side-eye as they passed. He lowered his voice and said, "They barely know I exist."

"They are going through a difficult time."

"And I'm *not*? It's no excuse."

Fierce Phantos stood and nodded. "Yes, you are again correct. There is never a good excuse to ignore your child." He glanced at his gloved hand. "But I think they will come around."

Tommy pulled on his backpack and shouldered the duffel. "Your calculations?"

He nodded solemnly. "My calculations."

✳ ✳ ✳

Tommy and Fierce Phantos hiked back into the forest of buildings. The sounds and smells of the city enveloped them in a comforting blanket of anonymity. Unlike his small hometown, no one knew him here.

Walking along the sidewalk—polka-dotted with old bubblegum and dark stains—he studied the other pedestrians carefully. At first, he watched out of fear they would ask what he was doing alone in the big, bad city. *Where are your parents? Isn't it getting late for such a young boy to be wandering the streets?*

Not only did no one ask these questions, but the adults ignored him completely. After a few minutes, Tommy spotted a pair of kids even younger than himself walking on the other side of the street. "Oh—"

"It's the same as riding your bike into town," Phantos observed.

"Huh?"

"Kids walking around this city is as innocuous as riding your bike around Branchville."

He wasn't quite sure what *innocuous* meant, but he got the gist. The tension in his shoulders loosened. "That makes sense, I guess."

Phantos boomed, "Not as conspicuous as we thought!"

Tommy grinned. "Yeah, well. One of us at least." Of course, Phantos was invisible, so he supposed the point stood. Still, the realization they were in no danger of being harassed by inquiring adults didn't change their predicament. Tommy was lost in Pittsburgh with no notion of where to go. The best idea he had was to try a bus or train and hope for better results than last time.

"Do you think we can ask an adult where a bus station is without them getting curious?"

Phantos rubbed the bottom of his helmet. Tommy thought this a funny mannerism, given Phantos had no accessible chin. "We had better not. Just in case."

The buildings closed in. Anemic trees poked out from tiny squares of earth otherwise surrounded by concrete. Their branches were thin and broken; their leaves drooped and dropped. Tommy sympathized with those trees, trapped in their concrete prisons.

"We can't just keep walking around, hoping to find a bus station."

"No," Phantos agreed. "The day is quickly passing, and I would hate to be stranded come nightfall."

Another small group of kids, laughing and pushing each other, passed on the other side of the street. "We could ask *them*."

Phantos pointed behind the group they were watching. Another trio headed in the same direction. "Where do you think they are going?"

Tommy shrugged. "Let's find out." A warm ball of excitement formed in his belly. What did city kids do for fun? Was it different from what youngsters did in Branchville, or would they be up to the same kinds of mischief?

In his excitement, Tommy stepped between two parked cars, intending to cross the street. A city bus blasted by and pushed him back with a gust of hot air. He stepped onto the curb, his heart thudding like a bass drum. "That's twice now. Twice I almost ended up like the kid from *The Toxic Avenger*."

Phantos placed a heavy hand on his shoulder. "We are not in Branchville anymore. Let us proceed to the crosswalk."

The kids on the other side of the street were already halfway up the block and getting farther by the second.

"Hurry," Tommy said. "We'll cross at the next corner and then double back behind the second group."

"Onward!"

Tommy smiled to himself as they jogged past pedestrians. He liked calling the shots for once. Until that moment, Fierce Phantos had been pushing him along a path without much choice. Now, he was making his own decisions, and it felt good.

His duffel bounced against his side painfully, and the backpack's weight felt as if it had tripled, but Tommy kept moving. He didn't want to lose the group of kids, and he couldn't be sure there'd be more coming behind them.

At the corner, Tommy hit the crosswalk button and waited impatiently for the light to change. The second group had walked halfway up the block, and the first was no longer in sight. "Hurry, hurry, hurry . . ."

A middle-aged woman stopped next to him and adjusted her glasses. She was short with enormous permed curls and chubby cheeks. She peered at his bags and her eyebrows lowered.

Great. Now *adults start to pay attention.*

Tommy knew this expression, and he could almost hear the questions forming in the lady's mind. She stepped a little closer, her eyes inspecting, her mouth twisting. She'd ask where his parents were, and why he had those big bags, and was he okay, and was he lost, and—?

The crosswalk sign flashed *WALK.* But Tommy didn't walk.

He ran.

Behind him, the woman called out, "Young man?"

Tommy did not turn. He kept moving, across the street, onto the opposing sidewalk, trailing the group.

Phantos said, "Close one."

This whole trip had been a close one, and he didn't think things were going to get any better.

Closing the gap, he saw the kids more clearly. There were three of them, one girl and two boys. They appeared to be a little older. Maybe seventh or eighth graders. They all wore jeans and had on light jackets. One of the boys had a blue windbreaker. The girl wore a pink scrunchie, holding her hair in a high ponytail, reminding Tommy of Miranda. Their laughter carried on the autumn breeze like fallen leaves.

Phantos held a hand in front of Tommy. "Slow down now. Let us leave space between us."

"But we have to ask for directions."

Phantos consulted his mysterious holographic calculator on his wristband again. He typed a few quick bleeps and bloops, then collapsed the image. "Let's see where they are going first."

"Your calculations again?"

"We have a better chance—62% to be exact—of arriving in Brooklyn alive if we follow them."

Tommy's stomach somersaulted. *Alive?* As in, they could *die?* Those numbers weren't high either. And that was only if they followed the kids?

"What are our chances if we don't follow them?"

Phantos had been pretty goofy for a hero. Tommy liked that about him, but in those intervening seconds, F.P.'s sudden stoicism scared the ever-loving crap out of Tommy.

He didn't bother checking his device this time. "No chance. None at all."

A weightless moment later, Tommy replied, "Yeah. Let's follow them." As long as they stuck to the calculations, they should be okay. *Right?*

At the next corner, the three kids turned left and dipped out of sight.

"You saw?" Phantos asked.

"I did. Come on."

They sped to a jog, pushing past a few people. Someone in a business suit said, "Watch it, kid."

Tommy said, "Sorry" and kept moving until he reached the corner. He spotted the three kids just as they were making another left at the end of the short avenue.

"Hurry!" This time they ran at a full sprint. The bags bounced and slapped with every step. The chill autumn air seared his throat as he breathed heavier, and even in the coolness, his brow speckled with sweat.

What if I lose them? What if I get even more lost? What if I can't find a bus station and have to sleep on the street? What if I get kidnapped?

He pushed the corrosive thoughts away. They came in the voices of his bullies. Of Evan and Jonathan. Of Ray and Steve. The words always arrived with exaggerated and mocking laughter. But Tommy ignored the words in his head and focused on nothing but running until he reached the corner.

Then he stopped dead. His eyes lit up with flashing neon. His mouth hung open in wonder. All dread thoughts fled before the fantastic electricity before him.

Kids in Pittsburgh weren't so different after all.

CHAPTER TWENTY-SEVEN

PANIC

Miranda paced back and forth in her room, stepping over Barbie dolls and kicking stuffed animals. Her whole body was shivering with competing emotions, many of which were unfamiliar. Most of all, she was afraid. Fearful her father wouldn't call Tommy's dad, and if he did, that he wouldn't express the urgency of the situation. The pink walls pressed in on her as her hands trembled.

"Stop. Just stop it." Tears and laughter vied for space simultaneously. Nothing made sense, her mind a frenzy.

Downstairs, her father yelled something, making her jump. She sneaked to her door and eased it open to hear better.

"—should have stayed out of it!"

Her mom said something low and indecipherable.

"I said I'd call. You won't make a liar out of me. Someone in this house has to keep their word."

Was that a dig at Miranda? She felt a strange stab of cold pain in her stomach.

"I'm calling now, I said!"

Miranda's heart raced as an impulse overtook her. She didn't have a phone in her room. Her father would never have allowed it. But her parents had a phone in *their* room, right across the hallway. She poked her head through the crack in her door and listened. Her heart sped even faster as she stepped through the door and peered over the landing that overlooked the living room. Her mom wasn't there, but her dad stood at the far end of the room, his back to her as he flipped through the White Pages.

She crouched down and crawled as quietly as she could manage to her parents' bedroom. The door was closed as always. This was a "no fly zone," as her father liked to say. *Off limits.* Grounds for another week of punishment if he discovered her. This thought caused her heart to beat heavier still, but it did not deter her.

She reached out, the brass doorknob cold in her hand, and turned it. The door creaked open like a blaring alarm.

Her breath caught. In the quietude of the house, she waited for the inevitable shouts of her father, but they didn't come. She peeked around the staircase railing and saw Cole still flipping through the book. He hadn't heard. A small blessing. Miranda took the opportunity to step into the room and close the door behind her.

The smell of her mother's perfume and father's aftershave filled the small space, reminding her of their old apartment in Jersey. The whole of the apartment carried these familiar aromas, the few rooms so cramped together there was barely space for privacy. Somehow, the close quarters hadn't broken the family. On the contrary, they had been a tighter unit, the proximity bringing them closer together, literally and figuratively. There had been understanding then, and unwavering love. Sure, her dad was strict. He'd always been strict. But the tough love had been different then. It had a different smell. A different texture.

Miranda pushed her way through thoughts of Jersey as though escaping a Jell-O mold. She found herself suspended in gelatin memories often, like an errant chunk of pineapple, and she hated the feeling. Hated it because of how good the memories were, and how bad her present had become.

She carefully lifted the phone off the cradle and brought the receiver to her ear. Her father was still dialing, which was a lucky break. No chance he'd heard her pick up. Miranda moved her hand over the mouthpiece and tilted it away to keep as quiet as possible.

On the fourth ring, someone answered. "Taylor Toyota, Bill speaking. How may I help you?"

"Dave there?" Her father's voice was distant. Disinterested.

"Dave Grant?"

"Yeah." The disinterest turned aggressive with the single-word answer.

"Right. One sec."

The line cut out and The Bangles filled the dead air. Miranda hummed along with "Walk Like an Egyptian" until a chunk of ice fell into her stomach as she remembered to keep quiet. Lucky thing she'd held the phone covered and away from her mouth. *So stupid,* she thought. *Quiet, Miranda. Quiet.*

The song stopped and Bill said, "Sorry, Dave's out on a test drive. Message?"

"No, forget it." Her father slammed the phone down.

Bill muttered a curse as he hung up on his end.

Miranda placed the phone back on the hook. "*Rude.*" Her shock at Bill's reaction faded quickly as two thoughts collided at eighty miles an hour. First, her father hadn't left a message and had seemingly given up trying to alert Dave of his son's missing status. And second, she'd better get the heck out of her parents' room!

She stumbled over her own feet in a race to the door. Had she made too much noise? Would her father check the commotion? She didn't know, and it didn't matter. There was only one way out.

Miranda opened the door much faster than before, and seeing no one on the staircase, quickly exited and ran as softly as she could manage back to her own room. Closing the door behind her, she collapsed onto her Strawberry Shortcake blanket and let out a mirthless laugh of relief and confusion. She pressed her hands over her face, wanting to scream and knowing she couldn't. She took the anger, frustration, and fear, and stuffed all three into the bottle where all of her repressed emotions lived. One day the genie would be let out of her bottle. And that day would be a scary one indeed.

Why didn't he leave a message?

The answer was clear. He didn't *want* to. Simple as that.

"We had a deal." It had been an unspoken deal, but a deal nonetheless. Miranda would be grounded, and her father would call Mr. Grant and tell him about Tommy. Cole had broken his end of the bargain.

In each of her hands, Miranda clenched huge bunches of blanket. Poor Strawberry Shortcake's face was mashed, making her look like a wrinkled old lady. She released the blanket, went to her bedroom window, and stared at the friendly maple tree. An idea as sweet as maple syrup coated her mind.

"If Dad won't keep his promise, then I won't keep *mine*."

✳ ✳ ✳

Before Miranda could execute her plan, Mom and Dad came to her room for another scolding. Mostly her father explained in great detail how she had fouled up, listing her many offenses as though building a federal case against her. Mom stood silent, an expression of melancholy her only contribution. Once they left and stopped lurking around the second floor, hours had passed.

This did not deter Miranda one iota.

Although her new jacket was downstairs in the hallway closet, she had old clothes stored in the bedroom. She sorted through a mess of hangers, pulling on layers of stretched shirts and sweaters until she began to sweat. Her sneakers were also downstairs, but her rubber snow boots hadn't been taken out yet. She pulled on extra socks to make the boots fit tighter, pulled on a musty wool hat, and went to her bedroom window. There was a small landing directly across from the sprawling maple tree, with branches that reached out like craggy fingers.

God made this tree for climbing, her father had said when they first moved in. Of course, it wasn't long before he'd expressly forbidden Miranda from climbing the tree. When she reminded him of what he'd said, Cole reasoned, *Maybe if you were a boy.*

These memories were much closer than the ones from New Jersey, and thus more real. Truer. Something had happened to her father between Jersey and Ohio. She didn't know what, but she didn't like it one bit.

Squinting at the beckoning branches, she said, "I can do anything a boy can do. And *better.*"

Without another thought, she was out her window and closing it from the other side. She stood on the landing tall and proud, gazing at the landscape below. This was an act Miranda had imagined in her head a thousand times. Ever since they moved in, she'd wanted to sleep on the landing cuddled in a sleeping bag and gaze at the stars. She'd wanted to sneak out at night and climb down the friendly maple, scores of fireflies lighting her way.

"They'll call you a tomboy, Panda." Her father's voice firm and unwavering.

Looking at her tree, she finally responded to his fearful warning: "I don't care what people call me."

Miranda stepped onto a thick outstretched branch that nearly connected with the landing itself, like the top stair of a natural staircase.

All of her confidence evaporated as her second step descended directly atop a wet leaf. Miranda's foot skidded and a dozen cold spikes of fear impaled her lungs. She windmilled her arms, attempting to find balance, her breath coming fast and hard. The lopsided moment of terror called forth waking nightmares. Cole's vindictive face hovered over her as she lay in a hospital bed with broken limbs and a red face of embarrassment and shame.

What did I tell you, Panda? Didn't I say climbing trees is only for boys? Didn't I tell you!

Paralyzed, she was doubly imprisoned in both her parents' house and in a wheelchair, where she grew old utterly alone. Tommy was never found, and Miranda spent her days wondering if she could have saved him. If only she'd been better. If only she . . .

. . . . regained balance.

Her eyes were wide; her arms held the tree in a bear hug.

She hadn't fallen.

Even in the light of the near tragedy, Miranda did not waver in her pursuit. Each following step was increasingly surefooted, each branch a solid descent, until she hopped off the last low-lying branch and onto the lawn. Her confidence grew like the sprawling maple she'd mastered.

With merely a glance over her shoulder to ensure no one could see her from a window, she grabbed her bike and raced toward Tommy's house. There she was sure she'd find a clue to his whereabouts.

I'm coming, Tommy, she thought, feeling relief with every push of the pedal.

CHAPTER TWENTY-EIGHT

THE LOST ARCADE

Dusk became a neon explosion, testing the limits of the setting sun. The colored light caused Tommy's eyes to glaze over. Deep bass notes thumped in his chest, and a chorus of synthesizers leaked through the building's doors. Above the doorway, the neon sign flashed in reds, purples, and greens:

THE ARCADE

THE ARCADE

The Arcade

THE ARCADE

THE ARCADE

The Arcade

THE ARCADE

The Arcade

The Arcade

"The Arcade," Tommy read. The words tasted like caramel apples and cotton candy. They sent great and wonderful shivers of joy along his arms and legs. They felt like jumping into a pile of leaves, or a summertime swimming pool all cool and blue.

"What is an . . . *arcade?*" Fierce Phantos asked.

His question yanked Tommy away from the wonderment of colored lights, but only briefly. "*Dude.* You seriously don't know what an arcade is?"

"Yes. I am serious, my dude." He tapped on his holographic keyboard. "Arcade. A covered passageway with arches along one or both sides." He investigated the brick building before them. His eyes shot wide, and he pointed at the flashing sign, accusatory. "Lies! Be warned, young Tommy. This is no arcade. The structure does not have a covered passageway *or* arches."

"Oh for—" Tommy rubbed his face. "This is a *video* arcade. A place where people play video games, you know? Like *Pac-Man?*"

Phantos shook his head, his ghostly face expressing wonder. "You will show me."

The idea reignited the excitement Tommy had experienced upon first laying eyes on the hidden arcade. He'd played arcade machines before. Of *course* he had. But those were usually rundown, older cabinets in the corner store. They'd only had one (*Pac-Man*) for as far back as he could remember, and it wasn't until the past year they finally got a second game, *Double Dragon*.

The looming deity before them was a thing Tommy had never known, and he didn't want to wait another second before experiencing The Arcade for himself. Even the name suggested this place was a shining beacon all other arcades strove to be. This wasn't *Bill's* Arcade, after all. It was *The* Arcade. And as luck would have it, that's where the three kids had been headed. Tommy figured this was where all those groups of kids were going. He knew for sure that if he lived here, that'd be his number one destination on a Saturday.

They walked to the double doors and pushed into a space out of time. The relative quiet of the outside world shifted. Tommy's ears became clogged with cotton as the cacophony of The Arcade descended in a mixture of ambient arcade sounds, music, and conversation. He stepped onto a floor covered with the deep blue of space and a multitude of vibrant galaxies. Several lines of arcade cabinets ran from wall to wall with wide lanes for foot traffic. In an alcove on the far left sat a dozen requisite skee ball, coin drop, and claw machines. A second-floor balcony running around the circumference of the room and lined by a metal railing boasted more games.

Tommy waded into the throng. The place was packed to the gills, barely a vacant game. People gathered in great groups to watch presumably the best players.

Fierce Phantos's holographic face glitched and digitized as he gazed at the machines. "Video games." His voice sounded uncharacteristically low.

"Yeah. *Video games.*" Tommy's eyes lit with wonder.

"Curious things. They—" He stopped talking and placed a hand on the glass of his helmet. "They look like me."

"Um . . ." Tommy recognized the tone in F.P.'s voice. His own voice had taken on a similar cadence as of late. "Are you okay?"

Phantos shook his head and forced a smile. "Of course, Tommy. Onward!"

"Right." He kept walking, and though he knew the reason he'd come here was to find directions to a bus station, his attention wandered to the games, many of which he'd either never played or never even *heard* of. There were banks of the standard fare: *Galaga, Centipede, Frogger,* and *Pac-Man.* But there were also newer games like *Bubble Bobble, Contra, Shinobi,* and *Punch-Out!!*

The demo for a game called *Maniac Mansion* played on a nearby cabinet, pulling Tommy's focus. "We've got to play a few of these."

"We are on a mission. We must not deviate."

"Come on!"

A kid playing the machine next to him glanced over. "Huh?"

"Sorry," Tommy said. "Ate my quarter."

The kid nodded and went back to his game. Tommy made a mental note to talk to F.P. more quietly or not at all.

He turned away from the kid and spoke through closed lips. "I'm getting change. We can ask for directions in a few minutes." He stepped away before Phantos could respond, but perceived the holographic eyes burning a hole in his back. He found a change machine and fished out a fiver from his Velcro wallet.

"A whole five dollars?" Phantos asked. "We only have $50. That's $15 in your wallet, $15 in your shoe, and $20 in your backpack."

Phantos had a point. He shouldn't spend a lot on video games, especially when they were still so far from Brooklyn and in need of a bus ticket. There was the possibility of using an ATM machine, but he didn't want to rely on that hope.

"Fine." He looked around to see if there were attendants making change anywhere. Across the room lay a glass cabinet with a bunch of trinkets people could buy with tickets. A woman stood behind the counter, staring at nothing with glazed eyes.

He pushed through clusters of kids, his duffel bouncing off people's legs, and stepped to the register. The woman wore heavy blue eye makeup and had teased brown hair sprayed into place. She looked like a dancer from the music videos on TV. The name tag pinned to her Van Halen T-shirt, which hung off one shoulder, read Heather.

The attendant didn't react to Tommy's presence, so he said, "Excuse me, ma'am?"

She blinked and her eyes came into focus. "*Ma'am?* Come on, kid."

"Um. Sorry . . . Heather?"

"Whatever. You want to trade in tickets?" Her eyes bounced around, looking at everything but Tommy, as if he'd been sprayed with some kind of lady repellent.

"Can I get five singles?" He put the five on the top of the glass counter.

Heather made change and went back to staring at nothing.

Tommy took his singles and left. "Guess she doesn't like her job."

"Guess she did not like your *face*," Phantos replied, then cackled uncontrollably.

"You're one to talk, aquarium head."

Phantos fell silent. Something was definitely off. Tommy wanted to ask, but there were too many people around, and he'd already attracted a few stares. Overhead, a sizzling electric pop caused Tommy to flinch. A few sparks fell from a light fixture.

Phantos held an arm across Tommy's chest, as if they were in a car about to crash. He stared at the lights. "Strange."

No one else in the place noticed. "Come on, let's play a game."

"We should not linger."

Tommy ignored this. There were plenty of kids his age there, but to Tommy's surprise, there were a lot of older kids too. Some of them were dressed like the punks he'd seen on TV, hair sprayed into spikes and points, stained jackets, clothing ripped to shreds. He didn't realize people actually dressed that way in real life.

"Have they forgotten what day Halloween is?" Phantos asked sincerely.

Tommy shook his head. "I think for them Halloween is every day."

A large glowing jack-o'-lantern appeared in his helmet. "I like that."

Someone tapped his shoulder, and Tommy nearly jumped out of his skin. He spun around and found one of the kids he had followed, the one with the blue windbreaker. Up close, it was clear Tommy had been wrong about his age. He was younger by at least a couple years.

He pushed a mop of black hair from his forehead. "Who are you talking to?"

"Huh?" Tommy replied dumbly.

"I said, who were you talking to just now?" The boy shifted from foot to foot.

Phantos boomed, "Retreat! Retreat!"

"I was just talking to myself."

The kid nodded as if the explanation made perfect sense. "That's what I thought. Imaginary friend?"

"Um."

"It's okay. I have an imaginary friend too." He continued to move around, but his expression remained stoic. "My friend's name is Leo, like the lion, *not* the Ninja Turtle. Sometimes I like to call him Leo the Lion because the name makes him sound fierce, but that confuses people because he's not a lion *or* a turtle, but actually a lemur, and I wanted to make sure you knew so you wouldn't be confused."

"Oh." The panic that had threatened to overtake Tommy eased away. He looked around. "Is Leo here?"

"Of course." The kid shifted and stared at his feet, then said, "I forgot. My name is Carlos." He shoved his hands in the windbreaker pockets. "I don't like to touch, so I won't shake your hand."

Tommy smiled and said, "I'm Tommy."

He spotted the two others that were with Carlos earlier as they rounded a corner. Tommy raised a hand and waved to get their attention. After a second, the girl saw. She smiled, flashing a set of braces with pink bands around them. She grabbed the boy's shoulder, and they made their way through the crowd.

"Hey," the boy said.

The girl nodded a greeting to Tommy but turned her attention to Carlos. "We lost you for a second there."

"This is Tommy, and he has an imaginary friend too, but he didn't tell me its name yet."

The girl's ponytail bounced as she nodded. She began to smile again, then quickly drew her lips over her teeth and closed her mouth.

The other boy said, "Hey, I'm Lane."

"Elliotte," said the girl.

Carlos lost interest in the greetings and investigated the arcade, tapping his leg with one hand.

"Sorry if he bothered you," Lane said. "He has autism and can get—"

"Don't do that," Elliotte said, cutting him off. She was no longer trying to hide her braces.

Carlos didn't acknowledge the exchange, though Tommy had an idea he'd heard everything.

"It's okay. He was just telling me about Leo the Lion."

"Who is not a lion but a lemur," Carlos reminded.

Lane chuckled, then caught Elliotte's glare again and sobered. To her, he said, "You're right, sorry."

"You go to school together?"

"Yeah," Lane replied.

"We're neighbors and we've known each other for a long time. Our parents are friends, so Lane and Elliotte are stuck with me." Carlos said this with no sense of hurt, but Elliotte's expression told another story.

"You know that isn't true."

Lane said, "We'd be friends no matter what."

Carlos cracked a smile. "I know. I was just joshing. I totally got you."

Phantos nudged Tommy and almost sent him sprawling. The others eyed the sudden lurch with concern.

Phantos said, "Ask about the bus. It is why we are here."

He was right, of course. "Do you know where I can find a bus station?"

Elliotte lowered her eyebrows, then looked at Lane.

Lane nodded and inspected Tommy for a moment, his eyes lingering on the large duffel bag. "Where you headed?"

"Don't tell him, Tommy," F.P. warned.

The sounds of the arcade swelled, encasing him in an atmospheric prison. The push of bodies around them, the dim overhead lights, and the music all worked on Tommy's nerves. "Nowhere really, just—"

"You're trying to find a bus to go nowhere?" Elliotte asked, the skepticism clear in her tone.

Carlos stopped tapping his leg. "He's running away. Like you did that time, Lane. When you went all the way to my house!" He laughed and slapped his knee, then explained, "Remember, we're neighbors. He didn't get very far at all. That was the joke." Carlos laughed again, even louder.

"Quit it," Lane said. He squinted at Tommy. "Is that true? Are you running away from home?"

Another light popped overhead, and something gold and spherical whizzed by. Tommy ducked and spun. "What the heck! Did you see—?"

Lane and Elliotte stared at Tommy like he'd just burst into song. They glanced at each other, features pinched.

"Didn't you see . . . ?" Tommy trailed off. Fierce Phantos wildly signed the universal *stop talking* signal.

"I'm taking that as a ginormous *yes*," Elliotte said.

Tommy's chest constricted. "No, I'm not—" Some kids nearby looked over from their games for a moment. He lowered his voice. "I'm not. I mean, I am, but I'm gonna go back, so I'm not *really* running away, you know?"

"You sound crazy," Carlos said.

Elliotte tutted. "So you're, what?" She waved her hands in the air. "Visiting someone without your parents knowing?"

Phantos grunted approvingly. "That is . . . That is *true*." He sounded surprised. "Yes, Tommy. Tell her yes, that is correct."

Tommy nodded. "In Brooklyn. Just for the weekend, and then I'm going back home."

"Brooklyn?" Lane asked, surprised.

Elliotte gave him another one of those knowing looks. They turned and dipped their heads together, speaking low so he couldn't hear. Carlos shrugged and started pulling stuff out of his pockets, maybe looking for more quarters.

"Tommy." Phantos tapped his keyboard. "71%!"

Lane said, "What if I told you I can get you a ride to Brooklyn?"

Another gold fastball cut a jet stream through the air between Tommy and Phantos. This time he tried not to react, as it was clear no one else saw the anomaly.

"Tommy," Phantos said calmly. "Say yes. Agree now, before—"

Two more spheres whizzed above their heads like birds caught indoors. Tommy stepped away from his new acquaintances. "That's great—"

The arcade fell into an alien quiet. Lane's lips were moving, but Tommy couldn't hear a word. He backed away, nodding, maintaining the ruse.

A veil of shadow fell as if an unseen hand dropped an interdimensional curtain. Everyone in the room became phantoms as the metallic orbs shot past his head, nearly taking him out. "Phantos! What's—?"

F.P. grabbed Tommy's arm and yanked him away just as another flying orb shot past. "Run!"

Tommy turned to flee but felt as though he were running in quicksand. Each step was an agony of millennia. People no longer occupied the strange space. Sweat prickled his scalp. The duffel pulled like chains of the damned. A strangled scream bubbled underneath every forced step, even as the buzzing orbs dipped and whizzed by his ears, threatening collision.

Groaning, he shrugged the duffel from his shoulder, the relief like releasing a cement block from around his neck. No sooner had he regained a running pace, than an orb glanced off the side of his head, clanging painfully. His ears rang and his vision went fuzzy. When it cleared, he found himself in a vast hall. Arcade machines stretched to the horizon of a dream-dark corridor.

Four glinting spheres flew in from a distance and circled.

"What's going on? What is this?"

Phantos watched the orbs. His hand fell to the grip of his gun. "We are not alone here."

Tommy appraised the mechanical spheres and realized what they were. He was, after all, a die-hard fan of *Order of Cosmic Champions*.

Through clenched teeth, he said, "*EyeSpy*."

* * *

The endless black of space enrobed Tommy and Phantos. They were still in The Arcade, only now they occupied the negative space of the building.

This was The Lost Arcade.

Video game cabinets were present on either side in two long lines that marched into the distance of forever like forgotten soldiers. They had multiplied infinitely with titles of nonexistent games. Distant arcade sounds bleeped and blooped all around, yet none of the machines were on.

Tommy tried to speak, but when he opened his mouth, the words became clogged, shooting back into his own head in a stream-of-consciousness cavalcade.

? what's going on ? what are we going to do ? where are we ? did I finally lose it ? why didn't I just stay home ? do I need a doctor ? am I stuck here forever ?

Phantos placed a hand on Tommy's shoulder and squeezed. "Are you ready?"

The question was like a slap across the face, knocking the shock from his system in one gallant blow. He laughed, and it sounded insane even to his own ears. A little too loud and a little too frantic. "Ready?" He buckled over and leaned on his knees, the waves of hilarity so sudden he thought he might pee his pants. Barely able to catch his breath, he said, "Ready for the asylum maybe."

"*Tommy,*" Phantos chided, the disappointment clear in his tone.

This sobered Tommy by degrees. He wiped tears from his eyes and straightened, taking in his surroundings anew. The four orbs above continued to circle. "Have you ever seen *Phantasm?*"

"No. Is it relevant?"

He chuckled to himself, but the uncontrollable laughter didn't return. "Not really." He straightened his shoulders and took a breath. "I'm ready."

As if a quarter had been dropped into the coin slot, a few yards away one of the machines flickered on. An ominous tune played through tinny speakers as the marquee lit solid red: *Polybius.* The four orbs deviated from their holding pattern and swirled down, crashing directly through the screen of the game and disappearing into the machine without breaking the monitor, where they were absorbed and digitized.

Tommy pointed to the line of machines on their left and the singular operating game.

Phantos nodded. "I see."

The game continued to play its haunting melody, just a little off key. Just a little *wrong.* On the screen, a geometric game of colors and shapes flashed in time to the beat.

"What now?" Tommy tugged on the straps of his backpack, feeling ill-prepared and younger than his twelve years.

A robotic laugh echoed through the machine's speakers. The screen bulged outward like a pregnant belly with each cackling report.

"I think we play the game." Phantos lifted his arm and called up the holographic keyboard. A small timer flashed on the floating screen for only a second before Phantos cleared the image and began to type. A series of beams shot from the wrist of his suit and scanned the arcade. F.P. made a sound low in his throat that Tommy did not like one bit.

"What?"

"EyeSpy has grown in power since I last faced him."

The sinking feeling in Tommy's stomach dropped another fathom. "Crapola."

"Yes," Phantos replied seriously. "Crapola indeed."

"Can't we just go? I mean, why play the game if we don't have to?"

The towering space phantom turned and fixed Tommy with an intense glare. "Is that what you want, Tommy? To leave? To run home?"

A strange feeling coursed through his chest and belly. A word he'd heard his dad say from time to time came to mind: *conviction*. Tommy had made a lot of questionable choices the past couple days, sure. Leaving home on this quest wasn't necessarily a smart move. And in a lot of ways, he knew, deep down, part of this decision was egged on by a desire to run. Not just run, but *hide*.

Still, the farther he went, the more he began to understand something powerful about his choice to leave home. The decision was about more than the *Order of Cosmic Champions* contest. And if he didn't show some conviction, he'd never learn what that "something more" was.

"No. I want to fight."

Fierce Phantos smiled wide and true. "Good."

"One question first."

"Speak."

Tommy took a breath and asked, "What's our percentage now?"

"We will check after our victory." He handed Tommy a quarter. "Onward. Let us reclaim reality. Let us move one step closer to Brooklyn."

CHAPTER TWENTY-NINE

EYESPY WITH MY LITTLE EYES

The quarter was cold in Tommy's hand, and the bulging, pulsing game monitor made the rest of him feel even colder. Warbling digital notes of the senseless song continued in psychotic glee. Every metallic-tinged tone stung like pixelated bees.

He placed his hands onto the joystick and buttons of *Polybius* and took a breath to settle his nerves. He'd never experienced terrifying tension like he had that day, and the anxiety had only gotten worse with every new encounter. Still, with every new challenge faced, he also felt more capable. More prepared.

Tommy dropped the quarter into the machine and pressed the big red *START* button. A satisfying game tone dinged, followed by a distorted voice that said, "Welcome to your doom." The screen bulged, and Tommy stepped back. Phantos remained by his side as they watched the arcade cabinet shift on unsteady flooring. Digitized notes played frantically as the glass screen continued to bloat.

The air grew dry and charged, electricity coursing through every particle. The hair on Tommy's neck stood on end, and when he reached for Phantos as if to steady his wavering head, the loud snap and pain of a static shock caused him to jump back.

Phantos peered down at Tommy, and as if reading each other's minds, they both stepped back another few feet. Arcade music crescendoed with a scattering of haunted house notes. The screen extended beyond realistic proportions, as if the surface had been superheated and allowed to stretch and transform, expand and inflate. Something pressed against the inside of the glass, showing the imprint of a monstrous hand, outstretched and grasping. An image right out of *A Nightmare on Elm Street*.

In the vast space of The Lost Arcade, thousands of video games burst to life in a deafening cacophony of light and sound. Tommy clapped his hands to his ears and fell back. Phantos yelled out in alarm, then frantically tapped at his holographic keyboard, perhaps attempting to lower the volume coming through his helmet.

The protruding glass screen of *Polybius* exploded into a million shards of glinting glass and dust, which swirled around the empty space of oblivion, becoming a tornado of refracted light and color.

"What—?" Tommy began.

"EyeSpy," F.P. replied. "He has learned some new tricks."

The tornado of glass made touchdown on the oily obsidian floor. Smaller twisters extended from the bottom of the funnel: arms and legs.

A broken voice grated through the twister: "*Eye. See. You.*"

The four golden orbs burst forth from the shattered glass prison and buzzed directly at Tommy's and F.P.'s heads, nearly knocking them over. Tommy ducked as two of the orbs shot blue lasers, scorching the floor at their feet.

Fierce Phantos rolled, recovering in a crouch with his laser blaster at the ready. EyeSpy's flying eyes tumbled out of range just as the glass tornado liquefied. The molten glass glowed red and morphed into the pyramid-shaped head and robotic body of the *OoCC* villain, EyeSpy, complete with his laser cannon arm, a solid cylinder of mechanized weaponry that hooked into his torso with wires and cords.

A chilling laugh erupted from the solidifying body as EyeSpy manifested gold and green. The flying eyes docked to their home base, one on each of the four sides of EyeSpy's pyramid head. The villain slumped forward, his mechanized form whirring and buzzing to life. "At last."

The arcade machines snapped off, throwing them into an uncanny silence.

"Your quest is at an end. You've failed." EyeSpy charged so suddenly that Tommy stumbled back and fell over his own feet. He scurried out of the way as F.P. stepped between them and blasted EyeSpy with his laser.

The villain's orbs launched from his head as he threw himself into a roll, avoiding every shot and laughing the whole way through. The whizzing orbs vanished into the bleak expanse, no doubt watching for an advantage. He leapt to his feet, shooting a flurry of blue lasers from his arm cannon.

Phantos scrambled to his left too late. Two shots ignited his shoulder and sent him sprawling. Black scorch marks sizzled on his suit, a noxious fume rising in wisps. He leapt behind one of the arcade machines and summoned his army of holograms. "Tommy, take cover!"

Tommy regained his feet and threw himself behind the line of arcade cabinets opposite Phantos. He watched as the squadron of holographic heroes scattered, running through the corridor, some diving behind other arcade machines, some serpentining through the main hall. After a moment, Phantos entered the fray and mingled so completely with his cohorts, even Tommy didn't know which was real.

The golden eyeballs reappeared and dove, shooting blue lasers at each hero in turn. The shots sailed through the phantasmic figures, burning little holes into the black floor, through which beams of brilliant white light shone. Each shot was like a slap across the face, attempting to wake Tommy from a terrible dream. But the vision had too firm a hold. Tommy could feel the hard shell of the arcade machine against his back, smell the burning floor, hear EyeSpy's maniacal laughter.

The various holographic heroes continued to evade EyeSpy's attacks, but the obvious drawback was these phantom fighters couldn't attack. Sooner or later, EyeSpy would discover the metaphoric queen in F.P.'s game of Three-card Monte.

EyeSpy fired another flurry of beams. "This is a losing game, Phantos! You forget, my vision is 20/20."

A waving hand caught Tommy's attention. One of the Phantos holograms waved from the other side of the hall, then darted out from behind an arcade machine. Overhead, one of the orbs dipped and fired three shots, two of which hit, actually *hit*, the hologram. Phantos collapsed next to Tommy, panting, holding his injured torso where big black scorch marks gave way to pale skin underneath, red and blistering. Not a hologram after all.

"Phantos! What are you doing?"

Holograms continued to run around the main hall, but it was only a matter of time before EyeSpy tracked the real Phantos to his hiding spot.

F.P.'s chest heaved, and his voice sounded ragged. "Tommy. He's too strong."

A panicked smile of fear stretched across his face. "No." His heart raced, and he felt cold all over. "The hero always wins. You *know* that!"

He heaved a broken laugh. "I am not a hero, Tommy. Not yet." His sad laugh was layered with static, like an old walkie-talkie running low on batteries. He knocked on his helmet, his face blinking in and out of view. A bad television signal. A broken video game. He wheezed, "I am barely holding my own here."

Tommy had no time to dwell on F.P.'s doubts. There were more pressing matters. "What do we do?"

"I need to regain my strength, but we can't let him find us cowering, defenseless."

EyeSpy bellowed, "Your little holographic tricks are almost defeated, Phantos!"

F.P ignored this. He grabbed Tommy's shoulders. "Summon forth your sword."

"My *what*?"

Phantos shook him gently, still grasping his shoulders, holding firm. "Your sword, Tommy. You have always carried it with you. Even now, the blade lies dormant within, waiting only for a sure hand to wield it."

"I don't know what—"

"You *do*. Think, Tommy. Think back to when we first met."

EyeSpy's lasers disintegrated two more holograms only feet away. Echoing footsteps of the villain strode closer.

Tommy tried to think, his mind muddied with fear. "When we met . . . in my bedroom?"

"No. In your *dream*."

His dream. That's *right*. Before Phantos had manifested in the real world, Tommy had dreamed of him. That was when he first conceived of his plan to find Aaron. And in that same dream, he had attacked Phantos with—

"My sword." He rubbed his eyes so hard that bright spots of light exploded behind his eyelids. "I have a *sword*."

Fierce Phantos smiled wide, though the pain behind the smile was clear.

Tommy stood and emerged from behind the arcade cabinet. He walked to the dead center of the forever-hall and turned to face EyeSpy. The villain stood gigantic, a towering golden god of chaos. His pyramid head spun and clicked into place with one glowing eye set deep in the dock of his head. He fixed his cyclopean glare on Tommy, considering this new opponent.

A couple of Phantos's holograms continued to dart around the hall, but EyeSpy ignored these. The remaining orbs docked in his head, and he stepped closer. His head clicked from one side to another, each eye inspecting Tommy in turn.

EyeSpy laughed. "I don't know what Skullagar sees in you, boy." His head spun from eye to eye. "But I do not perceive your potential, and I can see *everything*."

EyeSpy raised the arm cannon, the blue light of his laser building strength. "I won't try and turn you to our side as Munch Mouth did. As Skullagar has requested." There was no expression on the faceless pyramid, yet malice and villainy oozed like liquid cancer from his every molecule. He explained plainly, "I prefer to destroy you."

The words burned, like so many others had this past year. But there was something different about the fire they lit this time. The licking flames ignited something in Tommy that had lay dormant for far too long. His heart sped like the drums of war as a grim smile grew.

From somewhere far away, Phantos was telling Tommy to fight. He was urging him onward to battle. But Tommy didn't need further provocation.

Not this time.

Without looking—because he knew what his hand would find, for he felt the weight of his weapon on his side—Tommy unsheathed a glimmering blade.

His sword. Though sometimes forgotten in the waking world, he recalled its name with unrelenting joy: Lórien.

He tightened his grip on the dragon scale hilt and shifted his weight to an attack position. Around him, time slowed to an IV drip of hallucinatory clarity. Lórien spoke in the high-pitched singsong of metal, and Tommy knew the words for what they were: a battle cry.

EyeSpy flinched at the sight of Lórien. He retreated a step, one hand shielding his eye from the glare of pure metallic fire. In a halting tone, he said, "What is this? Where did you find that sword?"

Tommy recalled Fierce Phantos's words, and he repeated them with burning delight. "I've always carried it with me."

He let not another second pass. Tommy charged, his sword at the ready, his jaw set, his heart pure. Just as Lórien uttered its battle cry, Tommy too roared in attack.

EyeSpy fell back another step, then launched three of his four eye-orbs. They rained down blue fire from the sky.

Tommy did not hesitate, nor did he slow. He raised Lórien with a confidence he'd not known since the previous summer and blocked every attack. The lasers bounced off his sword and shot back at EyeSpy. Three missed by inches, and the fourth hit home.

EyeSpy let out a surprised cry. "You filth!"

Tommy, mere yards away, redoubled his speed.

EyeSpy leveled his arm cannon and fired a laser the thickness of a tree trunk.

"Tommy, watch out!" Phantos yelled from cover.

He dove forward, Lórien tucked back, and he fell into a roll. The force of the blast sent him sliding across the floor where he crashed against an arcade machine. Lórien clattered to his side as a sharp pain shot through his arm. He tested his shoulder. Not dislocated, but sore and throbbing.

EyeSpy pounced; his orbs fired again, missing by mere inches.

Tommy tried to stand, but his legs wouldn't cooperate, his back throbbing from the impact. He pawed next to him and snatched Lórien, lifting the blade in time to block two incoming laser beams. They bounced away as before and sailed into the black expanse.

EyeSpy limped forward. "You are not as useless as I thought, but that does not change the outcome. You are finished."

The words slid off Tommy as he struggled to his feet. These words, these insults. They meant nothing coming from a villain. "Then come and finish it."

EyeSpy raised his arm cannon.

"Young warrior!" Phantos appeared from behind the arcade and pointed his gun at Tommy. "Use Lórien!"

Understanding dawned. Tommy lifted the blade as Phantos fired a brilliant array of colored holograms. Tommy caught the light with his blade. The prismatic colors refracted on the ancient dreamscape metal, manifesting a river of white-hot light that exploded from Lórien and sliced through the lone eye in EyeSpy's head.

Molten metal sputtered, and electrical circuits sprayed sparks as the villain screeched in horror. He clamped his hand to the destroyed eye and released the charged blast from his cannon, firing wildly. The blast struck an arcade machine in an explosion of wood and circuitry. Smoke carried a campfire smell as splintered wood rained from above.

The three remaining orbs dove at Tommy as EyeSpy screamed incoherently, a venomous and garbled curse.

Phantos shot the moving targets, destroying only one in a blaze of fire and sparks. Tommy spun away from the other two as they attacked, slicing one in half with Lórien. Cruel screeches from EyeSpy sent a wave of chills through Tommy. It was the sound of a dying animal, equal parts fear, anger, and pain.

The remaining orb bounded around the room in utter disorientation. EyeSpy's head spun around, perhaps attempting to dock his last eye. "You should have died when you had the chance. The alternative will be so much worse!" The final orb crash-landed into EyeSpy's head. He turned and fled, yelling over his shoulder, "Skullagar will have his prize," before diving headfirst into the molten glass of an arcade machine, disappearing in defeat.

A glorious joy tore through Tommy's heart. A thing he thought he'd lost forever filled him completely. Happiness enveloped him as he howled victorious, holding Lórien above his head in triumph.

"You did it, Tommy! You defeated EyeSpy!"

The boy thrust his sword into the air once again, letting hope surge like a river finally free of its dam. He limped to F.P. and hugged him. Tommy backed away after a minute, feeling a little embarrassed. "*We* defeated him. As a team."

Phantos smiled warmly. "A team." He looked around at the expanse of The Lost Arcade. "Now, to find our way home."

Tommy glanced at one of the arcade cabinets and smiled. "Don't worry," he said. "I think I know the way." He sheathed Lórien, then dug in his pocket to retrieve a quarter. He approached an arcade cabinet and nodded at the title. "I'm pretty sure this one will take us home."

Phantos read the marquee and laughed. "Yes, Tommy. I believe you are correct. Onward, young warrior. To Earth and the completion of our quest."

He nodded solemnly. "To the completion of our quest." Tommy took the quarter and dropped it into the coin slot.

Then he pressed *START* on *Tommy and the Order of Cosmic Champions.*

CHAPTER THIRTY
BREAKING AND ENTERING

miranda straddled her bike in the Grants' driveway. The house looked exactly as it had before. All the lights remained off and there was no car in the driveway or the garage. Even more than before, she knew no one was home. Was she doing this? Was she actually breaking into Tommy's house?

She shook her head to the internal question. *No, of course not.* Because she wasn't going to *break* anything. Besides, Miranda didn't plan on stealing. She was investigating for Tommy's sake. For Tommy's *protection.* Her parents might not understand, but Tommy's would.

Miranda dismounted and dropped her bike without bothering to prop the kickstand. All her attention was on the house and deciphering the mystery that lay before her. Where had Tommy gone, and was he in trouble?

She strode to the front door, and even as she checked the knob, something deep inside suggested her intentions weren't all that pure. Finding the door locked wasn't a surprise, but the little voice that spoke in her head was. She was trying to protect Tommy. How was that not a pure intention?

Because at least some small part of you is more interested in the excitement. The mystery.

This voice of doubt, she recognized. And Miranda *hated* it with all her being.

She moved to the front window that looked into the living room. Leaning past the decorative gourds and window pots filled with sunburst mums, she grasped the frame and lifted.

The window didn't budge.

Give up now. Go home before your father finds out.

Miranda walked to the side of the house, these warnings playing through her head. She could still go home, sneak back in. No one would ever know. And besides, all of the doors and windows were locked so far. Doubt had arisen, suggesting perhaps there was no easy way into the house after all. She wouldn't go so far as to actually *break* in. Would she?

She kicked an errant stone that sailed into the backyard. The rock bounced into the dying grass, still covered with fallen leaves. Her own father had been much more diligent with the yard cleanup than Tommy's dad. She wondered if that's why her father held Tommy's in such high contempt. It didn't take much for Cole to form a negative opinion of a person.

On the side of the house was a small window overlooking the kitchen sink. It'd be a tight fit, but worth a try. Miranda stepped onto her tiptoes and placed a hand on the lower frame. She closed her eyes and thrust upward. The kitchen window slid open freely.

She stepped back, eyes wide and mouth agape. On some level, she didn't expect any of the entryways to be unlocked. A big part of her had assumed she'd never actually have to enter the house. But now the open space welcomed home invasion.

Gripping the bottom sill, she tried to lift herself and found the feat too difficult. She never had been good at pull-ups, and this was even harder. Around the rear of the house lay two garbage cans in a small corral. Running over, she became hyperaware of probing eyes. Tommy's house was at the top of a steep hill, but they did have a neighbor to the left, close enough that if someone looked out a window from the top floor, they might spy Miranda scurrying through the Grants' window.

She hesitated with her hands on the garbage can and inspected the neighbor's house from her vantage point. There weren't any obvious onlookers, and the windows were all dark. That wasn't exactly an "all clear," but Miranda wasn't about to stop now. She pulled the can to the window and scrambled on top. After a precarious balancing act, the flimsy plastic lid collapsed inward as the can slipped and threw her forward.

She squeaked, "Oh no!" and leapt for the open window headfirst. Half her body went through just as the can bounded away from her flailing legs. Her head dipped down into a sink of sudsy water. Pushing at the sides of the sink, she managed to lift herself and yank the rest of her body through the window. One of her booted feet slipped into the sink as she knocked juice glasses from the counter, shattering them across the linoleum floor.

"No!" Miranda scooted across the soaked counter in an attempt to dismount without further calamity. There were more glasses and a stack of bowls to her left, but she managed to slide herself to the edge of the counter and hop onto the floor without breaking anything else. Her boots crunched down on the shards of glass, and she let out a deep, sickening groan. "I'm in so much trouble."

No one had come running or screaming for the police. That was the good news. The bad news was considerable. Her face and hair were soaked, her pants and jacket covered in suds. Worse were the shattered glasses. She stepped away from the mess and searched for paper towels, her desire to clean momentarily greater than the lingering mystery of Tommy's disappearance. A half-used roll sat on the kitchen table, so she tore a few pieces off to dry herself before turning back to the mess.

There was glass everywhere. Light glinted off tiny shards as far away as the other side of the room. Some of the cups had old milk and juice in them, and the spreading mélange looked like a pastel nightmare. Miranda scurried over and tossed the used paper towels down to stop the spread of liquid. That done, she backed away slowly and made an executive decision. "I'll clean this after I figure out where Tommy went."

Her decision wasn't the most reckless she'd ever made, but it was up there. She tiptoed out of the kitchen, as though some unseen adult would appear through the wall to reprimand her. Of course, no such specter materialized. But the uneasy, fluttery feeling in her belly did not dissipate.

The layout of the living room was similar to her own. They had the same variety of itchy fabric couch with the television positioned directly across. Around the base of the TV sat a Nintendo, a few scattered games, and VHS tapes. She noted most of the tapes were for *Order of Cosmic Champions* and felt a giddy little sense of happiness.

An Ericofon telephone sat on a small table next to the doorway leading in from the kitchen, and the answering machine was blinking with a waiting message. Miranda thought about pressing play and listening in. The message could be from Tommy, after all. Her finger went as far as hovering over the button, but she resisted the temptation. Sneaking around Tommy's house was bad enough. She wasn't going to add snooping on phone calls to her list. Well, at least any calls other than her father's.

Nothing else in the room screamed "clue," so she glided up the staircase to the second floor. The bedroom to her left was obviously Tommy's parents', though she was surprised to see they had left the door wide open. Why her own parents kept their door closed off like a sealed vault, she didn't know. Especially after her earlier visit and the realization that there wasn't anything particularly special or secret in there.

To her right, down a short hallway, there was another room with the door ajar, and without getting any closer, she knew it was Tommy's. The secret allure of a boy's bedroom beckoned, and before she realized what was happening, Miranda stepped into Tommy's domain and clicked on the light. A strange wonderland of toys, posters, comics, and games greeted her. There were tons of *OoCC* action figures posed in different areas of the room, but the biggest gathering was on his desk. There, Skullagar was poised for attack with one of his most trusted minions Creecharr. On the receiving end of their fury stood Masculon himself, backed up by Defendra and Flip Grip! Weapons were at the ready: swords, ray guns, and magical staffs. An insane mash-up of all things cool.

OoCC magazines lay strewn across Tommy's bed, and there were a few items out of place, but the room wasn't nearly as messy as she'd expected. She thought all boys were supposed to be gross and lived beneath a pile of games and garbage. Maybe the image all her friends conjured wasn't completely true, though she suspected there were boys out there that fit the description. Some of her friends did, after all, have brothers. They'd know firsthand.

Her biggest surprise was the small bookshelf with actual books, not just comics and magazines. She ran her fingers across the spines, noting a few titles she recognized like *Hatchet*. He had a book called *The Princess Bride*. She had no idea the movie was based on a book and was thrilled to think she could revisit some of her favorite characters in a new medium. She also noted a book called *The Silmarillion*, written by the same guy who wrote *The Hobbit* and the other *Lord of the Rings* books, all of which Tommy owned. He was full of surprises.

Turning back to the desk, Miranda noticed there was an envelope underneath the three villains. She carefully moved the action figures, revealing the text scrawled there: *Mom and Dad*.

A clue!

Miranda nearly tore the envelope open in her haste to uncover the truth of Tommy's disappearance. Now her parents would see she was right the whole time.

The piece of paper slid out from the envelope as if leaping into her hands. She unfolded the lined sheet and read, her smile first faltering, then drooping completely. "Oh no." She flipped the paper over and found no other text, then turned it back and read again. She shook her head in anguish. "Oh *no*."

The letter was clear. Tommy had gone to spend the night at his friend Sammy's house. A *sleepover.* That explained everything: the bags, the bike ride into town, why he hadn't come back. And here Miranda was, standing in his bedroom after having broken in and created a firestorm of chaos in the kitchen.

"The kitchen!" she squeaked, putting a hand over her mouth. Without thinking, she shoved the letter into her jacket pocket. She had to clean up before—

Downstairs, the door creaked open. A woman's voice called out, "Tommy? Are you home?"

Miranda's heart sped to hummingbird speed. She felt like barfing.

Tommy's mom had returned.

✳ ✳ ✳

Miranda ran to Tommy's bedroom window, hoping beyond hope he had his own ledge and sprawling maple tree. Her throat tightened by degrees. No ledge, no tree, no escape.

"Dad is going to *kill* me." Saying this out loud made her impending doom real, and her entire body went cold. She ran to close the bedroom door and put her back to the barrier as if barricading herself in, even as she acknowledged the futility.

Tommy's mom called again from downstairs. "I've got good news, come on down for some Rax sandwiches!" She laughed and said, "The Rax isn't the good news."

A mercifully quiet moment passed. One in which Miranda was able to pretend everything would be okay. One in which her mind fled to the far reaches of reality, where the fantastical hope of escaping unseen was still possible.

Then Tommy's mom shattered the hope like Miranda had shattered the juice glasses. "Tommy!" Her voice had changed spectacularly. "Get down here *right now.*"

Miranda had heard her fair share of screaming parents, and this tone was definitely of the "you messed up big time" variety. His mom had found the kitchen disaster.

"Do you hear me? Don't make me come get you!"

Miranda's face grew hot. She pulled the sagging wool hat from her head, leaving a frizz of static-charged hair. The hat fell from her useless hands. Her vision blurred with tears, the terror and resignation of being found out collapsing in on her. She tried to respond, but her voice cracked and turned into a small sob instead.

She opened the door, her throat tight as if someone were strangling her. Fighting with the old jacket, she managed to open the zipper, but multiple layers of shirts had already soaked through with flop sweat. The hallway and stairs floated by with funhouse surrealism, bleeding into one another until Miranda found the living room.

Tommy's mother stood there, jacket still on, her purse hanging from the shoulder, and an expression of utter confusion on her face. "Who—?" She glanced toward the stairs. "What are you—?" Her eyebrows fell. "Is—?" She shook her head then stomped to the foot of the stairs. "Tommy! Get down here!"

"He's not here." Miranda spoke so low she doubted Tommy's mom heard.

243

But Mrs. Grant *had* heard. Miranda knew this because the woman's head snapped around so fast her neck should have broken. "*Excuse me?*" She approached, her hands in the motherly attack position, firmly planted on her hips.

"Tommy isn't here." She pulled the letter from her pocket and thrust it at the fierce blonde woman before her. Miranda had of course seen Tommy's mom before, but always at a distance. Up close, she reminded Miranda of Defendra, the heroine of *OoCC*. Not so much how she looked—though she had to admit that Tommy's mom sure did look a lot more feminine than her own mom—but the expression of protectiveness she wore. Her striking presence. As if she were ready to throw down with a street gang at any moment.

She took—no, *snatched*—the envelope from Miranda and tore the letter out. As she read, her expression went through a series of conflicting emotions. Mrs. Grant inspected Miranda then went back to reading. She flipped the page over to make sure she hadn't missed anything, shook her head, then read the whole thing again. All the while, Miranda stood frozen and sweating in her old winter clothes, too afraid to speak.

Finally, Mrs. Grant put her purse down and removed her jacket, then sat on the couch. Miranda thought she mostly appeared confused, but also a little scared.

"Sit." She patted the couch cushion, her expression softening.

The room became swimmy. Everything was underwater and muted.

"Take your coat off, honey. You look like you're about to faint."

Miranda obeyed. Yes, she was sweating and felt faint. But mostly she listened because an adult told her to do it, and she was in trouble. Big, serious trouble. This thought caused her head to float a few more inches above her shoulders. She dropped her coat on the floor, then struggled out of the top sweatshirt, feeling vaguely nauseated.

Please don't barf. Please don't barf. She'd made enough of a mess without showing Mrs. Grant what she'd had for breakfast. The feeling passed, and with a small sense of relief Miranda sat next to Tommy's mom.

Mrs. Grant gripped the letter in her hands, crinkling it into a cylinder. She took a deep breath. "What's your name, honey?"

"Miranda." This came out in a whisper. She cleared her throat and repeated, "Miranda Vitalis."

"*Vitalis.*" Mrs. Grant's face did something strange. She blinked rapidly and sat a little straighter. "From around the corner. Your father is Cole."

Even though these didn't sound like questions, Miranda said, "Yes."

"Do your parents know you're here?"

She looked at the big black rubber boots on her feet. "No."

"Okay. Right. And Tommy?"

Miranda pointed at the letter Mrs. Grant continued to strangle in her hands.

Shaking her head, "Explain this to me, sweetie. Because first of all, Tommy wouldn't just leave for a sleepover without having spoken to me first. And then I find you here, and broken glass all over the kitchen floor, and—"

"I'm sorry!" Miranda blurted. With the words came a flood of tears and long, ugly sobs. Her vision blurred completely. She wiped her nose. The embarrassment, fear, and shame all compounded into a storm of pure grief. "I made a mistake."

Mrs. Grant didn't move to comfort her. Instead she said, "It's okay. You go ahead and cry as much as you need to."

Miranda did just that. For what felt like a solid hour—but was probably only a couple minutes—she cried and cried until the tears tapered off. She wiped her wet cheeks and took in a few shaky breaths.

"Feeling a little better, hun?"

Miranda nodded without looking up.

"Do you think you can tell me what happened now?"

Again, she simply nodded. Then she spilled her guts.

✳ ✳ ✳

When Miranda had finished, Mrs. Grant got her a glass of orange juice. She drank greedily, her throat parched and sore from all the crying and talking. Only after emptying half the cup did she say, "Thank you."

Mrs. Grant sat back on the couch, her expression troubled. It was an expression Miranda's own mom had often worn these days, especially around the time Dad was supposed to get home from work.

"First of all, thank you for worrying about my son. What you did was wrong, but you did it for a good reason." She tutted. "That doesn't make your actions right. You know what they say about good intentions?"

She did. Her father loved that particular adage. She nodded. "The road to hell is paved with them."

"That's right." She rubbed her temples. "I don't know what Tommy was thinking running off to his friend's house, only leaving a note, but he'll get a talking to, as I'm sure you will when I bring you home."

Miranda's stomach sank. "You don't have to—"

"Oh yes, I *do*. Much as I'd rather avoid it, I'll need to speak with your parents."

That was a weird thing to say, she thought. *Much as I'd rather avoid it.* She thought about her father's reaction to speaking with Tommy's dad earlier. Something had definitely gone on between Tommy's and Miranda's parents, though she couldn't fathom what.

"Before we go," Mrs. Grant went to the phone. "I need to call Sammy's mom."

Miranda nodded and started gathering her outerwear.

Mrs. Grant dialed from memory and waited. She muttered to herself,

"A message," referring to the blinking light Miranda had noticed earlier. Boy was she glad she hadn't listened to that. It'd be just another thing to pile on the long list of offenses.

"Hey, Theresa. It's Suzie. Yeah? Oh yeah, just fine. Uh huh. Right, no, just wanted to make sure Tommy got there okay." A pause. Mrs. Grant lowered her head. "He left me a note. Uh huh. Yes, please." She turned and stared at Miranda for a moment. The expression caused goose flesh to raise over her neck.

"What? Are you *sure?*" Mrs. Grant no longer looked concerned. She was terrified. "Yeah, yeah. Please, just call me back if you do. Okay, bye."

Mrs. Grant swooped over Miranda like a bird of prey. "When did you say you saw him? And where?" She grasped Miranda's shoulders and got onto one knee.

"What's going on?"

"When? Where?"

"Riding his bike into town, but I lost him after that. Around eight this morning, I guess."

Tommy's mom shook her head and started pacing.

"What's going on? Mrs. Grant?"

"He's not there." She said this quick, like the words hurt to be in her mouth.

"At Sammy's? So the letter—"

"He lied. Or—" She nearly buckled over.

"Or what?"

"Or someone forced him to write it."

Miranda almost tumbled down the same rabbit hole, letting the worst-case scenario envelop her like a grasping maniac, but then some sense returned. "No, that can't be. He was alone."

Mrs. Grant stopped pacing. "Right. *Right.*"

Then something else occurred to her. "Mrs. Grant. The message." She pointed at the answering machine.

Tommy's mom smacked herself on the head. "Duh, Suzie. Get a hold." She ran to the machine and pressed play. There was a long beep followed by a message:

"I'm calling for Mr. and Mrs. Grant, about your son Tommy."

Suzie made a weird sound deep in her throat.

"He's asking to buy a ticket to New York City to stay with his grandmother. He has a note here, but the signature is suspect, and I thought it prudent to check in first. You can reach me at the Red Fox Bus Terminal. My name is Jim Franklin."

"New York? His grandmother doesn't—"

There was another long beep, then a new message:

"Hello, this is Jim Franklin again. Your son ran off while I was leaving the last message. He left his library card here. I think this means the note was in fact fake. I hope he has returned home by the time you receive these messages."

As the second message ended, Mrs. Grant had turned pale and seemed as though she might pass out or start hyperventilating. Her eyes were wide, and she was holding a hand to her chest. "I was out all morning. I was at a job inter—I got the job, I—why did he . . ." She turned to Miranda. "Why New York? What the heck is in *New York?*"

Something inside Miranda's head clicked, warming her face and belly, because not only had she been right all along, but she knew exactly where he was going. Miranda took Mrs. Grant's hand and held it until the woman looked her in the eyes. "He's going to find Aaron Beltzer."

CHAPTER THIRTY-ONE

A CAR RIDE

Tommy awoke in a quiet alcove of The Arcade, huddled against the wall. Carlos gently kicked his feet while Lane and Elliotte watched. Groaning and rubbing his sore shoulder, Tommy got to his feet with more effort than standing usually took. His back complained with every movement.

Lane held out Tommy's duffel bag. "You dropped this."

"Thanks." The weight of the duffel nearly dragged him back to the floor. He dropped it at his feet.

Carlos wasn't staring at Tommy, but next to him. He wore a peculiar expression.

Phantos said, "Tommy, what do I do? The boy detects me."

That was impossible, of course, so Tommy shook his head to quiet his imaginary friend. Carlos hadn't made any kind of meaningful eye contact since they'd met, always looking off in another direction. That he happened to be staring where Phantos stood was a coincidence. Besides, wouldn't he say something if he saw a space-suited android with a gun?

Lane was staring at Tommy the way Carlos gazed at empty space—his face a bit scrunched, nose wrinkled like he smelled something foul. He glanced around the quiet alcove where the change machines sat. "What happened?"

"Huh?" Tommy responded lamely.

Elliotte chuckled. "*Huh*, he says." She threw a thumb at Tommy and in a nasal voice said, "This guy right here. A real comedian."

Lane rolled his eyes. "Again with the weird voices."

"You love it."

"Whatever." To Tommy, Lane said, "You ran away from us, dropped your bag, and then disappeared for like five minutes. We thought you went outside, looked everywhere."

Tommy's heart raced faster with every word. "I was right here."

Lane and Elliotte exchanged a look. She said, "We looked here."

"Must have missed me. It's crowded."

Elliotte shook her head and made an exasperated sound. Then she laughed and blew a raspberry. "Fine, whatever. Let's say you were here the whole time. Why did you run away from us like a lunatic?"

Good question. He glanced at Phantos, who shrugged. *Real helpful.*

"I, uh." He shoved his hands into his pockets and kicked at nothing. "Got scared."

"Scared of *what*?" Lane asked.

Another good question, but Tommy was just a kid, and kids could be scared of all sorts of things, so he let his mouth do the talking before his brain formulated much of a response. "Getting in a car with strangers to drive to a different state. *Another* different state. Getting even farther away from home." As he spoke, Tommy realized he wasn't lying. These were all real fears lingering just under the surface. The deeply satisfying atmosphere of The Arcade—with its bleeps and bloops, its digitized wonderment, its smell of electricity and quarters—dissipated, leaving Tommy numb to the magic.

Lane reached across the abyss and patted Tommy's shoulder. "Yeah, I can see that."

Elliotte said, "Maybe you should go home?"

The idea greeted Tommy with a small shimmer, but there was no turning back. He'd already flip-flopped like a dying fish through the first half of his journey. There'd be no more questioning, no more second-guessing. Fear was one thing, a normal and expected response. But as long as he faced it head-on, Tommy knew he'd regret nothing.

"No," he said. "I'm going all the way."

"Well," Lane said, "if you're sure, then we better hurry. My brothers are leaving pretty soon, I think."

Tommy gathered his bag and shouldered it painfully. Why did his arm and back hurt? The whole fight had been in his head, yet he felt battered and beat, as if he'd actually been slammed against an arcade machine. He wondered briefly if he'd somehow fallen in the real world while his mind went walkabout. He pushed the questions away, afraid of what the answers would reveal.

"Okay," Tommy said. "I'm ready."

* * *

The walk to Lane's house wasn't far, but by the time they arrived at the row of brick houses packed tightly against one another like sandwich cookies, his arm was ready to fall out of its socket. Time had gotten away from Tommy, and the sun dipped below the horizon as streetlights and house lamps flickered on. Lane and Elliotte talked easily with one another, the way Tommy had with Evan oh so long ago. They gently ribbed one another with a playful slap on the shoulder or shove. Carlos would chime in now and then but spent a lot of his time glancing at Tommy and, even more often, *next* to Tommy. His expression gave nothing away, but Tommy thought there was curiosity lingering behind his eyes.

They slowed outside a brick house where two older boys were loading bags into the trunk of a yellow Oldsmobile. The two boys—nearly men from Tommy's perspective—came around to the sidewalk, smiling wide and giddy. They weren't twins, but with their matching black-and-yellow letterman jackets (he wondered what the giant "C" stood for) and closely cropped blond hair, they could have passed as the same age. Lane looked a lot like them too—what with his own blond hair and broad features—though he appeared somewhat less athletic.

"Hey, Butt-munch!" one of the boys said. He punched Lane's shoulder, and from the expression on his face, it hurt. "How's lady butt-munch and neighbor butt-munch this fine evening?"

Elliotte rolled her eyes. "Shut up, *Loch Ness Monster.*"

He grimaced at the insult, then narrowed his eyes at Tommy. He seemed about to dig into his obviously enormous bag of insulting nicknames to call Tommy something incredibly witty like *new butt-munch.*

Instead he said, "My name's Lachlan, but everybody calls me Lock." He took on an air of importance, standing a bit straighter, throwing his shoulders back. "Because I'm so deep, you need a key to figure me out."

The other brother burst out laughing, nearly toppling onto the sidewalk. "You wish!"

Completely straight-faced, Carlos said, "No one calls you that." He looked to Lane and Elliotte as if to verify, then said again, "No one calls him that."

The other brother pushed Lock out of the way and stuck a hand out to Tommy. "Don't mind him. I'm Levi."

They shook. It felt kinda weird shaking someone's hand where a high five would suit just fine. Maybe it was a Pittsburgh thing. Or a high schooler thing. "Tommy."

A woman with curly black hair poked her head through a window of a neighboring house and called, "Carlos! Dinner!"

The boy let out a long and exaggerated sigh. "I have to go." He took a few steps before turning back to Tommy. "Say goodbye to your imaginary friend for me." Before Tommy could respond, he ran off and disappeared through the door of his house.

"Imaginary friend?" Lachlan asked.

"Yeah, I don't know what he's talking about."

Elliotte checked her watch. "I should get home too. Mom and Dad start getting worried after dark."

"You live far?" Tommy asked.

"No, right across the street and down a few houses."

"Right," Tommy remembered. They were all neighbors.

"Nice meeting you. And good luck." After a second, she gave him a brief hug. "Be careful." Her face flushed and she hurried off without looking back.

"Aww, snap! New kid's moving in on your girl, Lane!" Lachlan punched him again.

Lane rubbed his shoulder. "Cut it out. We're just friends."

"Lame! Lame Lane, they call him. My kid brother the lameoid."

Now it was Levi who did the punching. Lachlan grabbed his shoulder and exclaimed, "Ouch! What was that for?"

"Stop picking on him." Levi dropped a wink at Lane. He was obviously the older and most mature of the three. He'd be the one to ask about taking Tommy along on the trip, and he hoped Lane knew this as well. Lachlan was more likely to give them both wedgies than a ride to Brooklyn.

"Mom and Dad home?" Lane asked, eyeing the front of their house.

Lachlan ignored his brother and retreated to the trunk where he put equal time into loading the car and rubbing his sore arm.

"What, you got gremlins in the brain or something? They have their Halloween party, remember? At the Greenes' place across town."

"Right."

"Don't worry, kid. They left baked mac and cheese. Just be careful heating it. Don't wanna burn the house down."

"Yeah, yeah." Lane shoved his hands into his jacket pockets and glanced around the darkening sidewalk.

"Dude. Don't worry so much. You're apt to go bald."

"Ha-ha. I'm not worried."

Lachlan slammed the trunk and shuffled back to the little powwow. He jutted his chin at Lane. "He's worried we won't be back in time to take him trick-or-treating tomorrow."

"Nuh uh."

Levi said, "We *will* be back, you know. No way we're missing Halloween."

"I said that wasn't it."

Lachlan laughed. "So you're bummed Mom and Dad won't let you come with us?"

"Like I care about that dumb band."

"Hey! Oingo Boingo is not dumb! And they barely ever play the East Coast, especially for a Halloween show."

Levi fished the keys from his pocket and started around to the driver's side. Lachlan seemed like he wanted to keep arguing the matter but checked his watch and made for the passenger side door. "You should have taken off work so we could leave earlier," he muttered.

The sky was the ominous deep violet of dusk, and Tommy's stomach was feeling fluttery at the prospect of navigating Pittsburgh alone and at night to find a bus station. He nudged Lane with an elbow.

Lane nodded curtly. "Listen, you think you can take Tommy along?"

The two boys halted on either end of the Oldsmobile and stared dumbly at the younger boys. Levi said, "Uh . . ."

"No way!" Lachlan looked at his brother, then pointed at Tommy. "He's just a kid."

Levi fiddled with his keys. "We don't have an extra ticket anyway."

"I don't want to go to the concert," Tommy said, feeling his mouth dry out with every syllable. "My grandmother lives in Brooklyn. I was headed there anyway, but Lane said you could save me the bus fare maybe?" The lies came easier than before, and this scared Tommy. At the same time, he had to admit it was exhilarating.

Lachlan shook his head fiercely. "*No way.*"

Levi asked, "What about your parents?"

"*Levi!*"

He held a hand up to quiet Lachlan. "They know you're traveling alone? They're okay with that?"

"Sure, they know. I *am* fourteen, almost fifteen," he lied. Another easy one, like slipping into cozy pajamas.

"Bull!" Lachlan said. "Thirteen, *maybe.*"

Levi came back around the car and approached Tommy, inspecting him the way a drug-sniffing dog might inspect a suspicious package. He squinted at Lane. "You trust him?"

"Just met. It's your call, but I did kinda promise him a ride."

Levi rubbed his cropped head of hair. "Bus terminal is like five miles from here, in the opposite direction." He checked his watch. "And we're already running late."

Lane said, "You can't just strand him."

Tommy could see the inner workings of Levi's mind plainly on his face. He wouldn't make for a great poker player. A full minute before Levi spoke again, Tommy already knew he had secured a ride.

The confirmation came with exasperation and conditions. "All right, kid. You can come."

"Come *on*!" Lachlan said.

"We're not leaving him to wander Pittsburgh at night by himself.

But if you want a ride in the Delta, here's the deal." He stuck a finger into the air. "One, we're bringing you straight to the venue and you'll have to catch a bus or call your grandmother to pick you up from there. We're already running way behind and can't be your personal taxi service."

Tommy nodded that he understood.

He stuck a second finger up. "Two, you sit in the back."

He nodded again, not having expected to get shotgun.

"Three." A third finger shot up. "If you're lying, you're dying."

Tommy didn't like the sound of that. "What does—"

"It means you take full responsibility for yourself. We're not shouldering the blame if the night goes sideways."

"Right. Anything else?"

Lachlan leaned over and whispered something into Levi's ear.

Levi smiled like a wolf. "You pay for the road snacks. Agreed?" He stuck his hand out.

"Agreed." No hesitation, no regret. They shook on the deal.

Fierce Phantos finally spoke, "Agreed!" He nudged Tommy with his elbow. "80%."

CHAPTER THIRTY-TWO

FINDING TOMMY

"**W**ho's *Aaron Beltzer*?" Suzie's head felt like an over-ripe melon. What the heck was going on, and why would her son run off like this?

The young girl said, "He won some *Order of Cosmic Champions* contest. You know, the one Tommy entered?"

Had Tommy entered a contest? Suzie wasn't sure. Either he'd never told her, or he had and she had forgotten. She wasn't sure which scenario made her feel worse, but neither would win her mother of the year.

"Mrs. Grant?"

She shook her head and repositioned on the couch. "I don't understand. Why would he go looking for this Aaron kid?"

Miranda drank more juice. She still looked flushed and nervous, but something else was going on behind her eyes, and Suzie thought the girl was excited. This idea caused a flash of anger, but understanding came quick on its heels. This young girl had broken into the house in an attempt to make sure Tommy was safe. Miranda wasn't excited that Tommy had run off. She was excited to help find him.

The girl said, "I'm not sure. I could be wrong, I guess."

"But you don't think you're wrong." It wasn't a question.

She shook her head with more than a little confidence. "No. I don't. Tommy is a huge fan of the show. He didn't say so, but I could tell losing that contest hurt. And he had this other comic with him that he said is worth a lot of money. Like $1,000! Plus he acted weird about telling me. And then there's everything happening at school. That would make anyone want to run away."

Another shock of cold regret ran through Suzie's stomach. What had been happening at school? This was yet another blind spot. Another unknown aspect of her own son's life she'd somehow missed. Her hands shook with nerves and adrenaline; her heart screamed for her to go find her son *right now. This very instant. Go, run, seek, find!* But her mind warned her to slow down, get all the information, and proceed cautiously. Rushing off blindly helped no one.

Teeth clenched, head beginning to ache, she said, "What do you mean? What's going on at school?"

Miranda's young features constricted in confusion. Her expression bordered on judgment, but Suzie didn't blame her, as she was judging herself far more harshly than this twelve-year-old girl ever could.

Miranda wiped the expression from her face too late, feeling a little ashamed of herself. "He didn't tell you?"

A flash of frustration. "*Miranda*—"

"Sorry. Well . . ." She tugged at her sleeves and looked everywhere but into Suzie's eyes. "He was being bullied. Like, a lot."

"*Bullied?*" She stood in a surge of anger. "By *who*?"

Miranda still wouldn't meet her eyes. "I don't know. Kids at school. I think one of them used to be his best friend or something."

"*Evan?*" She never did like that little snot-nosed—

"I think so, yeah."

A few choice words stood at the ready, but Suzie wasn't about to launch into a tirade in front of Cole Vitalis's daughter. The guy already had it out for Dave for some reason, and she wasn't about to give him any more reason to hate them.

"Miranda. You get yourself home."

She didn't budge from the couch. "What about the mess?"

"Honey." Suzie attempted to express a calm she didn't feel. "I have to find my son." She took the girl's hand. "And you helped with that. As far as I'm concerned, this little B&E never happened. Now get home, and not a word of this to your parents. I'm sure they wouldn't like knowing what you've been doing."

A small smile teased at the corners of Miranda's mouth as Suzie scooted her to the door.

Before leaving, she said, "When you find him, tell Tommy he owes me a drawing."

✳ ✳ ✳

Suzie grabbed the phone and called Dave's work. For once, he was the one to answer, wearing his smarmy car salesman voice. "Hello, and thank you for calling—"

"It's me."

"Oh, hey. What's up?"

The slight twinkle of hope in his voice made Suzie's throat grow tight. He'd been against the split from the beginning, even after they'd both agreed to take the time apart. Every time they spoke, he had that same syrupy gloss to his voice, as if he knew that *this* time, she would beg him to come home.

Suzie swallowed the lump and said, "Tommy ran away. I'm calling the police, but I want you to be here when they arrive."

There was a moment of silence on the other end. No doubt Dave was trying to process the sudden onslaught of information. He stuttered something unintelligible before finally getting words into the right order. "What happened? How do you know—?"

"Just come home. Okay?"

"Yeah, okay. I'll be right there."

He hung up without another word, and Suzie was grateful. She depressed the receiver and got a dial tone. She pressed 9-1-1, her heart thudding with every number.

As the phone rang, she prayed her son was okay.

She prayed Miranda was wrong about his running away.

She prayed she'd have a chance to make things right.

CHAPTER THIRTY-THREE

HOPE

Miranda didn't hesitate a moment outside Tommy's house. She got right onto her bike and kicked off. Partly, she just wanted to leave before Mrs. Grant changed her mind about not telling her parents. But also, the time was getting late, and her mom would be calling her to come down for dinner soon. She didn't want to think about what might happen if she wasn't there to answer.

As she pedaled, her ears quickly got cold. She'd forgotten her hat on Tommy's bedroom floor, but that didn't matter. The old hat wouldn't be missed in the Vitalis household. Stray leaves skittered across the pavement, reminding her of tomorrow's festivities. She'd nearly forgotten Halloween among all the excitement and worry. With the sun dipping below the horizon, some of the houses were already lighting up orange and purple. Big plastic blow molds of ghosts and pumpkins came to life. Fabric bats waved in the air from their fishing line restraints.

Perhaps the confused emotions were due to her age, but Miranda couldn't figure out if she was happy, sad, scared, or excited. Maybe some crazy mixture of them all? On the one hand, tomorrow was Halloween. Also, she had managed to actually help Tommy's parents figure out that he was missing. On the other hand, he *was* still missing and potentially in trouble. Worse was Miranda's intense desire to continue the search. To be a part of the retrieval team. To ride her bike to Brooklyn if required.

The steep hill took over and Miranda coasted, her mind locked into the realization that she was disappointed she couldn't help any further. Her part in the story was over, and it was hard to come to terms with that. There was little she could do at that point, and there was no way her parents would ever allow her to remain involved. In fact, if they knew she'd been *this* involved, her punishment might very well extend straight through Halloween. Never mind trick-or-treating, carving pumpkins, or watching a scary movie.

No, there was nothing left for her to do but hope Tommy returned unharmed. *Unharmed* being the operative word. Because in the vast dark of an October night, terrible faceless things roamed free, ready to devour little boys who strayed from the path. This Halloween, Miranda feared Tommy might face some of the world's true demons. And this scared her more than witches and ghosts ever could.

CHAPTER THIRTY-FOUR

THE ROAD TO BROOKLYN

Having said his goodbyes, Tommy, along with Fierce Phantos, Lachlan, and Levi, piled into the yellow Oldsmobile Delta and sped off into the deepening dark of dusk. Tommy shoved his bags onto the floor in the back. F.P. was scrunched, crunched, and crippled into the small space, turning the once towering giant into a hunched joke.

Phantos groaned and tried to shift, barely accomplishing the feat. "How far to Brooklyn, Tommy?"

He bowed his head closer to his imaginary friend and tried to reply as quietly as possible. "I don't know. Check your whatchamacallit."

F.P. bent his arm in what seemed a painful pursuit and tapped at the holographic keyboard until the alien language appeared. Again Tommy noted something that appeared to be a timer counting down.

Before he could ask about it, Phantos yelled, "No!"

Tommy's heart sped. "What's wrong?"

F.P.'s hologram face was the picture of terror. "The drive will take *six hours*."

He rolled his eyes. "You'll deal."

Though, that did cause Tommy to wonder. He checked his watch. *4:16.* "Hey, guys? When does that concert start? It's already past four."

Levi didn't turn away from the road. "It's a midnight Halloween show. We should get there for the gate opening."

He figured they knew what they were doing, but Tommy wouldn't have cut it so close. He lifted his backpack and dug around for something to eat, hours having passed since his last bite of food. Worse than the hunger, he was exhausted, his body aching from a long day of travel and battle. The first thing he pulled out was a BarNone candy bar, and he decided that was good enough.

"So, kid." Lachlan turned and stared. "You bring enough for the whole class, or what?"

Levi concentrated on driving, but he did glance into the rearview when Tommy started searching for other snacks. Apparently, they hadn't had time for dinner either. There were a bunch of different goodies, but no more BarNones.

"I have Shark Bites, cheese balls, Kudos, Hostess apple pies—"

"Apple pie me!" Lachlan cut in. He shoved his hand at Tommy and wiggled his fingers.

"Apple pie for Lock, check."

The older boy took the package, his mouth hanging open in surprise, but not because of the snack. His eyes shimmered. A smile teased at the corner of his mouth and he sputtered, "You . . . you called me *Lock*." He broke into a huge smile and excitedly pushed Levi's shoulder.

"Hey, I'm driving."

"He called me *Lock*!"

"He sure did, buddy."

Lachlan couldn't stop smiling. "No one ever calls me Lock. Not really." He nodded approvingly. "Okay. You're all right, Tommy. You're all right." As Lock tore into his snack, Tommy could hear him mutter, "*Lock*. Outstanding."

Even through the exhaustion and anxiety, Tommy brightened. The kid wasn't so bad after all.

Phantos moaned forlornly, "Are we there yet?"

"Are you kidding?"

"Huh?" Lock eyed him questioningly.

"Uh, nothing. Just thought I had more candy bars."

Levi said, "We'll have a pit stop in a couple hours. Then you can make good on your end of the bargain, get more candy, some other stuff. In the meantime, hit me with those cheese balls."

"You got it." Tommy handed the bag to Lock, who tore it open and handed it to Levi.

He munched on a few and said, "How'd you get hooked up with Lane anyway?"

Tommy's throat tightened. He was worried about this part of the trip. A full six-hour interrogation. Two teens ready to pull at the loose strings of his story. The different scenarios had already played through his head. In one, the trip took on the dread tones of a fever dream. The car became Travis Miller's red beast. And like that ill-fated ride home, Levi and Lock brought Tommy to a deserted parking lot in the middle of nowhere and proceeded to beat the crap out of him, then drive away laughing. In another scenario, the two strangers—and they *were* strangers, having only met minutes earlier—admitted they were never actually going to Brooklyn. No, they were out looking for *drugs*. And they were going to force Tommy to do the drugs too!

During his last year in elementary school, Tommy's teachers showed a string of scary videos, reinforced by guest speakers who discussed the dangers of drugs with a capital "D." The videos showed irreversible damage: sores, rotting teeth, weight loss, death. All from a single puff of a marijuana cigarette. What one speaker called a *joint*, twisting the word to express the appropriate outrage. They hadn't been able to get Nancy Reagan to come to their little school, but the "Just Say No" campaign had arrived in full force nonetheless.

His dad tried to explain that the presentations were mostly scare tactics. He said a lot of what the guests told him was overblown and some of it outright lies. But this admission only confused matters, because at eleven years old, you were supposed to believe everything your teachers *and* parents said. When they contradicted each other, Tommy didn't know who to believe. What with the guest speakers, after-school specials, and McGruff the Crime Dog, his dad's speech had sounded ill-informed. So, even with his father's good intentions, Tommy continued to fear Drugs like some unseen reaper, ready to steal his sanity, health, and life.

"Earth to Tommy. Earth to Tommy."

"Huh?"

Levi laughed. "How'd you meet Lane?"

Duh, the interrogation. "We were all at The Arcade."

"Righteous. Love that place."

"It was awesome. First time I'd ever been in one so huge."

"Seriously?"

"Wait," Levi interrupted. "Are you not from Pittsburgh?"

Crapola. They knew he was going to Brooklyn, but he hadn't mentioned the first leg of his trip. Would the omission matter? He glanced at Phantos for a little guidance, but his hero friend was busy sulking.

"Well," Tommy said. "No. I'm from Ohio."

"Dude," Lock said. "Kinda left that part out."

"Yeah . . ."

Levi tapped at the wheel of his car. "You're not supposed to be traveling alone, are you?"

That had fallen apart rather quickly. The small interior of the car pushed in, claustrophobic. The fake pine smell of the air freshener clung sickeningly to his nostrils, nauseating him. "My parents said it's okay."

"No way," Lock said. "How are they gonna let a kid travel alone across three states?" To Levi, he said, "Mom and Dad almost didn't even let us drive to the show tonight, and this kid's parents send him on a bus to Brooklyn?"

Levi eyed Tommy in the rear view. "Yeah . . . I dunno, kid. You lying to us?"

"No, I swe—"

"Just tell us the truth, man."

Tommy nudged F.P.

He stared back with half-lidded eyes. "Are we there yet?"

No help there. And really, there were only two choices. Double down on the lie or trust the two teens and tell them the truth. He wasn't sure it would matter either way. If he lied, they wouldn't believe him and would probably force him to call his parents from the next pay phone they found. And if he told the truth, the same result. He hated lying anyway, and he'd felt pretty awful about the ones he told.

"They don't know. I ran away."

"Great! That's just great! What did I tell you, Levi!"

"I'm gonna go back," Tommy amended. "It's not like I'm running away forever. I just . . . I need to do something."

"In Brooklyn?" Levi asked. "What could you possibly—?"

"It's hard to explain. But please, I promise. I won't tell anyone you brought me. You won't get in trouble."

The teens in the front of the car fell silent. Levi kept driving. Lock stared at his brother, probably expecting some kind of ruling. Tommy waited, his heart in his throat.

And Phantos? Well, Phantos said, "Are we there yet?" and passed out.

CHAPTER THIRTY-FIVE
INTERROGATION

Run off? Dave couldn't wrap his head around the idea. Where would Tommy go? And *why*? He strangled the steering wheel as he sped down the winding back roads, hoping he didn't slam into a deer. Getting into an accident was a real possibility because his mind kept wandering back to Tommy. He barely saw the blacktop before him.

"The hell were you thinking!" he yelled, then punched the horn, startling himself with the sudden honk. Of course, he had a pretty good idea what Tommy was thinking. Dave had dropped the ball. He'd messed up his marriage, screwed up being a father, and damn near lost his job in the process. Nothing much was going right for poor old Dave Grant these days if he was being honest, and he had let it affect the people he loved most.

Why had Tommy run away? He clenched his jaw and depressed the gas pedal even farther. "Because I wasn't there for him."

The words tasted like bile, but they rang true.

The only thing left to do was face the consequences and hope there was still time to make things right.

* * *

When Dave pulled up to the house, a police cruiser was parked out front. Floating in a daze from the car to the house, he entered and found Suzie on the couch. A lean young officer sat across from her on a kitchen chair she must have dragged in. There were two untouched mugs of black coffee on the table between them.

When Suzie's eyes locked with Dave's, for the briefest moment, he saw the woman he'd married. She jumped from the couch and ensnared him in a bear hug of desperation. She pressed her face against his neck, the wetness of her tears pooling there like lava. She mumbled something unintelligible. He squeezed her, saying nothing, only taking what comfort he could from the temporary ceasefire, and giving whatever he could back. After another moment, he realized what Suzie was repeating in garbled sobs: "It's our fault. It's our fault. It's our fault." Over and over again, like a mantra. Like self-flagellation. The pain came tenfold as he acknowledged, of course, that she was right.

When their embrace broke, the officer was standing with his head bowed, waiting patiently. His name tag identified him as Officer Randall.

Dave wiped tears away with the back of his hand. "Sorry," he said, not knowing why he apologized. "I'm Dave Grant. Tommy's father. Suzie's . . ." He trailed off, then sat on the couch.

Suzie followed, but the officer stopped her. "Actually, ma'am. If possible, I'd like to speak to your husband privately."

She puckered her face and drew away. "Why can't I stay?"

Officer Randall nodded as if he'd expected this. "You can, if you insist, Mrs. Grant. But part of the procedure is to speak to the parents separately. Would that be okay with you?"

She shook her head, a curt gesture. Suzie sat hard on the couch and crossed her arms. "No. Dave doesn't know anything, and there's no reason I can't stay."

He nodded and jotted something down in his pad before sitting once again. He watched Dave for a moment, assessing. "When was the last time you saw Tommy, Mr. Grant?"

He scratched his head and looked at Suzie. He knew exactly when it was but hated to say.

"Sir?"

"Yeah." A deep breath cleared frustration and fear, if only momentarily. "Last night. He walked in on me packing my bags."

"Because of the separation?"

"That's right."

"And did Tommy say anything that would have indicated his desire to run away?"

This question was like a stab to the heart. What had they talked about? Had Tommy been looking for help? Was there something Dave could have done? He shook his head. "I can't remember. No. I don't think so."

More scribbling in the notepad. More quiet nodding. No judgment there; at least none that Dave could see. He supposed police got used to things like this. Or at least became adept at hiding their thoughts.

"And who has custody? Have there been any disputes about this?"

Custody? Dave shook his head again. He'd never even thought about it. Hadn't considered where Tommy might live once the split was finalized. Once they were actually divorced.

Suzie saved him from answering. "We both have custody. There haven't been any disputes."

Officer Randall did some more nodding. He was very good at it. The man could teach a masterclass in the art of head movement. "And the last person to see Tommy?"

"I already told you—" Suzie began.

"The question is for Mr. Grant."

"Right. I'm not sure. Might have been me last night unless you saw him this morning?" He asked this of Suzie, who shook her head.

"I was in bed when he left. Then I went out on job interviews."

"Was this normal? For Tommy to leave so early?"

Dave said, "Sure. On a Saturday? Absolutely."

"Like I told you," Suzie jabbed.

The officer wiped his forehead and sighed, showing more expression than before. "I have most of what I need here. We've already broadcast the initial description you gave over the phone. Once I return to the station, I'll file a missing person report with NCIC-MPF. That is the National Crime Information Center Missing Persons File." He stood and put the pad away. "But first, I'd like to ask your permission to search the house."

Suzie stood fast. "Search the . . . *Why?*"

His professional demeanor broke. "Children sometimes find the darnedest places to hide, Mrs. Grant." The man quirked a bemused smile, perhaps remembering finding one supposedly missing youngster under the sink or in a closet. The expression made Officer Randall look even younger, as if he'd just graduated high school.

"I already looked around the whole house," she replied.

"Even so." He held his hands out. "With your permission? Wouldn't it be better if Tommy were here and not on his way to Brooklyn?"

"*Brooklyn?*" Dave exclaimed. "What are you talking about?" Now he stood, his legs shaky and barely there.

The officer examined Suzie.

She shook her head. "Okay, you go search." Then to Dave, "Come with me. I'll explain."

A sense of unease cascaded over Dave's skin like cold rainwater. A familiar pit opened in his stomach, reminding him of the lost years. The ones when he still strove to be an artist, still eked out a life on his own terms. In some ways, those were his happiest days. But mostly he had felt hollowed out by fear. Fear that he wouldn't be able to provide for his family. Fear that his father was right when he called Dave a waste of a man. A terror so great it tainted every moment with a black stain that remained long after he abandoned his dreams for a car dealership and a mortgage.

Despite the dire reminders of a not-so-distant past clawing at his insides, Dave followed his wife—*yes*, he thought defiantly, *she is still my wife*—to the kitchen. His eyes found a scattering of broken glass and dried juice. "What happened?"

Suzie peered past Dave and whispered conspiratorially, "Wait until he goes upstairs."

Officer Randall was touring the living room and taking brief notes, though what he could have possibly found worth writing eluded Dave. "Why—?"

"*Shh*. Just wait."

In the quiet of the kitchen, he had time to note Suzie's perfume. The floral expensive one she only wore for special occasions. He guessed interviews were as special as the occasions got these days.

"Okay." She backed away and pointed at the mess on the floor. "Miranda Vitalis broke into our house today. I left that bit out when Officer Randall was questioning me."

"*What?*" The last name echoed in his head. "Wait, you mean—?"

"Cole's daughter. Yeah."

The hollow pit in Dave's stomach filled with fire. "I *hate* that guy," he hissed.

"Yes, I know."

"And do you know he almost got me fired?"

She rolled her eyes. "Yes."

"Right." Of course she knew. He must have railed on about the incident after one too many drinks on countless nights. The raging lunatic almost smashed up a brand-new Mustang during a test drive, and somehow *Dave* was to blame? And now his daughter . . . ?

"Hold on. Why did his *daughter* break in?"

"Aha. Welcome back to the land of the living."

"Gimme a break. Just spill."

Another eye roll. If Officer Randall could teach a masterclass in head nods, then Suzanne Grant could lecture at a symposium for eye rolling. "Miranda was worried about Tommy. She had an idea he might have run away. If it wasn't for her, we wouldn't know about Brooklyn. A clerk from the bus station called and mentioned New York, but that might as well be New Guinea for all the good it would have done."

"How'd she know?"

"Something about a contest he entered for that cartoon, *Order of Cosmic Champions*. He entered and lost, but the kid who won lives in Brooklyn."

"So?"

"So, Miranda thinks—"

"She *thinks*? We're taking the guesswork of a twelve-year-old girl as fact now?"

"Yeah, but—"

"You know that's crazy, right?" Dave began to pace around the kitchen. "So Cole's daughter breaks in here, destroys the kitchen, and then tells you Tommy ran away to Brooklyn, and you just *believe* her?"

"Come on, that's not how—"

"Don't 'come on' me!" His raised voice caused Suzie to fall back a step. She looked past Dave and he remembered the cop. Shouting at his wife was a quick way to shift undue focus back onto him. Randall obviously thought Dave could have kidnapped Tommy. Why else the pointed questions and suspicious glares?

"*Dave.*" She used her chiding tone. The one usually reserved for when Tommy was in close proximity and she didn't want their fighting to reach his ears. *Tommy heard every fight*, he realized. They weren't able to hide a thing, and Tommy knew exactly how broken their lives had become.

"Sorry. Just . . . explain this to me. Make me understand."

Dave pushed his hatred for Cole into the recesses of his mind. He remained quiet and listened to his wife. She told him about the contest, the losing entry, and *Strange Tales #1*. She told him about the bullying and fights. She told him *everything*, and with every new piece of information, Dave began to understand.

Dave began to believe.

He sat with these new epiphanies about his son for quiet minutes, even as Officer Randall stomped around the second floor. Even as Suzie waited, watching him for some clue to his thoughts.

Finally, he said, "We have to go see Matty at Defender Comics. And then we're going to find our son."

CHAPTER THIRTY-SIX

REST STOP

T he glow of 7-Eleven in October's early dark tugged at opposing emotions deep in Tommy's gut. On the one hand, Halloween called with its tempting allure of candy and mystery. He thought about what he carried in his duffel bag, and memories of Halloweens past caused a happy little chill to race through his nerve endings. However, on the tail of the pleasant reveries, his current predicament rode swift and scary. Sharp claws of getting lost or abducted dug deep into his flesh.

Levi and Lachlan fueled the car while Tommy approached the store with his mental list of snack demands. Of course, he knew the real reason for the earlier-than-scheduled pit stop was for the brothers to discuss in private what to do with Tommy.

He pushed into the fluorescent interior of the store and caught the smell of sizzling hot dogs and cola. Another momentary surge of calm before the undercurrent of despair dragged him beneath the waves again. He tried repeating the list in his head to keep from worrying. *Reese's Pieces, Whatchamacallit, orange Slurpee, Big Gulp of Coke, Funyuns, and Cool Ranch Doritos.* A veritable smorgasbord of the refined teenage palate. The brothers were taking advantage of the deal struck, asking for so many snacks, but Tommy didn't dare refuse. Not when they had every right to force him to call home.

Phantos strode next to the boy and stretched his long limbs, yawning loudly. "Ah, it feels good to extract myself from that abysmal torture device. The trip to Brooklyn has been completed at long last. Favored by the Myragran, we are!"

"*Dude.*" Phantos's unbridled joy broke Tommy's heart, considering they were still at least five hours from their destination.

Tommy placed a hand on F.P.'s arm. "We're still in Pennsylvania."

F.P.'s expression collapsed into a toxic pit of anguish. He fell to his knees, and with outstretched hands, screamed, "*Nooo!*"

Tommy could almost see the camera perspective pull out for maximum effect. "Drama queen."

"The Myragran have forsaken me."

"Take a chill pill." Tommy rubbed his face. "We have more important things to consider than leg room."

Phantos reached out to Tommy like a starving man seeking sustenance. "Go without me, young Tommy. I have been . . ." He placed his hands at the base of his helmet and choked pathetically. "Defeated." Phantos fell onto his stomach, arms splayed.

"You're not getting out of this that easily."

F.P. peeked through a half-lidded eye.

"Enjoy your break, because if Lock and Levi don't rat us out, we have a long drive." Tommy left Phantos sprawled on the linoleum floor of the 7-Eleven and nearly bumped into the narrow-shouldered cashier. He peered with glassy eyes from behind stringy hair, leaning on the handle of his broom. "Who you talking to, kid?" He sounded genuinely interested.

Your mother sprung to Tommy's mind as a possible retort (a favorite of his junior high classmates), but he'd never actually say something like that to a stranger. Not even one that looked a lot like the people in those "Scared Straight" videos.

Instead he said, "Myself," without a hint of self-consciousness.

"Oh," the clerk said, nodding approvingly. "Cool." He swept at the clean floor.

"Bathroom?"

The cashier kept sweeping in the direction of Phantos, then moved around the splayed figure as if he sensed something there. "In the back corner." He pointed to the far right of the store.

"Thanks." He watched the clerk sweep for another moment. The broom never came in contact with Phantos, and the more Tommy thought about it, the more he became convinced that no one had ever walked through the space Phantos occupied. A strange chill ran through him and he hurried to the bathroom, having to pee more urgently than before.

* * *

The bathroom had only two stalls, a single urinal, and smelled strongly of sick. Black patches of filth spread across the tile floor, stall doors hung open revealing a graffiti-covered mass of black lettering, and the ceiling lights buzzed like dying flies. Though the filthy room was empty, Tommy perceived unseen eyes embedded in the walls.

He stepped to the urinal and, after a moment's convincing, relieved himself. Tommy pondered the likelihood of the brothers allowing him to continue the trip with them. Would they overlook the fact that he was a runaway? The notion that his parents had no idea where

277

he was? Would they actually consider taking him the rest of the way to Brooklyn?

A shift in the air—an alien displacement—caused Tommy to shiver. The lights buzzed and sizzled a hot electric warning. He felt like insects were scurrying over his skin, tickling the fine hairs of his arms and legs, probing his ear canal with tiny pincers.

"*Father*," a voice whispered, cold and dead.

Luckily Tommy had finished his business, because if he hadn't, the shock would have ceased operations. He barely had time to zip up before spinning around to confront—

No one.

The lights continued to buzz lazily, though it felt as if the reverberations were inside his brain. The room thrummed in time with the vibrations. The light grew dim and hazy, like a cemetery in the fog. A strange dizziness overcame him, and he stumbled a step. The idea of fainting onto the obscenely gross floor of a convenience store bathroom was the only thing that kept Tommy on his feet.

He stepped to the sink and peered into the greasy mirror, streaked and spotted with filth. His own distorted visage stared back from the reflected surface, but he was not alone.

Mechani-Ghoul stood behind him, the empty sockets of his skeletal face glaring from behind his gleaming blue armor. This was not Tommy's innocent sketch, or even a cartoonist's vision of the villain. No, this was Mechani-Ghoul manifest in reality, like Fierce Phantos before him.

Tommy spun and leaned against the sink in sickening shock.

Mechani-Ghoul remained. His creation smelled like a mechanic shop, all gasoline and grease. Imposing was barely big enough a word to describe how the mechanized bogeyman devoured the cramped space. He clenched his metal-clawed hand. His other arm, a giant cleaver from elbow down, swung impatiently. A true murder machine.

"What are you doing here?" His small voice was like the squeak of a chipmunk. His words fell tinny and hollow onto the floor.

The creature opened its bone jaw, and a clicking sound, like that of a beetle, echoed from deep within his throat. It would have sounded like laughing had the utterance not been devoid of humanity. By degrees, the insane ticking, clicking, tapping died. Mechani-Ghoul tilted his head and spoke. "Father."

Tommy's soul caught fire. How could such a word be so gruesome? He tried to back away but found he was already pressed hard against the cold porcelain sink. He said, "No." The word, barely audible, was not a response. It was a plea. A prayer.

Mechani-Ghoul ratcheted forward, slowly. Deliberately. Tommy could see into the hollow holes of its eyes. He could see straight through to the nothing inside.

The monster observed Tommy as it clenched mechanized claws. Sharpened teeth parted, and the insectile clicking resumed. From this unenviable distance, the *tuk-tuk-tuk* was a copious chorus of tiny beasts, abandoned to torment inside the abomination of Tommy's own creation.

Mechani-Ghoul closed the remaining gap and held its clawed hand beside Tommy's face. "Father." More threat than observation.

Tommy slid away from the sink, inching to the exit. "No," he said again. "It was a mistake."

"Father."

"No!" Stronger now, the fear gripping his heart and mind like talons, unwilling to release.

Metal feet scraped the tile floor, digging furrows into the ceramic. *Tuk-tuk-tuk-tuk-tuk.* The voice grated. "Father." Metal on a grinding wheel. "Father." A chainsaw chewing birch. "*Father.*"

Tommy grasped the door handle, ready to flee. "Why are you doing this?"

Tuk-tuk-tuk. "Father." *Tuk-tuk-tuk-tuk.* "You called us, Father. You *begged* for salvation. We have heard your plea." *Tuk-tuk-tuk-tuk.* "Now, Skullagar awaits."

When the thing's bony mouth contorted into something approximating a smile, Tommy's insides turned to liquid and the world threatened to swim away. It was a ruinous grin, imbibed with malice and devastation. Death on parade.

Tommy turned and fled, his legs under him like pipe cleaners, wobbly and bending at odd angles. He ran just the same. The false light of the store streamed by like headlights on a lost highway.

Tommy had no thought left. He had no fight. No hope.

Only terror.

✳ ✳ ✳

The brothers had told him not to take long, given their tight timeline, but when Tommy burst through the doors of the 7-Eleven and into the cool evening, he knew he needed time to get his head on straight. Levi was still pumping gas, and Lock stood off to the side, gesturing wildly as he spoke. His voice was muffled by highway noises and wind, but Tommy didn't need to hear the words to know Lock was lobbying for ditching the troublesome kid, handing him over to the authorities.

Tommy stepped to the side of the building, out of the brothers' line of sight, and wrapped his arms around himself. A terror wormed into his every cell, a fear he had become intimately acquainted with.

"I made a mistake," he whined, not liking the sound if his own voice. He swiped at wet eyes and cleared his throat, trying to ignore the welling emotions. The gruesome villain had called him *father*. Aaron Beltzer created a hero, and Tommy had created evil. Mechani-Ghoul had come to remind him of this. To remind him of his discourse with Skullagar. To revive Tommy's desire for revenge against the bullies of Ende Junior

High. Tommy was so embedded in the dogma of the blackguard that he, even then, was attempting to manufacture Mechani-Ghoul's action figure with the help of Aaron Beltzer.

He sniffed and wiped at his nose. "Because none of this is real." He said this out loud because he needed to hear the words, even if he no longer believed them. All that mattered in that moment was getting the brothers' requested snacks and making sure he still had a ride to Brooklyn.

Otherwise, he'd be on his own.

All by himself.

Again.

✳ ✳ ✳

Tommy was able to wrap up his purchases before Lock and Levi finished talking.

He approached them cautiously, a plastic bag jam-packed with snacks and a cup carrier with their two drinks (plus a medium Dr Pepper for himself) in hand. They eyed him for a moment, then relieved him of his burden.

Levi drank deeply of the Big Gulp. "We don't want to miss this concert, little dude."

"Okay . . ."

Lock held his orange Slurpee but didn't drink yet. He looked more worried than Levi, his age perhaps fueling doubt. "I don't like just leaving you in the middle of the night in Brooklyn."

"I don't either," Levi added. "I mean, what if you, like, get kidnapped or something. And your parents are probably freaking out right now."

"Maybe."

"But," Levi continued, "you've gotten this far without any trouble." He glanced at Lock with a strained expression. "And we *really* want to go to this concert. The tickets were expensive."

Tommy drank some of his Dr Pepper. He nodded thoughtfully and said, "So let's go. You don't have to worry about me. I'm not your problem once we hit Brooklyn."

"That doesn't make me feel any better," Lock said.

"Doesn't matter. I can take care of myself. Just pretend you never saw me. Lane never brought me to your place, you never agreed to bring me along. None of it ever happened." The cup chilled Tommy's hand as he waited for their response. No colder than his insides had been when Mechani-Ghoul manifested.

Levi checked his watch and glanced pleadingly at Lock. When his brother didn't say anything, Levi made the call. "Fine, let's just go already."

"Good," Tommy said.

Lock didn't look pleased with the decision, but he didn't say a word in contradiction. The two hadn't made a smart choice, but Tommy guessed kids their age weren't always keyed into the potential consequences. He had a reflective moment when he realized this applied to himself as well, but being even younger than Levi and Lock, he pushed away the notion twice as fast.

As they all piled back into the car, Phantos, who'd been strangely absent, groaned pathetically. "If I do not make it, I wish you luck on the rest of your journey."

Tommy rolled his eyes and got in.

CHAPTER THIRTY-SEVEN

BREAD CRUMBS

Every muscle in Suzie's body tensed. She could feel the tendons in her neck pop and her jaws clench. Dave was driving far too fast on the curvaceous back roads, but that wasn't what caused her body to coil like a snake ready to strike. She was pissed because Dave was doing what he always did and had shoved Suzie aside to take charge. Those were his words. *Take charge.* Like she hadn't had things under control when he arrived. Like she wasn't the one who had figured out Tommy was missing and where he had gone.

Now hold on there, missy. Suzie bit down even harder. The truth was she *wasn't* the one. Miranda had discovered Tommy's absence, and if Suzie was being brutally honest, she must also admit many more hours would have passed before she noticed anything amiss. So fractured and dismantled were her parental duties as of late, Suzie couldn't be sure she would have even noticed until she went upstairs to say good night to her sweet boy. After all, meals had lately been of the TV dinner variety and eaten in solitude. Dave of course was no longer there to pick up the slack either.

They were to blame for this, Dave and Suzie both.

"We'll get what we need from Matty." Dave said this without looking over, and it sounded more like he was convincing himself than talking to Suzie.

"I hope so."

He appeared frantic, his eyes darting around the road, his mouth twitching. *At least he was sober,* she thought.

"We will." This was uttered a bit too forcefully. A bit too defensively.

"Officer Randall said they'd contact the Beltzers and local police in Brooklyn."

"I know, I know." Dismissive. Annoyed.

"Maybe we should just let them—"

"No." He gripped the steering wheel, his knuckles turning white. "They'll do their job, but I want to be there."

"There's a reason they wouldn't give us the address or phone number, Dave."

He slammed his hand down on the steering wheel and looked over, eyes blazing. "Do you actually believe that, or are you just so against me that you'll contradict every damn thing I say?"

"Watch the road."

He huffed and chuckled dryly. "*Watch the road.* Sure." Dave took a breath, visibly calming himself over the course of a minute. A long minute through which Suzie dared not speak. No matter the intention of her words, or the calm tone in which they were spoken, he would take each syllable as a fresh attack and only grow angrier with each utterance. She'd seen him lose his temper plenty of times and knew the only way it'd cool was through silence.

Eventually, he said, "I'm sorry. I just . . . I can't sit back and do nothing."

"I'm sorry too." Her mind and heart were on fire, but she thought there was a shred of truth to what Dave said. She did sometimes go on the defensive right out of the gate. Searching her heart, she knew she felt the same way.

"You're right." They had to drive to Brooklyn and do what they could while the police did what *they* could.

He parked near Defender Comics. "Yeah?" He looked over, his expression soft again.

Her own expression softened then too. They had to be in this together. One last time. "Yes."

"Officer Randall knew we'd call information and get the phone number and address ourselves. He'd have to be a dope to think otherwise."

"Maybe he knew there'd be too many Beltzers in the listings."

Dave opened his door, placing one foot on the road. "Maybe. But we have an ace up our sleeve."

* * *

The comic shop smelled exactly as she remembered: a strange combination of a Grateful Dead concert and the library. She had a pretty good idea Matty was smoking dope in the back room and covering it up with incense. There were times she nearly forbade Tommy from patronizing the shop, until she reminded herself of her own youthful follies and Matty's friendship with Dave.

Matty had his feet on the counter and his nose in a copy of *The Beast House*. When he peeled his eyes away from the pages and saw Dave, the man lit up like a slot machine hitting jackpot.

"No way." He almost fell over trying to pry his legs from the counter. He dropped the book onto the floor and planted his hands, leaning over the glass. "Is this actually Dave Grant wandering into the forbidden domain of Defender Comics? And with Suzie, no less!"

"Hey, Matty." Dave's expression remained somber, and his voice relayed the seriousness of the visit.

"Whoa." Matty squinted as if a cop had just shined a flashlight in his eyes. "This isn't a social visit, I take it?"

"I wish it were, buddy."

Suzie cleared her throat. This was no time for reunions.

Dave said, "Tommy's gone missing. Run off."

To his credit, Matty appeared as crestfallen as a real parent. His mouth dropped open, and he went almost completely pale. He placed a hand over his stomach as if he'd become physically ill from the news, and maybe he had. "Tell me."

Suzie took over. "One of his friends from school told us he was upset about losing some contest—"

"*Order of Cosmic Champions*," Dave put in.

"Right. He entered one of his sketches and lost. And with everything else going on . . ."

Matty's eyes shifted to Dave for a second, questioning, but he didn't ask, and Suzie was glad for his discretion.

Dave said, "His friend thinks he went to find the winner. A kid named Aaron Beltzer."

"In Brooklyn," Suzie finished, feeling nauseated at the words.

Matty somehow grew even paler. Now both hands were over his stomach. His eyes shifted around. "He was here yesterday."

"To buy the magazine? We need a copy."

"That's why we're here," Suzie agreed.

Matty shook his head, his dreads jostling. "No. I mean, yes. He came in days before and got the magazine, but that's not why he was here yesterday." Matty rubbed his face. "I'm sorry, man. Dave, listen, if I thought for even a second—"

"Talk!" Suzie nearly leapt over the counter.

Matty's eyes became clear and alert. "Tommy was in here with the comic you gave him, Dave. *Strange Tales*. He was trying to sell it to me."

"*What?*"

Suzie put her hand on Dave's shoulder. They'd known Tommy had the comic with him. Miranda had said as much. But selling it? "I don't get it."

Dave said, "It's worth a lot of money. Like, hundreds at least."

"He fed me some line about using the money for his college fund, but I told him no. You think he was trying to get money to run away?" Matty's face went slack. He hit himself on the head. *Hard*. "Stupid! If I'd only been *thinking*. If I had any idea—"

Suzie stopped him by placing a hand on his wrist. She didn't want to see Matty pummel himself, but she also wanted to get out of there as quickly as possible. "There was no way for you to know."

Dave said, "We need a copy of that magazine. And then we need your phone."

He nodded his head frantically. "Of course." He stumbled out to one of the displays and tore a magazine from the shelf. "Last cah-cah-copy. It's yours, no ch-ch-ch—"

Suzie grabbed the magazine and ran through the pages. Dave had mentioned Matty would sometimes, when nervous, lapse into his adolescent speech impediment. She'd never heard it before, and whether fair or not, she saw Matty in a new light. His style, the way he wore his hair, the way he carried himself—she considered the possibility it was all camouflage. She'd heard stories about how kids who liked comic books and sci-fi were treated. Maybe Matty hadn't had an easy childhood.

Suzie refocused on the magazine and found what they needed. "Here!"

The page was a full spread with a picture of Aaron, his sketch, and an article. Right at the top was the information they already had: "And the winner is . . . Aaron Beltzer of Brooklyn, New York, with his entry *Fierce Phantos!*" Of course, if that were all Tommy had, he probably wouldn't be able to find Aaron. As they'd discovered when they called information, there were far too many Beltzers in Brooklyn to easily narrow down. But if they had . . .

"Here!" Suzie ran her finger over the spot in the article once more and found her place. She read aloud, "Aaron's parents, Fran and Benny, say they always knew their son had a wonderful ability to create."

Matty said, "Huh?"

"The parents' names, Matty." Dave's tone bordered on patronizing. "We'll be able to get the right phone number and address from information now."

"Assuming they aren't unlisted," he said.

A mild unease wormed around Suzie's thoughts. She hated Matty for saying it but couldn't deny she'd worried about that very issue. Because even if the cops could get the right address, Tommy *couldn't*, which would further mean he could be anywhere in Brooklyn, trying every Beltzer in the book.

If he arrived in Brooklyn at all. The interloper in her mind clawed at sense and reason, cavorting through the carefully nurtured garden of her plan, tearing out the flowering plants by the roots and flinging them with reckless glee.

Dave said, "Just give me the phone. Tommy is a smart kid. He's gonna be fine."

Suzie didn't realize how much she needed to hear those words, and her runaway heart slowed by degrees.

While Dave dialed, she asked Matty, "Is there anything else you can think of? Anything that might help?"

Matty pulled at his dreads and explored the ceiling. He took some deep breaths and Suzie got the impression he was suppressing his stutter. "I don't think so?" He yanked his hair some more. "I saw him on his bike headed out of town. You might want to check the bus station?"

"They called when Tommy tried to get a ticket. He didn't get on a bus. We know that much."

"Maybe he didn't even get out of town then?"

Suzie nodded. This is of course what she and Dave had hoped. That Tommy, frustrated and angry, had biked off somewhere in town and simply hadn't come home yet. "The police have units looking, and they put out, whatever you call it, you know. An alert?"

Matty nodded, finally dropping his hands from his hair. No more stuttering either. His mind was busy working on the puzzle.

Dave got through to someone and was getting the information they needed, but Suzie was focused on Matty. "What is it?"

"That obvious, huh?"

Something about his expression then, and everything since they'd come into the shop, caused a twisting knot of regret to bunch in her chest. She shouldn't have kept Dave away from this place, from Matty. She'd only wanted him to get his head out of the clouds and do right by the family, but she saw in that brief moment of illumination that she'd been too hard. Everyone needs an outlet, and she had stolen Dave's. He'd replaced the lost dream with liquor instead of family, and that was on him. But she knew then, she'd played her part too.

Suzie said, "Pretty obvious, yeah. What are you thinking?"

He nodded once, firmly. Decisively. "You're both going to Brooklyn to look for him?"

"Yes."

He nodded again. "And if he's here in town somewhere? If he comes home when you're both gone?"

Wouldn't be the first time, was her first, cynical thought. Of course, he had a point. One of them would have to stay behind, and she knew neither would volunteer for the job. They were both convinced Tommy had left town, but why? He obviously hadn't gotten on a bus.

Would he have hitchhiked? Ridden his bike to another bus terminal? Called a car service? But without the money from the comic, how would he have—?

"His college fund."

Dave hung up and held a piece of paper out. "Got it!" He tilted his head. "Wait, what did you say?"

"He didn't sell the comic, right? But he was still trying to get a bus ticket. So where did he get the money?"

Dave groaned. "His college fund."

Matty said, "That doesn't mean he left."

"Matty thinks one of us should stay behind, in case Tommy comes back."

Silence ensued, and Suzie thought, *Here comes the fight*. Dave would refuse to stay, and she'd double down. Her muscles tightened as if readying to jab and dodge. But before either could speak, Matty saved them all.

"I can watch the house."

They both turned and stared dumbfounded at the comic shop owner.

"What?" He pouted comically. "You can trust me."

Dave looked questioningly at Suzie. The decision was hers. She appraised the man. They'd known him for years, and of course Dave had been his close friend until she'd intervened. Tommy knew him and spoke to him on the regular. He was a fixture in town, albeit one of the weirder ones.

Suzie closed her eyes and placed her house keys on the counter. "No smoking in the house."

Matty beamed. "I don't smoke."

"*Sure*. No incense either."

He waved the idea away. "You can count on me."

Dave shook Matty's hand slowly. Purposefully. "I know we can, buddy. Thank you."

* * *

Outside the shop, Suzie found herself exploring her husband's face. A face she'd known and loved for a long time. She could almost see the younger version of the man she'd married in the neon light of the comic shop's sign. A man who had his life ahead of him and dreams to keep him afloat. Suzie didn't blame herself for his lost hope, and she didn't think Dave blamed her either. Suzie admitted to herself one last time that she still loved the man. And probably, she always would. But she also knew, undoubtedly, that their married life together was coming to an unceremonious end.

But before they could tear the family apart, they first had to bring the unit back together. "You ready?"

Dave stared into the dark recesses between streetlights on Oak Drive. The car waited. Tommy waited. The night waited. He looked at his wristwatch. "If we leave right now, we'll probably get to Brooklyn around two or three in the morning."

"Okay."

He turned to her, and the illusion of his younger self dissolved before her eyes. She saw, maybe for the first time since he arrived at the house, his five-o'clock shadow, the ruffled shirt under his light jacket. The deep bags, almost bruises, under his eyes. Some of his appearance was due to alcohol, but even more was life, age, and time. The circumstances of the crumbling marriage. She wondered what he saw as he looked at her.

Dave rubbed his eyes. "Should we wait until morning to leave?"

"Are you *kidding*?"

He rubbed his eyes again. "What can we possibly do at three a.m. after driving six or more hours overnight? Wherever Tommy is, he'd be asleep."

"And we'll be there when he wakes up." She laughed mirthlessly. "You were the one fighting to go in the first place!"

"I know." He pulled his hair in frustration. "I know. It's just, the more I think about it—"

"So stop thinking. Matty will be here, the police are on the case, and we're going to Brooklyn. We may not be able to do anything, but you know as well as I do that we can't just sit around waiting."

"We'd go crazy."

She nodded and took his hand. "We'd go crazy."

"Okay. Let's find our boy."

CHAPTER THIRTY-EIGHT

IN THE DARK OF NIGHT

"**H**ey. Hey, little dude?"

"Little? He's taller than *you*."

"Shut up. Come on, Sleeping Beauty. Time to get up."

"Tommy. Wakey, wakey, eggs and bakey."

"That's so dumb."

"*You're* dumb!"

Tommy opened his eyes a crack and watched the two brothers in the front seat attempt to wake him up. The car was dark except for the occasional set of passing headlights. "I'm awake." He realized his head was resting on F.P.'s lap, and he briefly wondered what that looked like to Levi and Lachlan.

"Finally," Lock said. "We made good time."

Tommy sat up and looked at Phantos, whose expression had gone slack and expressionless. Apparently traveling through dimensions wasn't quite as taxing as driving across Pennsylvania in the back seat of an Oldsmobile.

He rubbed the sleep out of his eyes and peered out the window. They were parked in a large lot with what appeared to be hundreds of other vehicles. There were people *everywhere*, most wearing some kind of costume, all walking toward the large building in the distance. "That's where the band is playing?"

Lock hooked a thumb at Tommy. "Sherlock Holmes over here."

He checked his *Order of Cosmic Champions* watch. Ten to eleven. They really had made good time. "How fast were you driving?"

Levi patted the steering wheel. "Fast enough." He turned in his seat and studied Tommy with an expression bordering on pity. "We have to figure out what to do with you."

Fierce Phantos tried to straighten his crooked back. "I do not like the sound of that."

Tommy stifled a laugh. "It's late and I have some money. Do you know how much a hotel room costs?"

Lock said, "Do you think they'll even *give* him a room? He's tall, but he looks young."

"He *is* young." Levi scratched his cheek. "We were planning on just driving straight home after the concert. But, I mean, it *will* be super late. And I'll probably be ready to pass out by then."

"Okay?" Tommy perked.

"Maybe we can all go get a room before the gates open. They'll rent me a room for sure. You can stay there while we go to the concert and then we'll have a place to crash until morning. How's that sound?"

Tommy was half asleep and liked the plan very much. "You think we have time?"

"Sure. We passed a budget motel a few blocks back."

"Looked like a fleabag."

"So what? We're only spending the night, and barely even that."

Tommy stretched. "I'm in."

Lock laughed. "He's in, he says. Like he has a buffet of choices."

Phantos said, "Tommy. If you don't get me out of this tortuous metal box of agony in the next five minutes, I will set off my self-destruct mechanism."

"You have a—?"

Levi turned with his eyebrow arched. "Huh?"

"Nothing. Let's just get to the motel so you don't miss your concert. Pedal to the metal."

Lock laughed again, slapping his knee. "This kid. You heard him, bro. Pedal to the metal!"

✳ ✳ ✳

The motel was indeed a fleabag, despite being a chain. Tommy had heard of the Econo Cabin, and it certainly lived up to its name in both cost and aesthetics. As soon as they pushed through the smudgy glass door, a musky smell of dirty carpeting slapped Tommy across the face. Half the light fixtures boasted burned-out bulbs, and the fabric chairs in the lounge were well worn, to put it nicely.

A curvy woman sat behind the counter with a copy of *Misery* opened to the halfway point. Her red Econo Cabin polo fit so snugly, Tommy felt uncomfortable for staring as long as he did. She placed the book down and teased her puffy black hair with long fingernails. She looked them up and down, apparently assessing, though Tommy couldn't fathom why. "Welcome to the Econo Cabin." She put her elbows on the counter and leaned closer to Levi. "Here for the concert?"

Lock's jaw dropped and he nudged Levi.

Phantos observed quietly.

"Uh, yeah. Came in from Pittsburgh."

She stuck a hand out, palm down. "I'm Lynette."

Tommy didn't understand. Why was she introducing herself? Cashiers never told Tommy their name or shook hands in greeting.

"I'm Levi." He took her hand awkwardly, apparently unsure if he should shake it or kiss it.

"Fascinating," Fierce Phantos said. "I believe we are witnessing some sort of teenage mating ritual."

"Oh, sick!" Tommy blurted, then slapped a hand over his mouth.

"Your little brother?" Lynette said, her tone suggesting she was inquiring about a plate of steamed broccoli.

"Yeah," Levi replied through clenched teeth. "Our parents made us take him, the little brat."

Now those blue mascaraed eyes assessed Tommy, her glossy lips pursed. "He's a cutie." The words didn't match the inflection. Obviously, she saw pickled Brussels sprouts where Tommy stood. She reached out with her Freddy Krueger claws and tapped the counter. "Unless two of you want to bunk together, you'll need adjoining rooms."

"Sure, okay," Levi said, going for his wallet.

Tommy turned away and dug into his backpack, retrieving the $20 he had stashed. He sidled up to Levi, keeping his hands out of sight behind the counter, and pressed the money into the older boy's hand. It was a lot to fork over. He'd never spent more than a few bucks at a time. Most big purchases like video games were made by his mom or dad.

"Excuse me? Lynette?" Tommy asked.

She raised a drawn-on eyebrow.

"Do you have a White Pages?"

"All the rooms have one. Dial 9 to get out. No long distance."

"Okay, thanks."

"So, what?" Lynette nodded at Tommy as she worked the register. "You make your little brother the official bellboy?"

Tommy didn't get it at first. Levi looked over. Understanding smoothed the creases in his forehead. "Ha, good one. Yeah, yeah. He wanted to carry the bags, the little booger."

"Dude," Tommy said.

He pushed Tommy's shoulder playfully, smiling his easy smile. "Just messing around, man. No worries."

Levi sounded awkward, and Tommy figured he was overcompensating, maybe even getting a little worried about the questions. He doubted Lynette cared, but it was perhaps a little strange that Tommy was the only one with baggage: his huge, stuffed duffel hanging from his shoulder, his backpack filled with all manner of road snacks and paraphernalia.

"I've scanned her," Phantos said.

Tommy arched an eyebrow, knowing he'd better not start talking to his imaginary friend out loud again.

"She poses no threat. Her questions are clumsy attempts at . . ." He raised his wrist and tapped his holographic keyboard. "Ah, yes. Clumsy attempts at flirting."

Clumsy?

The woman leaned against the counter again, speaking so quietly that Levi had to inch closer. She smiled and twirled her hair, saying something about the concert. No, there was nothing clumsy about it, Tommy thought. Levi certainly seemed to have become enthralled easily enough.

Lock dropped a wink at Tommy. He smiled back, and a strange sense of happiness flowed through him. It was warm and calming, like summer vacation should feel. The moment almost passed before he understood. Despite the age difference, the rocky start, and the little insults, Levi and Lock weren't treating him like a stranger. They were treating him like a little brother. Like one of the clan, the same way they had messed with Lane back in Pittsburgh.

Tommy didn't have any siblings. Maybe that's why he had been so clingy with Evan. Maybe that's why Evan ended the friendship. These revelations came fast and sudden, nearly dropping Tommy to his knees. He hadn't once considered he'd done something wrong. Evan had been the one to start acting weird. He'd been the one to make new friends and bully Tommy. But what if Evan, at first, merely wanted some space? What if Tommy had become too dependent?

Levi held out the room keys. "Come on. Second floor."

Lynette sat down. "See you after the concert!"

In the stairwell, Lock said, "You okay, Tommy? You look a little green around the gills."

The bags were weighing him down again. Most of the aches and pains had subsided during the long ride, and the nap had done him good, so why the sudden fatigue? "I just realized I may have ruined a friendship. That's all."

They entered through the second-floor landing and turned right.

Lock patted his shoulder. "There's not much in this world that can't be fixed, one way or another." He glanced toward Levi who nodded approvingly. "Our dad says that all the time."

F.P. said, "Good advice. You've chosen your travel mates wisely."

He didn't know about that. They were his companions out of desperation more than choice. But they had proven to be trustworthy and kind. Tommy figured he couldn't ask for much more.

❋ ❋ ❋

The two rooms were tiny and connected by a door next to the small television. They were mirror images of each other, two twin beds in each, a closet-sized bathroom with a standing shower, televisions, and coffee makers with packets of complimentary coffee. The smell in there was a little better than the lobby. Nothing was visibly gross or dirty, which was a relief. He'd expected to turn on the lights and see roaches scurry away.

Tommy held his hand out. "Key, please."

"Yeah . . . *no*." Levi pocketed one and gave Lock the other. "You and Lachlan are bunking up."

His brother turned on him with a glare. "What are you talk—" He cut himself off with a huge smile. "Oh! You actually think you're gonna score with that Lynette chick!"

"You were there." Levi smoothed out his eyebrows. "She's into me."

"She probably acts that way with all the customers."

"Then why did she suggest the two rooms? You're just jealous."

"Ha! Yeah, right. Like anything is gonna happen anyway." He checked his watch. "Dude, we better go."

Tommy looked around, feeling strangely lost again. "Guess I'll see you later."

The boys hesitated. Maybe they were feeling that same sense of emptiness, or maybe they were just worried about Tommy. The moment passed, and Levi said, "Don't do anything we wouldn't do."

"Later, little bro," Lock said, smiling.

Then they were gone, and Tommy was alone again.

Well, not completely alone.

Phantos jumped onto one of the beds and stretched his legs and arms so far that all appendages hung off the small cushion. This didn't seem to bother him one bit. He groaned happily and continued to stretch. "I will never get into another Old Man Mobile as long as I live. Not for all the riches of Evernitia."

"*Oldsmobile*." Tommy rolled his eyes. "Don't make any promises you can't keep. We have to get home somehow."

A strange expression crept onto Phantos's face and he sneaked a glance at his wrist terminal. Tommy didn't have a good view, but the timer was definitely continuing to count down. But to what?

Tommy dropped his duffel on the floor and placed the backpack onto the other bed. "What are you checking on?"

Phantos said, "We're at 87%, Tommy. We now have an 87% chance of completing our quest."

"Going in the right direction." Tommy thought to push the subject, but there were more important things on his mind. He retrieved the *OoCC* magazine and went to the small table where the phone sat. The White Pages was in a drawer along with a Bible, a pad, and pen. He retrieved everything but the Bible.

Phantos sat up. "What are you doing?"

Tommy flipped through the White Pages. "Looking for Aaron's address."

"People post their home locations publicly?" He sounded downright appalled.

"Well . . ." He continued flipping through the pages. "I guess some people don't have addresses in here."

"And if Aaron has no address?"

Only a day earlier, this notion might have sent Tommy spiraling down into a pit of worst-case scenarios. But a single day turned out to be a lot longer than he had ever realized, and Phantos's query barely penetrated his concentration. "One problem at a time."

When he reached the "Beltzers" section of the book, he paused, then counted. "There are twenty-three Beltzers in Brooklyn."

"Is that a lot?"

Tommy shook his head. "Doesn't matter. We have this." He flipped to the article about Aaron and skimmed for the parents' names. He read the important line to Phantos: "Aaron's parents, Fran and Benny, say they always knew their son had a wonderful ability to create."

"Fran and Benny Beltzer."

"Yup." Tommy smiled, feeling even prouder than when he was chosen to represent his elementary school at the county science fair.

F.P. went to Tommy's side. "Now what?"

"We hope there aren't too many *B. Beltzers* in the listings."

"And if there are?"

He chuckled. "What did I say? One problem at a time."

Tommy checked the listings, and this one time, there *were* no problems.

There was only one B. Beltzer, and the address was listed.

CHAPTER THIRTY-NINE
BROOKLYN

Tommy woke up on a bed covered with empty potato chip bags, a half-eaten candy bar, and enough crumbs to attract every roach in New York City. The blinds were drawn, but early morning light still managed to sneak through the gaps, peppering his face with tiny dots of sunshine. Each beam was like a warm kiss on the cheek. Halloween had arrived, and Tommy had big plans.

Stretching, yawning, and scratching, he scanned the small room. Phantos was wedged between the bed and the wall, fiddling with his gun. He had removed the exterior casing and was working on a nest of wires with tools from the side pouch of his holster. Levi and Lock, despite having their own beds spread across two rooms, were cuddled together like puppy dogs on the bed next to Tommy. They must have gotten in super late—or early, Tommy supposed—because he hadn't heard them enter. They both snored so loudly it was a wonder Tommy had slept as long as he did.

"Ah," Phantos said as he squirreled away his tools and snapped the cover back onto his weapon. "Brotherly love."

"Gross." Tommy wriggled out of bed quietly and headed to the bathroom for the old "Triple S," as his dad liked to say. Shower, shave, and . . . Well, he knew exactly what the last "S" stood for, but his dad liked to pretend it meant "smile."

He was so tired that the entire bathroom ritual felt like an extended part of his dreams, all blurred around the edge like watercolors. When he came back into the room, the brothers were still fast asleep. Tommy got dressed, packed his gear, and retrieved the address from the notepad. Levi and Lock's continued slumber made his decision to leave without telling them easy.

But not so easy that he didn't write a note:

Levi and Lock,

Sorry to leave without saying goodbye, but I have a lot to do today. Thank you for the ride and for not ratting me out. I promise not to tell anyone you helped me. I'm leaving my phone number so maybe you both (and Lane, Elliotte, and Carlos) can keep in touch. But please don't call until some time has passed, to make sure I'm back home.

   I hope you had fun at the concert. And sorry Lynette stood you up.

                             —Tommy Grant
                            (555) 095-1983

Tommy added that last part about Lynette with a smirk. Poor guy. He was so confident about his chances with her. At least he had his brother to cuddle with.

✳ ✳ ✳

Lynette wasn't at the front desk as Tommy left, which was a godsend. He had no explanation ready as to why he was wandering onto the streets of Brooklyn without his older brothers. Though, as he skulked through the lobby, he realized she probably wouldn't have cared one way or the other. She may not have even noticed him walk by. The old guy sitting at the desk in her place sure didn't. He just continued to pick his teeth with a torn piece of cigarette box while staring blankly at a small black-and-white television.

Outside, everything looked different in the daylight. He knew this wasn't exactly "The Big City," but Brooklyn was so far removed from his small Ohio town that it might as well have been another planet. There were storefronts everywhere. The sidewalks were lined with businesses just as the streets were lined with cars. Despite the early hour, people drove and walked and gathered. Again, not exactly Manhattan traffic, but more than he was used to.

A cold chill ran through him as he spotted a shadow skulking between parked cars on the other side of the road. Something fast and stealthy. When Phantos didn't react, Tommy dismissed the fantasy figure. He was still pretty tired, and it wouldn't have been the first time he imagined something into being.

He set off to his right and inhaled deeply of contradictory aromas. In one breath, he got exhaust and hot pavement. In another, coffee and bagels greeted him.

"Breakfast?" Phantos said, keeping stride.

"Can you even eat?"

Phantos tapped his helmet. "Do you ask because of the helmet or because I am an android?"

"Uh. Both?" Tommy veered to the bagel shop. *Follow your nose! It always knows!* He imagined Toucan Sam flying overhead.

"I have a nutritive slurry tap in my suit."

"*Slurry?* Ugh, grody, F.P. Totally gross."

"Just everything a growing boy needs."

"Whatever." Inside the bagel shop, the aroma of fresh-baked goods erased the image of a slime-filled feeding tube. Bacon and egg sandwiches floated across his vision, so real he considered reaching out and plucking them from his imagination like ripe apples from a tree. The notion only lasted a moment before he decided ordering a sandwich from the front counter was more realistic.

There were a few people on the other side of an open window presumably working a griddle, and after only a few minutes the bald man at the register called Tommy over for his order. When he took his money out to pay, Tommy glanced at the address he had written down the night before. "Do you know where Bath Avenue is?"

"Bath?" He pushed the wrapped sandwich to Tommy. "Sure, sure. That's in Bath Beach." His accent sounded almost exactly like in *The Godfather* (a movie his father let him watch as long as he never told his mother). Tommy had always thought the accents were a put-on, far too exaggerated to actually be real.

"Which way is Bath Beach?"

His thick black mustache covered both top and bottom lips, but his wry smile showed through somehow. "You gonna walk there, kid?"

"I guess." *Why not*, he thought. How far could it be?

The man chuckled and turned to the open window. "Yo, Bobby! This kid's gonna walk to Bath Beach! Whattaya say?"

One of the men at the griddle shook his head and laughed. "I say pack a bag lunch. It's a hike!"

"Yeah, kid. Take the train." He handed Tommy his change, then pointed vaguely in the direction he'd been walking. "Or else just keep going thataway and stop when you hit water."

The man yelled back to Bobby. "You hear what I said? I said he should stop when he hits water! You like that?"

F.P. said, "I think that man is being facetious."

Tommy wasn't sure what the word *facetious* meant, but if it meant he was being an A-hole, then yeah, he was facetious to the max. "How long to walk?"

The man smoothed his mustache and looked serious. "Kid, you're in Park Slope." He glanced over his shoulder at Bobby, but the cook was too busy to notice. He shrugged. "A couple hours. Maybe less."

A couple hours? What was the big deal? Tommy had gone on *real* hikes in the forest that took half the day one way. He guessed when you had buses and trains and cars, you didn't do much walking. The guy behind the counter made it sound like Tommy was out of his mind to even try.

"And which way would I go if I wanted to walk?"

Through a lot of head shaking, he said, "Turn right out the door, look for New Utrecht Avenue. That'll get you there." He rubbed his mustache some more. "But if that duffel gets heavy, I'd hit the 9th Street station and take the D down to 18th." He shrugged as if it didn't make much of a difference either way. "But that's just me. Whattaya gonna do."

Tommy almost answered him but realized as the man turned away to stock more bagels that it wasn't actually a question. He left in the direction indicated by the bagel guy. He'd often eaten an ice cream or a bag of chips outside the corner store in Branchville, but there was something so *city* about eating a whole sandwich while walking around that Tommy momentarily felt a decade older than his true age. There he was, on his own three states away from home, enjoying a real Brooklyn bagel after spending the night in a hotel. If that didn't make him a man, he didn't know what would.

"Are you enjoying your embryo, pig, and lactose sandwich?"

He stopped chewing and stared at F.P. "Dude, what the hell?"

Phantos appeared genuinely confused but didn't question Tommy's reaction. Instead he said, "This is endgame, Tommy. What is your plan?"

He checked his watch. It was still relatively early, almost eleven. He wasn't entirely sure when trick-or-treating started in Brooklyn, but he wanted to be ready outside Aaron's place well before then. In Branchville, kids were allowed to start heading out around six, so he figured trying to get to Aaron's a little before five would be prudent.

"Well, now we find Aaron Beltzer's house."

"Tommy." He placed a heavy, gloved hand on his shoulder. "Please tell me this is only step one."

"This is only step one," he mimicked.

They continued along the street, and though the day was new and the sun shined bright, a cold shadow remained fixed in Tommy's mind. A shadow in the shape of a lurking beast.

CHAPTER FORTY

WAKE-UP CALL

Dave got out of bed, confused and panicked. He didn't know where he was or what he was doing. There was something . . . something important. Something *crucial* he was forgetting.

Orange and red crushes of light poured in from every corner of the room. Riding these waves were devils. Spiked and horned mutations tore through the floorboards as Dave stumbled away, shielding his face from blistering heat. His legs were heavy and lethargic. He had to run, craved escape, yet he stuck fast like gum to a shoe.

He tripped, and his fall continued past the floor into empty space. His stomach spun round and round, a manic carousel spinning off its axis. The demons dove after him, insane eyes boggling in the splashes of white intensity. They fell like stones through water. Growls of hunger erupted, guttural and foreboding. The cackling insanity that rushed from the creatures' mouths made no sense. They were not words. They were madness.

Still, Dave somehow understood the crazed lamentations as warnings. Only, they were warning of mistakes already made. The uncorrectable past. Unlike the ghosts of Christmas, these beasts were not here to help. They were here to mock.

A scrambling creature made of malformed appendages like a mutant crab tore at him. It bellowed in putrid tones of Dave's forgotten comic book art. The path he might have taken through a yellow wood, where freelance work led to an independent developer, which led to steady income and a happy life.

Crashing between other, smaller denizens of hell came a molten red monstrosity covered in boils and pustules. A hissing torment rushed from within, and Dave knew it to be the portent of divorce.

A final blue creature tumbled into the fray and squealed morosely. The vile thing spoke of Tommy's disappearance. He'd never be found. He was lost, taken, disposed of. Gone. Tommy! Of course! The forgotten assignment. The *something crucial*. The thing that must be done.

The fall continued. A forever fall that led nowhere. This emptiness would never be filled, and Dave would plummet to his end without another moment of happiness.

* * *

"Dave!"

He sat bolt upright and nearly tumbled off the bed. He was tangled in unfamiliar blankets in an unfamiliar room with terror lodged in his chest. The scenario wasn't a new one. He'd woken up in strange rooms bathed in the sweat of crushing fear many times this past year. Different hotel rooms, friends' guest rooms, the living room in his own house. The only difference this time was that Suzie was with him, albeit in a separate bed.

He rubbed his eyes, an intense headache throbbing over his entire skull as if someone had caved his head in with a mallet. *This must be what people mean by crushing pain*, he thought.

"You were screaming." Suzie sat on the edge of her bed, wearing the same clothes they had left in the night before.

"What time is it?"

"We overslept. It's past noon."

"What?" He jumped up, the blankets falling in a tangle at his feet and almost tripping him. The room spun as if he were drunk, but this time it was due to the *lack* of alcohol. A warning sign, but one he'd encountered and ignored before.

"I already called Matty and Officer Randall to check in. Tommy hasn't been back home. There's no other news except that they're still looking." Suzie stood and went to the coffee maker.

"What are you doing?"

"You need coffee."

He stalked over but kept distance between them. The heat of anger sat heavy on his tongue. He bit down and attempted to retain control. "We need to find our son."

She remained focused on her task. "We keep doing this. Don't we?" Suzie sounded simultaneously amused and melancholy.

Another stab of anger, but less this time. "Doing what?"

Suzie began the brewing cycle and turned. She'd taken her makeup off before going to bed. She looked vulnerable, her eyes soft and plead-ing. "Taking opposite sides."

"I don't know what—"

"It's like I need to fight whatever you say. And whatever I say, you need to fight too." She threw her hands in the air. "Can you even track which one of us wanted to look for Tommy and which didn't? Because here's a hint. We took turns depending on what the other one wanted to do."

"That's not . . ." He trailed off. He was doing it again. Just what Suzie said. Taking the opposing view.

The coffee machine gurgled and sputtered. A warm, roasted morning smell filled the room.

The best part of waking up . . . The jingle played in Dave's head and he thought about the sappy coffee commercial. Sometimes Suzie would mimic the mother from the Christmas ad, repeating in her best soap opera voice, dripping with sentimentality, "*Peter.* Oh, you're *home!*" The bit always gave Tommy a good laugh.

The memory made Dave smile.

Suzie didn't comment on his disposition. Instead, she said, "We were out until seven in the morning, driving around the Beltzers' neighborhood, going block by block. We didn't find him, and we needed sleep. Just like we need to eat something before we do it all over again." She approached Dave and took his hands in hers. They were warm and familiar. "And we will. Until we find him."

He squeezed her hands. "I know. I'm sorry."

Her mouthed twitched. She squeezed his hands back. "No more of that. Okay?" She dropped his hands and turned back to the pot, half-filled now. "We can't keep hurting each other and apologizing."

She pulled the pot prematurely and filled two paper cups. She fixed his with two creams and two sugars. "Let's be kind to one another. We can do this—all of this—with compassion."

He knew she was talking about more than finding Tommy. She meant the separation, the divorce, and every hard thing that had yet to come. And she was right. He hated that the family was falling through his fingers like sand, but he supposed there was a way to rebuild the castle into something new.

"It's a promise."

CHAPTER FORTY-ONE

CREATURE FEATURE

T ommy should have taken the train. His bags weren't all that heavy on their own, but after long hours of walking with the weight, he was ready to fall into a giant waterbed and sleep through autumn. Halloween or not. Brooklyn or not. Grand quest or not. He was dog tired.

"How much farther?"

F.P. had gone silent thirty minutes back and continued to fiddle with his weapon awkwardly, adjusting wires and circuits as best he could midstride. Tommy didn't think the great hero minded walking (definitely no worse than the dreaded car ride), but something was bothering him. Tommy had learned how to read the expressions on F.P.'s face. Well, *expression* was probably the wrong way to describe the strange glitches and hiccups that indicated emotional distress. The longer Phantos remained quiet, the more he shuttered and stuttered.

Like a Nintendo game in need of cleaning, there were square arti-facts and pixels littered throughout his visage. Even more telling was the way he kept checking his holographic wrist display, twisted to the side, out of Tommy's view.

"Earth to Phantos. You still with me, big guy?"

F.P. painted on a smile, a digital effect that didn't quite reach the eyes. "Yes, young Tommy. I am with you." A giant thumbs-up appeared in the helmet, then morphed back to Phantos's pale face.

"Right. We almost there?" Tommy stretched his neck in antici-pation. If he could get a closer look at the display, maybe he could figure out what F.P. kept checking. He suspected it was the timer he'd previously noticed, though he still wasn't sure what the clock counted down to.

"Ten minutes by foot, and it is only three o'clock." He collapsed the display before Tommy could manage a clear view.

"Is everything okay?" He watched his friend for a hesitation in stride or a stress-related mannerism. But Phantos continued to walk in the same restrained way he always had. The spacesuit had taken damage. Bright white skin showed through the torn fabric. Phantos removed a rag from a suit compartment and cleaned the glass dome of his helmet, which was just as grimy as it had been when he first arrived.

"Of course, Tommy. We have almost reached the successful comple-tion of your quest. This brings me great joy."

"Really? Because you don't sound happy."

"I don't express emotion the same way you do."

Tommy scoffed. "Bull! I've seen you express emotion. Heck, crammed into the car like a loaf of Spam, you were totally annoyed. You turned into a little . . . a little . . ." He searched for the most devastating insult he could fathom. "A little whiny diaper baby!"

Phantos stopped walking. His mouth dropped open. Quietly, he asked, "What?"

Tommy could hardly contain the bubbling laughter in his chest. "I said." He paused dramatically. "You." Ruthless smile. "Were acting." Squinted eyes. "Like a little. Whiny. *Diaper baby!*"

"Take it back!" Phantos bellowed, pointing a finger in Tommy's face. "I was not a diaper baby! You take it back or else!"

"Or else *what?*"

"Or else . . ." He looked around for inspiration. "Or else I'll never speak to you again!"

Tommy pressed his lips together and nodded knowingly. "Just what a diaper baby would say."

"Well," Phantos said, a huge grin forming, "if I'm a diaper baby, then you're a baby's diaper!"

That did the trick. Tommy couldn't hold the cackles back any longer, and he doubled over in hysterical laughter as an older couple walked by, taking a wide berth. Tommy didn't care. The laughter kept coming, and he almost toppled over from the sheer intensity. "I . . . can't . . . breathe," he managed between guffaws.

"Why are you laughing?"

He wiped tears from his eyes and composed himself. He shook his head. "You don't express emotion?"

"No. I do not."

"You totally spazzed because I called you a diaper baby. Plus you actually sounded like a normal human for a second there."

"A normal human?"

"You're usually all like . . ." Tommy stiffened and started walking like a robot. "Do not resist my perfect grammar and fully formed sentences. Comply! Comply!"

He nodded once, briskly. "Point taken. But you are still a stinky baby diaper."

Chuckling, Tommy asked, "Do I smell like moldy cat food?"

"More like dumpster juice."

"Ha, good one." Walking again, he asked, "So you'll still talk to me?"

"I suppose."

"Then tell me, what's going on with you? You've been acting weird. Talking to me less. Having strange issues with your, uh, face?"

"My face?"

"You know what I mean. Your hologram. It's like a bad VHS recording lately."

They continued walking in silence, and Tommy allowed his friend time. New Utrecht Avenue was the most interesting street he had ever traversed. Above them, elevated train tracks ran as far as he could see, blotting out the sun and sky. Occasionally a train would rattle by and little droplets of water (or at least what he hoped was water) sprinkled across the pavement. At random intervals, metal staircases appeared on either side of the street, leading to the train platforms. He figured they could have climbed one of those staircases at any time and hopped a train, but Tommy wanted to experience every bit of Brooklyn he could.

As they continued, he noticed the borough had a particular smell, like a mixture of cement, gasoline, and steam. Trash cans were everywhere, each with their own peculiar stink. The smells would mingle oddly with various restaurant aromas. Here a bakery, there a pizzeria. Sautéed garlic and gutter water. Fresh-baked bread and burned rubber.

Through these observations, the probing fear that something followed them remained, causing Tommy to ask a question that had lingered on his mind. "The percentage? Has it changed?"

"Yes."

"Our chances got better?" Tommy knew the answer before Phantos spoke.

"No. They have gotten worse—41%."

A cold stone fell into his stomach. "But that's *way* worse than before we even started."

"I know, Tommy."

"We're *in* Brooklyn! How could the number have gone down?"

Phantos lowered his head as if defeated by some unseen entity. "I do not know, but I suspect some new player has entered the game."

Some new player. Like the slinking shadow Tommy sensed on his heels. He searched for anything out of place and found only the mundane. People entered and exited stores, stood by cars, talked, and lived their lives. Something deep within Tommy stirred as he watched these things play out. An emotion stronger than fear.

A longing for home, like a finger repeatedly plucking a lone guitar string.

Every pay phone he passed was a reminder of his parents and the worry and grief he'd caused. They'd been terrible lately, but they were still his parents. No matter how badly they'd screwed up, Tommy knew they loved him, and he loved them.

He slowed next to a phone booth and jingled loose change in his pocket.

"Go on, Tommy. They will be glad to know you are safe."

"Will they?"

Phantos knelt and placed his hands on Tommy's shoulders. "Do you doubt? Truly?"

Tommy stared into the shimmering eyes of his friend. He pulled at the sleeves of his jean jacket. The pinned and patched armor was a poor defense against his trembling chin and the sucking void of loneliness. The farther he traveled from home, the more frequently happy memories flooded his mind, washing away the tribulations of this past year.

Like the time his dad stopped at a hardware store to buy some nails. He had told Tommy to wait in the car, and he'd obeyed, wondering why he couldn't go in. The answer came when his dad returned with the deluxe Fortress Darkheart playset, an early birthday surprise he'd had on backorder for months.

Or the time his mom drove all the way out to South Side so they could eat at Witzenberger's. When Tommy saw the commercial for the limited edition *OoCC* plastic cups, he'd begged his parents to take him. One of his favorite tactics was to gleefully sing the fast-food chain's jingle—*Nobody does burgers like Witzenberger's*—as he walked through the room. Dad had to work, but his mom had relished the 45-minute drive and made a whole day of it, even stopping at Toys "R" Us for a Nintendo game on the way home.

There were the family camping trips, the movie nights, the holiday traditions. Most of Tommy's life had been a golden surprise, and he became sick with guilt that he'd judged his parents so harshly for a single bad year.

Phantos must have seen the tears coming. Must have understood what played out behind Tommy's glassy eyes. "Do you doubt they are sick with worry? Do you doubt they search for you even now, an icy grip on their hearts, longing only for your safe return?"

Tommy attempted to speak through the lump rising in his throat, through the tremors in his chest.

He failed.

Along with the word "No" came a flood of pent-up tears. The release brought only more grief, and Tommy sobbed heavy against his friend's shoulder. Through racked breaths, he said, "Why'd you let me do this?"

Phantos squeezed Tommy in a giant's embrace. "Sometimes our greatest moments of enlightenment come from our worst mistakes."

Tommy wiped his eyes and sniffled. "If I call, you have to tell me what's been bothering you. I know it's more than our chances going down to 41%."

"Deal."

Tommy regained some composure and was about to enter the booth when a monstrous voice pulled him back.

"Fierce Phantos! Your journey ends here!" Across the street, a hulking figure stepped from behind a parked truck. At first Tommy couldn't understand why the person appeared veiled in shadow. Everything about the man was dark, as if obscured from sight.

Phantos hissed, "*Creecharr.*"

Then Tommy understood. The man didn't stand in shadow; he was covered in thick fur from head to toe. Further, this was no man. This was the thing he'd witnessed as a slick blur. The thing haunting their every step through Brooklyn.

Creecharr crouched, smiling maniacally, bearing rows of yellowed incisors. It leapt into the air and soared over the railway, out of sight.

Phantos grabbed Tommy's forearm. He appeared stricken, and seeing the hero from another dimension this way scared the ever-loving crap out of Tommy.

Phantos said, "Creecharr is fast. He is formidable. He is deadly." He pulled Tommy closer, the gloved hand hurting his wrist. "*Run.*"

✳ ✳ ✳

Fear bubbled in Tommy's chest, but his feet wouldn't budge. Phantos pulled Tommy into action, even as he stole a glance over his shoulder.

A tawny streak cascaded over the side of the railway and onto the roof of a silver car. Creecharr stooped, enormous horns growing from each shoulder, its sinister yellow glare fixed on the retreating prey.

Tommy's bags caused each of his strides to slow and falter. The panic bit deep, mingling with his recent grief in a potent cocktail. Phantos drew his weapon and fired a few holographic versions of himself and Tommy, then pulled the real Tommy into the fray, blending in with the horde. Each pair split off to a different direction, the real Tommy and Phantos running to the other side of the street and crouching behind a car. They peered through the windows of the beat-up Chevy.

"He's not even looking at the holograms, Phantos."

Creecharr closed the gap and slowed. He fell to all fours and sniffed like a bloodhound. A moment later, the beast lifted its head and stared through the car windows, directly at Tommy.

"F.P.," he muttered, the syllables turning to mush in his dry mouth.

"I know. My diversions are no match. He is a hunter."

They scuttled to the next car.

"What do we do?"

F.P. pulled Tommy another car down the line. "We cannot keep running; he is too fast. We cannot keep hiding; he will sniff us out."

Tommy relinquished his backpack and duffel. "So we fight."

F.P. held him from standing, but Creecharr was surely mere moments from finding them. The notion gnawed at Tommy's calm. He tried to stand again, but Phantos would not relent.

"Tommy. My friend." There was a strange sentimentality to his voice that caught him off guard. "By now you know. They are here for *you*. These villains, they mean to snatch you. To spirit you away. Take you to *Skullagar*." The name oozed from Phantos's mouth like bile.

"We don't have time—"

"Listen. Creecharr will kill me, but he will not dare harm you."

"But EyeSpy—"

"Went against orders. Creecharr will not. He is loyal."

"Why are you saying this?"

"If I perish . . ." He turned away, as if overcome. "You must do what they say." He squeezed Tommy's shoulder. "You must survive. The others—Masculon, Defendra, Flip Grip—they will find you."

None of this made sense. Why were these villains after Tommy? What could Skullagar possibly want with him? Did their pursuit have something to do with Mechani-Ghoul? Aaron Beltzer? Worse than the myriad questions already swirling around his head was this new one: How much did Phantos know, and why hadn't he warned Tommy before?

The car beside them collapsed like a crushed tin can. The windows exploded in an aural firestorm of glass shards and metal. Tommy and

F.P. fell away, shielding themselves from shrapnel. A young couple behind Tommy yelped and scurried to the side of the buildings. Had they reacted to the car, or to the insane child throwing himself across the sidewalk? Tommy thought he knew the answer, but he didn't dare explore it any further. Whether in his mind or not, an enormous bestial monster crouched mere feet away, and it meant to destroy Phantos and to kidnap Tommy and take him to Teltam for unknown purposes.

Creecharr lowered himself from the demolished vehicle and prowled slowly closer, dragging an enormous rectangular mace behind him. The metal spikes ground deep furrows into the cement, sparks and pebbles flying from the destruction.

F.P. stood and drew his weapon, flicking the switch from *hologram* to *blast*. "Stay your hand, Creecharr."

The beast-man ceased his approach. His mouth opened in the approximation of a smile, baring endless rows of razor teeth, glistening with saliva. He licked his lips as if anticipating a gourmet meal. "*Fierce* Phantos." Creecharr's laugh was an eruption of lava and ash. "Your name does not suit you."

"Move any closer and I will end you."

He lifted the mace by its bone handle and toyed with the sharp barbs. "You don't kill. None of you *kill*." The malicious smile grew spectacular. "Why Masculon sent you as the boy's protector, I cannot fathom. Was he too fearful to come himself? Did he not dare spare another, more seasoned warrior?"

Tommy listened to the exchange with great interest as he regained his feet. Unlike during the previous battle with EyeSpy, the surrounding cityscape remained, though not entirely unchanged. A quietude had dropped like a veil, shimmering and hallucinatory. The atmosphere wavered as though an invisible curtain had been drawn.

"Masculon did not send me. *No one* sent me." His grip on the pistol tightened. An intensity heretofore unseen crept into Phantos's glare. His eyes narrowed to slits of fire. His jaw set like stone. Every muscle tensed, threatening to tear his suit apart from the inside. Fierce Phantos exuded savage passion. His every movement was a storm of power. His very expression spoke of brutal intensity.

Tommy finally and completely understood his moniker. And Creecharr was wrong.

Fierce Phantos was the truest name ever conceived.

✳ ✳ ✳

Voices came to Tommy from beyond the veil, thin and wispy. They were far off. Barely there. A train rumbled past on the elevated track, and even this was muted as though it were a mere toy. Overhead, the blue sky took on violet hues. Clouds of amber rolled across the ocean of air. Alien worlds collided with untold realities, stacked atop one another in layers of insanity.

None of this concerned Tommy. He had one job, and it stood before him like grasping, clawing death.

Fierce Phantos squeezed the trigger, and a blur of lasers seared the air.

Creecharr matched their speed, lifting the mace as though it were no heavier than a feather, deflecting every shot, sending them blazing wildly.

Phantos was right; the beast was fast. As if to prove his speed once again, Creecharr fell into a four-legged run and rammed Tommy to the side—breath punched from his lungs and arm skinned raw on cement—before lunging at Phantos.

His friend wailed as he fell back, the clawing animal landing cat-like on top, triumphant as king of the mountain.

"Run, Tommy! Leave me!"

Phantos should have known better.

Tommy's running days were over.

His arm throbbed, but he pushed to his feet and regained composure, taking measured breaths to settle the adrenaline. Trusting what his hand would find, he reached down and gripped Lórien's hilt. A surge of golden energy ran through his veins, overtaking adrenaline, fear, and doubt. His muscles thrummed with power. Divine heat flowed through his veins.

Beams littered the air like a laser light show as Phantos struggled beneath Creecharr, who tore at his fallen prey. He scratched and bit, revealing more of Phantos's white skin beneath the destroyed suit. Blue blood oozed from newly opened cuts, driving the beast wild.

Tommy drew Lórien in a blur of white light, and he thrust at Creecharr's back.

Again proving the sharpness of his senses, Creecharr rolled off Phantos and into a crouch, avoiding the blade. He crawled two steps forward. Blue blood dripped from his muzzle and claws, mixing with saliva in sickening streaks.

He cocked his head, eyes narrowed in concentration. Or perhaps confusion. "What is this?"

The sword blazed, bathing the trio in white light so pure it burned. "This," Tommy said, sending his will and hope stampeding through Lórien, "is your destruction." He exhaled these words like dragon's breath. The blade's light traversed the gap from hilt to hand, and living lightning wound around Tommy.

Creecharr shielded his eyes. "But you're just a boy. Only *human*."

Tommy felt a sickening smile crawl across his face. From strange depths, words flowed like a river of blood. "If that were true, why does Skullagar hunt me?"

A moment of doubt creased the villain's features, and Tommy knew the animal hadn't previously given that aspect of his mission a moment of consideration. But he did now. *Oh yes*, Tommy thought. *He sees now.*

The light of Lórien coursing through him, Tommy attacked with a sweeping chop. Creecharr sidestepped the deadly blade and rolled, claws flashing. Tommy scurried backward, almost tripping over his own feet. Though young and spry, he couldn't match the beast's natural agility.

Creecharr howled, and the barbed mace whiffed by Tommy's nose, mere inches away. "If only I were permitted to finish you," he growled. His lips twitched and tongue lolled.

Lórien continued to pump hope and purpose through Tommy, but the want and desire in Creecharr's eyes still managed to penetrate his protective layer. The villain's hate was a visible shimmer, rising from his body like heat waves.

A blast of Phantos's gun brought Tommy back to the fight. Creecharr jumped out of the laser's path with infuriating elegance. The shot knocked over a nearby garbage can, and a wave of stink rolled out along with rotting food.

"Tommy, look out!"

Creecharr flinched away from the fallen trash can, his nose wrinkled and eyes squinted. He recovered and charged, mace held over-head. "Submit!"

The beast swung, but Tommy dodged easily. He wasn't trying to hit him, only scare him. Skullagar's orders were clear, and Phantos had been right: Creecharr was loyal. As Tommy watched the beast-man sidle away from the spilled garbage, he realized Phantos had been right about something else as well.

"Phantos! The garbage!" He pointed.

Creecharr swung, and the barbed mace crashed into the cement inches from Tommy's feet. "You will *submit*."

Tommy scooted away a few steps and swung his blade frantically. Creecharr dodged left, right, left. Tommy lunged and caught the edge of the beast's thigh. A minor scratch, but he drew blood.

"*Phantos!* Shoot the garbage!"

His friend appeared confused. He glanced at the other cans along the sidewalk, then at their foe. A smile teased at his mouth.

Finally, Tommy thought. *He's got it.*

Creecharr rubbed blood-smeared fur. When his eyes found Tommy's again, they were hard and full of malice. "This is your last chance, boy."

He saw Phantos take aim and smiled. "No. It's *yours*."

F.P. shot, only this time he didn't aim for Creecharr. The contents of the fallen bin caught fire, a noxious black plume of smoke infecting the air. He turned and shot another can, and another. Secondary shots set more trash ablaze until the whole of the sidewalk was a smoking hell of litter.

The effect on Creecharr was immediate. He tripped away, eyes watering. If the stink could overpower Tommy, he knew it was *destroying* Creecharr's acute sense of smell. Once a boon, his senses now betrayed him.

Phantos called forth a holographic squadron of Tommys, all holding their own blazing blades.

Creecharr watched in a panic. He dropped to all fours and sniffed the air, then gagged and shook his head, trying in vain to clear his nose.

Invisible to the beast's senses now, Tommy joined the holograms in a flurry of slashes and chops. For every holographic miss, the real Tommy landed a devastating blow. A lightning slash across the beast's chest drove him back.

Creecharr swiped, but only hit a hologram. He swung the mace, but only attacked smoke, leaving him off balance.

Seeing his chance, Tommy lunged, Lórien trained on Creecharr's heart. The beast twisted at the last moment and took the blade in his shoulder. Waves of burning light cascaded over the blade and into the oozing wound. Tommy screamed and sent another flood of sizzling energy through Lórien.

Creecharr wailed, his fur smoldering and smoking as the crater grew. He twisted away and fell, his legs lame, his body trembling. He licked his wound, whimpering and pathetic.

But Tommy didn't see a wounded animal. He saw bullies. He saw Evan. He saw Jonathan and Travis Miller. He saw the eighth graders Steve and Ray. And yes, he even saw the abstract and looming deity of divorce. He saw these tormentors, and rage enveloped him like a fiery blanket.

Tommy raised Lórien with both hands, prepared to deal a deadly blow. Prepared to behead the great villain before him. Far back, mingled within the other ghostly voices from beyond the veil, Mechani-Ghoul said, "Yes, Father. This is your right. This is your duty."

His *right*. Yes. He perceived the truth of it, the power in those words.

Creecharr held his hands out, fur matted with clotted blood. His eyes glassy and unfocused. "*Mercy . . .*"

Mechani-Ghoul spoke through Tommy, using his voice and his body: "There will be no mercy. Only death." He reared back and summoned every ounce of anger, hate, and rage. He meant to kill Creecharr, and the decision tasted like justice.

"*Stop!*" Phantos stepped over the fallen villain, his hand out, his voice larger than God's. "*You will stop!*" He stood fierce and formidable, growing larger than his stature. Becoming more.

The words echoed and cracked something inside Tommy. A hard shell of hatred had formed around his heart, encasing all that was bad and vile. Separating the good, keeping it out.

Phantos swung again, forming more fissures. "You are Tommy Grant of Branchville, Ohio. You will not use this power to kill. That is not how we win."

Phantos and Mechani-Ghoul, like the angel and devil on his shoulders. Tommy had so much boiling, bubbling rage inside. He wanted to push out the pain. He wanted to quench the thirst for vengeance, if only for a modicum of relief.

"*This is not how we win,*" Phantos repeated. He touched Tommy's tensed arm, and by degrees, the world came back into focus. The devil slid from his shoulder like an oil slick.

Tommy dropped Lórien and stumbled away, tears blurring his vision. "I almost killed him. I almost—" He backpedaled another few steps and fell to his knees, weeping. Inside his stomach, the hollow place had been filled with poison. Tommy knew this now. Felt the infection of hatred. The rot of revenge. But as he knelt weeping, his tears began to purge the sickness inside.

He heard Creecharr dragging himself away, muttering evil incantations and warnings, but none so loud as to reignite Tommy's anger. When Tommy finally stood and wiped the tears away, Creecharr was gone, but Fierce Phantos remained. He held Lórien out. "You dropped this."

"I don't know if I should . . ."

"The sword is yours, Tommy. You've always carried it."

Phantos placed a hand on his shoulder. "Now you know how to wield it, and the danger that comes with its mishandling."

Tommy nodded and took his sword. "I do."

"Good." Phantos turned and pointed forward. "We have a mission to accomplish. And time has grown teeth."

CHAPTER FORTY-TWO

SKULL AND BONES

Before long, New Utrecht turned into 86th Street. Tommy and F.P. continued walking until they reached 18th Avenue, where F.P. paused. He checked his holographic wrist contraption and indicated they should turn seaward.

During this final leg of Tommy's long journey, Phantos's words repeated in his mind, echoing like a mantra.

Time has grown teeth.

F.P. meant they were running out of time, but the words had larger implications. The phrase was a perfect description of Tommy's imperfect year. One wrought with the pain of teething. Yes, time had grown teeth, and they bit and gnashed at his childhood, mashing memories to mush.

However, if time had grown teeth, Tommy matched this change with newly discovered fortitude and courage. He reached down and grasped Lórien's hilt, the power there no less in the absence of rage. If anything, the energy was stronger. More pure.

"One more block," Phantos said.

Tommy checked his watch. Almost five 'o clock. Right on time. They crossed Cropsey Avenue, and the neighborhood shifted from business to residential. The entire street was lined on either side by endless brick houses that connected to each other with no separation for alleys, side streets, or driveways.

Windows and doors were covered in die-cut Halloween decorations. Witches, pumpkins, black cats, and ghosts as far as the eye could see. There wasn't much in the way of front yards (instead there were tiny fenced-in squares of pavement and lawn with diminutive stoops), but most managed to jam in light-up blow molds. As the sky grew darker with approaching dusk, more of these decorative lights snapped on.

Already, younger kids waddled door to door with their parents. Revelers tasting their first Halloween perhaps. Many appeared too young to retain the memories, yet Tommy knew Halloween's magic would linger, if not as memory, then as an impression. A sensation that would burrow deep and remain untouched by age and time.

F.P. halted Tommy's progress and pointed up the street to where two police cars were double-parked.

"Is that—?"

"I'm not sure, but based on the house numbers . . ."

He read off a few numbers and counted up the line of brick buildings with his eyes. "It's Aaron's house."

Clouds rolled slowly through the darkening sky, devouring bits of daytime.

F.P. pulled Tommy around the corner of Cropsey. "Why are the police involved?"

Tommy thought this over. It could be a coincidence. Some unfore-seen tragedy at the Beltzers'.

A chill wind blew, and clouds stacked atop one another. Tommy drew his jacket closed, shivering, ghosts of the past haunting his thoughts. The sudden change in atmosphere. The hungry night winds. Something hid in the dark, and Tommy knew his fight was not over.

"Tommy?"

"I'm thinking." And he was, though his mind *had* drifted from the problem at hand. *Why are the police at Aaron's house?* Of course, Tommy knew the answer; he just didn't want to say it out loud. Didn't want to admit that as far and as fast as he'd run . . .

"My parents," he relented, knowing the words were true as soon as he spoke them. "They figured everything out. They called the cops to find me."

Phantos knelt beside Tommy. "Impossible. You left false leads. You were careful."

"Was I?" He rubbed his hair. It was greasy and matted from sweating through the long hike. "I'm not so sure. There was the clerk at the train station. He definitely called my parents."

"But how did they know of Aaron?"

A good question, but not impossible to answer. Both Miranda and Matty knew bits of his plan. Yes, he was sure his parents had figured everything out. Were they somewhere in Brooklyn too? The thought caused a sickening dizzy spell as his stomach plummeted and his mouth went dry.

Mom and Dad are here. They're looking for me, and they're scared. Probably think I'm dead. And when they find out I'm not, they'll never forgive me. They'll hate me forever, like they decided to hate each other.

A cascade of sick washed over his entire body. He'd really fouled up. They weren't supposed to find out about any of this. No matter how mad Tommy was about the split or about how they'd ignored him, he didn't want to hurt his parents.

And this, he knew, would hurt them. A word his mother had uttered to his father came back with stifling insistence: *unforgivable*. Were Tommy's actions unforgivable?

The pain he'd caused them echoed back and hit him full in the chest, like a blast from F.P.'s laser, stealing his breath and blurring his vision. Phantos put his arms around Tommy and spoke words he couldn't hear. Or maybe they were in another language. Whatever the case, understanding eluded him.

Yet, the syllables and tone soothed. The words eased his mind.

His breath came back in shallow sips, then gulps. He straightened as his trembling limbs stabilized. Tommy wiped sweat from his forehead, despite the cool of the autumn night's approach. "Holy cow." He focused on Phantos. "What did you say?"

The hero stood and brushed off his knees, somehow ignoring that his suit was a wreck from all the fights. His injuries had begun to heal, leaving only crusted blue blood and flaking scabs. "I told you only what you needed to hear. No more, no less."

"Fine. Be cryptic."

Phantos cracked a smile. "Now. How will we get to Aaron with the police at his house?"

Tommy smiled wide and bright. He may have mishandled parts of the plan, but he knew his endgame was solid. He removed the duffel bag from his shoulder and unzipped it to show F.P. the contents.

Inside lay his Masculon costume from the previous year. This was not one of those cheapo smock costumes they sold at the drug store with a flimsy vacuform mask. He'd saved for an entire year to purchase a full vinyl mask. His mom had sewn a professional costume—vest, arm bands, loin cloth, and all. Of course he wore clothes underneath, unlike the real Masculon, but even a year later he thought it was the best *OoCC* costume he'd ever seen. It was much tighter than the previous year, but it did still fit. His dad had even gotten him a plastic replica ax with an embedded blue gemstone.

Phantos picked up the mask and stared into its empty eyeholes. "This is disturbing."

He snagged it back. "Oh, cut it out."

"It is like you have the severed head of my friend in your bag. Do you not see how this might, to use your parlance, *freak me out?*"

"Then it's *really* gonna freak you out when I wear his face over mine."

Phantos recoiled at the suggestion. A quizzical expression crossed his face, then he said, "A disguise!"

"The cops are looking for Tommy Grant. Not Masculon." He shrugged the bag back over his shoulder. "My parents might recognize me if they're around, but it's a chance we have to take."

"The plan, Tommy?"

"Simple." He went to the corner and peered down the street where the police vehicles were still parked. "I put on the costume and . . ." His breath caught. Words sputtered.

"Tommy? What's wrong?" Phantos's voice was covered in layers of gauze. Muted, not by a physical disturbance, but by the complete consumption of Tommy's concentration.

Shadows pressed in, obscuring the buildings, oozing past the curb, devouring parked cars, light, and sense. Twin columns of living shadows wormed along brick walls. They slithered over windows and crawled onto roofs before erupting into the sky like obsidian towers. The dread shadow blotted out everything except a single lane of poison light.

Sandwiched by darkness, a purple sphere hung in the sky like a malignant tumor. Waves of virulent purple vapors leached into the air, coloring the world like a horror movie poster.

"Do you see it?" Tommy's words were thin and anemic.

"I do."

The toxic purple sphere was joined by two others, descending from the heavens like fallen angels. The three orbs were a hundred yards off and double that distance high, and still the inhabitant of the main orb was crystal clear.

The scourge of Evernitia.

The enemy of good.

The villain of Teltam.

"*Skullagar.*"

✳ ✳ ✳

As Phantos uttered the name, a flood of memories invaded Tommy's mind like swarming locusts. Months ago, before Fierce Phantos had taken his place, it was Skullagar's voice that guided Tommy. That whispered menace and venom into his ears.

The villain's words returned, tearing open old wounds.

Now they think you're a loser.

The torment of those ideas had been planted in his mind like seeds of deadly nightshade. They now bore fruit as fresh anguish infected Tommy's hard-won peace.

A big baby loser on his birthday.

Your best friend hates you.

You ruined your parents' marriage.

Worthless.

Friendless.

Unwanted.

"Shut up!"

Phantos brought Tommy close. "Do not listen. He is toying with you. It is what he does. What he has always done."

He shook the bad thoughts from his head and tried to focus on the present. He couldn't be distracted. Not now.

Tommy's blood congealed in his veins when he saw Mechani-Ghoul in the second bubble and Vile-Ette in the third. He didn't yet know the full power of Mechani-Ghoul, but if the cartoons and comics were to be believed, Skullagar and Vile-Ette were the two most powerful villains on planet Teltam. Capable of Myragran manipulation using their respective staffs of power. Truly, they wielded magic. With this ability, Skullagar had created the purple orbs that now made landfall then dissipated like so much fog. Perhaps also through this power, they had invaded his reality.

"Phantos. Do we fight?" He felt enervated, as if the darkness surrounding them fed on life force. Even Lórien waned in light and energy as the thickening pitch surrounded them like the edge of hell.

"We have no choice."

The villain's skull mask, bleached white, toothed and horned, stood in contrast to his fur-covered body. His clothes were different from Tommy's memory of the cartoon, reminding him of a cross between the Old West and science fiction movies: dusty desert boots, suede vest held by a gold chain at the neck, and worn khaki slacks. The clothes were both familiar and completely alien in construction.

Skullagar raised his staff into the air, its corona—a purple masked face—exuding infected light. "At last we meet, young Tommy."

Hearing Phantos's affectation from the lips of the evil stranger made Tommy's legs go wobbly and his stomach turn sour. He wanted to reply in the grand, operatic way a character in the cartoon would have.

But Tommy was a twelve-year-old boy of Earth, and he replied as one. "Eat me, barf bag."

Phantos tensed and placed a hand on his gun.

Vile-Ette, the purple-skinned sorceress, leveled her gem-tipped staff. The pigtailed hair and tight-fitting purple bodysuit did nothing to diminish her woeful potential. "Hold your tongue, boy! Do you not know to whom you speak?"

"Sure do," Tommy said. "Skully and I go way back."

At the utterance of his nickname, Skullagar slammed his staff into the pavement, sending a shock wave through the cement and nearly throwing Tommy off his feet. "I am not your pet hamster. You will cease calling me by that mawkish name."

Tommy had no idea what *mawkish* meant, but he did know Skullagar had weaknesses, and this was but one example. Even as the black edges of shadow bled inward, attempting to steal all will and courage, he knew they weren't beaten yet. He dropped his bags and drew Lórien. The blade blazed with divine light, and both Skullagar and Vile-Ette recoiled. The revulsion in their eyes gave Tommy great joy.

Mechani-Ghoul, however, stood as though a metal statue, unmoved by the blade's light. Its empty sockets were trained on Tommy like all-consuming black holes, endlessly starving. It leaned forward and opened its mouth to join the feast. They fed deeply of Lórien's light, dimming her again, taking strength from Tommy's limbs and mind.

Skullagar approached, his minions close behind. "I am not here to fight, Tommy." He held out a furred hand, his regal rings glinting in the low light. "I am here to save you."

"Don't listen, Tommy!" Phantos drew his weapon.

Vile-Ette uttered a phrase in a foreign tongue, and the gemstone atop her staff shot the gun from his grip with a pink beam. It landed yards away in a clatter. She smiled coyly. Her voice dripped like honey on fire. "The next one takes your hand from its wrist."

"You see, Tommy"—Skullagar had not withdrawn his proffered hand—"this worthless android cannot help you. And perhaps you've noticed, but none of the other so-called *Cosmic Champions* have come to your aid." He motioned around him at the bleak surrounding walls of shadow, the darkening sky, the fading world. Apropos of Halloween and no less terrifying. "Where is Defendra? Mace Ace and Flip Grip?"

He laughed. The sound was ill-fitting and gritty. "Where is your precious *Masculon*? Could they not be bothered to protect you? Have they truly placed their faith in this hastily built guardian?"

Tommy looked at Phantos. Where *were* the rest of the Order of Cosmic Champions? Why had only a single hero journeyed with him? Phantos shook his head, his holographic face glitching, the malfunction indicative of inner turmoil. No answers there.

"Meanwhile," Skullagar said, "I am here. My compatriots are here. And we want only one thing."

Tommy held Lórien slack at his side. Every moment brought the sucking, mewling darkness closer. Every uttered word was a spike through his barely healed mind. From within those injuries, from the dead center of his trauma, a voice asked, "What's that?"

The answer was exactly what Tommy desired to hear. "To welcome you like family. To treasure you." Skullagar reached out and took Tommy's hand.

✳ ✳ ✳

At Skullagar's touch, Tommy's body crackled and burned like a campfire. His mouth went dry and tasted of metal; his eyes blurred, and his head spun. Phantos, Vile-Ette, and Mechani-Ghoul were still there, but they became lenticular phantoms in a new landscape. The sinister shadows vanished and gave way to 18th Avenue again, complete with Halloween decor and capering children. Even the police cars returned, their red and blue lights no longer spinning.

But that was only half the story. Tommy looked up and found an alien sky. The Mafiltion Solar System beckoned from the unknown expanse. A blazing red dwarf star set over the ocean's horizon as two planets came into view overhead. The enormous purple and blue marbles dominated the dusk sky while blazing waves of the Enorem Cluster painted pinks and silvery whites against the black. There were so many stars they nearly turned the heavens white.

Tommy's stomach was light and fluttery. He knew the sensation as one of discovery and fear. A good fear. The kind he should have experienced as he started junior high school. Something akin to the moments before tearing into a birthday present, not knowing what was inside but bursting with untold hope and excitement.

"Where are we?"

Skullagar's grip tightened on his wrist, long nails biting into his flesh. "A liminal space, between worlds. Between dimensions."

Before him, 18th Avenue flickered. Superimposed over the pavement and sidewalks, a rocky pathway emerged. Where the Atlantic Ocean once lay, an enormous mountain range grew, stabbing the sky with razor spires. "The Black Matter Mountains."

"Yes, Tommy."

His mind tumbled. "This is Teltam?" Skullagar's nails dug deeper, and Tommy barely noticed the stinging pain.

"A glimpse. Yes."

He turned to Phantos, excitement energizing his muscles and mind. There must have been some kind of mistake. Skullagar wasn't a villain. He was trying to help. He wanted the best for Tommy.

Only, Phantos wasn't there. Not even the faded lenticular version of him. For that matter, Vile-Ette and Mechani-Ghoul were also missing.

Skullagar's grip tightened yet again, and when the first rivulet of blood cascaded over Tommy's wrist, his sense of well-being wavered. He thought, *Is that my blood?* Then, *Why doesn't this hurt?* The masked face of Skullagar's staff vibrated like a tuning fork as its eyes and mouth shined white with power.

"Why are you showing me this?"

He pulled the boy close, and the stink of rot and musk overwhelmed

Tommy's senses. At this proximity, tiny bugs could be seen crawling through Skullagar's matted fur. Dried bits of browned, nearly blackened detritus covered his hands and torso. "You are home."

Home. His mind bucked like a wild stallion. *Phantos. Where was his friend?* He pulled his hand away, but Skullagar held it with a vicious grip and would not relent. More blood spilled, and now he felt the sting and tear of punctured flesh. "Let go." With these words, something warm began to glow at his side.

"Your family does not want you. Your classmates *hate* you." Stringy pieces of meat hung between razored canines, and the smell of long-dead animals wafted with every utterance.

He pulled away again, and Skullagar's grip slipped momentarily from the slick blood. "It's not true."

"Even Fierce Phantos is only here for his own benefit. He cares not for you."

"Lies!"

Skullagar held his staff inches from Tommy's face. The thrumming energy made his teeth feel like he was chewing on foil. "You are coming with me, voluntarily or not."

Somewhere in the other world, outside that liminal space, Phantos bellowed a scream of attack. The cries and struggles of a far-off battle echoed in Tommy's ears. He had to break free. All of Skullagar's words were lies. There was nothing for him on Teltam but heartache. His life was on Earth, with his mother and father. Whether or not they stayed together, he knew they loved him. They'd called the cops in search of him, hadn't they? They'd probably gone through hell to find him. There was no way he would allow this villain to take him, *steal* him, away from his family.

The light at his side blazed again, clearing the fog of forgetfulness and manipulation. *Lórien.* He still had his sword in hand. He *always* had his sword.

Tommy drew Lórien in a single swift motion across Skullagar's chest, throwing him back. With the villain's manipulative grasp broken, Teltam, the Black Matter Mountains, and the alien sky disappeared.

"Tommy!" Phantos cried.

He spun to find his friend fending off both Vile-Ette and Mechani-Ghoul, barely holding his own.

But now Tommy was back.

And he had a score to settle.

CHAPTER FORTY-THREE

THE FINAL BATTLE

As Skullagar wailed behind him, Tommy sprinted to F.P.'s aid. Vile-Ette shot a barrage of pink beams from her staff. Phantos dove, barely dodging the attack.

Mechani-Ghoul leapt at Phantos, his bladed arm raised for a fatal blow.

"Phantos, look out!"

He obeyed, and the razor's edge hit the pavement with a shower of sparks mere inches from F.P.'s head as he rolled aside. Old wounds reopened, oozing blue blood. As Phantos rose to a knee, his holographic face appeared solid and steady—exhausted but not defeated.

Both Vile-Ette and Mechani-Ghoul closed on Phantos, their intentions plain. The infinite obsidian towers pushed in like the walls of a trash compactor. They moved deliberately, eating the remnants of Earth. What would happen if the two walls of shadow met? Would

Tommy and Phantos be crushed? Transported? Defiled? Tommy vowed to never find out.

The air sizzled above his head, filled with electricity and menace. With Lórien dripping blood, Tommy ran at the villains' backs. He didn't scream in attack like they always did in the movies, but his prudence didn't matter. They still heard his approach.

Vile-Ette spun fast. Too fast. Her staff was already glowing pink, her mouth moving silently in eldritch words of power. They burned his ears, causing his feet to falter as he ran. Brilliant beams of pink discharged, lighting Vile-Ette's manic expression, her mouth spread in a toothy grin, her crazed eyes wide, all whites.

Tommy stumbled and tried to correct course, but he was running too fast. The beams sizzled quick and relentless, no time to block or dodge.

In this split second of thought, the impossible happened.

Mechani-Ghoul dove in front of Tommy, taking the full force of the assault. Magical voltage radiated in a web of destruction, throwing Mechani-Ghoul like a toy action figure in a playset battle. He collapsed into a pile, mere yards away from the creeping wall of shadow.

The empty sockets of Tommy's creation stared at him, the blue metal shell dull. Small singe marks smoked where the beams had hit.

Skullagar roared, "We take him *alive*!" He limped into the fray, holding the bleeding slash Tommy had gifted him. Around the wound, his brown fur was darkened and slick with blood. Tiny insectile creatures scrambled through his matted hair to feast and revel.

He put his weight on the staff, using it more as a walking stick than a weapon. "Do not harm the boy!" he said, weaker now. The shadow walls had closed in, leaving only the width of the city street.

Phantos stumbled to his fallen weapon. Vile-Ette stood frozen with a look of shame and resentment on her face until she detected F.P.'s movement and spun to address the situation.

Mechani-Ghoul remained a heaped pile of motionless bone and metal, though Tommy knew better than to assume he'd been killed.

That only left himself and the hulking, wounded Skullarian king of Teltam. Skullagar limped closer, the malicious smile beneath his skull mask giving away the ruse.

Tommy glanced over his shoulder in time to see Phantos retrieve his gun ahead of Vile-Ette's attack. As much as he wanted to help, he had his own problems. Tommy leveled Lórien toward Skullagar and said, "Stop walking. And stop pretending."

Skullagar's smile grew wider. The sharp teeth in his mouth matched those of the mask, like the rows of a great white. He straightened and stood his full height.

"Not so hurt after all."

"Smart boy," he growled.

Even as his blade blazed, even as the shadows grew long, Tommy had to know. He had to ask. "Why me?"

Skullagar gave nothing away. Not a flinch of the mouth nor a tilt of the head. "Have you no inkling?"

He looked over at the motionless body of Mechani-Ghoul. "Because I created *him*."

Now Skullagar did show his thoughts. He narrowed his eyes, a quizzical smile appearing. "*You?*" He laughed spitefully, wickedly. "Mechani-Ghoul was born of my sweat, blood, and tears. *These* hands. *My* power. *My* knowledge."

The answer nearly knocked Tommy back.

Phantos called out, "We need to end this! The shadows!"

He ignored F.P. "But I drew him."

"And I *built* him." He stepped closer. The blood oozed from his wound. The corona of his staff glowed purple with power. "Though . . . you *did* divine his existence. Through layers of the many worlds, you saw him.

Just as others have seen before. Realities bleeding through realities. There have always been oracles."

"I don't get it."

"I am no more aware of my creator than you are of yours. But if you listen closely, you can almost hear the scribbling pencil filling in the details of your life."

What was he saying? That Tommy had been imagined by someone in a different reality just as Tommy himself had imagined Mechani-Ghoul? As Aaron had imagined Phantos?

"We live in a complex system of interweaving thoughts, each one imagining the next in a cosmic ouroboros. You crave the truth as I do. Come with us and we will pull back the curtain together."

Tommy's stomach sank. He hadn't realized until that moment how much he liked being special. Being sought after. Yes, even by villains. They had seen something in him, but what?

"I think you're lying. Why do you need me?"

Skullagar looked at Lórien, his smile fading in the divine light of the blade. He didn't say anything, but the expression spoke volumes.

"Something to do with this?" He thrust the blade closer, and Skullagar flinched back.

He brought his staff forward. "You *will* come with us."

Phantos cried out as Vile-Ette charged him. He shot twice before she knocked him back with her staff. They tumbled over each other in a pile.

A hand grasped Tommy's fighting arm, and again the world faltered. Skullagar had him once more. The walls of shadow were only yards away. The air was compressed and close. Sounds escaped the ether. Wailing, hungry sounds of the insane.

"Let go!" He pulled, but the Skullarian gripped with a giant hand.

"Once the shadow world closes in, your Earth will be gone. And we will be home."

"No!" He tried to swing Lórien, but Skullagar was too strong.

He leaned in close, the smell overpowering. "*Yes.*"

More laser blasts lit the air behind him. Tommy couldn't see what was going on, but he heard F.P. struggling. Vile-Ette too groaned with effort as they fought.

"Mechani-Ghoul. To me."

The metal monstrosity sprung to life, unfolding itself and obeying its master's command. Its every step was a mechanized whirring. The emptiness of its body echoed like a metal barrel. Black pitch slithered and oozed closer on both sides. Tommy's hands grew numb with cold.

Mechani-Ghoul spoke, a metallic insect. "Home." *Tuk-tuk-tuk-tuk.* "Father, home."

The words were colder than the freezing air. Stinging, biting cold. If what Skullagar said was true, why had Mechani-Ghoul called Tommy father? No, he realized. The Skullarian had lied. As Phantos said, manipulation was his bedfellow.

"Tommy!" Phantos called from behind. "Fight! You must fight, my friend!"

F.P.'s words acted as an antidote to the cold, replacing images of defeat and death with those of their shared journey, F.P. by his side through everything. When Tommy hopped onto the back of the pickup truck, hiding among the piles of pumpkins, the smell of Halloween all around him. When he discovered The Arcade and met his new friends, Lane, Carlos, Elliotte, Lock, and Levi. The car ride across states. Trying his first New York bagel. Their shared jokes and games of insults. Always Phantos. Always by his side, just like his sword.

Skullagar's grip tightened. He leaned ever closer. "Why are you smiling, boy? Don't you know your own defeat when you see it?"

Tommy waved a hand in front of his nose theatrically. "Wooo! Hey, F.P. This guy's breath smells like three-week-old roadkill!"

"What did you say?"

Tommy laughed. "Not talking to *you*, numbskull. I'm talking to my friend."

He couldn't turn, but he heard Phantos's laugh clearly.

"I'm telling ya," Tommy continued, heartened by Phantos. "This guy smells like a mangy dog fell into a vat of toddler puke."

Tommy pulled free enough to look over his shoulder. F.P. had Vile-Ette in a headlock. Her staff lay broken on the pavement.

Phantos said, "I can smell him from here. He smells like an armpit landfill."

Skullagar held his staff close to Tommy's face, the heated power of the masked corona poised for destruction. "You will cease your foolish prattle. This is *over*."

Shadows licked the edges of reality. The slate embankments were within feet, and the end was indeed close.

F.P. laughed hysterically and called out, "He smells like a baby's diaper!"

Skullagar flinched, his attention wavering for only a second. But a second was all Tommy needed.

He opened his right hand, dropping Lórien and catching the hilt in his left.

Skullagar swiped his staff, but he was too late.

Tommy dodged and plunged Lórien straight through Skullagar's stomach. The sword's light flooded into his body, erupting from his eyes and mouth as if an internal light bulb had been turned on.

Tommy withdrew the blade and fell back, stunned and sickened by what he'd done. He hadn't meant to kill the villain, but his hands had moved thoughtlessly in defense.

Phantos threw Vile-Ette at the all-consuming shadow. She tumbled through the air, screaming horror and malice, slinging curses like shuriken right until the moment the living shadow swallowed her whole. If Skullagar were to be believed, she'd be transported home, to Teltam.

Skullagar fell to his knees. Mechani-Ghoul stepped to his side, holding him upright.

Tommy sheathed Lórien. "I'm . . ." He sputtered, feeling strange about apologizing to a creature bent on kidnapping him. "I didn't mean to."

Blood poured from Skullagar's torso. He took a shaking hand and painted Mechani-Ghoul's face with his blood in a long diagonal stripe. "Nothing is over. Not until I say."

He grasped his staff and held the corona to Mechani-Ghoul's head, muttering words as Vile-Ette had before. Each syllable was a razor's edge. The words seared the air, consuming thought and reason.

F.P. took Tommy's arm and pulled him back. "What is he . . . ?"

Tommy said, "Look out!"

The walls of shadow and gloom lurched in, threatening to devour them. Skullagar continued his incantation, the staff vibrating in his hand so fiercely that it blurred. The purple light so bright it became a star. Wisps of shadow bled from the walls, flowing into the staff's crown. The wisps became rivulets. Then springs and streams.

Skullagar spit blood and continued the eldritch words. His staff consumed the shadow in rivers, feeding on the darkness to power the spell.

Tommy made to attack again, but F.P. held him back. "Whatever he's doing, it's clearing the black fog."

Tommy replied, "Yeah, but whatever he's doing, it's going to be bad."

They fixed each other with a knowing stare, then broke into a run, meaning to put Skullagar down for good.

Tommy drew Lórien, and Phantos drew his gun.

Skullagar raised his staff and recited a dire lamentation of bleeding words. The last of the shadow drew inward, imploding in a black diamond as Skullagar brought the staff down in a single, devastating motion.

The staff shattered. The black diamond exploded like an atomic blast of hate.

Tommy and Phantos were blown back by gale force winds. They tumbled over each other as the hot air blasted them against a parked car and held them there like the fist of God. Dirt and leaves cut Tommy's face. He held his hand up and yelled into the searing air, but his voice was stolen by the winds.

Just as Tommy thought the force of the explosion would squeeze the breath from him until he passed out, it died by degrees. In the last fading gusts, the two heroes found their feet.

Tommy steadied himself and wiped at his battered face, smeared blood coming off on his hands. "You okay?"

F.P. patted his torn suit and scuffed helmet. "I think so."

The real world had returned. Or perhaps, they had returned to the real world. There were children going door to door once again, trick-or-treating and eating candy. A few parents were staring at Tommy curiously but said nothing about the bleeding boy talking to himself.

"Tommy." The tone of his friend's voice was scarier than any of the Halloween costumes he'd ever seen.

Tuk-tuk-tuk.

Mechani-Ghoul stood in the middle of the street. Skullagar's body was nowhere to be seen, but the remnants of his staff were at Mechani-Ghoul's metal-clawed feet. And there was something else . . .

His *eyes.*

They were no longer empty sockets.

Mechani-Ghoul's eyes glowed yellow with Skullagar's soul.

✳ ✳ ✳

Skullagar's incantation had merged the two villains into a single powerful enemy whom Tommy inwardly named Skullaghoul. The metal housing bulged and creaked like a ghost ship lost on vacant waters. Escaping steam hissed like an angry snake as fissures of molten metal paved crooked pathways across the monster's joints. Fanged protrusions broke through tender areas of growth. Skullaghoul howled in torment as assorted alloy plates tore through his core, clicking into place like ingot scales on a robotic dragon. Lingering tendrils of living shadow squirmed over his body, stitching together disparate pieces. He was no longer a hollow thing of limited power. He was a Mafiltion god.

Tommy and Phantos limped to the middle of the street and stood side by side. The police cars must have departed while he'd been distracted. Had he also missed Aaron?

The hulking mutation before him became chief among his obstacles. There was no getting to Aaron without first dispatching Skullaghoul.

"Do we have a plan, F.P.?"

Phantos watched Skullaghoul's continued transformation in quiet awe. Shards of bone burst through the metal at his torso, then fused into spider legs, sharp as swords.

He shrugged. "Try not to die?"

"Try not to die," Tommy repeated solemnly. He held out a hand. Phantos took it and they shook.

"It has been a pleasure fighting with you, Tommy."

"Ditto." He smiled through the fear, knowing these could be his last moments. The blood on his hands and face. The fatigue in his muscles. The unimaginable beast before him. No matter his previous doubt, it was all real in that moment. Which meant he could die.

Skullaghoul fell to all fours, his skeletal head snapping back, the numerous spider legs tapping pavement spastically. He stretched his bone jaw in speech, though no English words came out. A series of metallic growls and grinding chatters spilled from the demon mouth.

Tommy didn't understand the foreign tongue, yet knew them to be words of war, and there was but one response. He sprinted at Skullaghoul without thought, summoning his best battle cry, feeling the sizzle of adrenaline and hope power his body like a deadly locomotive.

Kids dressed in their Halloween best stopped to watch. Tommy could only imagine how insane he appeared to onlookers but was beyond caring. *Far* beyond the ability to worry about embarrassment. How could he while charging a mechanized terror, brandishing a phantom sword?

Phantos fired his gun on hologram mode, calling forth a legion of identical fighters. It was a Hail Mary move and probably wouldn't confuse Skullaghoul, but they had to throw everything they had at him.

Cool autumn wind blew leaves across the field of battle and refreshed Tommy's spirit. He charged toward his doom, yet his mind reveled in the delight of life.

The first wave of holographic fighters reached Skullaghoul. Tendrils of shadow shot forth from the beast, stabbing a dozen holograms at once, erasing them from existence.

Tommy faked to the left, then spun to his right, swinging Lórien in a semicircle. He caught Skullaghoul across the chest, severing two of the spindly legs. But his metal-plated armor deflected any major damage as sparks erupted upon contact. The hard impact vibrated up Tommy's arm and into his teeth.

He fell off to the side as Phantos laid down cover fire with his laser. Like Tommy's blade before them, the blasts ricocheted off hardened armor, dealing no major damage. The villain's altered construction was like a titanium shell. Bone, metal, and shadow made whole.

Phantos drove forward, swinging at Skullaghoul's head. He made contact, then punched again and again until teeth flew from his skeletal mouth. Skullaghoul recovered and returned fire, pummeling Phantos in the stomach with mechanized force. Sharp spider legs grabbed at his arms while others stabbed him, perforating his suit and skin. His body was more blue than white with the spilled blood.

"Tommy!"

"I'm here!" He lunged, blade glinting with orange light from nearby Halloween decorations. He stabbed and sliced, creating a light show of sparks exploding around the villain like a grand Fourth of July fireworks finale.

Skullaghoul shrugged off Tommy's paltry attempt and skewered Phantos through the torso with his machete arm.

F.P. groaned and spasmed as Skullaghoul lifted him into the air by the blade.

Skullaghoul beamed down at Tommy, grinning like a delighted demon. "So ends the life of Fierce Phantos."

Fire shot through Tommy's gut in frantic defiance. He swung wildly with Lórien, hoping to stop the inevitable.

The Skullarian king punched Phantos's helmet; the force was so great it cracked the glass shell.

F.P. didn't look away from Tommy, even as his face pixelated and deformed. The cracks in his helmet grew, bisecting his features like a broken mirror. "Tommy." The words came out as broken as his face. "*Run.*"

Skullaghoul threw Phantos. The fallen hero tumbled limply through the air, collapsing into a heap in the street.

Tommy did as Phantos asked.

He ran.

Only he didn't run *away*. Instead, he ran to his friend's side and turned him over in his arms. "Phantos. You can't . . ."

"Can't what?" His face appeared and disappeared on the broken screen of the helmet. His voice crackled like a phone with a bad connection. "Die?"

Skullaghoul cackled and crawled toward them on all fours like a rabid animal. "Home. Father." *Tuk-tuk-tuk.* "Home." He spoke as if the fractured consciousnesses and personalities of the two villains had been fused in abhorrent construction, defiling both minds.

Phantos still held his gun. He padded at it with his free hand—flipping switches and pressing buttons—then pointed the gun at Tommy.

"What are you—?"

Phantos pulled the trigger, and Tommy saw his doom in the glowing red tip of the barrel. A string of thoughts whipped through his head: *what is he no Phantos wouldn't die I can't believe it can't be no Phantos no he's my friend this isn't . . .*

Nothing happened. The gun fizzled to a stop like a lawn mower running out of gas. "What the hell, Phantos?"

He turned the gun over in his hand. "I've . . ." Intermittent buzzing broke his speech. "Modified." He shook his head. "Not enough power."

Modified. He remembered F.P. working on the gun with his tool kit, but to what end? "What did you do?"

Through a staticky visage, almost gone, Phantos said, "Use Lórien." He held the gun out.

Tommy didn't know what Phantos planned to do or what kind of modifications he could have possibly made, but with every uttered word and every passing second, Skullaghoul crept closer. He had to trust Phantos.

Power surged through Lórien's hilt and into Tommy. A power of hope, will, and love. A power for all that was good in the world. He allowed the divine electricity to run through him as he placed the tip of the blade against Fierce Phantos's weapon.

Tuk-tuk-tuk-tuk. The mechanized clicking tickled Tommy's ears.

He released a surge of energy, and sizzling bursts of potential ran into the gun, through the casing, and into Phantos. He sat bolt upright, his face showing clearer, his eyes open wide.

He pointed the gun at Tommy once more, but this time, the boy didn't flinch.

"Finish it." Phantos pulled the trigger.

A golden blast of light struck Tommy. He fell back holding the wound, only it didn't hurt. He moved his hand and instead of finding a hole or blood, a small blue mark spread over his body like a blanket of warmth.

Skullaghoul paused, clicking and chattering insectile phrases to himself, watching the infection spread.

The blue shell, warm and welcoming, continued to envelop Tommy as he jumped to his feet. The ground looked farther away than usual, as if he were standing on a chair. He held his arms out, studying his hands as he continued to grow taller, bigger, heavier.

He grew inches, then feet, then yards. Tommy had always been tall for his age, but now he was a literal giant. Phantos appeared as small as an action figure on his bedroom floor.

So did Skullaghoul.

With his new stature, a sudden urge for vengeance gripped him. He could feel the grin, like that of a villain, overtake his face. He wanted to crush Skullaghoul like a bug. He wanted to tear him to pieces and listen to the screams, to lap them up like a dehydrated dog.

The heat of revenge and anger fizzled as he heard Phantos's words in his head. *Heroes don't kill.*

Tommy had been disgusted with himself only moments before when he'd stabbed Skullagar. No. He wouldn't make the same mistake again. Pointing at the Lilliputian creature below, he spoke in the booming voice of Zeus. "Go back to Teltam, and never come back."

Skullaghoul gibbered. "You're only a hologram. You can't—"

Below Tommy's enormous feet, the pavement cracked, ceasing Skullaghoul's words.

His yellow eyes went wide. "Impossible."

Tommy reached down and grasped Skullaghoul, bringing him within inches of his face. He squeezed and watched the tiny metal man squirm. "Nothing more than an action figure."

Tendrils of the devouring shadow emerged from Skullaghoul's shell and attacked Tommy. They stabbed and bit, but with each thrust, each advance and lunge, the shadow bounced off, deflected by an invisible parry.

Skullaghoul repeated with increased venom, "*Impossible*. You can't—"

But he could, and he *did*. Whatever modifications Phantos had been working on, they'd no doubt tapped into the same Myragran power that Skullagar and his cronies used, somehow fusing science and magic. Barbed shadows stabbed and lunged at Tommy. Some broke through, some drew blood, but the injuries were mere bug bites.

"I said," Tommy squeezed harder, deriving perhaps a bit too much pleasure from the frantic, trapped expression on the skeletal face of his enemy, "*leave*."

Skullaghoul screamed, panicked and incredulous, as if he couldn't believe what was happening. The attacking tentacles of obsidian puffed out in great plumes, enveloping Skullaghoul in a protective cocoon.

Tommy squeezed harder. "And never. Come. *Back*."

He held fast until the biting cold of nothingness caused him to release the villain. As he did, the cloud dissipated, vanishing from his hand and taking Skullaghoul with it. Hopefully back to Teltam, though Tommy admitted to himself, and only himself, that if the vile creep had been taken to hell instead, he wouldn't mind.

Below, Phantos shot Tommy again. Tommy paid little attention to how his body shrank and instead chose to focus on how Fierce Phantos, his friend, came closer and closer to his embrace.

CHAPTER FORTY-FOUR

AARON BELTZER

Tommy gathered Phantos close, his red blood mixing with the blue as if making an oath, blood brothers for life. They were both bruised and beaten, but F.P. had taken the brunt of Skullaghoul's attacks. His fractured helmet sparked and crackled, and a tiny puff of smoke erupted from one of the connecting tubes. His pixelated face was bisected with fissures and fading fast.

Phantos lifted himself into a sitting position. Some of the minor wounds were already healing and scabbing over, but the deeper ones still bled freely. Tommy pressed his hands against the sickeningly warm gore.

He sputtered, "What do I do?"

Phantos moved Tommy's hands away. He tapped at his wrist device, and a timer appeared—the one Tommy had spied Phantos checking in secret. He'd never been able to discern much, but now the numbers counted down mere minutes.

"What's the timer for, F.P.?"

Phantos closed the display. "I owe you some answers, Tommy. And I only hope you can forgive me."

"What are you—?"

He held a hand up, silencing Tommy. "I do not have much time."

"You're not going to die, damn it! We have to do *something*."

Again Phantos quieted Tommy with a single gesture. His words sounded more human then. Filled with emotion and hurt. "I don't have much time before I *leave*."

Phantos departing was better than him dying, but the revelation stung nonetheless.

"The technology we used to get me here, it's not like Skullagar's magic. It has limitations. One of them is time."

"The countdown," Tommy said. "You have to go back to Teltam."

"Correct."

Tommy may have been twelve years old, but the admission nearly caused an uncontrollable sob to overtake him. He held it in, but the pain of loss lodged itself firmly in his throat, and he couldn't speak for fear of loosening the painful tears.

"These limitations are also why only I could come. I was, quite literally, made for this mission. Masculon and the others trusted me to protect you from Skullagar." His smile was warped by broken glass. "I do believe I've proven myself."

Tommy took his friend's hands in his and held them tight, not wanting to ever let go. He spoke, freeing his grief in a heavy sob. "You have." The blood loss slowed but still looked dire. "Are you going to be okay?"

"When I get back, they can repair me. I will not die."

Tommy leaned in and hugged Phantos tight, the tears coming back, his chest feeling heavy with loss. "Don't go. You're the best friend I've ever had." The words reignited the storm of grief. He held tight until Phantos took his shoulders and held him at arm's length.

"You are my best friend too, Tommy. And nothing can take that from us. Not time, space, nor the infinite realities that separate us." F.P. began to fade, a glittery light enveloping him.

"Please say we'll see each other again."

Phantos smiled wide and bright. As he disappeared into the shimmering glow, he said, "We *will* see each other again."

"Swear it!"

Phantos was gone, but through the ether, Tommy heard, *I swear it.*

He fell forward into the street, letting the grief take him, feeling every ounce of sadness. But he knew, even as the tears fell, he wasn't experiencing despair. This wasn't hopelessness.

He just missed his friend.

"Yo, you okay?"

Tommy wiped tears away and turned to see Fierce Phantos staring back at him. Only, he was much smaller. And his suit looked shabby and ill-fitting. "*Phantos?*"

The kid lifted his makeshift helmet. "You know my character?"

Tommy jumped to his feet. The kid standing before him was the person he'd been searching for. The one he had traveled across three states to find.

Tommy had found Aaron Beltzer.

* * *

"That was some show you put on out there."

Show? Tommy looked to the middle of the street where he'd waged war against a mechanized alien from another dimension. "Oh, right." He wiped at his face, hoping he didn't look too ridiculous. His hands came away wet with tears and blood. Aaron probably assumed it was part of a costume. "Um. What did it look like?"

Aaron shifted his trick-or-treat bag from one hand to the other. "Like you were sword fighting an invisible monster." He looked around at kids walking by. "It was all for show, right? I mean . . ." He swung his bag nervously. "You're not, like, crazy, are you?"

The jury's out on that one, Tommy thought. "Just a Halloween prank."

"Oh, okay." He sighed, obviously relieved. "I came over because I saw that." He pointed where Fierce Phantos had collapsed. In his place lay Tommy's duffel bag, opened to reveal the Masculon costume. "Big fan?"

"You can say that again."

"Awesome." He looked along the street, passing the bag back and forth, probably anxious to get back to collecting free candy. What he said next took Tommy by surprise. "You're that kid, aren't you?"

He knew exactly what Aaron meant, but found himself saying, "What kid?"

"Come on. Tommy Grant, right?" He turned his gaze toward his house. "The cops are looking for you. They were at my house, had your picture and everything. They said you ran away, and they thought you were coming to my house for some reason."

"Oh." Tommy wiped his hands on his pants, trying to get some of the blood off. "Yeah, I guess that's me."

Aaron backed away. "So, like . . ." He shrugged, uneasy. "Why?" He pointed at the duffel bag again. "I guess something to do with my winning the contest, huh?"

"Yeah," Tommy agreed.

"What, you want an autograph or something?" He laughed at his own joke, but still appeared unsure of the situation. Unsure of Tommy.

"Actually . . ." He'd come all this way, nearly lost his friend to Skullagar, and put his parents through hell. Even though he no longer was sure of what he wanted from the boy, he knew he had to explain himself. "Can we talk?"

Aaron didn't say anything for a second. Maybe he was assessing Tommy, or maybe he was getting ready to run home and tell his mom that the crazy runaway was there. Tommy decided no matter what was going to happen, he'd roll with the punches. Like Phantos had taught him.

Finally, Aaron said, "Sure." He lowered his Fierce Phantos costume helmet over his head. "As long as we do it while trick-or-treating."

Tommy smiled. "Deal."

＊　＊　＊

As Tommy donned his costume, he noticed something glimmering in the street. He ran over and found the crown of Skullagar's broken staff. The purple-masked face stared at him with defeated malice, and despite the overwhelming urge to kick the vile thing into the sea, Tommy shoved it into his backpack along with the empty duffel. He retrieved his plastic treat bag, purchased from the corner store back home. The orange-and-black bag screamed *TRICK-OR-TREAT* in enormous yellow letters across the top.

Full dark had come, and the magic of Halloween was alive all around him. Dried leaves skittered across the pavement like frightened mice. Grinning jack-o'-lanterns winked with yellow flickers from porches.

Kids ran by, screaming in delight as they capered from door to door in search of treats and tricks. Whenever someone in an *OoCC* costume passed, Tommy's heart lurched, sure the villains of Teltam had returned for him in Phantos's absence. Around every turn, hiding in every shadow, Mechani-Ghoul waited with his skeletal grin and glinting blade.

The notion that Tommy had imagined everything didn't curtail the probing fear inside his chest. Halloween night, of all nights, was when your worst nightmares and greatest hopes could manifest. Even the cartoon witches beside doorways and plastic ghosts hanging from bare trees boasted a sinister air.

The first few houses were plundered in silence. Aaron appeared content to gather his haunted rewards alongside his new acquaintance. He didn't prod or probe for answers. Only for candy.

At the far corner of 18th Avenue, they crossed the street and began back the way they had come. Aaron lifted his helmet and said, "I'm not allowed to go out of the neighborhood. Especially tonight."

"How come?"

Aaron chuckled. "You know. There's some crazy runaway kid planning on breaking into my house." He shoved Tommy's shoulder playfully.

"Oh, right. Sorry." He glanced down the street, still in sight of Aaron's house. Mrs. Beltzer stood on the porch, handing out candy and watching her son from a distance. His time was limited. "So . . ."

They approached a door covered with fake spiderwebs and rang the bell. "Trick-or-treat!" Aaron held his bag out before the door even opened. "Yeah?"

"About my coming here."

The door swung open, and Frankenstein's monster groaned, "Happy Halloween!" He held out a giant bowl filled with full-size candy bars, and Tommy momentarily forgot what he was saying.

"Whoa!"

The monster winked. "Take two."

Snickers, Twix, Whatchamacallit, 3 Musketeers, Reese's Peanut Butter Cups, Clark Bars, PayDay: all the big hitters were there. Tommy grabbed a Snickers and a Whatchamacallit, and Aaron, apparently a big fan of peanuts, took the peanut butter cups and a PayDay.

"Thanks! Happy Halloween!"

They went down the stairs, passing Alf and a vampire on the way.

Before he could get distracted by candy again, Tommy said, "I entered the contest too."

Aaron stopped inspecting the contents of his bag and looked up.

"Oh . . ." He fidgeted with his costume, pulling at the fake tubes. "You're pissed, huh? Is that why you're here?"

"No." He pulled the Masculon mask off and put it into his bag. "I mean, I guess I was. Kind of."

Aaron removed his helmet. They were face-to-face now. No more hiding behind costumes. "Sorry."

He shook his head. "Don't apologize for winning. Fierce Phantos is *awesome*. I know what I'm talking about. He's seriously cool."

A heartbreakingly happy expression crossed Aaron's face. "Thanks." He looked down, kicking at some fallen leaves on the ground. "You know, my parents, they thought the contest was a waste of time." He hurried to add, "They were proud of me, I guess. But my dad especially, he said I *shouldn't get it in my head that I am an artist.*" He said this in a deep voice, pushing out his bottom lip and wagging a finger.

"That's bull. You won an art contest." Tommy puffed his cheeks, exasperated with the many ways parents could try to stuff ideas into their kids' heads. "That makes you an artist."

They walked along the sidewalk, taking their time even as other kids ran past. Aaron couldn't shake the smile that Tommy's approval had brought out. He hoped the rest of what he had to say wouldn't take an eraser to the boy's happiness.

With a deep breath, Tommy summoned will and courage. He'd traveled all the way from Ohio to Brooklyn on his own. Battled creatures from another dimension. Surely explaining *why* couldn't be so hard. He imagined Lórien where Masculon's battle-ax now rested on his belt. The warmth from its divine light radiated through him.

"I've been having a hard time." His voice caught, but he forged ahead. "My parents are getting divorced. They basically ignore me. Don't even know where I am half the time." With every new admission, the words came easier. His heart felt lighter despite the negativity of the words, as if he were sucking snake venom from a festering wound. "My best friend hates me. I've been getting bullied at school. My grades are total crap because I spend the whole day worrying."

Aaron's mouth hung open. He obviously didn't know what to say. He sputtered, "Oh, man. I mean . . . I'm sorry. That totally sucks."

They paused at the entrance to the next house. "The contest kept me going." He laughed to himself, shocked at the realization. "I don't think I even knew that until now. But I was feeling bad. Like, really bad. And then I'd come home and be safe in my room with all my *OoCC* friends and my character ideas. I'd lay there by myself, my parents wrapped up in their own crap like usual, and I'd draw. The world would disappear. I could be a superhero. I could be a villain." He swallowed back the tears, not wanting to cry in front of Aaron. "And I was okay. For a little while, at least."

"And then you lost the contest."

He nodded. "And then I lost."

Aaron nodded solemnly. "What can I do?"

And there it was. The reason he'd come. Tommy could pitch his big ask. But is that what he still wanted?

Tommy swung his backpack around and dug out the folded sketch of Mechani-Ghoul. "Here."

Unfolding the paper, Aaron's eyes lit up. "Whoa!" He glanced at Tommy, then back at the paper. "*This* was your entry?" He shook his head, tracing over the lines with a finger. "You should have won, Tommy. Like, seriously, I'm not just saying that. He's so cool!"

Warmth bloomed in his chest. The approval, especially from the real winner, felt better than he expected. "The reason I came—" He stopped himself and course corrected. "The reason I *thought* I came was to ask for you to use your power as president for a day at Telco Toys to get Mechani-Ghoul made into an action figure." Saying it out loud, after everything he'd been through, Tommy was struck by how childish the whole thing was.

"Oh." Aaron's expression tightened. "I mean, I guess I could ask—"

"No," Tommy interrupted. "Thank you, but don't." Was it that he didn't want a physical representation of his tormentor, or that he no longer needed the win? In that final moment of doubt, Phantos spoke through him: "I needed this trip, but I don't need to win. Not anymore."

Aaron smiled politely, though Tommy detected the skepticism hidden beneath. He ignored this because he didn't require outside acknowledgment. In his heart, he knew what he'd accomplished was greater.

Tommy and Aaron replaced their respective masks and went to the next house on the block. Tommy walked lighter, his spirit high and his soul bright. And why not?

It was Halloween night, and all was right with the world.

CHAPTER FORTY-FIVE

REUNION

Dave stared through the passenger-side window and tapped the glass. "That's the kid's mother."

"Fran."

"Right, right. Fran." He turned to Suzie.

She was gripping the steering wheel, watching the woman hand out candy to the never-ending parade of children climbing the stairs of her porch. "No police."

"They must have left. It *is* Halloween. I'm sure they have their hands full tonight."

Suzie scoffed, nearly *hissed*. "We're talking to her." She opened the door and put a foot out.

"The police said—"

She turned fast, her eyes fierce. "Do you *care*?"

Fair point. They'd driven from Ohio to Brooklyn, searched street after street, spent a restless night in a hotel, and had absolutely zero communication from the police since their first report. "No. I guess I don't."

As soon as Dave stepped out of the car, Suzie screamed bloody murder. His heart leapt into his throat. He, and everyone else in the vicinity, spun to see what had happened. In his nightmare imagination, he saw his dead son, run over by a car in the middle of the street.

Suzie broke into a sprint, but Dave couldn't tell who or what she was running to. There were tons of kids, and every one of them wore a costume.

Dave jogged after her. "Wait up!" Parents on the street gathered their kids close to protect against whatever the crazy woman was screaming about. Other kids, the unsupervised ones, bunched together and watched.

A few yards ahead of him, Suzie nearly tackled a kid wearing a Masculon mask. A tickle of recognition began in his stomach and crawled through his nerve endings. He knew that costume. He'd watched Suzie toil over it for weeks.

Dave caught up and grasped Suzie's arm. Her eyes were wide, and her face flushed. "Tommy?"

The boy removed his mask. Tommy's face was scrunched, red, and wet.

He started to say, "I'm sorry," but both parents attacked with violent hugs, squeezing him so hard he couldn't finish.

Suzie kissed his face and held his cheeks. "What were you thinking?" she said between kisses.

All three of them were crying and babbling their own threats and apologies.

"Thank God you're okay."

Kiss.

"I'm so sorry."

Hug.

"Grounded until you're thirty."

Hug, kiss, hug.

"I didn't mean to scare you."

"What happened to your *face?*"

Kiss.

"I'm fine."

Hug, hug, hug.

"You're okay, that's all that matters."

At some point, Aaron's mother came over. She and her son stood nearby, watching the display until Dave composed himself.

Tommy and Aaron stepped to the side and talked while Dave and Suzie spoke to Fran. The entire conversation felt like a dream, and later, all Dave could remember was a word salad that contained explanations and apologies until Fran begged off.

"Don't want the house to get egged," she said, taking Aaron back home with her.

That was fine with Dave. The sooner they got on the road home, the sooner they could put the whole ordeal behind them.

✳ ✳ ✳

Dave took over driving duties for the first leg. Having everyone in the car together was melancholy because he knew deep down, it might be one of the last times they took a road trip as a family.

He checked the rearview and delighted in the sight of his son. "You okay, kid?"

Tommy smiled sheepishly. "I'm okay. Just happy to have a ride home."

"Ha-ha." Dave shook his head. "You better tell us every single bit of what went on the past couple days."

"Yeah," Suzie chimed in. "We want every dirty detail."

After a moment of silence, Dave checked the mirror again and found Tommy fast asleep, curled up on the seat with his backpack. "That was quick."

Suzie turned to look. "He must be exhausted. I can't even imagine what he's been through."

Dave laughed. "Couldn't have been *that* bad. The kid was trick-or-treating, for crying out loud."

She slapped his shoulder. "Careful."

"All right, all right. Still . . ." He checked his son again, acknowledging the simple pleasure that may have been stolen from him if things had gone differently. "I think he's gonna be okay."

The Halloween moon shined bright overhead, and a sudden gust blew a few stray leaves across the roadway. Dave had never been a big fan of the holiday, but he thought there had to be at least a little sorcery in the autumn air. He cracked his window and breathed deeply, hoping to steal some of the magic for himself.

Part Five

FAMILY
TIES

CHAPTER FORTY-SIX
HOME AGAIN, HOME AGAIN

Tommy woke up in the dark back seat of the car as his father turned onto their Halloween-ravaged street. Streamers of toilet paper waved from treetops, and globs of shaving cream adorned mailboxes like fancy dollops of whipped cream. There'd probably be exploded eggs drying all over the house since they hadn't been home to appease the devils and ghouls of the neighborhood.

To Tommy's surprise, instead of a destroyed house, he found his bike propped in the driveway. The brief mystery was solved when his dad unlocked the front door, and Tommy found Matty snoring on the couch, a nearly empty bowl of candy cradled in his arms.

"Matty?"

The comic shop owner snorted himself awake. Upon seeing Tommy, he stumbled off the couch, knocked the candy bowl to the floor, tripped over it, and squished a Snickers. He grasped Tommy by the shoulders. "Am I dreaming?" He drew Tommy into a hug.

The embrace felt weird for a second. He'd known Matty for years, but they'd never been super close. Then he remembered his father's relationship with the man and that Matty had known Tommy since he was born, and he hugged back just as tightly.

"Man, you scared us, kid. You almost made the milk carton." He pulled away and stared Tommy in the eyes. "You *did* manage to score some prime real estate on a few telephone poles, though."

"No way." His heart sank. If there were fliers of him around town, it meant people at school would know. Which meant more bullying than ever.

His mom took Tommy's hand. "He should get to bed, Matty. It's been a long weekend. For all of us."

"Right, of course." He patted Tommy's shoulder. "Free comics for a week, bud. Anything you want."

"Seriously?" The offer took the sting out of the potential ridicule at school. Frankly, he was still waiting for the cascade of punishments to come from on high, so being rewarded for his crimes was strange. He looked at his mom, then his dad, expecting a rebuke.

None came.

Matty laughed. "Seriously."

He left the adults downstairs to talk. The moment he reached his room, Tommy collapsed onto the bed and descended into a dreamless sleep.

* * *

When Tommy left for school the next morning, he found Miranda waiting outside the front door.

"You're back!" She nearly tackled him when she ran in for a huge hug. Miranda held on tight for longer than Tommy had ever been hugged by a girl, and then he received another first. A big kiss on the cheek.

They both blushed, but the shock only lasted a heartbeat.

As they began their walk to the school bus, Miranda bumped Tommy with her shoulder. "Where's my sketch, you goon?"

He started to check his backpack. "Oops . . ."

"What?"

"I forgot it in Brooklyn. With Aaron."

Miranda frowned comically. "You gave my sketch away to some kid you hardly know?"

He dug deeper into his backpack and retrieved a worn woolen hat. "Yeah, but I did find this in my room. Look familiar?"

Miranda's eyes shot wide, and she grabbed the hat.

"So you were in my room, huh?"

"Yeah, well. You ran away from home, and I was worried."

Tommy bumped her with his shoulder this time. "I know. My mom told me what you did." A weird fluttery feeling filled his chest. "I can't believe you cared enough to—"

"Yeah, yeah, yeah. It was nothing."

"Not nothing. I'm going to draw you something new. Something better, just for you."

Some loose toilet paper flew across the street. With Halloween's passing, Thanksgiving would arrive before he knew it. Then Christmas with its lights and snow and presents. Not since the onset of the previous summer had Tommy been so excited for the future. Where once a dark pit of dread lay, there now resided a glimmering gemstone of hope.

Miranda put the old wool hat into her backpack. "A drawing just for me, huh?" She scratched her chin theatrically. "Hmmm. I don't know."

"You don't know?"

She shook her head. "My detective services are worth more, but the drawing will do as a start."

Miranda grabbed Tommy's hand. Her fingers were cold, but they warmed him all the same. They walked this way, swinging their arms in the morning sun, oblivious of time. Experiencing only that infinite moment of happiness.

CHAPTER FORTY-SEVEN

JOE COOL

By the time Tommy arrived at school, word of his big adventure had reached the ears of his peers. He'd known to expect this. He wasn't sure how much the kids knew but figured they would be happy to fill in the blanks with childish speculations.

Schoolmates stared at him as he walked through the halls, ducking their heads together when they thought he wasn't looking. Tommy stopped at his locker, and while he entered the combination, someone tapped his shoulder. The stocky boy, Randy, was an eighth grader he knew only by reputation. They'd never spoken, but the boy also never bothered Tommy, which made him better than about 15% of his classmates.

"Is it true you hitchhiked all the way to Brooklyn? By *yourself?*" His expression suggested he didn't quite believe what he'd heard, and that as an eighth grader, it was his duty to fact-check sources.

Tommy crinkled his nose. "Um. Well, yeah. Kinda."

"*Kinda.*" The kid nodded knowingly. "So you didn't go to Brooklyn by yourself. I figured." He looked over his shoulder at his friends who all nodded, looking relieved that the little sixth grader wasn't more courageous than the lot of them combined.

"No, I mean I didn't *hitchhike*. Not technically. I jumped onto the back of a pickup truck and hid behind pumpkins to get to Pittsburgh."

The kid's mouth hung open. "No way." He waved his friends over. Tommy was immediately surrounded by a group of kids calling out questions as if he were giving a press conference. Their skepticism melted away, but instead of being replaced by annoyance or anger, they became transfixed.

The students oohed and aahed at his recounting of the bus clerk chase. They cheered at his heroic leap onto the pickup truck and the subsequent confrontation with the driver in Pittsburgh. His description of The Arcade caused widespread discussion of organizing a road trip for winter break. They laughed with him as he joked about the woman flirting with Levi at the motel and begged for more stories even as the bell rang for homeroom.

He promised to tell them everything in time, though deep down he knew he'd never reveal the parts about Phantos and the villains of the *OoCC*. Those moments were his alone.

*   *   *

The rest of the school day continued in the same fashion. Tommy rode high on a wave of acceptance—and maybe even admiration—he had no longer thought possible. In every class, in the hallway, at lunch and during gym, kids that had never talked to him before were saying hi, asking questions, and treating Tommy like a celebrity. Even some of his classmates that had casually made fun of him earlier that same year showed a modicum of respect, if not the blatant adoration many others displayed.

Tommy felt good. More than good, he felt happy. The sheer velocity of change from a single weekend away made his head spin with giddiness. Though, deep down, a familiar voice whispered, *Mark your true friends, young Tommy. The ones who were always there. The ones who always cared.*

When the final bell rang, he left biology class with Sammy, who unlike everyone else hadn't grilled him with questions. In fact, the only thing Sammy asked was, "Are you okay?" He did so with concern etched on his face. Concern so true and deep, Tommy would have hugged him if they weren't in school.

The throng of bustling students, anxious to leave, created a kind of warm buzzing in the air. Kids pushed past, gathering their books and jackets so Monday could be over a little quicker. The siren call of Halloween candy no doubt put an extra pep in their steps.

Sammy followed Tommy to his locker while he swapped out his books for the ones he needed for homework. They were chatting about their ideas for the upcoming science fair project when a coldly familiar voice spoke behind them.

"I bet you think you're pretty cool now. I bet you think you're hot shit."

He turned to find Evan and Jonathan Miller. Jonathan's eyes were hard with hatred. Evan stood behind his new best friend, checking the hallway.

Sammy put a hand on Tommy's shoulder. "Let's go."

Something interesting happened then. Something unexpected.

Tommy wasn't scared.

He didn't feel embarrassment or shame. Nor did he feel anger or resentment. He felt only pity. Pity for a boy who had so much hate and anger inside him. What had happened to Jonathan to make him this way? He'd never thought about that before, instead wasting all his imagination on how to exact revenge.

"You're not going anywhere," Jonathan said, jaw clenched.

"No," Tommy agreed, stepping forward. "I'm not." Though no longer visible, Lórien's heat radiated into his leg, through his bones, muscles, and mind. He knew he could use this courage, this will, to do terrible things. But he also knew that was not how heroes operated. Phantos had taught him that. Even more importantly, it wasn't how a good *person* operated.

"Just because the other kids love you doesn't mean I won't kick your ass."

Evan appeared worried and uncomfortable, stepping away from the impending fight.

Tommy said, "You can't hurt me. Not anymore."

"I can knock your teeth in. That would hurt plenty." Jonathan grinned ugly.

"Let's go," Sammy whined, pulling at Tommy's sleeve.

Instead of retreating, Tommy took another step forward. He didn't avert his gaze. He stood straight and tall, towering over the bully. Looking at Jonathan in that moment, he was shocked to realize how small the boy was. As small as Skullaghoul had been at the very end, clenched in Tommy's giant grip.

"If I have to defend myself, I will. But I'm not running away ever again." He took another step forward, and amazingly, Jonathan stepped back, his eyes giving way to something other than hate.

"I'm not kidding. I'll do it!"

Diplomacy, he knew, would only get him so far with someone like this. He growled, "Try it."

Jonathan swung wildly, and Tommy stepped to the side as if dancing.

Jonathan stumbled forward into the lockers. He didn't waste any time before lunging back at Tommy, his face a mask of incredulity.

Tommy backpedaled a few steps and spun to the left so gracefully he could have been auditioning for *Guys and Dolls*. He stuck his foot out at the last second, and Jonathan sprawled face-first onto the vinyl tile floor. When he looked up, his mouth was bleeding, and his eyes were wet.

He stood unsteady, wiping at the blood and tears. "I'm not crying!" He looked at Evan who had completely disengaged. "I'm not!"

And maybe he wasn't at first, but the more he said the word *cry*, the more his voice tightened.

Tommy had been prepared for a real fight, but apparently Jonathan required an unfair advantage and a fearful opponent unwilling to defend himself. He considered offering a hand to Jonathan. He wanted to say something like *no hard feelings*. But as it turned out, he wasn't so enlightened that he could ignore the months of torment. Still, he hadn't beaten Jonathan to a pulp, as he had imagined doing so many times before, and he called that a win.

He knew Phantos would have agreed.

Evan slunk off without speaking a word. Perhaps in time, he'd grow the backbone needed to apologize. Tommy no longer cared either way.

He knew who his real friends were.

And he knew how to handle the bullies.

CHAPTER FORTY-EIGHT

CHANGES

Not all of the changes after Tommy's return were good. His father did stick around for weeks following his big journey, a decision no doubt made for Tommy's well-being. However, before long, the situation became untenable. There was a silent but palpable tension in the house.

Tommy's dad sat him down the Friday after Thanksgiving, his eyes soft and glassy. He had a few days' beard growth and a saggy look to his face, usually indicative of a hangover, but Tommy knew that wasn't the case. He hadn't even had a glass of wine with the big dinner. This time, the ragged expression was born of something else.

The moment played out as he'd imagined in his head so many times. His father took his hands, squeezed them tight, and said, "I have to leave, kiddo. Your mother and I . . ." He broke off and swallowed something back. "We wanted to stick it out until after Christmas. We thought we could." He rubbed his cheeks and it sounded like sandpaper. "But we can't."

Tommy wanted to ask why. He wanted to plead and beg and play Mr. Fix-it like a good son would. But by then, he knew better. He'd done a lot of growing up in a short period. Sometimes, there was no fixing things.

"What's going to happen?" The words came out quiet as Tommy tried not to cry. He knew if he cried, the weak dam his father had built around his own emotions would break too.

Dad squeezed his hands. "We're still a family. We'll see each other all the time." He forced a laugh. "You can't get rid of me that easily."

Tommy smiled as fake as his father's laugh.

"I know this sounds awful, and stupid, and probably a justification. But your mother and I have talked about it more than you know, and we both agree. This is better. For all of us."

"Sure." He pulled his hands away.

The sorrow on his father's face nearly broke Tommy. He'd never seen such vulnerability and pain, squeezed tight in every crease and wrinkle. "I never said it wouldn't be hard, but—"

Tommy cut him off with a hug. He didn't want to hear any more. He knew what the rest would sound like. All that was left to say was, "I love you, Dad."

"Love you too, Tommy. We'll get through this."

"I know." The change would tear him apart, tear them all apart. For a while. But he knew what his dad said was true. Time would pass, and the changes would become normality.

Maybe they'd even prosper.

✳ ✳ ✳

A few days later, Tommy's heartache was quenched by three unexpected surprises.

The first was his progress report from school, which showed vast improvement in all classes. Mrs. Jaffee had even scrawled a little note about how impressed she was with the turnaround in his schoolwork. His parents had finally met with Mrs. Jaffee the week of his return, and to Tommy's surprise, they'd shouldered much of the blame.

The second surprise came right before dinner, when the phone rang. Tommy ran over and answered, "Hello?"

After a moment of silence, a boy asked, "Is Tommy there?" The voice sounded familiar, but he couldn't quite place it.

"This is Tommy. Who's this?"

Off to the side, the caller said, "It's him. One, two, three . . ."

A chorus of voices exploded through the headset, "Brooklyn or bust!"

His heart thudded uncontrollably in his chest. "Lock? Is that—?"

"Yeah, buddy! It's all of us! But seeing as I'm the coolest, they voted I make the call."

In the background, Carlos said, "Actually, Levi is the oldest and so he's the cooler one, because everyone knows age equals coolness making you only the second coolest—"

"All right, all right already. Hey, Tommy, someone wants to say hi."

There was some shifting around and ruffling material before an excited voice said, "You have to tell us everything!"

"Hey, Elliotte." Tommy hoped his blushing cheeks couldn't somehow be detected through the phone.

In the background, "The kid disappears from the hotel and we're not supposed to freak out, right?"

"Did you find the boy you were looking for?"

Tommy laughed, his head spinning with excitement. There was so much to tell them. "Well, yeah. I did."

"Oh, wait, wait. Lane wants to tell you something important first."

The phone changed hands yet again. "Yo! Our parents said you could totally come stay with us if you want to visit during winter break."

In the background, Lock, or maybe Levi, yelled, "No hitchhiking, though! Ask your parents this time!"

He laughed, "Tell him I'm done hitchhiking for a while. I'll ask my mom if I can."

"Rad. This is going to be the best Christmas break ever."

The conversation lasted another twenty minutes, and it didn't get any less raucous, with the phone changing hands a dozen times. Eventually Lane said they had to go because of the long-distance bill but made plans to speak again about the trip.

Tommy hung up, his head buzzing. He couldn't wait to tell Miranda. And maybe she could even come along! Her father was pretty strict, but he had loosened up over the past weeks and started palling around with Tommy's father, having squashed whatever beef they had with each other. Miranda said her parents had even started going to a counselor.

Before he could run back up to his room, the doorbell rang.

"Tommy!" his mom called from the kitchen. She'd been incredibly busy with her new job but still managed to make some killer dinners.

"Got it, Ma!" He didn't know how she managed, but among the pantheon of *OoCC* heroes, she sat firmly at the tippy top.

He opened the door to the mail lady, running much later than usual. "Hey, Tommy. Got a package for ya."

She held a huge brown box out to him. The label did indeed have his name on it. He couldn't imagine what it was until he noticed the return label said Aaron Beltzer. Somehow, he made it to his room without lifting off and flying into space fueled by giddy excitement. He closed his door and sat on the floor with the box, running his hands over the edges before tearing the box open. On the top was his sketch of Mechani-Ghoul. Then a piece of composition paper with a letter:

Tommy,

You forgot your drawing! I asked about getting Mechani-Ghoul turned into an action figure, but they said they couldn't. But I wanted to send you something. It was so cool that you came all the way to Brooklyn to see me.

I hope you like what I sent. I know it's not Mechani-Ghoul, but I think it's pretty cool. They made a small batch of limited-edition figures just for me. These aren't the ones they're gonna sell, so they're collectible!

Anyway, write me back. Maybe you can come visit again sometime.

Your friend,
—Aaron Beltzer

Tommy's hands worked quickly to remove the packing material and found a second box. Only *this* box had black typeface on the outside that read *Telco Toys / Fierce Phantos / 6 / LE / 10-191928.*

He cut open the box and found six packaged Fierce Phantos limited-edition action figures. He took one out and, upon seeing the familiar face, a surge of grief overtook him. He hugged the figure to his chest.

"Phantos." His friend. Maybe the best friend he'd ever had. Tommy didn't know if he'd made the trip back safely or if he'd survived his injuries. There'd been no word from Teltam.

He sniffed and wiped his nose, placing the carded figure on the floor. "You're probably not even real anyway," he said to the toy, but it didn't make him feel any better. Real or not, he missed Fierce Phantos as much as he missed his dad on their days away from each other.

He took a breath and steadied himself, trying to focus on the good. And that day, there had been plenty of it.

CHAPTER FORTY-NINE

GOOD NIGHT

Tommy lay in bed, his mind afloat with thoughts of his friends in Pittsburgh, the surprise package from Aaron, Christmas, his parents, school assignments, Miranda, Phantos, and a million other little things. He pulled his blanket tighter and let out a contented breath. He thought this might be what growing up was like. Having both worries and joys flitting around your brain simultaneously and still managing to keep your wits about you. No wonder his parents acted the way they did sometimes, like the world had been pulled out from under them and they were floating in space.

The vast, bleak oblivion had gripped Tommy too, but he had found his center. In his friends. In his parents. In himself.

His door creaked open. "You asleep, sweetie?"

"Not yet."

His mom walked in, then sucked a tiny breath through her teeth. "You need to clean up in here, mister."

In the past he might have been annoyed at the request, but he saw how hard she'd been working. "You got it, Ma." He snapped and pointed his finger-gun at her with a wink.

"Silly boy." She came to the bedside and kissed his head. "Thanks for helping out around the house. Don't think I haven't noticed you pitching in."

"You're welcome."

She winked at him. "I think Santa has noticed too."

"Aw, come on. I know—"

"Shh, you just be quiet now. Don't even think about saying what you were about to say. You're not *that* old yet."

Upon second thought, Tommy decided maybe Santa *was* real, because that meant Phantos was real. And that meant he might see his friend again someday. "My lips are sealed."

"That's right they are. Love you. Get a good sleep." She went to the door and hesitated, eyes fixed on the corner of the room. She looked like she was about to say something, then instead only closed the door.

Tommy shifted in bed to look into the corner. There was nothing there except some schoolbooks and his backpack—where a faint light pulsated in the darkness. He got out of bed, unzipped the bag, and closed his hand around a familiar object, warm and alive with power.

Tommy removed the top of Skullagar's staff from the backpack and stared into the glowing eyes of an abstract face. Tiny wisps of purple light evaporated into the dark room like bioluminescent algae. With numb fingers, he released the heated corona, letting it fall back into his bag. He drifted to his bed like a ghost and drew the covers; only this time, he brought them all the way over his head. Gone were the millions of thoughts parading through his mind. Now only one notion occupied his attention. A single, ominous seed planted deep in the fertile soil of his imagination.

Outside, the late fall wind howled through bare treetops. Soon, frost would collect on the dying grass, and snow would fall as the season of death came. Tommy tried to turn back to thoughts of holiday lights and hot chocolate memories. Of Christmas presents and animated television specials. Time off from school, cookies, and stockings. He packed his mind tight with these images, and yet bleak winter dread had already grown like icicles in his heart.

Something was coming with the winter cold, and even before he heard the insectile laughter, Tommy knew what form his adversary would take.

He squeezed his eyes tight as tight could be, but that couldn't keep the devil out.

From the dark abyss, a final good night was spoken.

"*Father.*"

ACKNOWLEDGMENTS

Anthony J. Rapino

A little over a year ago, I was approached with a simple question: "If I had a story I was dying to write, would you be my ghostwriter?" When I said yes, I embarked on a yearlong exploration of 1980s Ohio that shattered my expectations of what a creative collaboration could be. I was not a ghostwriter. I was this man's partner. I can't thank Anthony Grate enough for tapping me to be his copilot on this extraordinary journey. It has been—as Tommy might say—totally awesome.

As always, I must thank my parents who will never not support me in all I do, and my brother, Mike, who is and always will be my best friend.

I've thanked Todd Keisling in every acknowledgment page I've ever written, and I'm not one to break with tradition (even if he hasn't yet read the novel). But that doesn't matter because Todd has played a much more important role: as my friend.

My deepest gratitude to the entire Geeky Writers Collective, who are always there with an encouraging word and a kick to the butt: Amelia Bennett, Nikki Nelson-Hicks, and Mercedes Yardley.

Thank you to the Candy Corn Apocalypse Army, who are a daily reminder that what I do matters.

Thank you to anyone reading this right now. You add the extra breath of life necessary to animate these dead pages. Make no mistake: Tommy's world does not exist without you.

Finally, I'd like to thank everyone who contributed to the making of this novel. All of the readers, editors, creators, artists, and supporters. I thank you all from the bottom of my heart.

Anthony D. Grate

It isn't often I see one of my creative endeavors through to the very end, but I'm grateful that this book has found its place in that exclusive group. This would not be the case if it were not for some important and influential people.

First and foremost, my wife Miranda. If it were up to her, I would be convinced I could do anything. But I'll settle for believing I do a few things above average, as long as she's there beside me.

And then there is our brood of four: Elliotte, Lane, Levi, and Lachlan. Each of them has made me a better person, and they remind me daily why it is I love being their father.

I'm thankful for my partner in this little adventure, the other Tony. I gave him a tiny seed, and he turned it into a tree. One we trimmed and nurtured into something we could both treasure for the rest of our lives.

I've been blessed by God to have had family members and friends who were willing to put up with me because they kind of liked me for whatever reason. They have given me memories I prize every single day. They include my mom, Karen, who I know is anxiously waiting for this book to arrive in heaven's library. Mom, I hope this somehow makes you even happier. My dad, David, who has never not been there for me when I truly needed him. My sister, Tracey, who will have to wait until Mom is done reading. Sorry, sis. My stepbrother, Brynn, who is still unable to grasp how wrong he is about his choice of Links. My best friend, Phil, who is still unable to grasp how wrong he is about which musical group truly dominated the 1987 charts. The Dewhurst family—I'm so very thankful they adopted my family into theirs and continue to show us unconditional love. My "retro" family—Adam, Mickey, Jason, Jeff, Victor, Jeremy, Justin, Ben, Johnny, Mr. Magic, Edd, and all the rest (you know who you are). If nostalgia nerds ruled the world, you would all be the top picks for the Planetary Retro Council. And then there is Josh Hayman, the world's okayest drummer. Out of all the dudes named Josh, he is the best.

I appreciate the hard work and efforts of the folks at Greenleaf. They have been a pleasure to deal with. Special thanks to Jen Glynn, Tenyia Lee, Pam Nordberg, Nick Stegall, Jessica Reyes, and Daniel Sandoval.

There are too many other family members and friends I am thankful for or who helped make this possible. Therefore, to those special people, pretend your name is listed here.

ABOUT THE AUTHORS

Anthony J. Rapino

Anthony J. Rapino resides in Northeastern Pennsylvania with his cats Luna and Poe. When he's not writing speculative fiction, Anthony can be found in the classroom teaching English or crouched in dark alleyways sculpting horrific autumnal creatures out of clay.

His short work has appeared in *On Spec*, *A capella Zoo*, *Black Ink Horror*, *Madhouse*, *Liminal Space*, and others. His novel, *Soundtrack to the End of the World*, and story collection, *Greetings from Moon Hill*, are both available now.

Proof of psychosis and a full bibliography can be found on his website: http://www.anthonyjrapino.com

Follow Anthony on social media:

Instagram: @CandyCornApocalypse

Twitter: @AnthonyJRapino

Anthony D. Grate

Anthony lived through the '80s, from age six to age sixteen, by surviving on steady doses of *Masters of the Universe*, Kool-Aid that he put way too much sugar in, and BarNones. Occasionally he put pencil to paper and created comic strips to entertain his friends. He dreamed of one day working for Marvel or DC. Once out of college, however, he found himself selling furniture. Life sure is funny. After a few failed attempts to use a new thing called "the internet" to find a nice lady to share life with, a nice lady found him. They married and soon found themselves raising four children together. Meanwhile, in his spare time, Anthony tried desperately to appease the creative spirit dwelling within him. Comic strips, websites, books, board games, interactive online games . . . you name it, he probably gave it a shot.

Nowadays Anthony juggles the responsibilities of a husband, father, business owner, and creator pretty well—or at least he thinks so. He lives in the same quiet corner of Ohio that he always has, with no plans of changing that. The guy's not much for change, which is probably why he still watches *Masters of the Universe* and eats too many BarNones. He did ditch the Kool-Aid, however.